P9-DNK-480

DREAMWORKS
GABBY'S DOLLHOUSE

KITTY SCHOOL

Adapted by **GABRIELLE REYES**

SCHOLASTIC INC.

ISBN 978-1-338-80446-1

10 9 8 7 6 5 4 3 2 1   22 23 24 25 26

Printed in the U.S.A.   40

First printing 2022

Book design by **SALENA MAHINA**

FREE DOWNLOAD
TÉLÉCHARGEMENT GRATUIT

Download on the
App Store

GET IT ON
Google Play

Télécharger dans l'App Store
Disponible sur Google Play

GabbysDollhouse.spinmaster.com

Hi, I am Gabby.

This is Pandy Paws.

We are playing Kitty School!

1

First, it is music time.

DJ Catnip is the music teacher.

We sing together.

Pandy Paws sings another song.

DJ Catnip sings along.

That was cat-tastic!

What is next in Kitty School?

Story time with Pillow Cat!

We play the Three Little Pigs with a twist!

I am Astronaut Pig.

Pandy Paws is
Basketball Pig.

Pillow Cat is
Chef Pig.

CatRat is the Big Bad Chicken!

The Big Bad Chicken is coming!

"Little pigs, little pigs, let me come in!" he says.

"Not by the hair on our chinny, chin, chins!" we say.

We love story time!

What is next?

Playtime is next!

We play a game with Carlita.

CatRat hides.

We follow the green kitty light to find him!

We find CatRat!

He hides again!

Now where is the light?

Can you help us find it?

I see it!

It is in the ball pool!

We find CatRat!

Playtime is purr-rific!

What is next?

Lunchtime with Cakey Cat!

Cakey Cat makes kitty pizza!

We eat lunch. The pizzas are tasty!

Now lunchtime is done.

It is a fun day at Kitty School.

Thank you for playing!

You are such a smart little kitty!

Printed in the U.S.A. PO# 5078338 04/22

TOP SECRET

Rickett, the senior counterintelligence man, and the Provost Marshal walked the perimeter of the debris field examining the wreckage scattered there. Most of the pieces were small, no more than a few inches long and wide, but some measured a couple of feet on one side.

They came to one piece that was about two feet by two feet. According to Rickett, it was slightly curved. He locked it against his knee and tried to bend or break it. The metal was very thin and very lightweight. Rickett couldn't bend it at all.

As they prepared to leave the crash site, the senior CIC agent turned to Rickett. "You and I were never out here," he said. "You and I never saw this. You don't see any military people or military vehicles out here either."

"Yeah," Rickett agreed. "We never even left the office."

Other UFO Reports from Avon Books

COMMUNION
by Whitley Strieber

THE GULF BREEZE SIGHTINGS:
THE MOST ASTOUNDING MULTIPLE UFO SIGHTINGS
IN U.S. HISTORY
by Ed Walters and Frances Walters

PHENOMENON:
FORTY YEARS OF FLYING SAUCERS
edited by John Spencer and Hilary Evans

REPORT ON COMMUNION
by Ed Conroy

TRANSFORMATION
by Whitley Strieber

UFO CRASH AT ROSWELL

KEVIN D. RANDLE
Capt., U.S.A.F.R.
& DONALD R. SCHMITT
Director of Special Investigations, Center for UFO Studies

AVON BOOKS ⬢ NEW YORK

UFO CRASH AT ROSWELL is an original publication of Avon Books. This work has never before appeared in book form.

AVON BOOKS
A division of
The Hearst Corporation
1350 Avenue of the Americas
New York, New York 10019

First Avon Books Printing: July 1991

Contents

Foreword

As I write these words, good news continues to arrive daily from Eastern Europe. More and more, the remaining remnants of the Cold War are being dismantled. Armies are reduced in size, citizens are seizing control of the secret police apparatus, and free elections are being held for the first time in over forty years.

The United States has not, of course, been immune to these changes. The amount of money to be spent on defense is to be reduced as our former adversaries become cooperative and non-Communist members of the world order. The Cold War is not over, but many of the excesses it spawned can now be curtailed.

The subject of this book by Kevin Randle and Don Schmitt is, I believe, directly connected to these recent political changes. Since this link may not be immediately clear, let me explain.

Randle and Schmitt write about what they have learned after an exhaustive investigation, one that still continues, concerning the events surrounding a single UFO case. That event—the crash of something *highly unusual* in the high desert of New Mexico in early July of 1947—becomes with the publication of this book one of the best-documented cases in UFO history.

Most UFO reports rely upon the testimony of one or two witnesses, so it is relatively easy for skeptics to disregard the thousands of sightings recorded since 1947.

Very few UFOs leave a physical trace after they disappear.

The Roswell event is not like most UFO reports. Although no one actually saw the object crash, dozens of men collected the debris that remained. Then several crews of military aircraft flew that debris to government installations around the country. The authors' reconstruction of the Roswell event does not rely upon one or two witnesses. Their almost heroic efforts have resulted in direct or indirect confirmation from over dozens and dozens of witnesses to various portions of the recovery effort.

This may all be interesting, says the reader, but what does it have to do with Eastern Europe? Just this. The Roswell UFO crash has one other feature that sets it apart: *It remains a government secret.* The military—the Army Air Force at the time—moved within a few hours on July 8, 1947, to conceal almost completely any evidence of the true nature of the debris. The authors have extensively documented this cover-up, hour by hour, on that fateful day. That web of secrecy has been extremely effective, but today it is beginning to unravel.

In the post-war climate that existed in 1947, one can understand and sympathize with the decision made then to conceal the Roswell crash from the public. But 1990 is not 1947. As the Cold War ebbs, the practices and habits of that era are becoming increasingly outdated. I believe this applies with special force to the excessive use of secrecy by all governments, including our own, to conceal activities from their citizens.

It is now time, I suggest, for the events of July, 1947 in New Mexico to be made public. The onus is not on Randle, Schmitt, and colleagues to demonstrate why the secrecy should be lifted. On the contrary, the burden is on the government and military to show why it should *not* be lifted. If it is important for national security that the Roswell event and its aftermath remain secret after forty-three years, let the government make its case. If the Roswell debris was a weather balloon, as was claimed, then why the continuing secrecy? But if it was not a balloon . . .

Sissela Bok, in her book *Secrets* on the use and misuse of secrecy, has captured my argument succinctly:

Rather, every effort must be made to press public officials to justify their case for secrecy, to produce reasons, and to show why particular practices of concealment are necessary.

It has been my personal and professional pleasure to assist the authors in their long and tireless investigation of Roswell. You will read about their many interviews, trips, and phone calls. The cost, both personal and financial, has been enormous. Their motivation, as I have observed, is not self-serving in any sense. Both wish only to discover the truth about the events at Roswell and bring them to public light.

Read this book with an open mind and remember that the investigation is not yet complete. By the time the book is in your hands, new witnesses will have been located. But I doubt that the authors' account of events at Roswell will be altered significantly. Over one hundred witnesses have painted a picture of an event whose contours are now clear. Randle and Schmitt's book is in the tradition and spirit of the best investigative journalism: exposing the practices of government officials who would prefer to avoid public accountability for their actions. The story they relate is at times unbelievable, sensational, and perhaps even unearthly. It is, however, the truth.

Mark Rodeghier
Scientific Director, Center for UFO Studies

Introduction

A UFO crashed northwest of Roswell, New Mexico, in the summer of 1947. The military acted quickly and efficiently to recover the debris after its existence was reported by a ranch hand. The debris—unlike anything these highly trained men had ever seen—was flown without delay to at least three government installations. A cover story was concocted to explain away the debris and the flurry of activity. It was explained that a weather balloon, one with a new radiosonde target device, had been found and temporarily confused the personnel of the 509th Bomb Group. Government officials took reporters' notes from their desks and warned a radio reporter not to play a recorded interview with the ranch hand. The men who had taken part in the recovery were told never to talk about the incident. And with a whimper, not a bang, the Roswell event faded quickly from public view and press scrutiny. It was not resurrected until one of the intelligence officers, thirty years after the fact, revealed his role to a reporter.

The above account is, in its bare bones, the reality behind the public face of the Roswell event. This book will flesh out the details with a huge collection of first- and secondhand accounts, documentary evidence, and reconstruction of the most probable course of events. Don't be surprised if there are moments of confusion as you read the book; it is not often that one is asked to juggle so many unfamiliar names, places and dates.

To aid your comprehension we have constructed a time line of events, placed in a separate chapter, that concisely presents our best reconstruction of all the important events of the Roswell recovery and its aftermath. There is also a comprehensive index to the book which should be helpful.

We are convinced that our account of the history of the Roswell event is as accurate as possible. Why, though, should you be convinced? Why should you believe the testimony of these witnesses? How could such an event be kept secret so long? Surely the real story would have leaked before now, as has seemingly happened to every government secret in the past twenty years. President Nixon himself, with all his powers and resources, wasn't able to prevent Woodward and Bernstein from uncovering the Watergate conspiracy.

Secrets surely do leak, but some secrets don't for long periods of time. Consider these instances:

1) The Stealth fighter aircraft was developed in secret and was flying at a time when the public was told the aircraft was *still on the drawing board*.

2) Project Ultra, the Allied World War II project that allowed us to break the codes of the Germans and thereby hasten their defeat, was a secret for almost forty years until revealed in the early 1980s.

3) Only recently have the numerous military accidents with nuclear devices been disclosed, not because of a desire by the government to admit the truth, but because of the dedicated probing of a civilian organization.

So it is certainly true that the government can keep secrets, but to what lengths are officials prepared to go to enact a coverup? We present copious details in this book about what was done at Roswell, but there is historical precedent for those actions. Consider this one instance from an event that occurred during World War II.

The Boeing Airplane Company was then secretly developing the B-29 bomber for the Army Air Force at its main plant near Seattle. On February 18, 1943, a prototype B-29 caught on fire during a test flight and crashed *in Seattle* onto a meat packing plant. The plane actually passed over downtown Seattle during its rapid descent. All members of the crew died, along with several employees of the plant and some of the firemen who fought the blaze that engulfed the plane and plant.

Thousands of people saw the plane coming down and the subsequent fire and rescue efforts. Did the story of the crash of a secret aircraft go out over the wires that same day, with accounts from these many witnesses? Although it seems unlikely, the FBI succeeded in preventing any but the most garbled information from leaking out. FBI agents went so far as to intercept all copies of *City Transit Weekly,* an employee newsletter that carried photos of the plane taken by a Seattle city bus driver.

So the government does keep secrets, and it will take extreme measures to protect those secrets in matters of national security. Could the Roswell event have been sufficiently important to warrant such treatment? We think so, and so must two men, still living, whom we have interviewed.

The Provost Marshal at the Roswell base, the equivalent of the chief of police, was in charge of all security at the crash site in 1947. When we located and then contacted him late last year (1989), it was the first time anyone had extensively questioned him about what had occurred. The Provost Marshal did not tell us the weather balloon cover story, nor did he give us a true account of the Roswell recovery. Instead, he told us that he considered himself *still* sworn to secrecy about the event—after forty-three years!

The second fellow we interviewed was an agent in the Counter-Intelligence Corps. He accompanied another intelligence officer on the initial trip to the crash site and, we believe, wrote a report on the incident for his superiors in Washington. At first, this intelligence agent refused to admit that the *event had occurred at all!* There had been no newspaper story, no fuss, not even the recovery of a weather balloon. After much prodding, he was willing to admit that something came down and was recovered, but that was as far as he would go. He admits no personal involvement, even though other reliable sources give him a central role.

We admire how seriously these gentlemen take their oaths of secrecy after several decades, but we must raise this question: Why the need to conceal the recovery of a weather balloon?

The government cover-up extends to the public records of the Air Force UFO investigation as well. Those records were released in 1976, and the file on Roswell contains but a single press clipping. No letters, no notes, no investigative forms, no official weather balloon explanation, nothing but that lone clipping. The file for the recovery of an actual weather balloon in Circleville, Ohio, a week before the Roswell event, contains far more documentation on its particulars. Where is the material that should be in the Roswell file?

The evidence we have begun to present here, and that we will discuss in subsequent chapters, establishes that the Roswell crash was one of those events that had to be kept secret by whatever means were necessary. Files and notes were confiscated from reporters, radio stations were warned not to air stories, a phony story was concocted, and men and women were sworn to secrecy.

As you can well imagine, it has not been an easy task to reconstruct what actually occurred in July of 1947. Many of the men (and the few women) involved are now dead, and those living are quite old. Human memory does not record events with complete accuracy, especially after years have elapsed. As Kevin Tierney has explained in his book *How To Be A Witness*, when someone has been asked to recount his memory of an event several times, "For the most part what he says will be the same, but there will generally be minor discrepancies between his recollection on one occasion and the next." This is certainly true for the accounts we have gathered concerning Roswell, and the natural errors that creep into an individual's memory mean that some inconsistencies exist in the testimony you will read. Nevertheless, the general pattern of events we have recorded from essentially all the witnesses does fit one consistent picture.

As those above the age of five at the time of President Kennedy's assassination can relate, the moment when they first learned of that gruesome event is permanently etched in their minds—a snapshot memory. Several of the Roswell witnesses have compared their memories of the 1947 event to that of the assassination: The Roswell memories are vivid and detailed, despite the passage of so many years.

Government secrecy is not always something evil and unjustified. We understand and support the practice of secrecy as it applies to certain types of information (one of us, in fact, worked as an Air Force intelligence officer). Some information should remain hidden, such as nuclear firing codes, court records, police files, and information about intelligence agents working undercover, but records documenting the recovery of a weather balloon hardly merit such treatment.

What could have happened so long ago at Roswell to cause former intelligence officers to abide by their oaths of secrecy today, even though previous accounts of the recovery have been published and broadcast? What kind of event required such high levels of security that the intelligence officer who participated in the initial recovery of the debris, and who was entrusted with the task of taking some of the debris to higher levels of command, was *not allowed* to read the written report upon his return? What caused the military to place the ranch manager who reported finding the debris under house arrest? Why have the military records of men involved in recovering the debris disappeared? Why, indeed?

We think we know why, and the story begins in the last week of June of 1947, as the public began to report sightings of strange objects in the skies: flying saucers.

Part I:

A Historical Perspective

The Summer: 1947

Kenneth Arnold started it all on June 24, 1947. Arnold, who sometimes flew search and rescue missions, had diverted to participate in the aerial search for a missing Marine transport plane, reported to have crashed in the mountains. According to Arnold, the air was so smooth and the sky so clear that he trimmed out the airplane and sat back watching the ground and sky around him. After an hour with no luck, he was heading toward Yakima, Washington when he spotted them.

It was a flash of brightness that drew his attention. As he searched for the source, he sighted a chain of nine objects flying north to south at about 9,500 feet. Because they were heading rapidly toward Mount Rainier, he believed, at first, they were jet aircraft.

As Arnold watched, the objects flew between Mount Rainier and Mount Adams, a distance of about 47 miles, at a speed he estimated to be 1,700 miles an hour. Every few seconds the objects changed course or dipped down, and when they did, they flashed, reflecting the sun. Arnold found them peculiar because he couldn't see the tail or wings. In drawings completed for the Air Force, the objects looked boomerang-shaped.

When he landed in Yakima, he told a few friends at the airport what he had seen. When he touched down in Pendleton, Oregon later, he found a group of reporters waiting. He told them that the motion of the craft could best be described as that of saucers skipping across the surface of a lake. Hearing that, one of the reporters, Bill Bequette, coined the term "flying saucer."[1]

The next day, newspapers around the country carried the story. The headlines, "Mysterious Objects Seen in Fast Flight,"[2] explained nothing. Government spokesmen, such as Edward Leach, senior CAA (later FAA) aeronautical inspector said that if the objects were as described, he didn't know what they could be. In Washington, a spokesman for the War Department (later the Defense Department) said only that they were interested in anything that could fly that fast.

But the damage had been done. Arnold, with his report, had told the world about the mysterious objects that moved like saucers on a pond. From that point, the newspapers were filled with stories of flying saucers and flying discs.

In fact, on the same day, June 24, Fred Johnson, a prospector in the Cascade Mountains, reported watching five or six disc-shaped craft fly by. He described them as round, with a slight tail, and about thirty feet in diameter. They were flying in no particular formation and as they banked once, they reflected the sun. As they came near, Johnson noticed that his compass was spinning wildly. This was the first report of an instrument affected by the close approach of the flying discs but it would not be the last. When the objects vanished in the distance minutes later, the compass settled down.[3]

During the next two weeks, hundreds of sightings would be made and most of them were reported in the local newspapers. On June 25, nine objects in a loose formation were seen over Kansas City, Missouri. Two oval-shaped objects, one flying after the other, were seen by Lloyd Lowry near Pueblo, Colorado. In Utah, a lone man saw a single object. In Oklahoma, C.E. Holman saw two illuminated discs, and near Glens Falls, New York, Louis Stebbins saw a reddish object.

Sighting reports continued on June 26th. They came from Utah, Arizona, Oklahoma, Texas, and New Mexico. In fact, the southwestern skies were filled with flying discs. In Utah, for example, Glen Bunting, a teacher near Logan, reported a single object flying at high speed to the east. Two hunters made independent reports of the same object.

Near Cedar City, Utah, Roy Walters watched one object moving at high speed. Like Arnold, Walters was flying, but he didn't give chase. He said the object took an easterly course and didn't make any maneuvers.

At the same time, Royce R. Knight, the airport manager at Cedar City, said he saw a lone object in rapid flight heading to the east. However, it was in sight for only a few seconds. Knight reported the object disintegrated into a ball of blue flame.

Charles Moore, driving north of the Cedar City airport, reported a single object flying eastward. He reported no exhaust or flames near it, but did say it looked like a bright meteor.

On June 27, there was also a series of sightings in New Mexico. Captain E.B. Detchmendy who was stationed at White Sands, reported he saw a high flying object that appeared "flame-like."

At the same time, 9:50 A.M., W.C. Dodds, who worked at White Sands, reported that he, too, saw a flame-like object. It was high in the sky and moving straight and level.

In Capitan, New Mexico, north of White Sands, Mrs. Cummins and her neighbor, Erv Dill, saw one shiny object that seemed to land on the nearby hills. They reported a yellow flame and a whistling sound associated with the craft.

The major change on the 27th was the distribution of sightings, which were now more widespread. The first sightings were made in Michigan and in Canada. In fact, sightings of flying discs were made throughout most of the United States. The first sightings were made in Australia and New Zealand. The phenomenon was becoming a worldwide problem and no one had any answers.

By June 27, newspapers now carried not only reports of the flying saucers, but the scientific explanations for them. The Science Service announced that they had made a quiet survey of the phenomena and said that the whole story of the flying discs might not be told by those involved in specific research. They pointed out that some aeronautical research was still under governmental wartime research classifications and regulations. The flying discs might be related to that research.

Sources involved in some of the classified aeronautical research programs, however, offered three educated guesses about the discs. One suggestion was the discs were supersonic aircraft with hexagon or diamond shapes that spun at high speeds giving the impression of a disc. A second theory was that they were remotely controlled rockets. And because of reported falling or landing discs, a third theory suggested they were controlled by some experimental station far from the centers of population.

One of the wildest theories surmised the discs were actually spots before the eyes. Some scientists said they were the afterimages caused by looking at bright light or the sun and then looking away. The problem with this explanation was that, if true, the discs should have been reported as black.

Another optical illusion is caused when a person leaves a darkened area and walks into a brighter one. That produces floating spots before the eyes, but those spots move erratically and do not travel at high speeds in straight lines as had been reported by most of the witnesses.

Scientists had already ruled out meteors because the discs were flying too slowly for that. And meteors wouldn't look like airplanes. Scientists also pointed out that the Earth was not moving through a meteor storm, and, therefore, the number of meteors striking the Earth's atmosphere was not higher than usual.

In one survey, the reliability of the observers was

checked. Many of them were people hard to disbelieve. Police officers, airline pilots, military officers, and scientists were among those sighting the discs.

David Lilienthal, the chairman of the Atomic Energy Commission, said that the flying discs had nothing to do with any atomic experiments. *Newsweek* suggested the Navy's "Flying Flapjack," might be responsible for some of the sightings but the Navy denied it. Their only "flapjack" was in Bridgeport, Connecticut and hadn't left.[4]

Finally, there were those claiming the flying saucers were from another planet. Mars and Venus were suggested as the most likely candidates, though a few thought the discs came from another solar system. With no evidence found to support any of the other theories, and with the objects outperforming the best military fighters, those who believed the extraterrestrial hypothesis seemed to be on the right track.

Interestingly, even with the newspapers across the country and around the world publishing every theory and explanation for the saucers, the numbers of reports continued to grow. Editorial writers began offering solutions of their own that ranged from a delayed war hysteria to extraterrestrial visitation. The only common thread was that no one had any answers. Everyone was talking about the saucers. They were taking the headlines away from events that were shaping the world, but no one could explain them.

Reports of flying discs didn't slow down on June 28. The majority of the reports came from west of the Mississippi, but the saucers were beginning to appear in large numbers in the east. In Montgomery, Alabama four military officers, Captain William H. Kayko, Captain John H. Cantrell, Captain Redman, and First Lieutenant Theodore Dewey reported a bright light in the late evening sky. It zigzagged through the atmosphere with wild bursts of speed and was airborne for about twenty-five minutes. On June 29, the flying saucers returned to the White

Sands Missile Range and were sighted by four men there. Two of the men, Doctor C.J. Zohn, and Curtis C. Rockwood were missile experts. John R. Kauke was on the White Sands staff. They reported a single disc or sphere seen first in the northeast traveling to the north. It was in sight for only sixty seconds. The Air Force, upon completing their investigation, claimed a balloon was responsible for the sighting. That was an explanation the Air Force used frequently and in the early days, before anyone asked the hard questions, people accepted it.

The military, particularly the Army Air Force, which was charged with the air defense of the United States, was not happy. The discs were mocking them by flying over the continental U.S. and there was nothing that could be done about it. During the July 4, 1947, weekend, the military had fighters on standby as far south as Muroc Army Air Field (now Edwards Air Force Base) in California, and as far north as Seattle in Washington. In Oregon, the fighters were not only equipped with gun cameras, they were airborne.[5]

It was during that Fourth of July weekend that the first report of flying discs was made by an airline flight crew. According to the pilot, Captain E.J. Smith, shortly after takeoff, five thin objects, smooth on the bottom, were seen silhouetted against the setting sun. Smith and his crew saw the discs clearly and watched them for about forty-five miles before the discs finally disappeared. Smith said they weren't clouds, aircraft, smoke, or weather balloons.

But Smith's sighting was only the beginning of the problems on that long weekend. In Portland, Oregon, there was a series of sightings that involved both civilians and police. The first was reported just north of Redmond, Oregon, when C.J. Bogne and a carload of witnesses saw four disc-shaped objects streaking past Mount Jefferson. They made no noise and performed no maneuvers.

At one o'clock, Don Metcalfe, an Oaks Park employee, said he saw more than one disc fly directly over the park.

Frank Cooley, a news reporter with KOIN in Portland, Oregon, watched twelve shiny, disc-shaped objects as they tilted and circled high overhead.

Five minutes after 1:00 P.M., Kenneth A. McDowell, a police officer near the Portland Police Station, noticed the pigeons around him were fluttering as if frightened. Overhead he spotted five disc-shaped objects, three heading east and two flying south. They were moving at high speed and seemed to be oscillating.

About the same time, Walter A. Lissy and Robert Ellis, the patrolmen in Car 82, reported three disc shaped objects overhead. They may have been the same three that the first police officer saw heading to the east.

Across the Columbia River, in Vancouver, Washington, Sergeant John Sullivan, Clarence McKay, and Fred Krives, sheriff's deputies, reported that twenty to thirty disc-shaped craft flashed overhead.

Not long after that, three harbor patrolmen on the river near Portland, reported seeing three to six discs traveling at high speed. According to the witnesses, they were shiny, like chrome hubcaps, and oscillated as they flew.

At 4:00 P.M., more civilians reported objects. A woman phoned the police, telling them that she watched a single object, "shiny as a new dime, flipping around." It finally faded from sight.

An unidentified man called police to report he saw one disc going east and two going north. Like the others, these were shiny, shaped like flattened saucers, and were traveling at high speed.

In Milwaukie, Oregon, not far from Portland, Sergeant Claude Cross reported three objects traveling to the north. Again, they were disc-shaped and moving at high speed.

The sightings in the northwest continued throughout the weekend. Newspapers around the country reported the sightings in Oregon as well as those in the rest of the country. Front pages were filled with reports and theories, though no one seemed to have a satisfactory answer. The radio news was filled with reports as more people saw the saucers, and the news magazines began covering the sightings.

According to the newspaper accounts, the mood in the country was one of interest but not fright. People wanted to know what was causing the sightings. To that end, three separate groups each offered a thousand dollars for a genuine flying disc. E.J. Culligan, president of a Northbrook, Illinois company; the Spokane Athletic Round Table; and the Los Angeles World Inventors Exposition all offered the money. Culligan said he would pay for the capture of a disc or for the true explanation, but the others said the money could be earned only by producing a flying saucer. And the Los Angeles group put a five-day limit on their offer. The Spokane Athletic Round Table thought that a little cash incentive was all that was needed for the proof to surface. But even with the promise of financial reward, no one came forward.[6]

It was also on the July 4 weekend that reports of crashes began. Sherman Campbell, of Circleville, Ohio reported to the sheriff that he thought the remains of a balloon recovered on his farm might explain the sightings. The balloon, covered with aluminum foil and flying high, could reflect the sun, giving it a disc-like appearance. It would move silently on the wind currents. The balloon was on display at the office of the *Circleville Herald* until public interest slipped. Pictures of Jean Campbell holding the kite-like appendage of the balloon were printed in papers around the country.[7]

Then, on July 7, newspapers reported the story of another alleged crash. According to Vernon Baird, he was flying in a P-38 above thirty thousand feet when he sighted a formation of discs behind him. He said that they were about fifteen feet in diameter and looked like yo-yos. As he watched, one of them broke formation, and flew at him on a collision course until the propwash ripped it apart. The craft spiraled down, crashing into the Tobacco Root Mountains.

A day later, Baird's boss, J.J. Archer, said the story was a joke. They had been sitting around in the hangar and after listening to stories of the flying discs, invented the tale. That was the end of it.[8]

It was also on July 7 that the first occupant report was made in the United States. Gene Gamachi and I.W. Martenson of Tacoma, Washington reported they had seen a number of objects, some of which landed on the neighbors' roofs. They said that "little men" climbed out of the objects but disappeared when reporters arrived.

An elderly woman in Massachusetts reported on July 7 that she had seen a moon-sized object fly by her window. Inside the craft was a slender figure dressed in what she thought was a Navy uniform.

On July 8, the last of the 1947 occupant reports were made. The witness, a merchant seaman in Houston, reported the landing of a silver saucer. The pilot of it was no more than two feet tall with a round head the size of a basketball. It greeted the seaman, climbed back into the disc, and took off.[9]

But sightings of the creatures from inside the flying saucers would not receive widespread play in the press. There was some talk about green men from Mars, but most sightings were of high flying craft. Very few of the flying discs were close to the ground and even fewer landed. Occupant reports would number fewer than a half dozen.

It was also on July 8, 1947 that the *Roswell Daily Record* reported that the mystery of the flying discs had been solved. Mac Brazel, a New Mexican rancher, had found the remains of a flying disc on his range. He brought pieces to show the sheriff, who contacted the military at the Roswell Army Air Field. According to the newspaper, the wreckage was being shipped to higher headquarters for examination.

For six or seven hours, the world waited. Stories about

the find appeared in newspapers as far away as London and Hong Kong. Reporters from everywhere called the Public Information Officer at Roswell, the local sheriff, and both daily newspapers, wanting details, but nothing newsworthy was being reported.

By 6:00 that evening, however, the answer was out. According to Brigadier General Roger Ramey, the commander of the Eighth Air Force, the flying disc was nothing more than a mundane weather balloon. Photographs of Major Jesse A. Marcel, the intelligence officer from Roswell, of Ramey, and of Ramey and his chief of staff, Colonel Thomas DuBose, were released. Finally, a picture of Irving Newton, a weather officer at Forth Worth Army Air Field, was also released. Each photo showed the torn-up wreckage of a weather balloon spread out on the floor of Ramey's office.

The next day, the official explanation was issued. The officers of the 509th Bomb Group had been swept up in the excitement of the situation and had not realized that the mundane might look extraordinary.

In fact, the next day the *Roswell Daily Record* carried a follow-up story. Mac Brazel was interviewed at the offices of the *Roswell Daily Record*. Brazel reported he had found the material in the middle of June and had thought nothing of it until he heard the stories of the flying discs. Then, at the urgings of neighbors and family, he drove the seventy-five miles into Roswell with a few pieces.

That had started the chain of events which lead to Brigadier General Ramey's announcement that it was nothing more than a weather balloon. At a press conference, Ramey identified the balloon as a Rawin target weather device. What had fooled Marcel and the others was the unusual configuration and the aluminum foil appendages. With the Roswell material identified, other reports of flying discs captured the headlines and continued almost unabated until over 800 sightings had been made. In an attempt to defuse the situation, General Ramey, on a radio station in Utah, pointed out that every state in the union was involved except Kansas. He then mentioned that Kansas was a dry state. No drunks in Kansas to see mysterious lights in the sky, even though seven sightings had been made in Kansas.

On July 9, the wave didn't seem to be ready to subside. Again, reports were coming from all over the country. Early in the morning in Chicago, Illinois, Thomas O'Brian and Timothy Donegan watched four or five dimly illuminated objects that were heading to the southwest. They also reported hearing a swishing noise and seeing a blue, gaseous trail.

Fifteen minutes later, William Valetta, also in Chicago, reported five or six domed discs in fast flight. He, too, reported the swishing noise, a blue flame and smoke. They were now heading easterly, out over Lake Michigan, and were in sight for only a few minutes.

Four and a half hours later, Marvin Wright and John Alinger of Springfield, Illinois reported a single, shiny gray disc that would fly straight and then dip, heading to the south. They, too, reported a bluish trail.

In Idaho, Dave Johnson was flying his own airborne alert. Johnson, taking a lesson from the military, had been searching for some of the flying discs from the cockpit of his private plane. Just after noon, he saw one flat disc that flashed once. He tried to film it but when the film was developed, no image appeared.

However, the number of reports was declining. By the weekend of July 12 and 13, there were few people sighting flying discs. The Army had grounded the planes that had been searching for the saucers and the newspaper accounts were nearly gone. It seemed the nation was no longer interested. If nothing had happened during the two or three weeks of excitement to prove that the saucers were real, then the explanation for them had to lie elsewhere.

Ed Ruppelt, former head of the Air Force's Project Blue Book, confirmed the sudden change in attitude in the middle of July and offered an explanation. "By the end of July 1947 the security lid was down tight. The few members of the press who did inquire about what the Air Force was doing got the same treatment that you would get today if you inquired about the number of thermonuclear weapons stock-piled in the U.S.'s atomic arsenal. No one, outside of a few high-ranking officers in the Pentagon, knew what the people in the barbed-wire-enclosed Quonset huts that housed the Air Technical Intelligence Center (ATIC) were thinking or doing," he said. [10]

Ruppelt had access to all the old memos, correspondence, and records when he took over Blue Book. He saw that in 1947 the generals took the situation very seriously. The documents also indicated a period of confusion. No one in the government, the Army Air Force, or at ATIC knew what to do about all the reports. But, by the end of the July, the brass had realized one thing. Too much information was being published in the press or reported on the radio. And that had to stop.

The *Las Vegas Review-Journal* confirmed this view when it reported on July 9 that the reports of flying saucers "whizzing" through the sky fell off sharply as the Army and the Navy began a concentrated effort to stop the rumors. The newspaper reported that Army Air Force Headquarters in Washington delivered a blistering rebuke to officers at Roswell, New Mexico for suggesting they had found a flying disc. Interestingly, no other officers were rebuked or admonished for any of the other statements they had made about flying discs. There were half a dozen reports of crashes and investigations of them, and there were other areas where military officers were making statements about saucers. None of those officers were criticized by the Pentagon. [11]

By the end of 1947, the flying discs weren't being seen as often as they had been in the summer and the few reports being made were not carried by the newspapers. The attitude, cultivated by the military and the government, was that if there had been anything to the flying saucers they would have discovered it. And, having learned the truth, they would have reported that to the people. When no such report was forthcoming, the perception was that there was nothing to the reports.

The flying saucers, for whatever reason, seemed to have gone away. They wouldn't stay away, but by the time they returned most of the 1947 reports would be forgotten. And buried deeper than most was the strange story that had come from Roswell, New Mexico on July 8. It would be almost three decades before anyone would again even look into the Roswell sighting, but by then the trail would be very cold.

Roswell Revisited

The world learned of Roswell, New Mexico on July 8, 1947, when First Lieutenant Walter Haut announced that the Roswell Army Air Field was in possession of a flying saucer. His press release, carried in whole or in part by more than thirty afternoon newspapers, left no question about what they had found. It was a flying saucer.

Haut's release said, "The many rumors regarding the flying discs became a reality yesterday when the intelligence office of the 509th Bomb Group of the Eighth Air Force, Roswell Army Air Field, was fortunate enough to gain possession of a disc through the cooperation of one of the local ranchers and the Sheriff's office of Chaves County.

"The flying object landed on a ranch near Roswell sometime last week. Not having phone facilities, the rancher stored the disc until such time as he was able to contact the Sheriff's office, who in turn notified Major Jesse A. Marcel of the 509th Bomb Group Intelligence office.

"Action was immediately taken and the disc was picked up at the rancher's home. It was inspected at the Roswell Army Air Field and subsequently loaned by Major Marcel to higher headquarters."[1]

Haut's release caused a nationwide stir and then a worldwide sensation. Telephones at the sheriff's office, the newspapers and the radio stations were ringing constantly. All the lines to the base were tied up. No one could make any outgoing calls as the world press tried to get any information they could on the flying saucer.

The next day, Mac Brazel, the man who had found the device, was taken to the offices of the *Roswell Daily Record,* where he told the waiting reporters exactly what had happened. According to that story, he had been in his pastures on June 14, 1947, and came across an aluminum foil and balsa wood balloon. He thought nothing of it until he heard the stories of the flying discs. Then friends and relatives urged him to take the find to Roswell and claim the three thousand dollars in rewards the papers were talking about. According to the *Roswell Morning Dispatch,* Brazel waited until Monday, July 7, to make the long trip into town. There, the sheriff called the military, who were momentarily excited by the find.

But now, a couple of days later, after a special flight to Forth Worth, the answer had been found. It was nothing more than a weather balloon. The rancher couldn't be expected to identify it because of the unusual nature of the balloon. The officers at the Roswell Army Air Field should have made the identification, but it wasn't until Warrant Officer Irving Newton at the Fort Worth Army Air Field saw it that its identity was established.[2]

The Army had moved rapidly to bury the report. They presented a cover story that answered the questions and that would remain intact if no one examined it too hard. The cover did what it was supposed to do. It diverted attention.

With the answer out, and with pictures of the weather balloon circulated to various newspapers, the pressure was off. Interest in the flying discs shifted elsewhere, and in a matter of days, they were gone from the newspapers altogether. By the end of July, 1947 there were no new sightings reported.

Most people considered the Roswell event to be a non-UFO case for the next thirty years. However, during a lecture in Indiana in 1956, Frank Edwards was asked if there had ever been a crash of a flying saucer. He answered, "I'm not sure that some of them haven't. Way back in 1947, at Roswell, New Mexico, a farmer reported that he saw something strike a mountainside and crash. According to what I was told, they threw troops in a circle all around that place, and would let nobody in for five days. Finally they came up with a picture of a man holding a little crumpled kite with aluminum foil on it—a radar target—and they said this was it—believe it or not."[3]

Edwards also mentioned the Roswell case in his book, *Flying Saucers—Serious Business*. There isn't much more there, except that the rancher had called the sheriff to report the discovery. Edwards never took it any further.

Then, in the late 1970s, Jesse A. Marcel, the intelligence officer of the 509th Bomb Group, broke the silence. Marcel, in several published interviews, said that he had been the intelligence officer who had picked up the material on the ranch near Roswell. He had taken some of it to higher headquarters where the cover story had been invented. Now it was time to reveal the truth.[4]

As that story was pieced together (at first with no regard to accuracy), W. W. "Mac" Brazel, a ranch foreman in the Corona, New Mexico area, was examining the range on July 3, 1947, when he came to a field filled with metallic debris. It looked as if something had crashed, scattering the debris over an area about three quarters of a mile long and two or three hundred feet wide. Pieces of thin metal, along with wire, I-beams, brown parchment-like paper, and lead foil littered the pasture.

Brazel didn't know what he had found, but picked up a few samples to show his closest neighbors who lived ten miles away. They suggested he take it into Roswell. Brazel followed the advice and showed it to Sheriff George A. Wilcox who, according to the story, was unimpressed. He suggested that Brazel call the military at the Roswell Army Air Field. Once the military arrived at the office, they took over and Wilcox lost interest in the event.

Two Army officers and a civilian, who was identified as a member of the Counter-Intelligence Corps (CIC), responded to the phone call. Jesse Marcel was one of them. Colonel William Blanchard, the commander of the 509th Bomb Group, the other officer, suggested that Marcel and the CIC agent accompany Brazel to the ranch and see what was there.

The trip to the ranch took the rest of the afternoon and they were forced to stay the night in a small cabin that had no electricity and no running water. The next morning they headed out onto the field where Brazel had found the debris.

Marcel would later say that the material was like nothing he had ever seen. The metal was as thin as newsprint and as light as a feather. It was slightly flexible but very strong. He tried to dent it with a sledgehammer but couldn't. Marcel and the CIC agent tried to burn it but it would not burn. It was lighter and stronger and more fire resistant than anything either of them had ever seen. Marcel, along with the counter-intelligence agent, picked up as much as they could and began loading it into Marcel's convertible and the counter-intelligence agent's jeep carryall, a vehicle with a rear box.

According to Marcel, loading it took all day. The material was hard to find because it did not reflect sunlight, and most of it was broken into small pieces. At dusk, Marcel and the agent headed back to Roswell, leaving Brazel alone at the ranch. On the way to the base, Marcel stopped at his house and showed some of the debris to his wife and son. He thought that it was something extraordinary and he wanted his family to have an opportunity to see the debris before someone classified it as top secret.

Jesse Marcel, Jr. later recalled an I-beam inscribed with strange writing. The symbols were more like geometric objects than any recognizable language. Jesse Jr.

remembered that his dad had been excited by the find and didn't know what it was. Marcel sat at the kitchen table with the material spread out, examining it closely but unable to identify any of it.

The next day, Walter Haut, the Public Information Officer at Roswell, released the statement that caused the worldwide interest. Haut, who said that he never had the opportunity to see the wreckage or tour the crash site, believed that something extraordinary had happened out there. He just didn't know what it was.

Marcel was ordered to fly some of the debris to Eighth Air Force headquarters in Fort Worth. There, the plane was met by armed men. The material was transferred to another aircraft for transportation to the Air Technical Intelligence Center at Wright Field, according to some of the sources. Once the debris was off the Roswell plane, the crew was ordered to return to their base and then forget that they had made the flight.

According to dozens of newspaper accounts printed on July 9 and 10, Brigadier General Roger Ramey, commander of the Eighth Air Force, and then one of his officers, identified the material as that of a weather balloon. Marcel, in interviews conducted in 1978, said that was only the cover story. It wasn't a weather balloon. Ramey had told reporters in 1947 the special flight had been cancelled, but Marcel said that it hadn't. The material continued on to Wright Field despite what newspapers reported in 1947.

Marcel, first located by researcher and nuclear physicist Stanton Friedman in 1978, said that he was ordered by Ramey not to say "anything to anybody," including his family. He was ordered not to talk to reporters. He returned to Roswell and pretended that he knew nothing else. But Marcel had handled the material and he knew that it wasn't a weather balloon. He knew that it was "nothing from this Earth."

Friedman alerted a newsman, Steve Tom, of Chicago, who in turn told Len Stringfield. Interviewed by Stringfield in 1978, Marcel said no radiation had been detected at the crash site. He again described the debris field, saying it was much too large for a weather balloon. Even after all these years, Marcel still hadn't thought of an explanation for the debris.

Both Friedman and Stringfield had been investigating stories of crashed saucers and the retrievals of them. Both had some accounts from sources who demanded their names not be used, but nothing like the story told by Marcel. And more importantly, Marcel allowed his name to be used. Coupled to some of the things Friedman and Stringfield had learned in the past, they began to believe that the government had recovered at least one flying saucer.

The story got even stranger then. A man, Grady L. "Barney" Barnett, claimed that he had come across the wreckage of a disc-shaped craft some time on July 3. According to friends of Barnett, he had been working near the Plains of San Agustin, known locally as "The Flats." That was about a hundred and twenty miles from the Brazel ranch.

While Barnett was there, a group of university archaeologists drove up, though Barnett couldn't remember which university they were from. All of them, including Barnett, saw four dead bodies lying outside the craft. He said the bodies were not human and he was close enough to touch them, had he wanted to do so.

Barnett later described the bodies to a close friend. They were small creatures with large, pear shaped heads, skinny arms and legs, and no hair. They wore metallic-like, formfitting, gray suits that had no buttons or zippers or snaps.[5]

Moments later the military arrived. They ordered Barnett and the archaeology team to step away from the craft. The officer in charge told the civilians it was their patriotic duty to say nothing about what they had seen that day. Barnett told no one but his wife, his boss, and a couple of very close friends.

The theory, in 1978, reasoned that the debris Brazel had found was associated with the craft and the bodies Barnett found. The craft had come apart and the alien creatures had ejected, landing near the Plains of San Agustin. They were killed when their escape pod failed.

Stringfield received other information about the recovery of bodies. Norma Gardner had been a typist with a top secret clearance at Wright-Patterson Air Force Base. One of her duties had been to type the autopsy reports on an alien being. Most UFO researchers, along with the general public, found the story incredible and refused to believe it. But, coupled with what both Marcel and Barnett were saying, it suddenly wasn't that hard to believe, especially since her descriptions of the body and the clothing matched those made by Barnett.

At the same time as Barnett's encounter, Mac Brazel, the rancher, was being held by the military. They took him around to the local media, the newspapers, and the radio stations, where he told the reporters a story about finding the balloon on June 14. The military's idea was that Brazel would tell the cover story and the reporters, no longer interested, would go away.

Later, Brazel confided to friends and family that there was more to the story, but he couldn't reveal it. He told his son, Bill, that he had taken an oath that he wouldn't tell in detail what he had seen. He did tell reporters at the *Roswell Daily Record* that he was sure it wasn't a weather balloon and that if, in the future, he found anything short of a bomb, he wouldn't tell anyone about it.

Blanchard, the base commander, went on leave on Tuesday, July 8, just as the story was breaking. That convinced some reporters that there was no substance to the report. In 1978, UFO researchers were sure that it was all part of the cover story.

There weren't many facts available in 1947. Marcel now provided some of the story, but he had been cut out of the loop on July 8 when he flew to Fort Worth with some of the wreckage. On his return, Marcel challenged the CIC man who had remained at the base, asking to see the CIC agent's report. Marcel was told that the report was now classified, that he wasn't authorized to see it, and it was on its way to the Pentagon. If Marcel had a problem, he could take it up with Washington.[6]

But the newspapers of 1947, and Jesse Marcel in 1978, had told enough of the story and had provided enough of the facts to get a new investigation started. Marcel, because he was the intelligence officer and because he had been in Roswell, was an important source of information. There was no reason for him to lie about it. He would gain nothing. The few facts that could be checked verified what Marcel said and Marcel was saying that he had found an alien spaceship.

That was all the information available at the time. Only a few people were saying things in direct conflict with what the Army had said. There were only a few witnesses available, Marcel among the few living firsthand witnesses, and almost no supporting documentation. Marcel's story was interesting, but that was all it was.

Those few facts, available in newspapers from 1947 and provided in interviews with Marcel, were the starting point. They suggested that something interesting had happened, but not what it was. In 1980, The *Roswell Incident* by Charles Berlitz and William L. Moore would generate worldwide attention. A brief, though somewhat inaccurate, chronology of events was constructed and a few of the participants had been identified. For the moment, that was all there was to the story. It did not prove that an alien spacecraft crashed near Roswell. Later investigations would have to correct the mistakes before the real work could begin.

Part II:

Roswell, the Real Story

July 3–14, 1947:
Mac Brazel

According to meteorological records, on the evening of July 2, 1947 a thunderstorm hit the vicinity of Corona, New Mexico. July and August are considered the rainy season because most of the moisture received by the region falls during that time. Thunderstorms are not uncommon, but they are spotty. One field might receive five or six inches of rain while another, no more than a mile away, receives nothing. July, 1947 was no different. It was hot and dry and there were sporadic thunderstorms in the region.[1]

During the storm of July 2, Mac Brazel heard a crash, one that was louder than thunder and sounded different than the other rumbling. Brazel would later comment on it, but at the time, he wasn't too surprised. In New Mexico, there had been a lot of strange rumblings heard since atomic research had begun during World War II.

The next day, Brazel and Timothy D. Proctor, a young neighbor boy, were on horseback, riding the range to determine which fields had received rain.[2] Brazel wanted to move the livestock into those fields because the grass would be softer and greener due to the moisture.

During that ride, Brazel came upon a field filled with debris, located south of the ranch headquarters. It extended from the top of a small circle of hills, ran down the arroyo, up another hill, and disappeared on the reverse side. There was quite a bit of debris—some of it was shiny but most looked like dull metal. There were big chunks and little pieces. The material was packed so densely that the sheep refused to cross it. To Brazel, it looked as if something had exploded while still in the air.[3]

Brazel and young Proctor rode down and examined the field. There was no indication of passengers in whatever had crashed. There was debris but no sign of a body or bodies.

Brazel closely examined some of the material, surprised by the properties it exhibited. The debris was so thin and so light that it stirred in the wind. It was so strong that most pieces wouldn't flex. Brazel couldn't cut it with his knife and he couldn't burn it with matches.

Brazel picked up some of the smaller fragments and, with Proctor, headed off to his nearest neighbors, Floyd and Loretta Proctor, who lived about ten miles from the ranch headquarters. At the Proctor house, Brazel showed his neighbors a sliver of the material. Loretta Proctor said she "didn't know what the stuff was." According to Loretta, her husband tried to whittle on it but couldn't make a mark. Brazel held a match up to it to show that not only wouldn't it burn, it wouldn't even blacken.

Brazel suggested they drive down to look at the debris field, but the Proctors declined. Today, Loretta Proctor says, "We should have gone, but gas and tires were expensive then. We had our own chores and it would have been twenty miles, round trip."

Brazel didn't know what to do about the material in his field. Tommy Tyree, who began working for Brazel a month or so after the event, said that Brazel was irritated about the situation. Because the sheep wouldn't cross the field, Brazel had to drive them the long way around to get them to water. He wanted to know who was going to clean up the mess because he was too busy to take the time to do it.[4]

During the Fourth of July weekend, Brazel talked to friends and family. Norris Proctor remembered that someone suggested Brazel should try to claim the rewards being offered for proof that flying saucers were real. Others told him to notify the sheriff or the government, because it was probably one of the military's experimental projects. Brazel again approached the Proctors, asking them to drive down to see the debris field. And again they decided that they didn't have the time. It was too far. They suggested that it might be an experimental craft and that the military would want to know what happened to it. Brazel was reluctant only because neither he nor his neighbors had phones and it was a three or four hour trip into Roswell.[5]

On Sunday, July 6, Brazel decided it was time to make the trip into Roswell to see the sheriff. He stopped to tell Sheriff George A. Wilcox what he had. Brazel showed Wilcox a small piece of the debris. Wilcox suggested that they call the local air base.[6]

During this time, Frank Joyce, an announcer and reporter for Roswell radio station KGFL called and asked the sheriff if he had "anything going on." Wilcox put Brazel on the line and Joyce interviewed him over the phone. Today, Joyce will not disclose what was said, only that it was significantly different from what Brazel told him three days later.

The military responded quickly to the sheriff's phone call. Major Jesse A. Marcel was in the officer's club eating lunch when he was told that someone had showed up in the sheriff's office with parts of a flying saucer. Marcel, along with Colonel William Blanchard, and a plainclothes counter-intelligence agent responded, each in his own vehicle.[7]

It was only a few minutes later that Marcel arrived, followed by the CIC man and then Blanchard. Wilcox said afterward that it seemed as if the military men were waiting for the call because they got there so fast.[8]

They all, the military men and the sheriff's deputies, examined the pieces Brazel brought in. No one could identify the material and Blanchard, still at the base, ordered Marcel to accompany the rancher back to Corona. The CIC man said that he was going, too.

Brazel led them back out to his ranch, using the back roads, including the Pine Lodge Road. Because it was nearly dark when they reached the ranch house, they had no choice but to spend the night. They ate a cold dinner of canned beans and crackers and spent the night waiting for the sun to come up.

Early the next morning, July 7, 1947, Brazel took them out to the crash site. Marcel said that the debris was scattered over an area three-quarters of a mile long and two to three hundred feet wide. Marcel also said that there were pieces of material as thin as newsprint that couldn't be bent or dented. There was some lead-foil-like material, I-beams, and parchment-like paper.

Marcel closely examined the debris. According to Marcel, he picked up a piece about three feet square. It was as light as a feather but so strong that he couldn't bend it or flex it. It was dull gray.

Marcel also picked up one of the small, two-foot-long I-beams. The inside of the I was covered with symbols, most of them geometric shapes. The I-beam was lightweight, would flex slightly, but was very strong.

Brazel watched Marcel and the CIC agent examine the material and then left. According to Marcel, the two men spent the day picking up the debris. They loaded it into the rear of Marcel's '42 Buick convertible and into the rear of the CIC agent's jeep carryall.

As it began to get dark, they gave up on the idea of collecting it all. There was just too much of it. They found Brazel and told him they were returning to Roswell, but someone would probably return the next day to retrieve the remainder of the material.

The next morning, the CIC agent, accompanied by another agent, Lewis S. Rickett, and several MPs, cordoned off the area. The two CIC men went in search of Brazel while the Provost Marshal, Major Edwin D. Easley, began stationing his men around the crash site.[9]

When Brazel was located, they took him to Roswell and kept him at the base. His son, Bill Brazel, said, ". . . He was asked to stay down there and he agreed. If the old man had said, 'Hell no, I'm not going,' I don't really know what would have happened. But he said, 'Yup.' They just asked him to go down there and to stay for a day or two and he stayed."

When asked how long Mac Brazel might have been held, Bill Brazel then said, "I was living in Albuquerque at the time. I got the paper and I looked at it and here's my Dad's picture. I said to Shirley (Brazel) 'what the hell did he do now?' I read about it and they said that he wasn't being held but they had asked him to stay in Roswell for a few days and I told Shirley, Dad needs help. So I proceeded out to the ranch. I think that it was two or three days before my Dad showed up. I said what did you get into and he said, 'Oh, I found a thing out there.' "

On July 9, 1947, Brazel was escorted by military officers into Roswell to talk to reporters at the office of the *Roswell Daily Record*. Two reporters from Albuquerque had brought a portable wire photo transmitter with them so they could transmit pictures over the telephone lines.[10]

Brazel told reporters that he had originally found the debris on June 14, while on the ranch with his daughter, Bessie, his son, Vernon, and his wife. In that interview, while the military officers watched and listened, Brazel now claimed the object was smoky gray rubber and that it was confined to an area of about two hundred yards in diameter. While no words were visible, there were letters on part of it along with a little Scotch tape and some tape with flowers printed on it. Although no strings or wires were fastened to it, a few eyelets in the paper indicated an attachment might have been used.

The new story ended with Brazel saying he had found weather observation devices on two other occasions but this object didn't resemble those. "I am sure what I found was not any weather observation balloon," he said.[11]

The escort officers then took Brazel out of the newspaper offices. While they were walking toward the car, two of Brazel's neighbors, Floyd Proctor and Lyman Strickland, saw him. Both were surprised that Brazel didn't say a word to them. Proctor said later that the military was keeping Brazel on a short leash.

They weren't the only ones to see Brazel under escort. Leonard Porter, who lived on the ranch south of Brazel, and Bill Jenkins, another neighbor, reported they saw Brazel in downtown Roswell. According to Porter, Brazel was surrounded by the military. Brazel, according to Porter, kept his eyes down, pretending that he couldn't see anyone.

Brazel got into the car and was taken to radio station KGFL, where he went inside alone. According to Frank Joyce, Brazel stood against the wall and told the cover story that the Army had given him. It was a balloon that had come down.

Joyce said that he knew the story wasn't true. He listened to it and then pointed out that it was not the same story that Brazel had told a couple of days earlier, before the "Army had gotten to him." Specifically, Brazel had mentioned nothing about his family being with him or that the debris field was only two hundred yards in diameter.

Joyce said that Brazel kept on repeating the new story but then said, "It'll go hard on me." Joyce could tell that Brazel was agitated.

Joyce remained at the radio station control board throughout the discussion. Finally, Brazel turned and walked out of the building. The military officers were waiting outside the station. With the new story firmly in place, Brazel was taken back to the base.[12]

Marian Strickland, a neighbor of Brazel, said later that Mac Brazel had been held in jail. They hadn't let him leave the base. She remembered him sitting at her kitchen table in late July or early August, talking about being held by the military. They had kept him in Roswell and refused to let him even call his wife to let her know where he was.

Brazel remained in custody in Roswell for approximately eight days. Bill Brazel said originally that his father was in Roswell for two or three at the most, but when a time line is worked out, two or three days doesn't cover the period adequately.

According to Bill Brazel, he learned his father was in Roswell on July 10. That was the first time he'd seen his father's name mentioned in either of the Albuquerque newspapers. Bill Brazel did not arrive at the ranch until two or three days after that, on the weekend of July 12–13. His father did not return for another two or three days. That meant Mac Brazel returned sometime between July 14 and July 16. He was in custody on July 8 and therefore was held for six to eight days.[13]

When Brazel returned, he didn't talk much about what had happened to him in Roswell. Some of his neighbors reported that he now talked about finding a weather balloon. Tommy Tyree said Brazel told him that it had been one of the Japanese Balloon Bombs launched during World War II.

But privately, to his family and to his closest friends, Brazel told a slightly different story. Bill Brazel said, ''My Dad found this thing and told me a little bit about it. Not much because the Air Force asked him to take an oath that he wouldn't tell anybody in detail about it. And my Dad was such a guy that he went to his grave and he *never* told anybody.''

All Mac Brazel would say what that whatever it was, it wasn't any type of balloon. He told Bill Brazel that he was better off not knowing a thing about it.

His neighbors noticed a change in Mac Brazel's lifestyle when he returned from Roswell. Brazel suddenly seemed to have more money. Loretta Proctor said that ''Mac never had two nickels to rub together.'' But when he returned, he drove a new pickup truck. Norris Proctor said that Brazel also had the money to buy a new house in Tularosa, New Mexico, and a meat locker in Las Cruces.

Tommy Tyree said that Mac Brazel was a frugal man and that he and his wife saved almost all his pay from working the ranch. However, Paul Brazel, another of Mac's sons, was angry when neighbors began to claim Mac had been paid off by the government. Paul Brazel said that the government had given his father nothing.

None of the witnesses still living know exactly what happened to Mac Brazel while he was in Roswell. Marian Strickland claims that Mac was held in jail and asked the same questions over and over again. When pressed on that point, Strickland made it clear Brazel wasn't in the jail in Roswell, but he wasn't allowed to leave the base, either. Others agree: Mac Brazel was detained by the military for about a week.

By the time Mac Brazel returned to the ranch, all signs of the debris were gone. The wreckage had been packed into trucks by the military and taken away.

Months later, while riding the range, Brazel spotted a piece of the debris in a sinkhole. He pointed it out to his ranch hand but neither man climbed down from their horses to retrieve it. At that time it seemed to be more trouble than it was worth. But even had Brazel picked it up, he would never have been able to hold onto it. The military was still watching.[14]

July 6–10, 1947:
Chaves County Sheriff

Years later George A. Wilcox, the Chaves County sheriff in July, 1947, would complain about the way the military handled the retrieval of the "flying saucer." He was angry with himself for bringing in the military because they claimed jurisdiction, and completely cut him out of it. If he'd had it to do over again, he said, he would have notified the press first, and let the reporters get to the crash site before he told the Army a thing about it.[1]

Brazel arrived at the jail sometime on the afternoon of Sunday, July 6, 1947, according to the witnesses. Deputy B.A. Clark took the initial report and then turned it over to Sheriff Wilcox. Because Brazel was an old-time cowboy, dressed in old clothes and scuffed boots, Wilcox didn't pay much attention when Brazel walked in. But Brazel not only brought a story of a crashed flying saucer, he had some of the material with him. Material neither Wilcox nor Clark could identify.

Although Brazel's ranch was in Lincoln County, Roswell is in Chaves County. But Roswell was the hub of that area in New Mexico. The ranchers and the people around didn't worry about fine lines between counties. Roswell was the place where business was conducted and it would have been natural for Brazel to go there rather than Carrizozo.[2]

Wilcox figured the best thing to do was call the military at the base. According to his daughter, Phyllis McGuire, the military arrived at the office almost as the sheriff got off the phone. There had been no discussion about Brazel being crazy or whether the sheriff was sure if the material was unusual. The military officers came as soon as they were notified.

Now McGuire doesn't remember who arrived. She was chased out of the jail while the men discussed what Brazel had found. They were in a small room, off the main office, with Brazel and a box of the debris that he brought with him. She did remember, however, that her father sent two of his deputies out to the ranch.[3]

The two deputies left the office for the Corona area. Although the military officers might not be familiar with the ranches outside of Roswell, the sheriff's deputies were. Brazel had described the location of the debris field and they felt confident that they could find it.

They returned, however, saying that they had seen no debris. They had come upon an area of blackened ground. It looked as if something large and circular had touched down. The ground had been baked to a hardness that surprised them both.

Jay Tulk, the husband of one of Wilcox's daughters, arrived at the jail after the military arrived. He asked the sheriff what was happening. He'd seen the military vehicles parked outside. Tulk and Wilcox went into the small room and talked about it there.

The military and Brazel left the office about dusk, before the deputies returned. Wilcox called the base but no one there had any new information. With Brazel and the military officers gone, and because the deputies had found nothing but the circular burn on the ranch, things quieted down.

On Monday, July 7, they heard nothing new about the debris or what the military had found out there. But on Tuesday, July 8, things changed radically.

Wilcox, wondering what had happened, dispatched another two deputies to the ranch. McGuire and her sister, Elizabeth Tulk, thought that the sheriff might have traveled out there himself. It doesn't matter now whether it was two deputies, or the sheriff and a deputy, because they couldn't get close. The Army had cordoned off the roads and was stopping and turning back all traffic, even deputy sheriffs. Since they were from Chaves County, they had no real legal status in Lincoln County, not to mention the fact that the Army was a federal agency.

Wilcox then tried to get more answers from the military at the base but, again, no one had much to say. Then, about noon, Walter Haut issued a press release. From that point the sheriff and his deputies were busy fielding phone calls from around the world. McGuire said that her father was up all night taking calls from Germany, England, France, and Italy as well as every state in the union.

Soon afterward, July 9 or 10, Wilcox was visited by military officers. They wanted to retrieve the box of debris that had been left in the small room. The sheriff had made sure that it had been guarded. Now the military wanted that and they wanted to order the sheriff to say as little as possible about the events, and to refer all calls to the base.[4]

Although Wilcox was a civilian law enforcement officer, he did have a working relationship with the base. When one of the men there got into trouble in Roswell, the sheriff would alert the Provost Marshal. Because of that, and because it seemed that the crash was a military matter, Wilcox felt obligated to keep the facts to himself.

Phyllis McGuire wanted to know more about what happened. She pestered her father, asking questions about what Brazel had found, what the military had been doing there, and about the flying saucer itself. Finally, her mother, Inez Wilcox, knowing that the military had told the sheriff to keep quiet, told Phyllis to stop asking the questions.

Wilcox never found out what Brazel had discovered. The only contact he had with the military after he'd called them was a warning against talking about the discovery. They would answer no questions from him. Wilcox had no need to know and the military wasn't about to share the information with him. Wilcox's role was minor, but important. Without his phone call, the information might have spread farther faster so that the Army would not have been able to contain it. With that one phone call, Wilcox helped create a mystery that continues to endure.

July 7, 1947:
The Debris Field

Because Marcel and the CIC agent arrived about dusk on the evening of July 6, 1947, there was no opportunity to see the crash site. The area where it happened is desolate even today. There are no streetlights and, in fact, the few roads are little more than areas scraped clean by road graders. Fence lines and gates make it difficult to get from one place to the next. It is a cross-country drive to the actual site.[1]

In 1978, Len Stringfield interviewed Jesse Marcel about his role in the recovery operation. Marcel said that they had arrived too late to do much the first day. Brazel showed them the largest chunk he'd found, a piece about ten feet in diameter that he had dragged from the field. It gave them an idea of the approximate size of the craft that came down. It also gave them some idea of the find's unbelievable nature. But at night, in an old house that had no electricity, there was nothing for them to do with the material except check it for radiation. Marcel found none.

At dawn, Brazel took them to the debris field. According to neighbors including Norris Proctor, Brazel was an early riser and was normally up an hour or two before the sun. He usually sat around drinking coffee until it was light enough to go to work. The morning of July 7, 1947 would have been no different.

Without breakfast, they headed to the crash site. From the ranch house where they had spent the night, it wasn't far. However, there were no roads and the country was rough. They had to drive to the east, then south and finally back to the west.

The debris field was oriented northwest to southeast.[2] Marcel said it was about three-quarters of a mile long and two to three hundred feet across, with a gouge at the top end of it that was about five hundred feet long and ten feet wide.[3] Debris littered the ground, lying on top of it. The wind blew some of it around because of the material's light weight.[4]

Marcel first checked the area for radiation but, again, found nothing to suggest anything was radioactive.[5] Marcel and the counter-intelligence agent then slowly moved across the field examining debris. A dull, foil-like material was scattered everywhere. Marcel picked up a small lightweight I-beam. A wire-like material that, according to Bill Brazel, resembled monofilament fishing line was found. Marcel mentioned some parchment-like material strewn on the field. Neither Marcel nor the CIC man found many pieces of material longer than six or seven inches. There was nothing on the field that would account for the gouge.

"The metal fragments," Marcel told Stringfield, "varied in size up to six inches in length, but were of the thickness of tinfoil. The fragments were unusual because they were of great strength. They could not be bent or broken, no matter what pressure we applied by hand." In fact, only a few pieces were bigger, and Brazel had removed the largest piece, dragging it off the prairie on July 3.[6]

There was nothing on the field that Marcel or the counter-intelligence agent recognized. All the fragments had unusual properties. Marcel, as an intelligence officer, was familiar with nearly all foreign aircraft and rockets because he was assigned to the 509th, the only atomic bomb group in the entire world at the time. Although he had access to information that most intelligence officers wouldn't have had, he still didn't have a clue about the identity of the material.

Together, Marcel and the counter-intelligence agent walked around the entire perimeter, searching for clues. It took them most of the morning to do it because of the size of the field. At one point they came to a sinkhole that had a small cave-like entrance and they had to climb down to examine it, searching for more of the wreckage.

After finishing the survey, they began collecting the material, loading some of it into Marcel's '42 Buick and into the jeep carryall driven by the CIC man. They started collecting the material at the outer edges of the field and moved in toward the center.

Although most of the debris was silvery, it did not reflect the light. It had a dull surface which made it hard to see. They could easily step over the smaller fragments without seeing them.[7] The thick grasses, the yucca plants, the outcropping of stone, and the sinkholes helped to hide the debris.

As darkness approached they left, and drove back to Roswell. Marcel stopped at his house even though it was after midnight. He said later that he was so impressed with what he had seen that he wanted to show some of the debris to his wife and eleven-year-old son, even if he had to wake them.[8]

He brought some of the wreckage into the house and spread it out on the kitchen floor. There his wife and son, Jesse Jr., examined it.

Marcel brought in samples of all types of the material: I-beams, foil, some of the wood-like material, and a few strands of the fiber-optics-like material. There was nothing in the pile any of them recognized. Marcel told his son that he didn't know what it was.

Jesse Jr. noticed writing on one of the beams. It looked like purplish, geometric symbols, squares and circles and triangles, and was embossed on the inside of the beam.

When the family had finished examining the wreckage, Marcel, with the help of his son, loaded it back into the Buick and drove it to the base. Marcel went first to the Intelligence Shop and, after dawn, on to Blanchard's office, where the material was temporarily stored.

There were others who saw the debris. Bill Brazel didn't see the field where the debris was found until a few days after the military had finished cleaning it up. Like Marcel, he talked about a gouge with the northwest-southeast orientation.[9]

Bill Brazel said that his Dad had been sworn to secrecy by the military but he would, occasionally, talk about it to his son. "The only thing, actually, he said, (was) 'Well, there was a big bunch of the stuff. There was some tin foil and some wood and on some of the wood it had Japanese or Chinese figures.' Evidently it was some sort of inscription on part of this wood. Now I found a little piece of it but there was no writing on it," Bill Brazel said.

In the months after the event, when riding the range near the crash site, Bill Brazel would find small pieces that the military had missed. He said, ". . . oh, not over a dozen and I'd say eight. Just different little pieces. There were only three items involved. Something on the order of balsa wood and something on the order of heavy-gauge monofilament fishing line and a little piece of . . . it wasn't really aluminum foil and it wasn't really lead foil but it was on that order. A piece about the size of my fingers with jagged edges."

He also mentioned something that sounded suspiciously like fiber optics. "Actually, this was before monofilament fishing line was a popular item and that's the nearest I could compare it to. Now there's this plastic . . . they put a light in the one end and it transfers the light down that thing and comes out the end."

He also mentioned the "wood," although he said it wasn't really wood. It was a neutral, tan color. He described one of the pieces he found as about five inches long, as light as balsa, but so strong he couldn't break it, only flex it slightly. Using his buck knife, he couldn't cut it or even scratch it. It was much tougher than any wood that he had ever seen.

And he remembered the lead foil. "The only reason I noticed the foil was that I picked this stuff up and put it in my chaps pocket. I had it in there, two, three days, and when I took it out and put it in the box I happened to notice that it started unfolding and flattened out. Then I got to playing with it. I would fold it or crease it and lay it down and watch it. It was kind of weird.

"The piece I found was a jagged piece. I couldn't tear it. Hell, tin foil or lead foil is easy but I couldn't tear it. I didn't take pliers or anything. I just used my fingers. I didn't try to cut it with my knife. I didn't even get a little sliver off it."

A key question, of course, is if Bill Brazel didn't see the debris field before the Army had cleaned it, how can it be determined that what he found was from the crash?

"He (Mac Brazel) looked at it and said, 'Yeah, that looks like some of the contraption I found.' "[10]

Bill Brazel wasn't the only person to see a piece of the debris after the military had finished the cleanup. Tommy Tyree remembered seeing a small piece in a sinkhole. Mac Brazel told him it was material from the crash. Tyree said that some time he might go back and see if the metal was still in the hole.

Both Floyd and Loretta Proctor saw a small piece that Mac Brazel brought to their ranch house when he brought their youngest boy back. Mac Brazel showed both Proctors the strange material and both said they'd never seen anything like it.

Today, Loretta Proctor said that it reminded her of plastic, although in 1947 there wasn't much made of plastic. However, plastic, especially small pieces of it, will burn when a match is held close to it. The material that the Proctors saw did not react to the flame.

Once Marcel and the counter-intelligence agent got the metal back to the Roswell Army Air Field, some preliminary tests were carried out. Using a sixteen-pound sledgehammer, they tried to dent one of the larger, metallic chunks. They couldn't even scratch the surface.[11]

They tried to burn it using a torch, but the metal seemed to dissipate the heat. There was no sign that the torch had touched it.

Their tests seemed to prove one thing: The material was not the flimsy stuff it appeared to be. Although it might look like aluminum foil and balsa wood, it was neither of those things.

Marcel then showed the material to Blanchard, taking more of it into Blanchard's office. Other members of the immediate staff, the Operations Officer, the Executive Officer, the Deputy Commander, and Marcel, were there for the meeting. They were discussing exactly what they should do now that all of them were sure that they had found something extraordinary.

Blanchard called Brigadier General Roger Ramey, the Eighth Air Force commander, and briefed him on what was going on. Ramey ordered some of the debris brought to his headquarters for inspection.

Interviewed over thirty years after the event, Marcel said, without any qualification, that the material was "nothing from the Earth." He said that because of his training, and his position as an air intelligence officer, he was familiar with all types of aircraft, rockets, balloons, and even the top secret experiments that were being conducted in New Mexico. Given all that, he still didn't know what he had seen that day north of Roswell. He went to his grave believing that he had held the pieces of spacecraft from another planet. The evidence, as it has been gathered, supports that view.

July 8, 1947:
The Morning Briefing

It was after three in the morning when Marcel arrived at the base. He headed for his office, a small wooden building. Across the hall from his office was the counter-intelligence office where the agent who had accompanied him to the field waited. They discussed what to do then.

Blanchard was an early riser and there was nothing critical in what either Marcel or the CIC man knew.[1] Nothing that couldn't wait a couple of hours until Blanchard was awake. The area of the crash was isolated and to that point not many people knew where it was or that it had happened. If it hadn't been compromised yet, the odds were that it would not be compromised by waiting a couple of hours.

While sitting there, drinking coffee, both men knew that they had stumbled onto something extraordinary. Neither man had been able to recognize any of the material scattered over the desert. The properties of it, the foil that could be rolled into a ball and then unfold itself without a crease, the sheets of metal that were paper-thin but that couldn't be dented or bent suggested that it hadn't been made on the Earth.

If the object, whatever it was, had been terrestrial in origin, but from a secret project, it might have been something that neither Marcel nor the CIC agent knew about. There has been discussion that it was the aluminum foil parachute assembly from a V-2, for example. Since neither man, nor anyone at the base, would need to know about the V-2 testing at White Sands, they might not have known what it was.

Marcel, with a top secret clearance, and the CIC agent with a need to know anything he deemed necessary for the completion of his work, could have learned about the V-2 testing. Both would have known who to call at the various bases and installations around Roswell. They could have gotten an answer. Had it been anything from any of those facilities, they would have been told either to mind their own business because there was nothing to worry about, or they would have gotten a classified briefing on the matter. Marcel, for example, knew all about the atomic bombing of Japan before it happened. Years later when President Truman read a speech about the Soviet development of atomic weapons, it was Marcel who had provided the text.

But that does not address the real point. Even if Marcel and the CIC man had not known about the V-2 testing, or any of the other secret projects, they would have recognized the material as something terrestrial. Aluminum foil used as a parachute on a V-2 nose cone is still aluminum foil. Copper wiring and vacuum tubes used in radios and avionics are still copper wiring and vacuum tubes. What they found on the desert did not resemble those things except in the grossest sense.

So, knowing that they had something extraordinary, but also knowing that the time between three and six in the morning wouldn't compromise the crash site, they waited for Blanchard to get up.

Blanchard lived on the base.[2] He had the big house that was just inside the gate. As soon as they thought he would be awake, they drove over to the house and then, sitting in the kitchen, told Blanchard what they had. Marcel had brought a couple of the smaller pieces of the wreckage, including one of the I-beams with the markings on it.

They then planned their strategy. They knew how desolate the area was, but there were people living in it.

Marcel and the CIC man had picked up as much of the material as they could, but they hadn't come close to cleaning the field. Debris was still scattered out there for all to see.[3]

Blanchard's first act was to get on the phone to call the Provost Marshal. Although it was next to impossible to direct someone to the debris field, it was possible to get them into the general area. Blanchard ordered the Provost Marshal to block all the roads that led into the crash site.[4] That would keep the curious from stumbling over it.

He also called the Base Adjutant and told him to bump the normal 9:00 staff meeting to 7:30. It would be limited to the primary staff including, of course, Marcel and the CIC man. They had to decide on a course of action.

With the commander alerted, Marcel and the CIC man left, Marcel heading home to take a shower and get cleaned up. He had enough time for a quick breakfast and then drove back out to the base.

At the staff meeting, Marcel showed some of the material that they had found. In discussions later, it was pointed out that some of the wreckage was in Blanchard's office. He, along with members of the staff, handled the material.

The major concern then was that someone else, someone outside the military, would get their hands on some of the wreckage. Blanchard decided that the fastest way to keep people out of the general area was to tell them that it had been picked up. Blanchard acting on orders issued in Washington, D.C., ordered Walter Haut, the PIO, to issue a press release saying they had recovered a "flying disc."

Haut later said that Blanchard worried about the relationship between the base and the town. He knew the value of maintaining good relations. He also knew, from the newspapers and the phone calls that were coming into the base, that the public was concerned about the flying disc reports. In fact, the unit history of the Eighth

Air Force, of which the 509th was a part, mentioned all the phone calls that had been fielded dealing with reports of flying saucers and questions about them in late June, 1947.

Blanchard's orders to Haut had three purposes. First, it was to alert the townspeople that the military at the base was now in possession of a flying saucer. Answers about it would be forthcoming. Second, the press release was worded so that it sounded as if the recovery operation was over. And third, it was damage control to suppress the remarks flying around Roswell. There was no longer anything to see out there. The first release, in fact, did not mention Brazel's name, did not mention the Foster ranch where he worked or the town of Corona. It said that the object had been recovered seventy-five miles northwest of Roswell.

Marcel, it was decided, would take some samples of the material to Forth Worth to show Brigadier General Ramey. In the meantime, the CIC man would head back to the crash site with some MPs, showing them exactly where the debris field was if they hadn't found it, and to round up the rancher. There were now additional questions for him.

Arrangements would be made to collect all the debris and transport it back to Roswell. Based on what Marcel and the CIC agent said, Blanchard knew there was a great deal of debris out there. He planned to use as many men as could be spared from their other duties.

It's important to remember that they knew they had something unusual and that almost everyone who has described the material has used the same words. They believed that what they had found was nothing from Earth. Wreckage that was strange just did not have a radical impact on them.

Blanchard detailed who would take what action. The military police would be used in the cordon. The area was large enough that it nearly depleted the staff. Photographs of the crash site would be taken.

Sometime during the meeting someone mentioned the possibility of a flight crew. Marcel said that the thing had been so torn up that anyone inside it would have been shredded. They all knew of aircraft accidents where the crew had been "collected in a bucket." The sudden destruction of an aircraft tended to destroy the humans inside and there was no reason to believe that the object that had disintegrated on the desert would have been kinder to anyone or anything inside it.

While talking about aircraft accidents, someone asked why they assumed they had found all the wreckage. There were cases where parts of an airplane were scattered over miles. More of it might have come down elsewhere.

Blanchard agreed and decided that they would also make an aerial search. They had the aviation assets to do it, from the B-29s stationed there down to a few small, twin-engine aircraft used by the staff to maintain their flight time and their flight pay. They could easily make an aerial search. Marcel pointed out that there were only a few yucca plants and almost no trees in the area of the crash. The searchers would be able to see, easily, any wreckage on the ground.

With no landmarks out there, it might be hard to direct the ground forces into a second site, if they located one. The rancher could be helpful. He was in charge of the ranch, he worked on it, lived on it, and probably knew every arroyo, sinkhole, and rattlesnake.

They also discussed what should be reported to the higher headquarters. Blanchard knew Ramey was going to want to see the material and he was going to want to know exactly what had been done. The only person who could answer the questions about the location, what the site looked like, and what the rancher had said was Marcel. He had been in on it from the moment that Sheriff Wilcox had alerted them. Marcel would go to Fort Worth and the CIC man would stay behind to lead the cleanup detail to the site.

Another reason to send Marcel was that the CIC had

their own chain of command. They reported to Kirtland in Albuquerque rather than Fort Worth.[5] Although Blanchard outranked the CIC agent, a phone call to Kirtland could have gotten his orders overturned. In the end, Blanchard's only choice was to send Marcel.

July 8, 1947:
The Debris Field

With the staff meeting over and with everyone having his orders, the men began to file out of the conference room. According to Lewis S. Rickett, one of the CIC agents, he, with the commander of the CIC shop, drew a staff car from the motor pool and returned to the crash site. They were followed by a second car carrying several MPs.[1]

Before they reached the debris field, they ran into the first of the cordon. It was nothing more than a military car pulled to one side of the road with two MPs sitting inside it.[2] As a vehicle approached, one of them would get out and stop the car, telling the driver not to enter the area. Naturally, military vehicles were not turned back, but an MP did ask for their identification because neither of the counter-intelligence men were in uniform.

When they reached the debris field, the MPs were already posted in a ring around the crash. The base Provost Marshal saw the approaching cars and walked over to see what was happening. Before he reached them, another MP had demanded to see some identification, even though the MP knew who the counter-intelligence men were. Military regulations demanded that everyone be identified as having a need to know.[3]

The MPs had circled the gouge, standing back from it slightly. There was a ring of men around the debris field itself, and there were more guards on the low hills around the crash site. They would be able to see anyone approaching from a long distance and would be able to dispatch a jeep or car to intercept the intruder before he could get too close.

Rickett, the Provost Marshal, and the senior counter-intelligence man walked the perimeter of the debris field, examining the wreckage scattered there. Most of the pieces were small, no more than a couple of inches long and wide, but there was still some larger debris, a few measuring a couple of feet on a side.

They came to one piece that was about two feet by two feet and Rickett crouched to look at it. He said that it looked like metal and asked if it was radioactive.

The CIC officer said that it wasn't. He told Rickett to pick it up.

According to Rickett it was slightly curved, but it was such a slight curve that the only way he could be certain was by putting it next to a flat piece of metal. He locked it against his knee and then used his arm to try to bend it or break it. The metal was very thin and very light-weight. Rickett couldn't bend it at all.

The senior CIC man said to the Provost Marshal, "Smart guy. He's trying to do what we couldn't."

Rickett said that it wasn't plastic and that it didn't feel like plastic but that he had never seen a piece of metal that thin that couldn't be bent.

The edges of it were not jagged like those exposed after an explosion but were straight and were sharp. Some of the edges curved back on themselves. Rickett thought the object might have disintegrated once it had touched down.[4]

Walking the site, Rickett recognized the men from Marcel's office gathering the debris.

Rickett walked over to one of the MPs that he knew and they talked for a moment. Then, according to the Rickett, the MP said, "I don't know what we're doing here but I do know that I never talked to you out here."

As they prepared to leave the crash site, the senior CIC agent told Rickett, "You and I were never out here. You and I never saw this. You don't see any military people or military vehicles out here.''

Rickett agreed, saying, ''Yeah. We never even left the office.''

The Provost Marshal picked them up in a jeep and they drove the perimeter of the field, searching. Rickett was told the crash site had been photographed from every angle before the men were allowed to walk it. No one touched a thing until the photographs had been made. In that respect, they were treating it like an aircraft accident. But, according to Vernon D. Zorn, the NCOIC (noncommissioned officer in charge) of the Third Photo Unit at Roswell, the photographs were not taken by his men. Someone came in from Washington to do that. No film was processed by the Roswell photo lab. It was all flown out, probably to Washington, where it was processed, classified, and filed so that no one without authorization would ever see it.[5]

Once the field had been photographed, the troops who had been brought in to search moved in. According to Robert Smith, a member of the 1st Air Transport Unit at Roswell, the soldiers walked across the field, one side to the other, collecting the biggest, easiest to spot pieces. Some of the men had wheelbarrows, and once they were loaded they were pushed to a central collection point near one of the sentries.[6]

When the soldiers had swept across the complete crash site, they did it again from another angle, trying to find anything they might have missed. Rickett said the foil was dull, like the back side of aluminum foil, and because it didn't reflect the sun, it was hard to see.

Finished a second time, they moved across it again, now on their hands and knees, searching for the tiny pieces that they missed on the first two sweeps. The ''fiber optics,'' the foil, and the metal that was left were tucked up against the yucca plants, trapped in the thick clumps of prairie grass, and had slipped into the holes dug by the various rodents and snakes that inhabited the field.[7]

They checked the gouged area carefully, searching the dirt and rocks, making sure nothing was embedded. The gouge itself was nearly five hundred feet long and ten feet wide at its widest but not very deep. The ground just under the surface of the earth was shale. The dirt was scraped away, leaving the bare stone. Those cleaning up the debris had to make sure there were no telltale marks left on the rock.

Those participating in the retrieval described the characteristics of the material just as Jesse Marcel had: metal pieces that were as thin as the foil in a pack of cigarettes, as lightweight as a feather, and so strong that men couldn't bend them. One man set a piece on the ground and jumped on it, trying to dent or bend it, and failed.[8]

The small I-beams were all taken to a single point for collection. Other debris was taken to other points. Trucks were brought in and the debris was thrown up, into the rear. One driver rolled over a piece of the metal but even the weight of the big Dodge truck didn't bend it or break it. This was a piece of metal thinner than paper.

The important thing was that none of the wreckage looked conventional. Had it been an aircraft accident, the debris would have been familiar. There would have been fragments that the men would have recognized. The avionics might not have survived intact, but there would have been bundles of wires, vacuum tubes, control heads. The metal, even ripped to pieces as described by the men out there, would have looked like conventional metal. There might have been thin sheets of metal, though nothing as thin as that described, and it would have been easy for them to bend it.

Had an aircraft crashed four days earlier, there would have been a search underway for it.[9] Brazel found the debris on July 3 but didn't report his discovery until July 6, and Marcel didn't see it until July 7. During those four days, no one reported any aircraft missing. No one instituted any searches for overdue airplanes. There are no records, no news accounts, no rumors to suggest that it was an aircraft. The military hadn't lost one and no civilian airliners were missing.

Any conventional craft, whether an airplane, an experimental rocket or even a weather balloon, would have left material that was recognizable by the men on the field. Dr. Jerry Brown, a NASA engineer, suggested Duraluminum, an alloy that is strong with good high-temperature properties.[10] Had they used a blowtorch on it, there probably would have been no noticeable results. The problem is that Duraluminum is fragile. Banging on it with a sledgehammer would cause it to shatter. The Roswell material did not react that way.

The CIC agents spent more than an hour on the field and failed to identify anything. Rickett said his boss told him he'd wanted another CIC man to see the crash because everything on the site was so strange.

Both of them went to find Brazel. They told the rancher he was going to have to return to Roswell with them. Brazel, knowing that there were things to be done on the ranch, didn't want to accompany them at first, but they convinced him that it was his patriotic duty. It was a matter of national security. Brazel finally agreed. Brazel and the CIC agents left the ranch to return to the base.

While the men were cleaning the field and Brazel and the CIC agents were heading into Roswell, the aerial reconnaissance was being carried out.[11] There had been flights over the field during the day.[12] The aircraft fanned out from the point of impact, circling outward and then expanding to the north, south, east, and west. The reconnaissance flights were made by the smaller single or twin-engine aircraft assigned to the base.[13]

Later in the afternoon, Colonel William Blanchard arrived at the crash site. After two days of receiving the reports of others about the nature of the field, he wanted to see the crash site for himself.[14]

Again, the Provost Marshal explained what had been accomplished in the last few hours. He told Blanchard about the efforts to collect all the material. Blanchard told him everything there was now classified top secret. Everyone who was there would be cautioned about the new classification. No one could say a word about it under the penalty of law. Anyone who talked could be jailed and fined. At the moment, Blanchard's biggest worry was security. Too many people were out there and too many people had seen too much.

The Provost Marshal accepted his instructions. Nothing had been given to him in writing and he wrote nothing down. According to him, Blanchard didn't want anything in writing.[15]

Blanchard had been there for only a few minutes when there was a radio message that a second crash site had been located. The radio transmissions, because there was a possibility that someone could listen in, didn't contain much information. These men were veteran wartime pilots, and knew all about radio security procedures.

The aircraft circled the second crash site and the pilot provided instructions to the men on the ground. The number of men who were sent to the second site was restricted by Blanchard. He, a small number of the MPs, and one or two of his top officers left the debris field, disappearing to the east as they crossed one of the ridgelines and then vanished into one of the many canyons.

The men who remained behind continued to search the site for more wreckage. The men who were there have indicated that they worked hard to make sure they picked up all the pieces. The officers wanted nothing left for the curious to find.

At dusk, they secured the site. There had been some discussion about bringing in lights. Because the base mechanics sometimes had to repair aircraft quickly in the field, where there were no electrical outlets, the military had carts that held huge, bright lights. Setting them up on the hills around the crash site, they could have illuminated the whole field and proceeded with the cleanup through the night. However, the lights would have been visible for miles. It would have easily pinpointed the crash site for the local ranchers and for any of the curious who might drive out to see if anything of interest was still happening. Blanchard decided that it wasn't worth the risk.

Blanchard, with a number of other officers, stayed on the ranch that night. With Brazel back in Roswell, there was no one at either the ranch headquarters or in the shack where Marcel and the CIC man had stayed that first night. The officers stayed there while the enlisted men camped out near the crash site. They ate C-ration type meals that night, but no one had hot food. Again, Blanchard didn't want to make fires or give anyone any additional clues that the military was camping on the range.

Blanchard kept the men out there so that they could inspect the field the next day. He wanted no signs of anything left behind. He wanted them to sweep the area one more time. Then he would get everyone out, returning to the base at Roswell.

July 8–10, 1947:
The Press Briefings

When First Lieutenant Walter Haut made his rounds in town on July 8, it was among the first indications that the newspapers and radio had that something unusual was happening in Roswell. According to a plan worked out at Colonel Blanchard's insistence, Haut normally took the press releases issued by the base to one of the two radio stations or one of the two newspapers first, based on a rotating system. That way he could not be accused of playing favorites.[1]

This press release, published in more than thirty afternoon papers, said, in part, "The many rumors regarding the flying disc became a reality yesterday when the intelligence office of the 509th Bomb Group of the Eighth Air Force, Roswell Army Air Field, was fortunate enough to gain possession of a disc through the co-operation of one of the local ranchers and the Sheriff's office of Chaves County.

"The flying object landed on a ranch near Roswell sometime last week. Not having phone facilities, the rancher stored the disc until such time as he was able to contact the Sheriff's office, who in turn notified Major Jesse A. Marcel, of the 509th Bomb Group Intelligence office.

"Action was immediately taken and the disc was picked up at the rancher's home. It was inspected at the Roswell Army Air Field and subsequently loaned by Major Marcel to higher headquarters."[2]

The press release was fairly straightforward. The officers and men of the 509th Bomb Group had a flying disc. Details were sketchy, but that said it all.

Walter Haut, interviewed years after the fact, said that the press release was issued because Blanchard had "a very sincere interest in the relationship between the base and the community. If anything unusual happened or anything he felt the community should know about, he would call me and say, get this thing out. He did that with many, many things."

Haut explained that Blanchard told him, "Jess Marcel has brought something in that looks like a flying disc or a flying saucer or parts of it. Put out a press release on this that it was discovered on a ranch outside of Roswell, near Corona. Basically that's all I'm going to tell you. Jesse's going to take it and is flying it down to Fort Worth."

Haut made it clear that Jesse Marcel and Colonel Blanchard thought they had something very unusual. Haut said that Marcel told him, "It was something he had never seen and didn't believe that it was of this planet. I trusted him on his knowledge. He felt very sincerely about it. He felt that it was something that was not made or mined or built or manufactured here on this earth."

Blanchard, as the Group Commander, would have known everything that Marcel knew. He would not have ordered the press release unless he felt it was justified. If Marcel had somehow been fooled by mundane wreckage picked up under extraordinary circumstances, Blanchard, or one of his staff, would have been able to identify it. Certainly, before they announced to the world they had a flying saucer, they would have made sure that it couldn't be explained by the mundane.[3]

"Once it got to Fort Worth it became a weather balloon," Haut said.

"As a matter of fact, I guess it was a rumor they started about how dumb we were . . . the fact that it was released from here (Roswell), on the base, that there was a detachment that came over from Holloman (actually it was the Alamogordo Army Air Field, New Mexico) and released the balloon here to pick up the winds going in that direction.''

Haut, armed with the release ordered by Blanchard, made his rounds. Art McQuiddy was the editor of the *Roswell Morning Dispatch* in 1947 and he remembered Haut coming into the office about noon. Unlike some of the witnesses contacted, McQuiddy said, ''I can remember quite a bit of what happened that day. It was about noon and Walter brought in a press release. He'd already been to one of the radio stations and I raised hell with him about playing favorites and he said there were four media in the town and he took turns.

''By the time Haut had gotten to me it hadn't been ten minutes and the phones started ringing. I didn't get off the phone until late that afternoon. I had calls from London and Paris and Rome and Hong Kong that I can remember.''

McQuiddy said that the *Dispatch* was a morning paper and before they could get on the streets, the story had died. ''The story died, literally, as fast as it started.''

McQuiddy talked about filing the release, ''which for me was setting it on my desk.'' There was a possibility the release might still be filed somewhere. The *Dispatch* was sold to the *Roswell Daily Record* and the *Record* moved from its old building to a new one. In all the transferring of files and records, McQuiddy thought that it had probably been tossed out.

That is, if they still had it. McQuiddy said that he had it in his mind that someone from the military, from the base, had come into the office to retrieve the press release. McQuiddy didn't remember much about it except that he believed he had surrendered the press release to the military.

McQuiddy said that he never got the chance to interview Mac Brazel. By the time their morning edition was ready, the weather balloon answer had been released.

"It happened very fast and it was very, very exciting around here as far as the media goes. And then it stopped as fast as it started. There just wasn't any story."

In later years McQuiddy had the opportunity to talk to Blanchard about the crash. McQuiddy said that Blanchard told him that they had put the wreckage on an airplane and flew it to Fort Worth and from there it went immediately to Wright Field.

McQuiddy said that Jud Roberts had worked at one of the local radio stations, KGFL, and it was there Walter Haut had gone first.

While McQuiddy was answering the phones in his office, Walt Whitmore, Sr., majority owner of KGFL, and one of his friends were out trying to locate Mac Brazel. Whitmore found Brazel in Roswell and took him to Whitmore's house on West Second. According to Roberts, Brazel was kept there overnight and during that time, made a wire recording of his story. Whitmore had wanted an exclusive and that was the reason behind the maneuvering. Whitmore was well aware of all the calls coming into Roswell from news organizations around the world. Brazel told him everything.[4]

The next morning, July 9, Whitmore and Roberts decided to take a trip out to the crash site and look around for themselves. Roberts said they couldn't get close because the military had the perimeter cordoned off.

They returned to Roswell. The Army was upset that Brazel had disappeared and they were searching for him. Whitmore finally turned Brazel over to the military. It was about this time they started getting phone calls from Washington, D.C. According to Roberts, New Mexico senator Dennis Chavez called and suggested that they not air the recording. If they did, they would lose their license.

While the press was being silenced in Roswell, Brigadier General Roger Ramey was doing everything he could to stop the story in Fort Worth. The plane from

Roswell had already been dispatched and there were people in Fort Worth who were interested in its arrival.

J. Bond Johnson was a staff reporter for the *Fort Worth Star Telegram* in July, 1947. He said the story that the airplane was on the way came in over the AP wire. He had just walked into the office because he worked as the night police beat reporter and was the backup photographer. The city editor, Cullen Greene, asked him if he had his camera, a Speed-Graphic, and when he said that he did, the editor told him to get out to Brigadier General Ramey's office. The editor told him that they had a flying saucer and they were bringing it from Roswell.

Johnson arrived at the base. The guard at the gate was ready for him, knew that he was coming, and knew where he was supposed to go. Johnson arrived at Ramey's office and saw the wreckage spread out on the floor. It wasn't an impressive sight, just some aluminum-like foil, balsa wood sticks, and some burnt rubber that was stinking up the office. "It was just a bunch of garbage anyway."[5]

"He had a big office as most of them (generals) do. And he walked over and I posed him looking at it, squatting down, holding onto the stuff."

Johnson took four pictures. Two had Ramey by himself and the other two show Colonel Thomas J. DuBose (Ramey's chief of staff) in it, sitting in a chair, looking at the stuff. According to Johnson, he talked to General Ramey for fifteen minutes and then left for the newspaper. Ramey was already spreading the word that the wreckage from Roswell was nothing more than a weather balloon. According to Johnson, Ramey told him "Oh, we've found out what it is and you know, it's a weather balloon."

"That was it," he said. "I got back to the newspaper. The newspapers had gotten excited. The AP had sent over a portable wire photo transmitter. Everybody wanted an exclusive and I'd taken only two pieces of film."

Johnson was sent into the darkroom immediately to develop the film and make the prints. The editor was so excited about it that he made Johnson bring the dripping prints into the city room.

Technicians from the AP were already waiting for him. Johnson mentioned they had been brought by bus over from Dallas. That was where the wire photo transmitter had been located.

The phones in the press room there were ringing, too. Johnson said that he if had taken more pictures he might have become rich. Everyone wanted their own print, but he had taken only four.

And, by this time, the weather balloon story had been released. Interestingly enough, the material, as shown in the photographs in Ramey's office, doesn't match at all the descriptions of the material made by those who had been at the crash site or who had held the material in Roswell.

There were accounts of a single press conference, and then two, held in Ramey's office. According to Marcel, reporters were never allowed into the office but were kept standing at the door, shouting questions. Johnson said he was the only reporter and that he questioned only Ramey. Marcel told his story quickly and was photographed with the weather balloon by the base PIO and that might be where the confusion came in. When Johnson went out, he didn't see any other reporters but he was not the only civilian called in.

Irving Newton, the weather officer, said that when he arrived at Ramey's office, there were ten or twelve people waiting for him. Newton had been alone in his office when a colonel called. When Newton refused to leave the office empty, Brigadier General Ramey called him, telling Newton to ''Get your ass over here now. Use a car and if you have to, take the first one with keys in it.''

When Newton arrived, he was briefed in the hallway by a colonel. Newton couldn't remember who it had been, but did say the message had been clear. ''These officers from Roswell think they found a flying saucer but the general thinks it's a weather balloon. He wants you to take a look at it.''

Newton walked to Ramey's office and saw the balloon lying on the floor. According to Newton, there was no question about what he was seeing. It was a Rawin target balloon.[6]

Newton also talked about other reporters in the room. They were standing back, out of the way, listening to what was happening in front of them. Johnson said that he was the only reporter there when he talked to Ramey. Later, when there were more representatives of the press available, Newton was called. Newton said there were five or six reporters, along with Ramey, a couple of colonels, and a major who was supposed to be the one who had flown up from Roswell.

According to Newton, the reporters didn't ask questions and Marcel had said that he was not allowed to speak with the reporters. But Marcel did point to portions of the balloon and asked Newton if he was sure that these features would be found on normal balloons. Newton said that he thought Marcel was trying to save face and not seem to be a jerk who couldn't tell the difference between a balloon and something extraordinary.

After Newton had identified the balloon, Ramey told his aide, Captain Roy Showalter, to cancel the special flight. Newton left as quickly as he could because there was no one in the weather office.

DuBose underscored Newton's statements. According to DuBose, the weather balloon story was designed to get the reporters ''off the general's back.'' And, although Ramey, in front of reporters, ordered the special flight cancelled, it was not. In fact, according to DuBose, General Clements McMullen ordered Ramey to cover up the whole thing. They wanted ''to put out the fire'' as quickly as they could.[7]

DuBose knew even more about it. According to DuBose, some wreckage from Roswell had transited Fort Worth ''two or three days earlier.'' DuBose had received a phone call from General McMullen. According to DuBose, "He called me and said that I was, there was, talk of some elements that had been found on the ground outside Roswell, New Mexico . . . The debris or elements were to be placed in a suitable container and Blanchard was to see that they were delivered . . . and Al Clark, the base commander at Fort Worth, would pick them up and deliver them to McMullen in Washington. Nobody, and I must stress this, no one was to discuss this with their wives, me with Ramey, with anyone. The matter as far as we're concerned was closed."

That had been on Sunday, July 6, after Brazel had gone into Roswell to talk with the sheriff. Material from the crash had gone to Washington and then, probably on to Wright Field where there were facilities to test and analyze it.

DuBose was quick to point out that the weather balloon ". . . was a cover story. The whole balloon part of it. That part of it was a story that we were told to give to the public and news and that was it."

But what about the special flight from Roswell to Wright Field that Ramey had ordered cancelled while the reporters were there? UFO researcher Brad Sparks, working through the Freedom of Information Act, was able to secure additional proof that the special flight to Wright Field had not been cancelled. An FBI document from the Dallas office, dated July 8, 1947, and with a time of 6:17 P.M. said, "Disc and balloon being transported to Wright Field by special plane for examination. Information provided this office because of national interest in case and fact that National Broadcasting Company, Associated Press, and others attempting to break story of location of disc today."[8]

The reporters never had the opportunity to see the real debris. Marcel said that he had brought it to Ramey's office, where the general examined it and then decided that he wanted to see exactly where the object crashed. Marcel and Ramey left for the map room and while they were gone, someone carried the wreckage out, replacing it with the weather balloon long before any reporters were allowed into the office.[9]

Then Ramey, in an attempt to "put out the fire," apparently arranged a radio hook-up in his office. He broadcast the news that the flying saucer found in Roswell was nothing more than a weather balloon. Reporters for the broadcast medium were right there looking at the balloon as Newton identified it and they heard Ramey cancel the flight.

Johnson, the newspaper reporter, said he never met Marcel. The only people in the office were Ramey and his chief of staff. He took the four pictures, two of Ramey with the balloon and two with both Ramey and Colonel DuBose. Johnson said that no other reporters from the *Fort Worth Star-Telegram* went out to the base because there was no one else to go. It was his story and if there had been another press conference, he would have been the one to attend.

Because more than forty years have elapsed, the exact sequence of events is difficult to reconstruct. Based on the testimony of the individuals, and based on the photographic evidence, it would seem that Ramey, on orders from McMullen in Washington, created the balloon answer in Forth Worth. To underscore the validity of that statement, he had a balloon brought to his office, and Marcel was posed with it for photographs. Two were taken, both by Major Charles A. Cashon, the base public information officer.

A teletype message based on Walter Haut's press release caused additional interest. Cullen Greene dispatched J. Bond Johnson to the base to interview the participants. When Johnson arrived, he was allowed to take photos of the balloon and to interview Ramey. Marcel was not there and wasn't a participant in that meeting, according to Johnson.

Later, more reporters arrived. With the press continuing to hound him, Ramey reluctantly granted them an interview. This time, he called on Irving Newton to identify the balloon. Marcel was still in Fort Worth and was in the office, but under orders not to speak.

With the reporters present, Ramey ordered the special flight cancelled. Newton went back to the weather office, and Marcel was sent back to the BOQ.

At some point, and again the sequencing hasn't been exactly established, Ramey made an appearance on radio station WBAP. On the air, he again gave the weather balloon explanation. He claimed the object found in Roswell wasn't all that mysterious. According to Ramey, the officers in Roswell had been swept up in the excitement of the moment and made an honest mistake.

The reporters in Forth Worth accepted the answer. Ramey had been willing to show the wreckage, had brought in his local expert to identify it, and Marcel, the man who had started it all, had seemed satisfied with the answer. Or rather, he was not objecting to the explanation.

In fact, it wasn't the first time in those few days that someone had claimed to have found a flying saucer that turned out to be a weather balloon. Sherman Campbell of Circleville, Ohio reported to the sheriff he found what he thought was the solution to the mystery of the flying discs. The picture of Campbell's daughter, holding part of it was published throughout the country on July 6, 1947. That photograph might have suggested the cover story to the military. The difference was that everyone in Ohio knew it was a weather balloon when they saw it, while at Roswell, the officers were unable to identify the wreckage.[10]

Attention shifted from Fort Worth back to Roswell. Reporters calling from around the world were told that Colonel Blanchard was now on leave.[11] Mac Brazel was in military "custody," and on July 9, he was taken to the offices of the *Roswell Daily Record*. He was interviewed by reporters from that newspaper and by two men from Albuquerque.

Local weatherman L.J. Guthrie said that he was sure

that the so-called disc found by Brazel belonged to the weather service. Based on the descriptions he had heard, he was sure it was one of the "several styles (used) to measure wind velocities in the upper stretches, and that some of them had been designed in triangular shape, with a radar target disk attached."[12]

Newton, still in Fort Worth, was quoted as saying, "We use them because they go much higher than the eye can see."[13]

The military, however, wasn't through. They had taken Brazel to the newspaper office for one interview and then took him to KGFL for another. Frank Joyce, an announcer and newsman for the station reported that Brazel, accompanied by a number of military officers, came to the station late in the afternoon. While the escort waited outside, Brazel walked into the control room and told Joyce a new story about the crash.[14]

Joyce said that he'd talked to Brazel while Mac was still in Sheriff Wilcox's office on Sunday, July 6. According to him, he had called the sheriff to see if there was anything interesting happening, and Wilcox handed the phone over to Brazel. Joyce had the story, according to him, a full day before anyone else.

Now, a few days later, Brazel was back, telling him a different story. According to Joyce, Brazel was under a great deal of stress. He could tell that Brazel was saying things that he didn't believe.

Newspapers around the country were carrying the explanation of the Roswell saucer. Even papers that hadn't reported the capture were telling readers that the disc found in New Mexico was nothing more than a weather balloon. The pictures, those of Ramey, Ramey and DuBose, and Jesse Marcel, were printed throughout the country. The debris spread out on the floor of Ramey's office looked just like a weather balloon. Everything seemed to be open and aboveboard. The military, both in Roswell and Fort Worth, seemed to be telling the truth.

The reports of saucers and related stories began to

disappear from the papers. Explanations for them grew to include hallucinations and illusions. On July 9, the *Las Vegas Review Journal,* among other newspapers, reported that the Army and the Navy had moved to stop the rumors of flying saucers.

As far as the press around the world was concerned, the Roswell saucer was nothing more than a weather balloon. The radio reporters in Roswell, who had talked to the people involved, knew better, but their broadcast licenses had been threatened.[15] They had been told that the minute they finished their reports, they would be off the air. No one challenged that authority, especially when it came from New Mexico's own Washington congressional delegation, including the powerful Senator Dennis Chavez.

But Frank Joyce knew the weather balloon was a quickly manufactured cover story. When his second interview with Brazel ended, the rancher walked to the door. Then, according to Joyce, Brazel turned to him and said, ''Frank, you know how they talk of little green men? . . . They weren't green.'' Brazel then opened the door and left with his military escort.

July 6–12, 1947:
The Flights Out

Wreckage from the crash site was brought to Roswell by Mac Brazel, in the back of Marcel's '42 convertible, the jeep carryall, and in subsequent days, a variety of trucks. The first wreckage recovered was scrap, the result of either the explosion that had stripped the outer surface from the craft, or from the rip in the hull that had sucked debris from the interior. However it happened, the debris field was covered with those scraps.

The first of the wreckage was flown out of Roswell on Sunday, July 6, on orders from General Clements McMullen. It was some of the material that Brazel had brought in to show the sheriff. According to Colonel (now General) Thomas DuBose, he received a call from Washington sometime between two and three in the afternoon of July 6, and was told that the men in Roswell had found something on the ground. ". . . the debris or elements were to be placed in a suitable container and Blanchard was to see that they were delivered . . . and Al Clark . . . would pick them up and deliver them to McMullen."

When the flight from Roswell arrived at Fort Worth, both DuBose and Colonel Alan B. Clark were waiting. DuBose said that he saw the container that held the debris. According to DuBose, "I saw only the container and the container was a plastic bag that I would say weighed fifteen or twenty pounds. It was sealed. (A) lead seal (was) around the top and the only way to get into it was to cut it."

DuBose never talked to the pilot of the aircraft from Roswell. Clark took the plastic bag and then walked over to the command B-26. That was the plane he used to fly the first of the wreckage to Washington so that McMullen and the others could examine it.[1]

It was two days before any more of the wreckage was flown out. Marcel, who, along with a counter-intelligence agent, had picked up more of it, remained at the Roswell base. On Tuesday, he was told by Blanchard that he would be going to Eighth Air Force Headquarters in Fort Worth later that day with more of the material. This was the second of several flights carrying wreckage.[2]

According to Robert Porter, a crewman on that flight, there were only four small packages. They had checked the aircraft, a B-29, and then a staff car from Building 1034 had brought the material out to load on the plane. Porter said they handed the material up to him, through the hatch. The largest of the pieces was two and a half feet to three feet across, three to four inches thick, and was triangular-shaped. The other three packages were about the size of shoe boxes and all felt as if they were empty.

According to Porter, the flight was ordered by Major Ralph R. Taylor, the 830th Squadron Operations Officer. The flight crew consisted of Lieutenant Colonel Payne Jennings as the pilot, with Lieutenant Colonel Robert Barrowclough in the bombardier's seat. Porter said that he thought TSGT George Ades and TSGT William Cross were on the plane and he knew that TSGT Sterling Bone was there. And, Jesse Marcel.

Once the packages were on the plane, they were passed to the rear of the forward compartment. Porter said that he could no longer see them.

When the plane arrived at the Fort Worth Army Air Field Porter and the other enlisted men were told to stay with the aircraft until a guard was posted. When that was done, they were allowed to go to the mess hall to eat. According to him, the material was transferred to a B-25 and flown on to Wright Field. As they got back to the plane, they were told that the material in their B-29 was nothing more than a weather balloon. Then they flew back to Roswell.

Once they arrived in Fort Worth, Porter lost sight of the material. He didn't see it loaded onto the B-25 and knew only that it had been removed from his aircraft after the trip. Jesse Marcel took it with him as he left and it was Marcel or someone at Eighth Air Force who loaded it on the B-25.

And there wasn't much of it. Hardly enough to account for the debris that Marcel had described earlier. Just enough material to make the story of a weather balloon sound plausible. Certainly not enough material to make up a spacecraft.

But Porter's flight wasn't the only one. In the days that followed, other crews flew material out of Roswell. Captain O.W. "Pappy" Henderson flew a C-54 load of wreckage on to Wright Field. He kept that flight a secret from everyone including his wife, Sappho, until the early 1980s. Then, after seeing an article in a tabloid, he told her, "I guess I don't have to keep it a secret anymore."[3]

Henderson, who died in 1986, told Sappho that he had wanted to tell her about it for years. He knew that flying saucers were real because he had flown a planeload of wreckage on to Wright Field. He didn't tell her much about it except that the wreckage was strange. The flight's destination had been Dayton and back again. She said that it had been a C-54.

Sappho Henderson said that she had never asked her husband for the details. He had told her the material was strange but did not elaborate. He said the article he saw, including the descriptions of the bodies, was accurate and he described the bodies to her.

Henderson was a member of the First Air Transport Unit which was assigned to the Roswell Army Air Field. Colonel Jennings was the deputy base and group commander, Barrowclough was base executive officer, and Marcel was the group intelligence officer. All were in the 509th Bomb Group headquarters. The first flight taking the material to Fort Worth had been a very special one as evidenced by the make-up of the crew. Too many of the top men at Roswell were assigned to that crew. The second flight was not quite as special but was as highly classified. Henderson later said that it was a routine flight except for the high classification.[4]

Henderson kept the secret as long as he thought it was required of him, but once the information was published, he didn't mind sharing it with his friends. In 1982, at a reunion of his flight crew from World War II, he told them about flying the wreckage of a spacecraft out of Roswell. There, at the reunion, he mentioned that he flew the airplane to Wright Field and he mentioned the bodies. And again, because of the nature of the story, those listening were skeptical until they saw Pappy was serious. The discussion then went to other UFO sightings.[5]

Pappy made comments about flying saucers on other occasions, always telling his listeners that he believed in them because so many other pilots reported seeing them. He never broke his silence about his own role, until he saw that article.

Sappho remembered that while they still lived in Roswell, Pappy had been outside with Mary Katherine, his daughter, staring into the night sky. When asked what he was doing, he told her, "Looking for flying saucers. They're real, you know."

Porter's flight to Fort Worth with a small sample of the material and Henderson's special flight to Wright Field weren't the only aircraft dispatched. Like Henderson, other members of the First Transport were involved in moving wreckage from Roswell to other locations. Robert E. Smith was a sergeant with the First Air Transport in July, 1947. According to him, he spent one day loading three aircraft with the material that had been picked up at the crash site.

In a recent interview, he told about the scene at the airfield on the morning of July 9, 1947. "We started out in the morning, say about eight or nine o'clock. Seems like it lasted up to nearly four o'clock with a break for lunch. The reason I say it took so long is the weight and level guy worked to determine how much each crate weighed. He had to counterbalance the aircraft."

The crates were made of plywood with one-inch furring strips on the edges. The crates were from four to six feet wide, eight to ten feet long and three or four feet high. There was a variety of them and they were all fairly light. The problem wasn't the weight but the size. Smith said that some of them were hard to handle because they were six feet tall and three or four feet wide.

According to him the crates were marked, but he couldn't remember what the markings said. He did know that the crates were top secret and that several armed guards were posted around the hangar where they were working.

When Smith and his men finished, the three aircraft were sealed. Smith said that the procedure required any aircraft flying on to Los Alamos to land at Kirtland Air Force Base first. "The pilot would leave the aircraft and go to base ops (operations) and receive a sealed envelope. He would be escorted into base ops and escorted back by MPs. We would get airborne and he would have to open the envelope for the passage code. There were three codes in there. We had three positions that we had to answer. At one time we had a green (inexperienced) pilot and he stumbled on one of the passage codes and they fired some warning shots at us and we had to go back to Kirtland. Security was extremely tight. I would assume that when these planes went up there, went to Kirtland, they got their passage codes to go in. All I know, they went up there and they weren't up there over a day."

A few points, however, demand clarification. If the crates were sealed, how would he know what was in them? Lightweight crates loaded into a C-54 under an armed guard might be interesting but it didn't prove that they had contained the wreckage picked up at the crash site.

Smith and a couple of the other sergeants discussed the nature of the cargo as they were loading the aircraft. Smith said, "We were talking about what was in the crates and so forth and he (another of the NCOs) said, 'oh do you remember the story about the UFO? Or rather the flying saucer.' That was what we called them back then. We thought he was joking, but he let us feel a piece and he stuck it back into his pocket. Afterwards we got to talking a little bit more about it and he said he'd been out there helping clean this up. He didn't think taking a little piece like that would matter.

"It was just a little piece of metal or foil or whatever it was. Just small enough to be slipped into a pocket. I think he just picked it up for a souvenir.

"It was foil-like, but it was a little stiffer than foil that we have now. In fact, being a sheet metal man, it kind of intrigued me, being that you could crumple it and it would flatten back out again without any wrinkles showing up in it. Of course we didn't get to look at it too close because it was supposed to be top secret. He just popped it out there real quick and let us feel it and so forth while everybody was doing something else."

Explaining how the man might have gotten the piece, Smith said, "I know there was a pretty good gathering of them and they went across the field, about a couple of feet apart, and they just kept going across picking up the pieces. They were loading them into wheelbarrows and things like that and carrying them to the sentry point."

Smith said that the pieces were crated elsewhere on the base. He thought that the material was stored on the eastern side of the base, near the salvage pool. Smith added that the hangar didn't have a double door. It differed from the other hangars because they all had double doors that could be opened to catch the breeze.

The three flights, all C-54s from the First Air Transport, were not the last of the flights out of Roswell. One man said that he was involved in a special flight on his B-29. That plane flew directly to Forth Worth, was there only long enough for the crate to be unloaded, and then returned to Roswell. The flight log showed the whole trip took just under two hours on July 9, 1947.

And there was a final flight that carried some of the material out of New Mexico along with passengers. The counter-intelligence people came in to Roswell on a special flight from Andrews Army Air Field on July 8. This flight, described by Lieutenant Colonel Joe Briley, Frank Kaufman, and Lewis S. Rickett, also carried material out of Roswell on its return to Washington, D.C.

According to the testimony of the participants, there were several flights carrying wreckage or bodies. One flew to Fort Worth and then on to Wright Field, another flew to Wright Field directly, three flew to Los Alamos, and one flew to Andrews in Washington.[6] If what Mac Brazel found was only a weather balloon, would the Army have wasted so much time and effort transporting pieces of it all over the country? If it had been a weather balloon, wouldn't they have just thrown it away when they realized what it was? If it was a weather balloon, why were there so many flights made under such tight security?

July 8, 1947:
The Bodies

The story gets muddled when the search for the bodies begins. For years there have been rumors of alien bodies from crashed saucers, but no one ever offered any proof that they existed. There was even talk of cryonic suspension at Wright-Patterson Air Force Base and there were rumors of special rooms with special equipment, none of which could be confirmed.

The logical extension of the crashed disc theory was that the craft also contained a flight crew. Although only a few people had ever mentioned seeing bodies, there were enough solid leads to warrant further investigation.

According to the currently accepted version, Grady L. "Barney" Barnett and the members of an archaeological team who followed him into the site saw bodies during the summer of 1947. Barnett, while working near Magdalena on the Plains of San Agustin, said he had come upon the wreckage of a disc-shaped craft and saw the dead bodies of the crew. Within minutes the military, lead by a red-haired officer, had arrived, sworn him, and the archaeologists, to secrecy. The archaeologists never publicly revealed what they saw, and Barnett told only a few of his closest friends.

According to that version of the story, Barnett found the crash on July 3.[1] If the military had found bodies on July 3, they would have realized that they had discovered an extraterrestrial craft. Given that, and five days to make plans, it is doubtful that Colonel Blanchard would have told Walter Haut to issue a press release about the debris Mac Brazel found. In other words, the cover-up would have started on July 3, 1947, and there would have been no story in the July 8 newspapers.

In July, 1947, a number of people were in the Datil, Magdalena, and Plains of San Agustin area of New Mexico. Many of them are still alive, and none of them remember any stories circulating about alien ships and dead bodies.

Doctor Herbert Dick, an archaeologist still living in New Mexico, was working around a place called the Bat Cave on the eastern edge of the Plains of San Agustin in July and August of that year. He said that he knew nothing of other archaeological groups working in the vicinity. He reported that he had been questioned about it, ten or fifteen years earlier, by someone else, but was unable to remember anything new that would shed light on the crash.

Dick did say that he remembered a woman by the name of Francis Martin who was living in Datil, New Mexico, in 1947. She owned a bar and everyone who was working the flats eventually stopped in. "If anyone would know anything, it would be her," Dick said.

Francis Martin was 91 in 1989, but still remembered the summer of 1947 quite well. According to her, nothing like the crash, any crash, happened around Datil. She confirmed that all the people working near the Plains of San Agustin eventually stopped by her bar and she was aware of everything that was happening.

According to her, no military people ever came in and no military vehicles were seen in the area. And there were no strangers anywhere. Even if the strangers hadn't stopped by the bar, those living or working in the area would have seen them. She would have heard, from the locals at the very least, about something as extraordinary as a crashed flying disc.

That seemed to effectively eliminate the possibility of

a second crash near Magdalena, but there is another, more devastating piece of evidence. Ruth Barnett, the wife of Barney, kept a daily diary. According to that document, Barney spent the day of July 3, 1947, in the office. There was no time for Barney to be in the field, find a crashed flying disc, and get home.

That, of course, did not rule out the possibility of a second crash site. Research suggests that the second crash was not near Magdalena, but much closer to the first site, no more than two or three miles from it. And, the bodies were not found on July 3, but late on July 8.

Mac Brazel had been picked up by the counter-intelligence agents on July 8.[2] He was taken back to Roswell, where an aerial search was arranged. Because the country around the Brazel house has few landmarks, those unfamiliar with it can become lost in a matter of minutes. One arroyo, one draw, one canyon looks like the next. It was hoped that Brazel would be able to direct ground parties to any debris spotted from the air.

The first aerial survey discovered a second crash site about two and a half miles to the southeast of the first. That was where the ship came down and where the bodies were located.

But before the military on the ground could be directed to the new site, Barney Barnett and the archaeologists stumbled onto the wreckage. The references to the Plains of San Agustin and Magdalena had been inaccurate.

According to L.W. ''Vern'' Maltais, Barney Barnett told him a few years later that he had seen the bodies of beings from another planet. They were three or four of them, all wearing one-piece gray suits with no sign of buttons, snaps or zippers. They were small creatures, four to five feet tall, with large, pear-shaped heads, small bodies, and skinny arms and legs.

Maltais said that Barnett never really described the object, saying only that it was metallic, dull gray and was "pretty good sized." Barnett said that it seemed to have "burst open." It was jammed up against a ridgeline and there was no wreckage scattered around it. But because there were bodies outside the craft, Barnett's attention had been drawn to them. He was close enough to touch one, had he wanted to.

Moments after he had found the bodies, a small group of people appeared. Barnett said they were archaeologists who were working in the area. They, too, saw the bodies and the craft, but before anyone could do anything, the military arrived.

Barnett never learned who the archaeologists were or where they were from. He didn't have the chance to talk to them. The military warned everyone that what they had seen was a classified project and that it was their patriotic duty to keep what they had seen to themselves. They were then escorted off the site.

Ruth Barnett's diary for July 8, 1947 said that Barney was in the Pie Town area, on the far side of the Plains of San Agustin—as far from Barnett's home in Socorro as the actual crash site near Corona is. According to the diary, Barnett got home about 8:30 P.M. The question becomes: Because of the orders of the military officers, did Barnett mention Pie Town because it was so far away? Was he covering his tracks by suggesting he was more than 300 miles from the crash site? Was he actually in Lincoln County on July 8?

After the civilians were gone, the military brought in trucks and a few dozen men to clean the site. The bodies were loaded into the back of one of the trucks, in which there were several large blocks of ice. About dusk, Sergeant Melvin E. Brown and one other soldier were stationed in the truck with orders not to look under the tarp. Brown could not resist the temptation and as soon as his superiors moved away, he pulled the tarp aside. There, he saw the bodies.

Like Barnett, Brown described them as smaller than human. He said the skin was yellowish-orange, but that might have been an effect of the lighting or decomposition. He said that the skin was similar to that of a lizard, meaning it was leathery and beaded, but not scaly.

But Brown was not the only one to report bodies at the crash site. Captain Darwin E. Rasmussen, the 718th Bomb Group Operations Officer, (part of the 509th) told family members that four bodies had been recovered at Roswell. Elaine Vegh, Rasmussen's cousin, reported she had heard Rasmussen tell her father that he had no doubt that flying saucers were real because he'd helped to retrieve the bodies from one that crashed.

As soon as the bodies were loaded into the truck, they were driven from the crash site to the Roswell Army Air Field where they were taken to the base hospital. Brown and the other soldier remained in the truck during the trip. Once there, Brown was dismissed and the bodies were taken inside the building.[3]

Shortly after the bodies arrived at the base, a mortician from Roswell, Glenn Dennis, also arrived. All afternoon the doctors at the base had been calling the mortuary asking questions about preservation techniques: "What's this going to do to the blood system? What's this going to do to the tissue?" The mortician was told by the military doctors that the bodies had been out on the prairie for a couple of days, maybe a week.

The mortician stressed that the military doctors at the base hospital called him repeatedly, asking different questions each time. He described some of the embalming techniques but was told that wasn't what they wanted to know. They were more interested in the best way to move the dead. The implication then, according to him, was that the dead were humans killed in a plane crash.

According to the mortician, he was told there were three fatalities. Two of them had been mangled in the crash but the other was in fairly good shape. The officers at the base wanted to know if they could get all three into a single, hermetically sealed casket.

Records available for the time, however, show that no personnel at the Roswell Army Air Field died. The unit history for July, 1947 states there were no deaths recorded at the hospital.

But the mortician was told that there were casualties. The mortician, assuming there had been a plane crash, climbed into the hearse and drove out to the base. He was waved through the gate because he had been out there often on official business and was easily recognized. At the hospital he parked next to one of the old box-type military ambulances on the back ramp.

He got out of the hearse and walked up the ramp. At the top were two MPs staring down into an ambulance that had its rear doors open. Inside he could see some metallic wreckage that he didn't recognize. It didn't look like the material normally found at an airplane crash site.

Inside the hospital he was met by another MP who demanded to know what he was doing there. The mortician told the MP who he was and the MP let him pass, apparently believing that someone at the base had summoned him.

As the mortician walked down a corridor, he was seen by one of the base hospital nurses. She wanted to know how he had gotten into the hospital and told him to get the hell out. She said, ''My God, you are going to get yourself killed.''

Dennis couldn't understand her sudden fright and told her that the MPs hadn't stopped him. She was still agitated and told him to get out. Before he could respond, two MPs grabbed him by the arms, lifted him from his feet, and carried him outside. He was escorted off the base and followed to his parent's home.

The next day, the nurse explained what had happened in the hospital. Bodies had arrived, just as Dennis had suspected, but the bodies were not human. She didn't know what they were or where they came from.

She said that they were little, smaller than an adult human. She said that the hands were different, too, that they only had four fingers with the middle two protruding longer than the others. She saw no opposable thumb. She also said that the anatomy of the arm was different. The bone from the shoulder to the elbow was shorter than the bone from the elbow to the wrist.

The heads were larger than a human's. The eyes were large and had a concave shape. She said that all the features, the nose and the ears and the eyes, were slightly concave.

The nurse added that the bodies were very delicate. The skulls and the bones were very fragile. She said that it reminded her of pictures of the mummies she had seen, thin, spindly, and fragile.

She said that the bodies had been exposed to the elements and to predators for several days. There was no indication of any sex organs but she didn't think that was strange given the circumstances. She mentioned that it looked as if predators had attacked the bodies and the soft tissues of the genitals were normally the first areas destroyed.

She also said that the bodies were frozen once they arrived in Roswell. They were sealed in rubberized "mortuary" bags and nailed in a crate for shipment possibly because of the stench they gave off. She said that she heard the final destination was Wright Field and she was sure they were sent there eventually, but once they left the hospital, she lost track of them.

Pappy Henderson, a captain with the First Air Transport Unit assigned to Roswell, also saw the bodies. Given the scenario, there is only one point where Henderson could have seen them, and that is on the crash site. Henderson, as a pilot, would have no reason to be on the site, but as one of Blanchard's most trusted officers, it stands to reason that Henderson would have been called in by Blanchard to fly one of the reconnaissance planes. It seems likely that Henderson saw the bodies as he flew over in an aircraft and, possibly, directed the ground parties to the second site.

Henderson told a close personal friend and fellow military officer, Doctor John Kromschroeder, about the bodies in early 1978. According to Kromschroeder, Henderson and he were sharing stories while on a fishing trip. After several hours, Henderson mentioned that he had seen the bodies of alien visitors and the remains of their craft.

Kromschroeder said that Henderson was clearly nervous about it. Henderson, according to the source, didn't like being around the dead or injured and wanted to get away from them as quickly as he could. The source quoted Henderson as saying, "I really couldn't look at them."

But he did see enough to say that they were "kinda little guys." Henderson said that they had been put into the deep freeze and that as late as 1986, Henderson thought they were still at Wright-Patterson Air Force Base.

Naturally Kromschroeder wanted to know more about it. Henderson would only repeat the descriptions and then said, "I just can't talk about it."

Kromschroeder, having been a good friend of Henderson's for years. believed the story. He said that Henderson was clearly uncomfortable talking about it. Henderson said that he'd never even told his wife, Sappho, because of the top secret classifications of the information. Henderson talked only because his friend was another military man who understood the significance of the information and the restrictions of military classification.[4]

Kromschroeder would have believed Henderson even if he'd had no proof of what he said. But about a year later, in 1979, Henderson showed Kromschroeder a small piece of metal that Henderson said was from the craft. Kromschroeder had studied metals and metallurgy for years and had never seen anything like it.

The metal, according to the doctor, was gray and resembled aluminum but was harder and stiffer. He couldn't bend it but had to be careful because the edges were sharp. He said that it didn't seem to have a crystalline structure and based that on the fracturing of it. It hadn't been torn.

Kromschroeder said that Henderson claimed the metal was some of the lighter material lining the craft. He said that when properly energized, it produced perfect illumination. It was a soft light with no shadows.

Henderson, after seeing an article about the Roswell event in 1982, mentioned the bodies to his daughter, Mary Katherine Groode. He told her a little more about them, saying that they were little men, gray, with slanted eyes and tiny mouths. He didn't tell his daughter how he happened to see the bodies, only that he had.

Henderson hinted that the bodies were at Wright-Patterson Air Force Base. The nurse thought it was the final destination for them. Neither Henderson nor the nurse knew what happened to the bodies or the crate once it left the hospital. Others, however, did have that information. According to Frank Kaufman, the bodies were sealed in a wooden crate while still at the hospital. Under the cover of darkness, the crate was loaded into a covered truck and driven to a hangar on the flightline. Once there, it was unloaded and carried inside.

Kaufman said that MPs were stationed around the interior of the hangar and that a searchlight was set to shine on the crate. It remained there overnight.

Brown, who had ridden with the bodies from the crash site, was added to the guard detail outside the hangar. While he was standing guard, the commanding officer of Squadron K of the 509th Bomb Group, Captain John Martin, walked up and said, "Come on, Brownie, let's have a look inside."

There was nothing to see except the wooden crate. Brown said that it all had been packed up for shipment to Fort Worth. Martin and Brown walked back outside.

Years later, on the days when Americans first landed on the moon, Brown told his family the story of the crash at Roswell. They were reluctant to believe him, but each of them remembered that Brown told them to tell no one else because "Daddy will get into trouble."

In 1986, as Brown was on his deathbed, his daughter, Beverly Bean, said that Brown talked about Roswell extensively. He mentioned, over and over, that "it was not a damn weather balloon."

Brown's wife still will not talk about it, nor will his oldest daughter. Both are afraid that it will reflect poorly on Brown's military record and that the Army could retaliate.

Beverly Bean, however, wanted everyone to know what her father had told her on his deathbed. He had seen the bodies. He had escorted them into Roswell, and he knew that it was not a weather balloon.[5]

The crate containing the bodies remained in the hangar overnight. About noon the next day, July 9, it was loaded into another truck and driven out to bomb pit number one on a remote part of the air base.

The bodies remained there for another two or three hours. Then, according to a witness who requested anonymity because he was afraid he could lose his job, the crate was loaded onto a B-29 to be flown to Fort Worth.

According to him, the flight crew, including Second Lieutenant Joe C. Shackelford, Second Lieutenant Elmer L. Landry, CPL Thaddeus Love, SSG Robert A. Slusher, and PFC Jesse M. Delozier, were on the skeet range after lunch. All of them had heard the rumors that a flying disc with bodies had been found on a ranch near Roswell. Although Walter Haut's press release had already been printed in the local newspaper, Ramey's explanation wouldn't be published for another few hours. They left the skeet range and returned to the squadron area. Most of the other flight crews had already been sent home for the day, but the squadron operations officer,

Edgar Skelley, told the aircraft commander to keep his crew together because there might be a special flight.

Once it was decided to ship the bodies, the flight crew went out to preflight the aircraft, a B-29, but didn't have the usual time allotted for the task. They were forced to rush through it. About an hour later, they were ordered to taxi to the "pit" where the bombs were normally kept. This time the pit was covered with a canvas tarp. When the tarp was removed, they saw a large wooden crate sitting on a platform used to carry cargo. It was loaded into the bomb bay along with an armed escort of six military police, an officer, two sergeants, and three enlisted men. All were armed with .45s and one of the enlisted men had an M-1 carbine. Normally they didn't fly with carbines because the weapons could become entangled in the control cables. They never allowed the crate out of their sight.

Before takeoff the officer crew members reported to base operations for their flight briefings and clearances. When they returned only the bombadier was allowed to look into the bomb bay to make sure the load was properly secured. The flight engineer and the crew chief weren't concerned about the weight because they had been told the load did not weigh more than five thousand pounds and therefore no ballast in the tail was required.

"Everything about the flight was unusual," said the source. "So tight was security that we knew the crate contained more than the general's furniture."

He described the crate as made of wood, unpainted and unmarked. It was about five feet high, four feet wide, and fifteen feet long, certainly large enough to contain the three or four bodies recovered at the crash site.

The witness said that the afternoon was hot and muggy and that they were looking forward to getting airborne. The flight was ordered to stay at eight thousand feet rather than at the routine twenty-five or thirty thousand. The escort and the crate remained in the bomb bay.

According to Curt Platt, a member of the 509th Bomb Group, transporting cargo and passengers in the bomb bay wasn't unusual. He said there were rails or racks that fit into the bomb bay so that both cargo and passengers could be transported. Because the bomb bay was not pressurized, they had to stay below ten thousand feet. According to Platt, they frequently carried people and cargo in that manner.

The plane flew directly to the Fort Worth Army Air Field. There, they were met by a contingent of officers from Fort Worth, including a man that the bombardier recognized as a mortician. According to the bombardier, he had gone to school with the man and knew that he had become a mortician.

Once the crate was unloaded, the crew was ordered to return to Roswell immediately. No time was spent in Fort Worth. They just turned the aircraft around and took off. The bombardier told the crew they were all now "part of history" because of the cargo they had carried.

After seeing a copy of the 509th yearbook, the witness said that he believed that Jesse Marcel had been on the return flight. He said he was sure there had been an intelligence officer on the return flight. Robert Slusher who was also on the flight confirmed that view.

Later, Jesse Marcel, Jr. said he remembered that his father had been gone for more than twenty-four hours. In other words, Marcel took a flight to Fort Worth on July 8 with some of the wreckage and returned on July 9 with the B-29 that had brought the bodies.

The source, who still has his flight log books, confirmed the July 9 date. He had flown in a B-29, tail number 7301, on a cross-country flight from Roswell to Fort Worth and back again. Total flight time was one hour and fifty-five minutes including the short period they were on the ground in Fort Worth.

According to all the stories, once the bodies were discovered, they stayed in New Mexico only a few hours. Through witnesses, they have been traced from the crash site near Corona, New Mexico to Roswell and then on to Fort Worth. The base nurse said that their final destination was Wright Field in Dayton, Ohio. At that point they seemed to disappear.

July, 1947 – Present:
The Bodies

If there were bodies in the crate loaded into the B-29 at Roswell, once they arrived at the Fort Worth Army Air Field they disappear. A chain of witnesses taking them from the crash site to Roswell and then to Fort Worth had been found. But once the bodies arrived in Fort Worth, the chain was broken. The assumption was that the bodies, like some of the wreckage, would have gone on to Wright Field, but there was no concrete evidence of that.

Over the years, stories were told about alien bodies at Wright Field and it was believed they were the bodies recovered outside Roswell. Len Stringfield, in his research, had located a number of witnesses to the presence of bodies at Wright-Patterson Air Force Base.[1]

One of the people whose report found its way to Len Stringfield was from a woman named Norma Gardner, a one-time employee at Wright-Patterson Air Force Base. In 1959 she retired for health reasons. She hinted to friends that she knew more about the "flying saucer" situation than the government was comfortable with her knowing. Given a top security clearance, she had been given the chore of logging in all UFO-related material, which included parts of the interior of a craft that had been brought to the base in the past. Everything had been photographed and tagged and labeled and all the documents had to be filed by someone. Norma Gardner had that task.

At one point, she saw two bodies as they were moved from one location to another. The bodies had been preserved in some kind of chemical solution. She said that they were small, four or five feet tall, with large heads and slanted eyes and obviously were not human. In the course of her duties, she also typed the autopsy reports on them.

Her story, told years earlier, had been ignored by researchers. Without corroboration, there was no reason to accept Gardner's story. But now, with the reports from Roswell, there was that corroboration. Barnett and Brown, among others, confirmed that bodies were found. Marcel and others told of something from another world that had crashed. Each story, coming from independent sources, helped to confirm the next.

Gardner is important for one other reason. She was at Wright-Patterson Air Force Base. She was one of the first sources to confirm that corpses had been brought to the base. It didn't prove the bodies were from Roswell, but it provided a starting point for investigators.

Gardner, however, is not the lone source about the bodies and their location. Others have, over the years, hinted of inside knowledge. Again, according to Len Stringfield, he was told by a man that he had attended a high-level, secret conference at Wright-Patterson and saw, in an underground facility, a body in deep-freeze preservation.

The source described the body as having long arms positioned at its sides. It was about four feet tall and the skin on the face appeared smooth and gray. The eyes were open and there was no hair visible.

It wasn't much, and without confirmation, almost useless, but it did address the question about the location of the dead. It also suggested that the bodies had not been buried or burned, but were being preserved.

Truman Weaver, a former Air Force major, provided some additional information. He showed researchers a letter from a friend who claimed to have worked across the alley from the building where the bodies were kept. The source claimed that on some days a strong odor drifted across the alley, and when he asked about it he was told that it was embalming fluid.[2]

A strong odor of formaldehyde drifting on a breeze at Wright-Patterson isn't enough to even suggest alien bodies or that bodies were there. The source went on, however, explaining that his boss, a man named McAdams, showed him an interim report that confirmed the rumors of the bodies and the captured craft.

It was another piece of the puzzle that provided a little confirmation. The McAdams report is, unfortunately, secondhand, but a few of the details mesh with those of other, firsthand accounts and lend some support to these cases.

Another source, an electrician, was employed by General Electric and accepted a job at Wright-Patterson. He was taken into an icy room that had a strange, offensive odor. There was a number of cases in the room that had electrical connections and air ducts hooked to them. The source managed to sneak a look at one of the cases. Inside, resting on a marble slab, was a body that wasn't human.

The source, once he finished the job at Wright-Patterson, returned home. He told his family of the pungent odor in the cold room. The source's daughter said that she remembered her father's clothes having a strong odor of ammonia on them.

Such reports provide clues about the locations of the bodies and, coming from widely separated sources without knowledge of the other reports, suggest they are true. The people are reporting, as accurately as possible, their personal experiences.

The problem is that none of those stories connects the events in Roswell with the bodies seen at Wright-Patterson. John Timmerman, a researcher who is on the board of directors for the J. Allen Hynek Center for UFO

Studies in Chicago, may have provided some of the connecting material.

Timmerman has a traveling UFO exhibit he sets up in malls, schools, and shopping centers. Along with the displays of photos and other material, Timmerman has a small cassette recorder, and he asks those who stop by to share any of their UFO experiences with him.

On January 13, 1990, he had a brief, taped interview with a man who refused to give his name. He said that he knew something about the bodies recovered at Roswell in 1947. He said that he knew the victims of the crash had been taken to Wright Field. The source said that the bodies were not from this planet. He had worked with a doctor who had been involved with the medical research on the dead.[3]

That evidence by itself is nearly worthless. An unnamed source talking about the bodies at Wright-Patterson provides nothing that can be verified. But when coupled to the other reports where firsthand witnesses have told what they saw, it becomes convincing.

It is important because the source said that the bodies were from the Roswell crash, and that they were taken to Wright Field. It completes the chain of evidence. The link isn't strong until it is added to other reports coming from Wright-Patterson.

John G. Tiffany said that his father was assigned to Wright Field in the summer of 1947. They supported many of the activities of the 509th Bomb Group. They had, for example, built the special bomb racks required for the atomic weapons. At the time they didn't know what they were for—other than the destination of the 509th.

In the mid-1950s, Tiffany said that his father first mentioned that he had been on a flight crew dispatched from Wright Field to a destination in Texas. Once on the ground there, they picked up some of the debris and a large container that looked like a giant Thermos jug, that was specialized military equipment.

The debris was all very lightweight and very tough. Tiffany said that it had a glasslike surface, and everything that the flight crew did to mark it, bend it, or break it, failed. According to Tiffany, they beat on it all the way back to Wright Field, and were unable to affect it. When they heard the weather balloon answer later, they all laughed about it because it was so ridiculous.

Tiffany wasn't sure if his father had seen the bodies himself, or if he had heard about them from others, but he did describe them. Two were intact and one had been dismembered. They had smooth features and skin, and all wore some kind of flying suit.

Tiffany stressed that carrying that cargo bothered the entire crew. They all felt as if they just couldn't get clean. They could not "get over handling something beyond a foreign device."

Once they arrived at Wright Field, everything—the debris they carried and the Thermos jug—were loaded onto trucks. Once the trucks were gone, the whole flight crew was told by a high-ranking official not to mention the flight to anyone. They were told, "It didn't happen."

Helen Wachter said that she was a nursing student at a school in Dayton, Ohio, in the summer of 1947. According to her, she was visiting a friend when the friend's husband returned in an agitated state. He dragged his wife into the bedroom and told her, in a voice that could be easily overheard, that something of a top secret nature had happened at the base. Bodies of alien creatures had arrived. Four of them. He had been one of the guards posted when the plane had come in with them.

That was all that was said about it. Four bodies had come into the base during the summer of 1947. Another suggestion that the bodies recovered at Roswell went to Ohio.[4]

The problem with the stories is that none of the people telling them, other than Norma Gardner, had much to do with the bodies. They saw them in connection with other duties and didn't have an opportunity to examine them.

Or they saw them under less than ideal conditions. One source had to look through the glass top of a freezer that had frost on it. But even with those problems, they were able to describe, sometimes in detail, what they had seen.

And there were a few people who had the opportunity to examine the bodies at length. Jesse Johnson, M.D., who was at Roswell in July, 1947, was the base pathologist. It is believed that he made some preliminary studies when the bodies were first brought to the base. When coupled with the information provided by Len Stringfield, a comprehensive description of the bodies can be drawn.

According to the doctor, the bodies measured between three and a half and four and a half feet and weighed about forty pounds.

There were two large, almond-shaped eyes without pupils that were under a heavy brow ridge. The eyes were elongated and appeared slightly slanted, giving the face an Oriental look. They were set deep and wide apart and without an eyelid, just a slight fold.

The head was large by human standards, which meant it was not in proportion to the body. Instead of ears, there were small openings on the side of the head. The nose was indistinct, almost invisible, with only a slight protuberance. The mouth was small and described as a slit without lips. According to the doctor, the mouth didn't function as a means of communication or as a way of eating. In fact, the mouth appeared to be a wrinkle-like fold and was only about two inches deep. The head seemed to be hairless, with a slight fuzz. The bodies themselves were hairless.

The torso was small and thin. The arms were long and thin, reaching down to the knees. The length from the shoulder to the elbow was shorter than the length from the elbow to the wrist. The hands had four digits and no opposable thumb and seemed to have sucker pads at the end. Two fingers appeared longer than the others. This is consistent with the descriptions given by the nurse at Roswell.

The legs were short and thin. The feet were covered, though one source did say that the feet didn't have toes. That impression might have been given by a webbing between the toes that a few of the sources had described.

The skin, as everyone who ever saw the bodies pointed out, was not green. The skin was a pinkish gray, though Melvin Brown thought it was yellowish. The skin itself was tough and leathery. Under magnification, it had a mesh-like structure.

Many of the sources talk of an overpowering odor associated with the bodies. Tiffany said his father felt as if he couldn't get clean. The nurse at Roswell said the stench was so bad that it was making them physically ill.

Most of the firsthand sources who reported seeing the bodies had no opportunity to see any internal structures. One of Stringfield's sources did. He said there were no teeth and no apparent reproductive organs. The Roswell nurse said that those soft tissues are among the first attacked by predators and there was evidence of predator damage to the bodies brought into Roswell.

There was a colorless liquid prevalent in the body but without red blood cells. There was no evidence of a digestive system or upper gastrointestinal tract and no lower intestinal or alimentary canal or rectal area.

The doctor provided one of the most comprehensive descriptions of the bodies. He had the opportunity to work on them and examine them. He was able to spend time studying them.

There are others, however, who have had firsthand experiences, but who did not see the bodies. They, through their work with the military, saw files containing notes about the crashes and photographs of the bodies.

One of those is a man who said he worked at NORAD in Colorado Springs. In the course of computerizing some of the files, he came across one labeled, ''USAAF (United States Army Air Force) Early Automation.'' The file dealt with the recovery of several small bodies and included black and white photographs of them. The man said the bodies were small, no more than four or five feet tall, with big heads.[5]

All this leads to one conclusion. The bodies were moved from the crash site, packed in ice at Roswell, and flown to Fort Worth. Unloaded from the plane there, they were put on another aircraft and flown on to Wright Field. Once there, they were examined, one was autopsied, and all were frozen for study as the techniques for genetic tracking, cellular mapping, and biological explanation were improved.

Are they still there? Possibly. Do they still exist? Absolutely. They would not destroy samples that were unique.

July, 1947:
The Wright Field
Connection

Numerous reports suggested that the material recovered by the officers and men of the Roswell Army Air Field went to Wright Field in Dayton, Ohio. Almost everyone who knew anything about the bodies suggested that Wright Field was the ultimate destination for them. Evidence had been presented and a few witnesses had been found but the proof was still far from conclusive. Then, Brigadier General Arthur E. Exon came forward.

Exon is a pilot with 135 combat missions and over 300 hours of combat flight time during World War II. His aircraft was severely damaged by an exploding ammunition dump and he was forced to bail out over enemy territory. Captured, he spent just over a year in German prisoner of war camps. He was liberated in April, 1945.[1]

After the war he completed an industrial administration course at the Air Force Institute of Technology and was then assigned to the Air Materiel Command (AMC) Headquarters at Wright-Patterson Air Force Base. (It should be noted that General Nathan F. Twining was the commander of the Air Materiel Command which controlled various intelligence functions. Twining's letter of September 23, 1947 has been quoted by many. It was Twining's conclusion then that flying discs were real.)[2]

Over the next several years he held a variety of positions finally arriving at the Pentagon as a full colonel in 1955. In 1960 he became Chief of Ballistic Missiles and was responsible for establishing the Jupiter Ballistic Missile system for NATO in Italy and Turkey. In July, 1963, he left Europe for an assignment at Olmsted Air Force Base in Pennsylvania. In August, 1964, he was assigned as commander, Wright-Patterson Air Force Base. On August 20, 1965, he was promoted to brigadier general.

General Exon has had a most impressive military career. Officers are not promoted to flag rank (general officer) without having proven themselves as competent. Those who make it while on active duty, who are not rewarded with the promotion on retirement, are in a small minority. Only the top officers achieve the privilege of wearing stars.

General Exon, as a lieutenant colonel, was assigned to Wright Field in July of 1947. He was there when the wreckage from the Roswell crash came in and was aware of the recovery in New Mexico. He knew that it was brought in and knew where it was sent. A few of his colleagues performed the tests on the metal, trying to determine what it was. And he learned from other colleagues that the bodies had arrived on the base. All in July, 1947.[3]

According to Exon, "We heard the material was coming to Wright Field." Testing was done in the various labs. "Everything from chemical analysis, stress tests, compression tests, flexing. It was brought into our material evaluation labs. I don't know how it arrived but the boys who tested it said it was very unusual."

Exon also described the material. "(Some of it) could be easily ripped or changed . . . there were other parts of it that were very thin but awfully strong and couldn't be dented with heavy hammers. . . . It was flexible to a degree."

According to him, ". . . some of it was flimsy and

was tougher than hell and other almost like foil but strong. It had them pretty puzzled.''

The lab chiefs at Wright Field set up a ''special project'' for the testing of the material. ''They knew they had something new in their hands. The metal and material was unknown to anyone I talked to. Whatever they found, I never heard what the results were. A couple of guys thought it might be Russian but the overall consensus was that the pieces were from space.''

Exon's involvement wasn't strictly at Wright Field. He flew over the crash site. And, he confirmed some of the reports that had been made in the years since.

''(It was) probably part of the same accident, but (there were) two distinct sites. One, assuming that the thing, as I understand it, as I remember flying the area later, that the damage to the vehicle seemed to be coming from the southeast to the northwest, but it could have been going in the opposite direction, but it doesn't seem likely. So the farther northwest pieces found on the ranch, those pieces were mostly metal.''

When asked about the bodies, he said, ''There was another location where . . . apparently the main body of the spacecraft was . . . where they did say there were bodies . . . they were all found, apparently, outside the craft itself but were in fairly good condition. In other words, they weren't broken up a lot.''

When asked if they went to Wright Field, Exon said, ''That's my information. But one of them went to a mortuary outfit . . . I think at that time it was in Denver. But the strongest information was that they were brought into Wright-Pat.''

Exon also knew something about the coverup that began on July 8, 1947. Because he knew Blanchard, he said, ''Blanchard's leave was a screen. It was his duty to go to the site and make a determination.''

Concerning the coverup, Exon pointed out that there were no secret balloon or weather devices at that time. The balloon explanation was ready-made. ''Blanchard could have cared less about a weather balloon,'' Exon said.

"I know that at the time the sightings happened, it went to General Ramey . . . and he along with the people out at Roswell decided to change the story while they got their act together and got the information into the Pentagon and into the President.''

According to Exon, the instant they understood the nature of the find, Ramey would have alerted the Chief of Staff, Dwight Eisenhower. Once they had the information in Washington, control of the operation would have come from the Pentagon. The men at Roswell would have been tasked with the clean-up because they were there, on the site, but the responsibility for the clean-up would have moved up the chain of command and into the Pentagon and the White House.

According to Exon, the outgrowth of this was a top secret committee to study the phenomenon found at Roswell, an oversight committee whose responsibility it would be to protect the data, to control access to it, and to design studies to exploit it. It was a small group with control, a secondary group made up of the aides, assistants, and staff from the first group, and then a third level where actual testing was done.

Exon was sure that the material, at least some of it, would still be housed at Wright-Patterson. There would be reports, probably filed in the Foreign Technology building, that would describe everything learned in the last forty plus years. There would be photographs, from the debris field and the crash site, of the bodies and of the autopsies, filed away. Everything needed to prove that Roswell represented the crash of an extraterrestrial spacecraft would be found, if those reports were ever to be released.

Like others who had been on the crash site in July, 1947, who had been in Roswell at the time of the recovery, or who had been in Fort Worth when Marcel brought the material in, Exon was convinced that this was the wreck of a spacecraft. It was not something manufactured on Earth. "Roswell was the recovery of a craft from space."

July, 1947:
The Archaeologists

There were never many witnesses to the discovery and recovery of the bodies. Access to that portion of the crash site was severely limited. While the debris field was literally filled with the men assigned to clean it, the second site was nearly empty.[1] Blanchard realized the importance of that find and wanted to keep it as quiet as possible. The fewer men on it, the better it would be. The debris itself could be explained in an ordinary way. Metal was metal and wires were wires, even if that metal and those wires seemed to be extraordinary. Bodies, however, could not be explained so easily.

Firsthand witnesses to the bodies were few and almost all of them were military personnel, except for Barney Barnett and the group of archaeologists that Barnett claimed arrived shortly after he did.

The problem with the archaeologists as witnesses was that scientists interested in the history of New Mexico said there was nothing of archaeological interest in the Corona area. Most of the state was rich in archaeological sites, but there was nothing near Corona that would interest anyone other than a souvenir hunter. The ranchers claimed the archaeologists wouldn't be interested in their land for any reason.

When it was believed that part of the craft crashed near Magdalena, New Mexico, it was learned that a team from the University of Pennsylvania might have been in the area in the summer of 1947. Research, however, showed that no one was working the "Flats" in July, 1947.[2]

The Museum of New Mexico did say that two groups were operating in the general area in that time frame and that both had produced monographs about their work. J.H. Kelly led one of the digs, but when contacted about the possibility of her group being in central New Mexico, she said that she wasn't there in the summer of 1947. In fact, she didn't think that anyone had been there then.[3]

The other dig was led by Donald Lehmer. His name was also provided by the Museum of New Mexico. He was responsible for a short monograph published in 1948. Donald Lehmer, unfortunately, is dead.[4]

All efforts to track any of the archaeologists who would admit to having been involved have failed. Everyone contacted denied knowing about a crash and denied having ever heard of it. A few would not even admit they were there, although there was evidence that they had been. It was similar to the situation developing with a few of the military people. There was proof they were in Roswell and were involved in some aspect of retrieval, but they wouldn't admit it. All they would say was that it had to be someone else.

In October, 1989, Mary Ann Gardner, a nurse who had worked in the cancer ward in the St. Petersburg Hospital in Florida, came forward to say that she might know something about the archaeologists. According to her, she had been watching NBC's *Unsolved Mysteries* when the story of Roswell was aired. She said she turned white as she watched because she had heard the story of the alien ship years before.

She said that she had treated a terminally ill patient, a woman, who claimed to have been with the archaeologists. The patient said that when she was in school in the late 1940s, she was involved with a site survey in New Mexico. The dying woman then told the story of discovering the wreck of the alien ship and the dead bodies of the crew.

Gardner, assuming that the story was some kind of a drug-induced fantasy, never gave the account much thought, or questioned the woman about it in depth. In fact, she thought nothing of it until the *Unsolved Mysteries* broadcast because she hadn't heard anything else about it.[5]

A second source was also developed through *Unsolved Mysteries*. Iris Foster lived in the Taos area in the early 1970s. She said she might have information regarding the identity of the archaeologists. She said that at the time she owned a small cafe and a fellow known locally as Cactus Jack made it a habit to stop in frequently for coffee. Cactus Jack was a pottery hunter, an amateur archaeologist who searched for Indian artifacts in the desert. In 1971 he told Iris Foster that "he had been there when the spaceship had come down."

Foster, who was interested in the subject, listened to everything that Cactus Jack told her. He said that he had seen the "object which was round, but not real big." He saw four bodies and said that they were small. Their blood, according to Cactus Jack, was like tar, thick and black, and stained their uniforms. Cactus Jack was positive that they had been wearing silver uniforms.[6]

Foster was sure of the date because it was during the time she owned the cafe. And it was long before there was any significant publicity about crashed saucers and the bodies of the flight crews. She added that she had heard rumors of a crash since she was a child. Although everyone took the stories seriously at first, it all became a big joke as the years passed.

Further confirmation of the archaeologists came on February 15, 1990. A firsthand source who was one of the archaeologists came forward, but because he was worried about professional repercussions, he didn't want his name used. He was sure that if he told stories of crashed saucers and a dead flight crew it could come back to haunt him.

According to the source, they had been surveying the area north of the Capitan Mountains in central New Mexico, searching for signs of occupation that pre-dated both the arrival of the Americans and the Spanish. He said they were driving when they came up over a rise and saw what looked like a crashed airplane without wings. He said it looked like a fat fuselage that was badly damaged. He saw no sign of a dome, portholes, or a hatch and there were no markings on it anywhere.

As they approached the craft, he saw three bodies. The one closest to him was in the best condition. It was small, with a big head and big eyes. Its head was turned to one side so that it was difficult to see the facial features. He saw a mouth, but he couldn't remember seeing a nose. It was wearing a silvery flight suit and had one arm bent at a strange angle, as if it had been broken.

He hadn't been there very long when a jeep arrived carrying soldiers. He believed one officer rode in the jeep but didn't know. All of them were armed with pistols and some of them had rifles. The officer ordered everyone away from the craft and then told them that it was an issue of national security and that he was asking them, ordering them actually, not to tell anyone what they had seen.

The witness said the officer stressed national security and then took their names and where they were going to school. He told them that if anyone talked, their government grants would disappear and they would never receive any further funding. He made the threats very clear to them.

The civilians were then escorted off the site. The archaeologist stressed that they were escorted rather than simply told to leave. They were taken to the nearest road and then told to drive east. They passed an Army car parked by the side of the road with two soldiers standing near it.

That was all he knew and he refused to answer any further questions. He did say that he thought the information should come out and that was why he was telling it at all. He wanted everyone to know that the story was true.

All the facts as presented by all the sources—Foster, Barnett, and the archaeologist—when compared agree, in general. Descriptions of the bodies, descriptions of the military, and descriptions of the crash site all match the facts.

Although the archaeologist mentioned nothing about trucks but concentrated on the jeep with the officer, that doesn't mean trucks weren't there. It means only that he never mentioned them.

All the sources mention silver or gray suits with Foster describing them as uniforms. The archaeologist mentioned gray flight suits and flight suits are uniforms. Different words that mean the same thing.

It is important to note that these stories don't match exactly. If they did, it could be argued that each of the sources read the current literature on Roswell, or had all seen the same programs about it. But the variations suggest the witnesses are not being coached by anyone for any reason or that they were influenced by media exposure. They are relating experiences as they remember them.

This information establishes one more area of proof. It establishes another group of witnesses who were not related to the military activity around the crash sites. But most importantly, it establishes just how powerful the government threats have been. Those threats have silenced people for more than forty years.

September, 1947:
Rickett and LaPaz

By September, it had quieted down in Roswell. The activity that had followed the discovery and recovery of the wreckage and the bodies had been forgotten by almost everyone. The job of flying took precedence.[1] But, there were things that had to be accomplished.

During World War II, Doctor Lincoln LaPaz, an expert in meteroritics, had worked for the government. He worked on the Manhattan Project, was trained in mathematics and astronomy. Because of the work on the Manhattan Project, he held various security clearances up to and including top secret.

He had been hired as a consultant during the Japanese Balloon Bomb raids on the United States.[2] His job was to help the military discover a way to quickly find the balloon bombs and destroy them before they could cause damage on the ground. LaPaz had been involved in several top secret projects during the war and there was no indication that any of his various clearances had lapsed in the two years since the war ended.[3] When the military needed someone to make a followup investigation of the event at Roswell, LaPaz was the perfect selection. He was already in New Mexico and he already had the clearances.

LaPaz had been successful finding meteorites that hit the ground.[4] He could move into an area, interview the witnesses, and by using maps of the region, chart the apparent path of the object. If it hadn't burned up, he could locate the point where it struck the ground. With the Roswell event, he could work backward. He knew where it had touched down, now he had to figure out the trajectory and the speed.

Rickett wasn't sure where the idea had come from but LaPaz had the various permissions and clearances to search the area. The CIC Headquarters ordered them to send someone and the senior man volunteered Rickett. He was told to pack his clothes and to take as long as was necessary. If he needed money, he was told to call. He was ordered to take care of LaPaz by driving him to the ranches, finding accommodations, and paying for the trip.[5]

According to Rickett, he drew a staff car and they drove off, looking for the ranchers and the ranch hands who might have information to share. LaPaz had a topographical map and they used it to mark their progress, sometimes backtracking, talking to the old ranchers and cowboys who had never heard of flying saucers or flying discs and who rarely got into a town of more than two or three hundred people.

According to Rickett, LaPaz could speak fluent Spanish. Many of the ranchers in the more desolate parts of New Mexico were Mexicans who spoke very little or no English. LaPaz could talk to them like a native.

Rickett said they would hit the bars and ask the men if they had seen anything strange, any lights or any objects, in the last six months or so. More often than not they found someone who had seen something strange but who had never mentioned it to any of his friends.

According to one of the ranchers, he'd seen a light that looked as if it landed on top of a hill momentarily. LaPaz plotted the information, combined it with sightings from other sources, and headed out, searching. They found a touch down point, in the woods on top of a hill, just as the old rancher had told them. They didn't know if it had anything to do with the crash site or the debris field. Rickett and LaPaz could see where the object, or the light, or whatever, had come in and cut the tops off the trees.[6]

According to Rickett, a pattern started to develop. As they continued the investigation, they located a few people who talked about two or three lights moving together. Some of them said the lights were in formation, flying rapidly. Others, closer to Corona, said they had seen one of the lights peel off. The other two lights circled it.

Rickett said, ''The best we could figure out, this one was in trouble. Maybe the guidance system on it happened to fail, but it was touching the top of a hill, losing altitude. Maybe fifteen, twenty miles from there (the debris field).''

They had found a touch down point, this one closer to the debris field. Rickett said that there was an area where it looked as if something had been dragged along the ground. They asked the rancher what might have marked the ground that way. The rancher didn't know what had caused it.

Rickett and LaPaz tracked the light as far as they could. Rickett thought that the lone object had stayed aloft as long as possible and then it had landed or crashed on the debris field. He thought that it had self-destructed. Rather than exploding, the object had just come apart, scattering the small pieces of material.

Rickett, however, never took LaPaz out to where it had finally hit the ground. They circled the area, and when they found a place where the ground had been crystallized, a little bit of the foil-like debris was discovered.[7]

According to Rickett, LaPaz believed that the stricken craft, which might have been followed by one or two others, had landed once. The crew had tried to repair it. When it seemed that the craft would fly again, it took off, but as it did, it was destroyed. Maybe it exploded, as some thought, or maybe it just disintegrated, as Rickett believed. It hit about five miles away, skipped across the ground leaving the debris that Mac Brazel found.

Later the majority of the craft, or some kind of an ejection pod, crashed onto the ranch two to three miles from the debris field.

Rickett wrote an informal report about what he and LaPaz had seen and done. LaPaz, on the other hand, was required to submit an official report. Everything went to Kirtland and then to Washington.

Rickett did, however, see LaPaz again. During that discussion, a year later in Albuquerque, LaPaz said that he thought the craft contained no occupants. It was remotely controlled. It had touched down briefly as those controlling it tried to make some long distance repairs. Maybe they failed or maybe they thought they had succeeded. Either way, they wanted to get it up, out of that field, and as it took off, it was destroyed. LaPaz believed the object was unmanned but that it was some kind of extraterrestrial probe. LaPaz had seen nothing that would change his mind during the year. (Interestingly, LaPaz would later become a secret consultant and a honorary member of APRO.)[8]

According to Rickett, they barely discussed the possibility that the probe might have contained a flight crew. LaPaz was sure that it was remotely controlled and he was satisfied with that theory.

LaPaz never told Rickett if he had determined anything about the trajectory or the speed. They spent three or four weeks driving through New Mexico searching for the answers but once LaPaz went back to Albuquerque and then on to Washington, that was the end of it. Except for the one brief conversation, Rickett heard nothing more from LaPaz on the subject.

Part III:

The J. Allen Hynek Center for UFO Studies Investigation

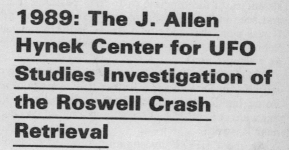

1989: The J. Allen Hynek Center for UFO Studies Investigation of the Roswell Crash Retrieval

Fall, 1988

No government secret seems safe these days, and the Roswell crash is no exception. Until Major Jesse Marcel confided in Stanton Friedman and decided to reveal his role in the event, most UFOlogists had put little credence in stories of the "crash-retrievals" of UFOs, with the exception of Friedman and Len Stringfield. Marcel's story was so convincing and he was such a compelling witness that several researchers decided that the Roswell case deserved further attention.

Interest among researchers increased greatly in the 1980s, and the crash was discussed in both the print and broadcast media with some frequency. This was how matters stood in the fall of 1988, when CUFOS became involved in the investigation.

Donald R. Schmitt, CUFOS Director of Special Investigations, learned, contrary to everyone's understanding, the investigation of the Roswell event was incomplete. This startling information came to CUFOS' attention at a fortuitous moment. A CUFOS associate in Chicago, interested in government involvement in UFO investigation, had been studying the details of the Roswell crash as published and broadcast.* He found inconsistencies in the timeline of events, puzzling omissions, and seemingly odd behavior on the part of the military. It was clear that additional investigation was necessary. Schmitt's report that more witnesses were available came as welcome news.

Also in the fall of 1988, Schmitt began working closely with Kevin D. Randle, a former helicopter pilot and Air Force intelligence officer. Both were initially skeptical but were convinced that something unusual had happened near Roswell.

As the CUFOS investigation proceeded, two shortcomings in the prior investigation of Roswell became quickly evident. The first was that many of the primary witnesses had not been interviewed systematically or in depth. The second was that the actual site of the crash had not been studied. CUFOS planned to remedy both those problems.

It was at the end of 1988 that Schmitt and Randle planned their first trip to New Mexico. Schmitt knew a New Mexico contact had to be arranged and selected Don Mitchell of Santa Fe. Mitchell would be able to arrange some of the local interviews and provide advice on the operation in New Mexico.

During the trip, interviews with the principals would tell them if the case was worth pursuing. One of the first witnesses contacted was Bill Brazel. He was reluctant to talk because of the number of people who had questioned him in the past. Meetings with Frank Joyce, the Proctors, and others were also arranged.

---

*Because of the complex nature of the investigation and because we sometimes were working independently, it was decided to use the third person in the narrative rather than the more conventional first person. We hoped that this would make it easier for the reader to follow the various aspects of the investigation as they unfolded.

Upon arriving in Albuquerque, Schmitt and Randle met with Mitchell. Mitchell had talked to Joyce, who had interviewed Mac Brazel before Brazel had surrendered his pieces of the craft to the Army and had then led the military to the crash site.

Plans to meet with Joyce had to be postponed. Joyce was ill. And with the interview cancelled, the only thing to do was make the two hundred mile trip from Albuquerque to the Roswell area. From there they had to drive to Carrizozo to meet Bill Brazel.

The first thing Bill Brazel said to them was, "I've thought about this and thought about it and I don't really know what I could tell you guys.

"My Dad found this thing," he said, "and told me a little bit about it. Not much . . . . because the Air Force asked him to take an oath that he wouldn't tell anybody in detail about it. And my Dad was such a guy that he went to his grave and he *never* told anybody.

"I found a few bits and pieces later on. And the Air Force came out . . . they didn't confiscate it. They just put it to me in such a way that I should give it to them or they would have. And I had no use for them and Dad had told me that he had taken an oath that he wouldn't tell in detail anybody. He told me that I didn't need to know and probably I'm better off."

Brazel talked about his father finding the material, and what he did after he'd made the discovery. "He went out there and he loaded it all up onto his truck. He took it into the headquarters of the ranch. He had a jeep pickup. And it completely filled all that he could get on this jeep pickup. He picked it up and hauled it in. Now, he very likely did, though I don't know, when he got into headquarters he might have took it all and pushed it under a shed. Very likely he did that to get it out of the pickup because he used his pickup. Later on then, he went to Roswell. He didn't haul it down there because the Air Force came up and picked it up. They picked it up in a station wagon or a van and it completely filled that. All they could carry."

"That was Major Marcel and the CIC man," said Schmitt.

"Yeah. Major Marcel, and I never met the man, but that name is . . . yeah, he's the man who talked to my Dad."

"How soon after the incident were you able to go to the ranch itself?" asked Schmitt.

"I got up one morning and was living in Albuquerque at the time. I got the paper and I looked at it and here's my Dad's picture. [Actually the newspaper contained only a story about Mac Brazel and no picture.] I said to Shirley (Brazel) what the hell did he do now? So I proceeded out to the ranch. I think that it was two or three days before my Dad showed up. I said what did you get into and he said, oh, I found a thing out there. The worldwide press was after him. I said it looks like you're rich and famous, or famous anyway. I said I'll stay here and take care of the ranch but nothing happened so I went back to Albuquerque to my own business.

"You asked me a question and that is the first time I thought about it. I know he hauled it into the ranch and we had some sheds there and he backed the pickup to it and pushed all the stuff off it."

"We've heard that a number of neighbors were involved in some fashion," Randle said. "You're not aware of anyone like that at all?"

"Probably he told them that he found a bunch of stuff. Now Floyd Proctor might have come down. He might have. There might have been more than that who came out and looked at the stuff and Dad just didn't say anything about it. By the time I talked to him the Air Force or the Army had already had him and he just wouldn't tell me very much about it.

"I'd ask him a question and he told me a little about it, naturally. But if I asked very many questions, he'd just say, well, I told them I wouldn't tell and you don't need to know. That's the way he was.''

"Did your father seem different after he came home?" asked Schmitt.

"No way.''

"That he knew something but he still couldn't talk about it,'' said Schmitt.

"My dad knew a lot of things that he wouldn't talk about. He might know who stole the calf but he . . . I don't know how to put it across to you people. He was an old time western cowboy. He didn't do a lot of talking. His philosophy in life was if you can't say anything good about a person, don't say anything.

"It's been kind of hard for me to explain this to all the people who've called me about this thing. I says . . . one lady, a newspaper reporter from El Paso, and she said you mean your own father didn't tell you. She said, didn't you ask him. And I said, yes ma'am, I did ask him. But he had given his word to the Air Force that he wouldn't tell about in detail. And I said, no, he didn't tell me. She said, I don't believe that. Then why did you call me? I told her he took an oath not to tell and he didn't.''

"Did you find many pieces?" Randle asked.

"I imagine about . . . oh not over a dozen and I'd say eight. Just different little pieces. There was only three items involved. Something on the order of balsa wood and something on the order of heavy gauge monofilament fishing line and a little piece of . . . it wasn't really aluminum foil and it wasn't really lead foil but it was on that order. A piece about the size of my fingers with jagged edges.''

"After the Air Force came did you ever go out there and look for anything else?" asked Schmitt.

"Oh yes. Every time I was out there I looked.''

"Did you ever find anything?"

"No, I never did find anything else. Riding horseback you see far better than you can even walking. Walking, you've got to watch where you put your feet. Riding a horse, you can really look. Well, naturally I was curious. This thing made quite a track down through there. It took a year or two for it to grass back over and heal up.

"Then I rode up there, probably on an average of once a week. When I was riding through that area, hell, I was looking. That's why I found these little pieces. I never did really go looking for anything. I didn't figure it was worth it anyway. But just curiosity, and I'd see something that didn't belong out there and I'd get off and stick it in my chaps pocket. I might keep it in there for a week before I'd reach in there."

"Did your father know you were collecting the pieces?" asked Schmitt.

"Oh, yeah. I showed it to him. He said, oh yeah, that's some of that thing I found."

"But he didn't tell you to be quiet about it?" said Schmitt.

"What the hell good is a little old scrap? A little piece of garbage? I was in Corona in the bar and the pool hall that was kind of a meeting place for that little town. That's where everybody got together when they went to town. Everybody was asking me . . . they'd all seen the papers . . . and they were all asking me about it. I said I'd picked up a few little old bits and pieces and fragments. Well what are they? I said, hell, I don't know. And lo and behold, here comes the military."

"In uniform?" asked Randle.

"Yeah. I still am not really sure, but I'm almost positive that the officer in charge, his name was Armstrong. A real nice guy. Now he had a sergeant with him that was real nice. And I think there were two other enlisted men. They came out to the ranch and they was talking to me and they said, we understand your father found this weather balloon and I said yeah. And they said we understand that you found some bits and pieces of it. I've got a cigar box that's got a few in there. And this, I think he was a captain as best I can remember, said, well we would like to take it with us. I said, well. He smiled and he said, your father turned the rest of it over to us. You know he's under an oath not to tell anyone. I said who knows better than I do. Well, he said, we came after those bits and pieces. I kind of smiled and I said it's kind of like when I was in the Navy. We want volunteers. We want you, you, and you. I said okay, you can have the stuff. I have no use for it.

"He said, how well have you examined it? I said well enough to know that I don't know what it is. He said we would rather that you wouldn't talk much about it. And I really didn't. After that, people would ask me and I'd just say, well . . ."

"Did you ever see any of the neighbors out in the field?" asked Schmitt.

"Not anybody," said Brazel. "As far as I know, the only people who have been out there and looked was the Army or the Air Force, whichever it was. I think they did come out there with quite a few troops and they walked and really kind of combed the area. But, as far as anybody else going out there . . . Floyd Proctor might have. But to my knowledge he didn't find anything."

"Was you father the only one you ever showed the pieces you found?" asked Schmitt.

"Yeah. He looked at it and said, yeah, that looks like some of the contraption I found. Actually, this was before monofilament fishing line was a popular item and that's the nearest I could compare it to. Now there's this plastic, fiber optics. It could have been (that). But it was about like the heavy gauge nylon fishing line. That's the closest comparison as I can give you. And there were some pieces of wood. I had several of those."

"Real wood or like wood?" asked Schmitt.

"No, they were like wood. They were like balsa wood. Real light, kind of a neutral color, kind of a tan. And I couldn't break it."

"Would it bend at all?" Randle asked.

"Flex a little. The longest piece I found, about six

inches, would flex a little. I couldn't break it and I couldn't whittle it with my pocketknife. The only reason I noticed the tin foil was that I picked this stuff up and put it in my chaps pocket. Like I said, I had it in there two, three days, and when I took it out and put it in the box and I happened to notice that when I put that piece of foil in the box it started unfolding and flattened out. Then I got to playing with it. I would fold it or crease it and lay it down and watch it. It was kind of weird. Other than that, that's the three items I found. Piece of this balsa wood, some of that string, and some of that foil."

"Were the edges straight?" asked Schmitt.

"No. The piece I found was a jagged piece. I couldn't tear it. Hell, tin foil or lead foil is easy but I couldn't tear it. I didn't take pliers or anything. I just used my fingers. I didn't try to cut it with my knife but I did try to whittle on that piece of wood. I didn't even get a little sliver off it."

"Any color variations?" asked Schmitt.

"The color was consistent throughout the pieces I found. It was a dull color."

"Was it the same on both sides?"

"Yeah. And it was about the gauge of lead foil. Thicker than tin foil. It was pliable. Real pliable. I would bend it over and crease it and if you straighten back up, there would be a crinkle in it. Nothing. It would flatten out and it was just as smooth as ever. Not a crinkle or anything in it."

"Without making a sound."

"Nope."

"When you bent it over, would it slide against itself? Was there any friction? Was it smooth to the touch?"

"Yeah, as best I can remember, it was smooth. I wasn't intrigued with any part of it until I discovered the foil and what it would do. Then, I got to looking at the rest of it. It wasn't too long after that that they came out and said, hey, we'll take that off your hands."

"In the course of your later trips out into the fields you never found any more?" Randle asked.

"Never found any more. No, I never did. But that thing, whatever it was, had to come to earth with a *terrific* force to ever leave any little pieces at all. But I never found any more of it."

The thing about the interview was, Brazel had confirmed everything that Schmitt and Randle had ever heard from him or about him. There were a few minor discrepancies in his stories, little changes that were explainable by the time between his telling of the stories. These little changes suggested a story told from a memory of the events rather than a rehearsed story told to convince the gullible that something untrue had happened.

Schmitt, upon returning from New Mexico, briefed the CUFOS board in Chicago. Impressed with the preliminary report, Mark Rodeghier, the Scientific Director, initiated plans for the first scientific excavation at the crash site since 1947.

Ten months of research went into substantiating the actual crash site, that included two trips into Corona, New Mexico. Meetings were arranged with scientists Carl Bebrich and Sue Ann Curtis, who worked for a major laboratory. The effort would result in an expedition to New Mexico later.

March, 1989

Both Schmitt and Randle realized shortly after the first trip to Roswell that there was much more to do. One witness had provided a lead to the mortician who prepared the bodies of the aliens for shipment. Bill Brazel had told them a little about Tommy Tyree and the Proctors. They knew that Walter Haut, the PIO at Roswell in the summer of 1947, still lived in Roswell, and they had not been able to talk to Frank Joyce. These were all things that had to be done.

Because there was work to do in Albuquerque as well, Randle arrived a day early on the next trip. One thing to do was check out the newspaper files. Copies were needed of all the articles that ran in both Albuquerque newspapers. Finding the picture of Mac Brazel in the paper would tell them exactly what day Bill Brazel had read about it and that would give them a time frame for his return to the ranch.

And the lead to the mortician could be examined. According to a source in Roswell, the mortician worked in Albuquerque. He shouldn't be that hard to find.

At the library, Randle pulled the Albuquerque papers and read through them quickly. No picture of Mac Brazel, but there was a story on July 10 that identified Brazel as the man who had found the balloon that caused the trouble. That helped them fill in some of the details.

Next Randle tried to track down the mortician. He found the man identified as the mortician easily. But that was the last of the good luck. The man denied that it was him. He'd never been a mortician and had never lived in Roswell. He'd been to Roswell on vacations, but that was the best he could do. Someone had given Schmitt and Randle bad information.

The first day in Albuquerque had not worked out. No picture of Mac Brazel in the paper for Bill to see, but there was an article for him to read. And then the man identified as the mortician had not been involved. That was the most disappointing. If they could have found him and had received a firsthand statement from him, they would have had some very convincing testimony.

The next day both Schmitt and Randle were ready to interview Frank Joyce. This time he had agreed to met with them. Randle took out a tape recorder and asked if Joyce minded if the session was recorded.

"I'd rather you didn't," he said.

Randle turned off the recorder and Schmitt asked, "Do you mind if we make notes?"

"Nope."

The first thing Joyce did was show them a number of documents, letters and a teletype message to establish his credentials. He had been working at a radio station KGFL in Roswell in the summer of 1947.

He also unfolded a sheet of teletype paper that had a question on it from the AP headquarters. On July 7, 1947, in response to the information coming out of Roswell, it asked, "Is this the same ranch where there was a halla-balloo last week?" Joyce had no explanation for that comment.

Joyce went on to explain that he would call the office of Sheriff George A. Wilcox in the afternoon to see if there was anything of interest happening. According to Joyce, Wilcox was unimpressed with the story that Bra-zel was telling, but handed the phone to Brazel, telling Joyce, "Here's something that you might find interest-ing."

Joyce claimed that Wilcox didn't believe the story and Brazel wasn't sure what to do. Joyce suggested that he call the air base because the military was involved with all things flying and the officers might know what Brazel had found.

Joyce said that Brazel had told him everything on the phone, but when asked for clarification, Joyce re-sponded, "W.W. is dead and I don't want to put words in a dead man's mouth." He refused to answer questions about what Brazel found, only that Brazel was in the sheriff's office and it was Joyce's idea that Brazel call the military.

The next day, according to Joyce, Walter Haut, the PIO from the base, arrived at the station with a press release. According to Joyce, "Haut told me, I'm giving you an hour on this." After Haut left, Joyce took it, read it over, and then called Haut right back. He said, "Wal-ter, you don't want to send this out like this."

According to Joyce, there were procedural errors in it. Haut was making statements in the name of higher headquarters without permission to do it. Haut said that Colonel Blanchard had told him to release it.

The release was issued and Joyce claimed that a Colonel Johnson called him from the Pentagon, screaming at him and demanding to know who the hell told him to issue the release. Joyce finally managed to convince Johnson that he was no longer in the army and there was nothing Johnson could do about it. Johnson responded, "I'll show you what I can do to you."

After he got the call, Joyce decided that he had better have some proof that he hadn't made up the story. He found the press release that Haut had given him. He showed it to the station owner, Walter Whitmore, Sr.

According to Joyce, Brazel came to the radio station on July 9. Brazel had a new story about his discovery that differed significantly from the one he told before the military had interviewed him. According to Joyce, Brazel was under a great deal of stress and said that it would go very hard on him if he didn't cooperate.

During the second interview with Brazel, Joyce noticed that there were several military officers waiting in the lobby of the station. They didn't say anything and didn't accompany Brazel into the control room.

As he was leaving, according to Joyce, Brazel turned and said, "You know how they talk about little green men? Well, they weren't green." With that, Brazel, with the military officers surrounding him left the station.

After that was all over, Joyce claimed that someone came into the station and cleared out every scrap of paper that had anything about the event on it. They found everything, including those duplicates that Joyce had tried to hide. Joyce claimed that Jud Dixon, the AP man in Santa Fe, reported the same thing. Someone was pulling the paper trail apart. Dixon's files on the Roswell event had vanished.

Schmitt and Randle quizzed Joyce for another twenty or thirty minutes but were now covering the same ground. Joyce didn't remember anything new. They thanked him and all left the hotel room. Joyce drove back to work. Schmitt and Randle left for Capitan, New Mexico where they would meet Bill Brazel. Brazel had promised to take them out to the crash site.

In Capitan they waited at a small cafe for Bill Brazel. They were there for no more than ten minutes when Brazel drove up. They climbed into the back of his truck and headed out to the crash site using the back roads. These were gravel, and, for the most part, in good condition. There were a couple of places where it seemed that the road disintegrated so that it would have been next to impossible to get a passenger car through but Brazel's truck made it easily.

On the way there, they learned little about the events of July, 1947, but more about the Brazel family. Bill confirmed that his father had been living alone at the ranch headquarters while the rest of the family was living in Tularosa, New Mexico. The ranch house where Mac Brazel lived was without electricity and had no phone service. The newspapers were periodic and there were days when they didn't arrive at all.

As they had seen during the first trip to New Mexico, the area was desolate. There was no real sign of humans. There was a fence line on the horizon and scattered windmills, but as they slipped down into the valleys, all that disappeared, too. The land was as it had been a hundred years, a thousand years ago.

Brazel now drove along county roads that were nothing more than plowed tracks through the ranges. The county had erected a few signs designating routes and Brazel said that they periodically came out to plow the roads again, sometimes altering them so that a road that had led to one place five years earlier might no longer be there.

Brazel turned off the road and used a smaller track across the prairie. This was a rutted road cut by the wheels of vehicles. It climbed a hill and disappeared. Now he drove cross country. There was no road to the crash site, just open ground where there were rattle-snakes, deer, sheep and cattle.

They came out on the side of a hill. In front of them was a shallow, narrow valley with a rounded, rocky area at one end. The other end opened gradually until it was nothing more than a pasture sloping down into another, bigger valley.

"The gouge started up there and moved down in that direction," said Brazel.

He described the gouge as running from the northwest to the southeast. It looked as if the thing had hit and bounced, scattering debris in the field. The gouge wasn't very deep but was about ten feet wide in places. The whole thing was about five hundred feet long.

"Where'd you find the scraps?" asked Schmitt.

Brazel pointed outside the truck and said, "Around here. All over here."

Schmitt and Randle got out and walked down into the draw. They kept their eyes on the ground, knowing full well that they probably wouldn't spot any of the metal. They weren't worried about snakes yet. It was too early in the year and too cold for snakes.

Schmitt and Randle walked around on a patch of land that would become historic someday. This was the first place where the people of Earth learned that they were not alone in the universe. There was life on other planets. This was the place where the proof came down and if it hadn't been for governmental secrecy, the world might have learned it. Attitudes toward space travel would have been different. Attitudes on a number of subjects would have been different if the military and the government had not decided to hide the truth.

But in March, 1989, there was nothing to see. The gouge had grown over, according to Bill Brazel, within two years. The material, the lead foil and balsa-like wood and the fiber optics, had been cleaned up by the military. There was nothing to mark the field as an extraordinary place. Just the normal tough grass, cactus, yucca plants, and Joshua trees.

They returned to the pickup. Bill Brazel was sitting there, waiting for them. "Nothing to see," he said.

They returned to Capitan using the back roads again. Brazel pointed out some of the landmarks, some of the places where houses or cabins had stood and that were now abandoned.

In Capitan, they thanked Bill for taking his time and driving them out to the crash site. He said, "If there is anything else I can do for you fellows, you give me a call."

That afternoon they arranged to meet Walter Haut in Roswell. As the Public Information Officer, he had been in a position to know a lot about what was happening on the base in July, 1947. And it had been Haut who had issued the famous statement saying that officers at the Roswell Army Air Field had captured a flying saucer.

They met Walter Haut at his home on a Saturday afternoon. He invited them into the living room. He told them to go ahead and ask their questions.

The very first thing Walter said was that he could sum everything up he knew in one word. "Nothing."

Randle started the official interview. "You were, well, we all know you were the PIO out at Roswell when the thing came down."

"Yes. Blanchard said Jess Marcel has brought something in that looks like a flying disc, or a flying saucer, or parts thereof," Haut said. "Put out a press release on this that it was discovered on a ranch outside of Roswell, near Corona. Basically that's all I'm going to tell you. Jesse's going to take it and fly it down to Fort Worth."

"So he was scheduled to go to Fort Worth?" Randle asked.

"Marcel was going to put it in an aircraft and take it to Fort Worth. That's after they had looked at it and everything else. I didn't hear about it until, I guess, Jess was on his way to the flightline. And that's about it.

That's all I know. As I told you, I could tell you all this over the telephone."

"So Blanchard called you," Randle said, "told you we have one, put out your press release . . . you didn't ask him if you could see it. You just put out the press release. The next day the phones began ringing off the hook and you said wow, am I famous or what?"

"I was famous enough that if you . . . this is all before your time. At one time they had clipping services that would send you a postcard that would say your name appeared in such and such paper and if you will send us fifty cents, a dollar, whatever it was, we'll send you a copy of the paper . . . I had two stacks of postcards that tall (he indicated a stack about six inches high) from all over the world. I wasn't even smart enough to save the stamps."

"Did Jesse Marcel ever tell you anything about it?" Schmitt asked.

"Nope."

"Did you ever see Mac Brazel?"

"Nope."

"Did you ever discuss it with Frank Joyce?"

"Nope."

"Did he call you after the press release, before it went out over the wire, and say that you didn't want to say it that way?" Randle asked.

"No."

"Advising you that this was a mistake. . . ." said Schmitt.

"No." He hesitated and then said, "I hate to be this way but you're asking me pointed questions."

"Did you see Marcel after he came back from Fort Worth?" asked Schmitt.

"Yeah. As a matter of fact I used to see him quite regularly. He lived right down the block here. One block."

"Right after he returned?" asked Schmitt.

"No. I think the most interesting part of this whole

thing, and you can verify this by going down to the newspaper office and looking at the newspapers . . . (is) the time frame. For two days it was front page and then it disappeared. The thing died extremely fast.''

''Especially after Fort Worth with Brigadier General Ramey,'' said Schmitt.

''Well, even local interest here. Nobody called me locally and said anything about it. Nobody, frankly, cared.''

''What was the feeling on the base after Marcel came back from Fort Worth?'' Randle asked. ''I mean, there must have been some interest in it when he went to Fort Worth.''

''Basically it was a dead issue. And when it was stated that it was a weather balloon, that was it. We screwed up. Simple as that. The old man didn't know what he had seen. I never asked Marcel and as I said he lived down the block here from me.''

''Why do you think that Blanchard was so quick to order you to make the report?'' asked Schmitt.

''You would have to have known the man. He had . . . I'm trying to think of how to phrase this. He had a very sincere interest in the relationship between the base and the community. If anything unusual happened or anything he felt the community should know about, he would call me and say, get this thing out. He did it with many, many things. If he thought of things like when you take releases into town don't stop at the first one and give it to them every time. That was the *Morning Dispatch* on Main Street and there was KGFL and KSWS and then the *Record*. He wanted them alternated so that no one could say that we're showing partiality. There was no preselection. And all of them knew about it.

''But basically, I very rarely questioned him on anything that he came up with. I think . . . he'd tell me what I need to know and if I get into hot water he'll get me out of it. So there we stood.''

"Looking back on this from a perspective of forty-two years, what do you think they found?" asked Randle.

"A bunch of stuff that Jess Marcel took to Fort Worth. I think actually, they found something that they actually, and I've got to base what I'm going to say on what Jess Marcel told me. It was something that he had never seen and didn't believe that it was of this planet. I trusted him on his knowledge. He felt that it was something that was not made or mined or built or manufactured anywhere on this planet. He was explaining things (to me) . . . a little, thin, paper-thin piece of foil that you couldn't burn and you couldn't bend and couldn't cut . . . He explained a whole bunch of this stuff to me . . . at the time, (we thought) oh Christ, weather balloon, that's good."

"Everybody accepted it as a weather balloon," said Schmitt.

"As a matter of fact, I guess it was a rumor they started about how dumb we were . . . the fact that it was released from here, on the base, that there was a detachment that came over from Holloman (Air Force Base, NM) and released the balloon here to pick up the winds going in the direction."

"Were you aware at that time of recovery effort itself?" asked Schmitt.

"No, I was not."

"So there was no activity on the base which indicated that . . ." said Schmitt.

"Not that was known to the average people. Carry this one step further. It was never mentioned in a staff meeting. And I used to sit in all the staff meetings."

"Was that unusual?" asked Schmitt.

"Oh, someone would have heard it from someone. Apparently the thing was bottled up when they found out actually what it was."

"So as far as staff meetings go there was no mention of the detainment of Mac Brazel at the base? Questioning him?" said Schmitt.

"Oh we heard there was, I think I heard it from some

of the other news media about Walt Whitmore had practically kidnapped him. Walt was an old, old time newsman. You never could quite tell whether everything he was saying was all the truth.''

''So you didn't hear that Brazel had been held incommunicado on the base for a while,'' Randle said.

''No. Not on the base. In town, yes.''

''In Whitmore's home?'' asked Randle.

''Well, in town. I think the rumor was that Walt was moving him from place to place. This was a big . . . it's a much more interesting story when you move a man from place to place.''

''And the military is hot on his heels,'' Randle said. ''Mac Brazel was apparently kept in Roswell for five or six days. With military authorities but you're saying he wasn't kept on the base.''

''To my knowledge. I did not know he had been on the base.''

Haut was quiet for a moment and said, ''I'm like my wife. I think there was one gigantic cover-up on the thing. I think that somewhere all this material is stashed away. The only thing that I cannot comprehend is how, with all the people, and I start talking about people . . . I know that Jess Marcel did not go out to that airplane and fly it alone. He had to have a co-pilot and a crew. I don't think there was a one of those crew members who would have strained themselves to load this on an airplane. The truck drivers, people that . . . the maintenance people and when it gets to Forth Worth there are more people involved and at Wright Field there are more people there. In all this time no one has stolen a piece?'' said Haut. ''Jess Marcel, this I can understand. He was not the kind who would.''

''But,'' Randle said, ''you think that there was some kind of a cover-up?''

''I think there was a giant cover-up,'' said Walter.

Schmitt and Randle had run through the questions at that point and were beginning to repeat themselves. They had to get back to Albuquerque and it was a two hundred mile drive. Haut told them that he would be glad to help in any way he could. If they had any further questions, they should feel free to call. They thanked him and left.

Interlude: Spring, 1989

There were dozens of things that could be done between trips to Roswell and the interviewing of witnesses. Now that it looked as if something more than just a weather balloon had come down near Roswell, Schmitt and Randle would have to start building the paper trail. The *Roswell Daily Record* of July, 1947 would be one of the sources searched later. Finding the records of the 509th Bomb Group might help. Randle told Schmitt that the military abhors a vacuum and into that vacuum, they throw paper.

The 509th Bomb Group had been stationed at Roswell Army Air Field. Late in 1947 the name was changed to Walker and once the Air Force was created, it became Walker Air Force Base. The 509th and its records remained there until the government closed the base in the 1960s. Then everything, including the 509th, was transferred to Pease Air Force Base, New Hampshire.

The history of the 509th is available on microfilm. This was a gold mine. The unit, under the direction of Eighth Air Force Headquarters had started preparing a detailed history in the beginning of 1947. Available, in detail, was everything that had gone on at the base, with very few exceptions, for July, August, September, and November, 1947. After that the histories deteriorated until the summer of 1949 when a provisional group deployed to England for training.

The notations for July, 1947 were disappointing. There was a single paragraph that said, "The office of Public Information was kept busy during the month answering inquiries on the 'flying disc,' which was reported to be in possession of the 509th Bomb Group. The object turned out to be a radar tracking balloon.''

Here was story that had been front page news around the world for three or four days. Newspapers from London, England, and Hong Kong carried the report. Nearly every newspaper in the United States mentioned it in some fashion. The *New York Times* reported on the discovery of a weather balloon and the *Los Angeles Herald Express* claimed that it was a flying saucer in the earliest editions. The point is not whether it was a balloon or an extraterrestrial spacecraft, but what happened when the story was announced. The 509th Group chose to refer to the chaos of that first full week in July with a one paragraph mention in their unit history.

The other thing that was interesting was that the microfilm carried copies of the base newspaper, *The Atomic Blast*. The issue of July 4, 1947 wouldn't be of interest because the object hadn't been reported to the military until July 6. But the issue of July 11 should be filled with stories. After all, it was the thing that all Public Information Officers and the editors of base newspapers want. A real story. Something that would make the troops sit up and take notice. Here they were, sitting on a story, a front page story from around the world. They knew names of the participants. Walter Haut lived down the street from Jesse Marcel and was a member of Blanchard's staff. He knew about the plane flights and the recovery. He could call the participants on the base phone or talk to them in the officer's club. It would be the biggest story that *The Atomic Blast* would cover.

And there is not one word about it in the base paper. Not one word.

The lead story on July 11, 1947 was that one of the base's softball teams was in the bid for the ''El Paso Crown.'' The second story was that they had retained the lead on Mills' one hitter. And the pictures on that page were of a Sikorsky YR5A, a helicopter that had landed at Roswell.

In fact, the base newspaper carried nothing about flying saucers or flying discs until August, when they published a picture of the Navy's Flying Flapjack, an experimental aircraft, saying that it might be responsible for some of the sightings of flying saucers around the country.

There would be no explanation for this, except that Walter Haut told Schmitt and Randle that after the balloon answer came out of Fort Worth no one at Roswell ever discussed the crash again. No one brought it up in the staff meetings, no one joked about what a bunch of jerks they were when they couldn't identify a weather balloon or a radar reflecting balloon as something mundane. Word of that event dropped from the minds of everyone at Roswell. Haut would not go so far as saying that Blanchard had ordered the silence. He just indicated that everyone knew the topic was suddenly taboo.

Going through the unit history, Randle learned that Lieutenant Colonel Joe Briley had taken over duties of the Operations Officer in the middle of the month, replacing Lieutenant Colonel James I. Hopkins, who became the commander of the 830th Bomb Squadron.

Randle also learned that two intelligence officers, Captain James R. Breece and Lieutenant Charles V. Swanson, had been transferred.

Randle found a list of visitors to the base that included General Nathan F. Twining on July 16 and Ramey a number of times. Ramey, as the commanding general of the Eighth Air Force, could be expected to go to Roswell often. Twining, as the commanding general of the Air Materiel Command, could be expected to visit, but not as often as Ramey.

There were many such little interesting tidbits, but nothing that could lead to the recovery of a crashed saucer in July. What wasn't present was more interesting. The lack of anything relating to all the activity made both Schmitt and Randle suspicious.

Because the Eighth Air Force was the parent unit to

the 509th, Schmitt and Randle decided they should look into those records too. For one thing, Schmitt and Randle wanted to find out who the Public Information Officer of the Eighth Air Force was because he might be able to answer a few questions.

Like the 509th, the Eighth Air Force had complete records for 1947. The microfilm contained June, 1947 and at the end of that month there was a comment about how busy everyone at Eighth Air Force Headquarters had been answering questions about the flying discs.

During July, 1947, there were no mentions of the flying saucers. No mention that Major Marcel had brought wreckage to Fort Worth and no mention that Irving Newton had told them it was nothing more than a weather balloon. There was no mention of Ramey on the radio in Fort Worth giving the story or that the special flight had been cancelled.

Not one word about the event.

During the time between trips, there were other questions to be asked and interviews to be conducted. During both trips to Roswell, Schmitt and Randle had failed to visit with Loretta Proctor. Her role in the event was as a spectator on the sidelines, but she was one of the first to learn that Mac Brazel had found something. There were things that could be learned from her.

Finally reaching her by phone, the first thing Randle wanted to know was whether she and her husband, Floyd, had gone out to look at the debris field. Because they were the closest neighbors to Brazel, living only ten miles from the ranch headquarters, Randle was hoping to locate another civilian who had been on the field.

"No," she said answering the first question. "Back then, why gas, tires, time, and everything was real short."

"Then you weren't expecting to see anything extraterrestrial?"

"Oh no. We just figured it was a weather balloon or an experiment or something," she said.

"Did you talk to Mac Brazel about it afterwards at all?"

"Well, before he took it in, but after he took it to Roswell he wouldn't talk about it."

"Do you remember anything he might have said before going to Roswell about it? Did he visit you?"

"Yes, he came up and wanted us to go down and see it. We told him that if he thought he had something . . . you know, we'd heard there was a reward for a UFO, he might take it and report it down there (Roswell). I guess he did."

"Did Mac describe what he'd found to you at all?"

"Well, yes. And he did bring a little sliver of a wood looking stuff up but you couldn't burn it or you couldn't cut it or anything. I guess it was just a sliver of it, about the size of a pencil and about three or four inches long," she said.

"Do you remember the color?"

"I would say it was kind of brownish tan but you know that's been quite a long time. It looked like plastic, of course there wasn't any plastic then but that was kind of what it looked like."

"When he brought it up did you try to cut it?"

"No, we didn't. He did and he was telling us about more the other material that was so lightweight and that was crinkled up and then would fold out. He said there was more stuff there, like a tape that had some sort of figures on it."

"Did he talk about finding something that might have been more intact than the pieces of it that he mentioned?"

"He never did say what he had. But anyway, he went into Roswell and reported it and they flew him back out there to show them the location. They took him back to Roswell and kept him down there until they got it all cleaned up."

"Did you see any military people?"

"Oh no. It's maybe twenty miles down there," she explained.

"Do you know if there was more than one area of material found or was it all in that one place?"

"That was the only one I knew of."

"Do you know who all might have been at the ranch?"

"There weren't many there. Our seven-year-old son was with him (Brazel) when he found it but he can't remember where it was at and he can't remember what it looked like."

"Was Bessie (Brazel Schreiber) with him (Brazel)?"

"No, she wasn't at the ranch when this happened. Some of them kind of got their stories mixed up. No, she wasn't there."

"Did you ever ask Mac about it after he got back from Roswell?"

"He just said it was a weather balloon. Whatever they told him down there. He wouldn't talk about it. He did say that if he ever found anything he wasn't going to report it. They convinced him or something."

"Is there anything else that you can remember about this that might help us out?"

"No. I know that the day after Mac went to Roswell it made all the news. And then it was hushed up real quick. You just never heard any more about it."

While Randle worked in one direction, Schmitt and his assistant, Brad Radcliffe, worked in another. Their task was to track down new witnesses. An emphasis was placed not only on the military personnel at Roswell, but also on those at both Fort Worth and Wright Field.

Schmitt had realized from the very beginning that new witnesses were needed. Those who had never been interviewed could corroborate the testimony of the participants who had already told their stories.

As Schmitt and Radcliffe located potential leads, they turned the information over to Randle for the interviews.

As a result, more than three dozen new military witnesses were confirmed. Unfortunately more than fifty of the participants in the events of July, 1947 had died.

Research took both Schmitt and Randle in strange directions. Randle, while in Las Vegas, decided to see what the newspapers in Nevada had to say about the Roswell event. Randle looked them up and found a long chronology of what happened.

According to the *Las Vegas Review-Journal*, "The excitement ran through this cycle:

"1. Lieutenant Warren Haught (Walter Haut), public relations officer at the Roswell base, released a statement in the name of Colonel William Blanchard, base commander. It said that an object described as a 'flying disc' was found on the nearby Foster ranch three weeks ago by W.W. Brazel and had been sent to 'higher official' for examination.

"2. Brigadier General Roger Ramey, commander of the 8th air force, said at Fort Worth that he believed the object was the 'remnant of a weather balloon and a radar reflector,' and was 'nothing to be excited about.' He allowed photographers to take a picture of it. It was announced that the object would be sent to Wright Field, Dayton, Ohio, for examination by experts.

"3. Later, Warrant Officer Irving Newton, Stessonville, Wisconsin, weather officer at Fort Worth, examined the object and said definitely that it was nothing but a badly smashed target used to determine the direction and velocity of high altitude winds.

"4. Lieutenant Haught (sic) reportedly told reporters that he had been 'shut up by two blistering phone calls from Washington.'

"5. Efforts to contact Colonel Blanchard brought the information that 'he is now on leave.'

"6. Major Jesse A. Marcel, intelligence officer of the 509th bombardment group, reportedly told Brazel, the finder of the object, that it 'has nothing to do with army or navy so far as I can tell.'

"7. Brazel told reporters that he had found weather balloon equipment before, but had seen nothing that resembled his latest find."

That brought up a number of questions that neither Schmitt nor Randle had asked Haut. The quickest way to clear up the problems was to give him a call.

Randle asked, "Do you have a couple of minutes to answer a couple of new questions."

"Shoot," said Haut.

"I found in a newspaper that they had quoted you as saying that you had received two blistering calls from Washington. Do you remember anything like that at all?"

"Nope."

"Nothing whatsoever?"

"Nope. I hate to be that way. I think that had I really gotten any calls from Washington, a first lieutenant getting calls from the big boys, I'd remember it."

"We came across a witness who says you were on the first airplane when it took Marcel to Fort Worth. Any truth to that?"

"Ah . . ." There was a hesitation. "I think there's an expression, not only no, but hell no. No, I actually, I had no connection with it whatsoever."

The last thing Randle asked, "Did you ever meet Brazel during that time frame?"

"Nope. Nobody told me nothin'."

Interlude: Summer, 1989

Throughout the summer months, the focus remained on locating and interviewing new witnesses. Schmitt, however, was also submitting Freedom of Information requests to various agencies of the government. Letters were sent to FOIA officers at the Pentagon representing the Army, Navy, and the Air Force. Other letters were forwarded to the National Archives in Washington, D.C., Holloman Air Force Base in New Mexico, and Kirtland Air Force Base in Albuquerque.

Specific information was requested regarding Dr. Lincoln LaPaz; Mac Brazel's medical record created at Roswell; and maps and photographs of the crash site. None of the requests dealt directly with Roswell. To date, no letter of response acknowledges any information about Roswell.

August, 1989: Corona, New Mexico

Schmitt and Randle reached Albuquerque on Friday and used the time to talk to Merle Tucker, who had owned radio stations in New Mexico for years. Tucker himself was not directly involved. While everything was happening, he was out of town. When he got back, he was upset to hear that Johnny McBoyle, his station manager, and Lydia Sleppy, his secretary, had tried to put a story out over the wire. Tucker was sure that he was going to get into trouble over it.

According to Tucker, he knew that McBoyle had tried to get out to the site of the crash and that he had been intercepted by the military. Once McBoyle returned to Roswell, the sheriff went to see McBoyle and told him not to talk about it.

Tucker mentioned that McBoyle had been giving information to Sleppy over the phone, that he had talked about a "crushed" dishpan and about burn spots on the ground. But when Tucker asked him about it specifically, McBoyle said he couldn't talk about it. McBoyle refused to say anything more.

Tucker had no contact with either of the New Mexican senators or anyone else. He did hear that someone "official" had gone into his Roswell station and cleaned out all the paper about the event. That was all that he knew.

Finished there, Schmitt and Randle drove down to Corona, New Mexico. Many of the ranchers who had known Mac Brazel still lived in the area. Schmitt and Randle called Tommy Tyree, who had worked with Brazel just after the Brazel made the discovery. He agreed to meet with them and they drove out to the Tyree house. They met with Tyree and his wife, June, and interrupted an afternoon baseball game on the television.

Tyree's information, for the most part, was second-hand. Mac Brazel had told him a couple of things about the crash. Tyree, in fact, had said earlier, to Don Mitchell and Ralph Heick, that he thought Brazel had found a Japanese Balloon Bomb. Brazel, under orders by the military, had told him that it was a balloon.

According to Tyree, Mac had gone into Corona before heading into Roswell. He talked to his brother-in-law, and was told he should take the debris into Roswell. Several others in town gave him the same advice.

Tyree also told Schmitt and Randle that Brazel was angry about the debris because the sheep wouldn't cross the field. Brazel had to drive them around the field to get them to water. It took him a mile or more out of the way.

Now that Schmitt and Randle were there, Tyree's story changed slightly. He believed that Brazel had found something unusual and in fact, he had seen a piece of the material in a sinkhole. He and Brazel were riding the range and Brazel saw the piece floating at the bottom of the hole.

"Neither of us wanted to climb down after it," Tyree said. At that time, more than forty years ago, there was no reason to do it. "I might go out there and see if it's still there."

June Tyree listened patiently for a few minutes and then interjected, "If it was real, why didn't any of the boys from the high school head out there? Nobody'd keep them out of there if they thought there was anything interesting to see."

That seemed to be a legitimate question. In 1947, with no radio or television,. any diversion, even if was only a weather balloon, would be enough to draw the kids out to the crash. She even mentioned that when a secret plane had crashed in the mountains to the west, they had gone out to see it.

"I don't believe it happened," she said. "The kids didn't go out there and no one ever talked about it."

Tyree also said that Paul Brazel, another of Mac's sons, was upset because everyone said that his father had been bought off. Tyree pointed out that Mac Brazel was frugal. He didn't come into money suddenly, but saved everything he earned. He also mentioned that Mac had been a guard in a bank to earn extra money.

Finished with the interview, Schmitt and Randle drove to Roswell for the night. It was there they got the answer to June Tyree's question about the kids trying to find the wreckage. They also got good information from a number of new sources. And from Ralph Heick, they learned that one of Sheriff Wilcox's daughters, Phyllis McGuire, was still living in the area. She was willing to talk.

On Sunday Schmitt and Randle called the the witnesses on the list. Randle talked to Jack Rodden, whose father had been a photographer in Roswell in 1947. Although he didn't know much, he remembered his Dad's disappointment as the story turned from a flying saucer to a weather balloon.

"They killed it," he told his son.

Rodden also said that the rumors around Roswell had been thick. There was even talk about one of the "green" men being alive and running loose in the town. He said that he'd never heard or seen anything to confirm it but the town had been filled with such rumors.

The important thing, however, was that as a photographer Rodden often dealt with the ranchers from all over that area of New Mexico. One of the ranchers told him that his three kids had come home one day frightened to death and refused to talk about what they had seen.

Rodden pressed the issue and the upshot was that they had either been on the field and seen the debris, or they had gotten close to the second site where the bodies were found. They never said much to their family because someone in the military had scared them badly. They wouldn't say a thing to outsiders.

That could be the answer to June Tyree's question. The local kids did try to get in and those who got close enough to see something were intercepted by the military. If there is one theme that runs through the whole story, it's that secrecy was to be maintained. Those military guards who saw civilians told them that it was a classified matter and anyone who talked could expect jail time and heavy fines. Even the adults in the area were told not to talk and many of them were frightened by those threats.

Schmitt also talked to Terry Wilmot about the UFO sighting by Dan Wilmot on July 2, 1947. He said there was no doubt that Dan Wilmot had seen something.

While Randle talked to Rodden, Schmitt was talking to Phyllis McGuire, Sheriff Wilcox's daughter. She mentioned that her father had been excited by the discovery and the story told by Brazel, and regretted that he had ever called the military. The military had come in, taken over, and cut the sheriff out. They wouldn't answer any of Wilcox's questions and they had told him to forget all about it.

Schmitt asked her why she hadn't said anything before and she said, "Because no one ever asked me."

The important point, however, was her father's reaction to the story. Contrary to what had been printed in the past, he was interested in it. Wilcox had done what he thought was right at the time, and then wished he'd called the newspapers first.

That was the last bit of good information Schmitt and Randle received on that trip. The rest of the time was spent confirming statements that witnesses had made in the past. Nothing startling had been found but a dozen good leads had been developed and they had moved farther down the road.

September, 1989

The crash site had been identified by Bill Brazel. It was based on what his father had told him and on his observations of both wreckage and the gouge cut by the craft as it came down. Using that information, and the fact that no scientific study of the site itself had been tried, the J. Allen Hynek Center for UFO Studies decided that it was time to do just that.

The team put together by Mark Rodeghier consisted of ten members including two scientists, Carl Bebrich and Sue Ann Curtis, with training in archaeology and the collection of soil samples. Also included was Mimi Hynek, the widow of the CUFOS' late director, J. Allen Hynek, Tim Rodeghier, Jerry Vermeulen, M.D., and Don Schmitt and Kevin Randle.

Three days were spent on the site, the first photographing the area and marking the primary site with a square grid pattern a hundred feet on a side. With the grid complete, the entire site was surveyed carefully and likely spots for the entrapment of debris were marked. These included yucca plants that looked to be forty years or older, outcroppings of rock, and sinkholes.

The preliminary survey yielded nothing of interest. There were no signs of debris or even of the military presence forty years earlier. A single rusted and crushed can was found. It had been opened with a knife but there was no way to tell how long it had been lying there.

On the second day, the team dug test holes to various depths in a systematic pattern in the area of the gouge. The team also screened the dirt, searching for anything as small as a quarter inch in size. The team managed to sink about two hundred test holes.

Other team members also dug around the bases of the plants and surveyed the sinkholes carefully. An area on the hillside, where Bill Brazel said he'd found a couple of pieces of debris was marked and raked carefully. Again, nothing was found.

Schmitt and Randle left the site about noon to conduct a few interviews and attempt to arrange for Tommy Tyree to join them. While at the ranch headquarters, they learned that one of the ranch hands had seen a military vehicle on the range within the last year. Since there was no reason to expect the military to return to the crash site, they wanted to talk to the ranch hand.

Jim Parker told them that his son came from school one afternoon and reported that he'd see a strange pickup truck on one of the roads on the ranch. Parker climbed in his own truck and went in search of the strangers. Parker chased them down and reported that it was a crewcab Air Force pickup truck. The Air Force markings were clear on the doors, though he didn't know what base they came from. (It could have been Holloman, near Alamogordo, Kirtland in Albuquerque, or Cannon near Clovis, to name the three closest.)

The men, whom Parker described as being in their late twenties or early thirties and who were fairly low ranking, said that they were out there surveying the area for a low level aircraft radar site. Parker saw maps in the truck and four attache cases on the backseat.

But, before the men drove away, they asked Parker about the Roswell crash, wanting to know if they were close to the site. Parker, at the time, had heard nothing about it and told them he didn't know what they were talking about.

Checking with both the ranch owners and the Bureau of Land Management, Schmitt learned that the Air Force had never approached either the ranch owners or the BLM for permission to survey the site.

On the final day, the team made measurements and a drive around the entire crash site. The last thing was to collect all the flags, fill all the test holes and leave the site as close as possible to its original condition.

While that was going on, Schmitt and Randle drove to

Roswell to interview additional witnesses. They spent the morning tracking down the ice house where the military might have bought ice in July, 1947. Unfortunately, the ice house had changed hands four or five times and the only records the current owner could find were for 1927 and 1928. There was nothing there to suggest that a large purchase of ice had been made on July 8, 1947, but then, there was nothing to suggest it hadn't happened.

Late in the day, they linked with the rest of the team in Corona. The preliminary site survey was completed. Again, nothing startling had been learned, except that two members of the Air Force had expressed an interest in the location of the crash site within the year preceding the expedition. That, in and of itself, could be significant.

Interlude: Fall, 1989

As usual, between trips, there were things that could be done. Schmitt briefed attorneys and solicited their advice on the course of the investigation. They assured Schmitt that the weight of the testimony, from the dozens of first-hand witnesses, would be enough to win a judgment if the case went to trial. Suddenly, the talk of Congressional hearings became serious.

Schmitt also received from Stan Friedman, a reunion list from the 509th Bomb Group and passed it along to Randle. By cross checking the names on the list with the yearbook, they could determine who had been in Roswell at the time the crash occurred. Since the list contained only names and addresses but no phone numbers, Randle spent time in the library looking those up. With that completed, he could then begin to call the names on the list.

Joe Briley was in the yearbook as the Operations Officer (S-3), and according to the official unit history, Briley took over in the middle of July, 1947. He told Randle that he wasn't the S-3 when the crash occurred and that he really didn't know that much about it. But, in the course of the conversation he said that Colonel Blanchard had gone out to the crash site. That was something new, but as soon as he said it, Randle knew it was right. It made sense. Blanchard went on leave on the afternoon of July 8, and now Randle knew where he had gone. To the crash site.

But Briley wasn't finished. Randle said, "You heard stories . . ."

"Right. And then the story was changed and hushed up immediately. As soon as the people from Washington arrived."

Randle repeated that and Briley said, "Right."

Briley went on, ". . . you've probably got this thing (newspaper interview) of Roger Ramey's that refuted the whole thing and said that his over-ambitious or, I don't remember how he said it but it made Butch (Blanchard) sound like a first grader, which I don't buy."

Briley went on to deny that he had any firsthand knowledge of the crash. He said, "When we read the local paper the day that this happened there was a big flap and then this was all discounted and I think was even turned into a hoax that some reporter had stretched it way beyond the truth. And then it was hushed up real well."

Randle, wanting to be sure that he had the information correct, asked again if Briley was positive that Blanchard had gone out to the crash site.

"I'm sure of it."

In October, Schmitt traveled to Florida to meet with Lewis S. Rickett, one of the counter-intelligence agents who had been stationed in Roswell in July, 1947. Rickett and Schmitt talked of many things concerning the find by Brazel. In the course of the conversation, Schmitt asked, "What was your first impression while examining the material at the crash site?"

"This was the strangest material we had ever seen . . . there was talk about it not being from Earth."

Later in the four hour interview, Rickett said, "A year later I was talking to Joe Wirth, a CIC officer from Andrews Air Force Base in Washington D.C. I asked what they had found out about the stuff from Roswell. He told me that they still didn't know what it was and that their metal experts still couldn't cut it."

In the interim, Randle also talked to Art McQuiddy, who had been the editor of the *Roswell Morning Dispatch,* the other daily paper in Roswell in 1947. Only a few researchers had talked to McQuiddy or used his newspaper because all the good information had already been buried by the time the morning editions came out.

McQuiddy told Randle that "It was about noon and Walter Haut brought in a press release. He'd already been to one of the radio stations here and I raised hell with him about playing favorites and he said, well, there were four media here and he took turns taking the release first. The radio station put the release on the Associated Press radio wire. By the time Haut had gotten to me, it hadn't been ten minutes, and the phones started ringing . . . I never got off the phone until late that afternoon. I had calls from London and Paris and Rome and Hong Kong that I can remember."

But McQuiddy never got to talk to the rancher or any of the others. According to him, "The story died literally as fast as it started.

"Haut told me that he had some training in weather and that he didn't think it was a radiosonde or a weather balloon." He went on for a moment and then said, "Of course they came in and disclaimed the story so fast after that.

"As I recall, Walter didn't come in and ask to have the release back or anything although it sticks in my mind that he did but he says that he didn't and he ought to remember it."

"But you remember him coming in and asking you for the release back?" Randle asked.

"Well, I thought he did and he says he didn't."

Again McQuiddy said that he just wasn't that involved in it because the *Dispatch* was a morning paper. By the time he could get an issue out, the weather balloon story had been around for several hours. It was suddenly old news, though the *Dispatch* did carry a story about Wilcox and how busy he had been answering questions from around the world. Obviously, since Walter Haut, Art McQuiddy, and Sheriff Wilcox all talked about phone calls from around the world, there was a great deal of interest in the Roswell story.

Later Randle tracked down Frank Kaufman, who had been in Roswell during the event. When Randle talked to Kaufman on the phone, he admitted, reluctantly, that he had some firsthand knowledge of the crash but that he didn't want to talk about it.

Instead Randle asked about the activities in Roswell in 1947 and who might know something. Randle decided Kaufman might be able to help locate some of the other members of the 509th who had been directly involved. And then Kaufman mentioned that no one talked about the crash after the special flight from Washington came in.

Trying to confirm that, Randle said, "No one talked about it after the special flight got there from Washington?"

"Yeah, that's right."

"You're familiar with the special flight from Washington?"

"Yeah."

They talked for nearly thirty minutes more, but there was nothing interesting that came out of the discussion. Kaufman knew enough that he would became an important source. He knew more than he was willing to say over the phone.

During the fall, thanks to Brad Radcliffe, Schmitt established a direct link to a ranking officer in Army Intelligence, stationed at the Pentagon.

Schmitt submitted names, gave the Pentagon contact some information, and was assured that files would be pulled. In fact, Schmitt was told that Roswell was occasionally mentioned at the Pentagon, though he wasn't told in what context.

To date, Schmitt has been told to "leave it alone," and that there's nothing at the Pentagon about Roswell. Yet in March, 1990, Schmitt was told by an intelligence colonel that Project Blue Book was not the only government investigation during Blue Book's existence.

"All classified reports are still part of that department," the colonel said. "Maybe that's where your Roswell report is."

Archivist Ed Reese at the National Archives in Washington, D.C. seemed to confirm that. He told Schmitt that he had always been surprised that Roswell was not part of the declassified Blue Book material.

"We have all of the other explained reports, many of them involving weather balloons, but not Roswell. That always struck me as strange," said Reese.

January, 1990

Mark Rodeghier had an opportunity to re-interview Rickett in late January. There were dozens of follow-up questions and because Rickett had been on the site, his statements took on added weight.

Rodeghier spent the first hour learning about the function of the Army's counter-intelligence corps in the late 1940s. With the background established, Rodeghier began to question Rickett about Roswell.

According to Rickett, "There were four or five military vehicles at the crash site. The MPs checked our IDs.

All of them had .45s and some of them had Thompsons or old grease guns.''

''Anybody have any special equipment?'' asked Rodeghier.

''No. No special equipment. The MPs, four or five in the first group, were close to the gouge. There were twenty-five or thirty others scattered around the perimeter. The Provost Marshal didn't want anyone just wandering up on it.

''My boss said that he thought it advisable that someone else from our outfit see it. I said, it looks like metal and then I asked if it was hot (radioactive). My boss told me no, go ahead and pick it up.''

Rickett also said, ''The Provost Marshal said that he 'didn't want anyone coming out until you fellows saw this. Everything you see is already on film.' ''

''What did the material look like?'' asked Rodeghier.

''There was a slightly curved piece of metal, real light. It was about six inches by twelve or fourteen inches. Very light. I crouched down and tried to snap it. My boss laughs and said, 'Smart guy. He's trying to do what we couldn't do.' I asked, 'what in the hell is this stuff made out of?' It didn't feel like plastic and I never saw a piece of metal this thin that you couldn't break.''

Rickett continued, saying, ''As we walked around, my boss said, 'you and I were never here. You and I never saw this. You don't see any military people out here.' And I said, 'Yeah, that's right. We never left the office.' ''

Schmitt and Randle realized that there were things that needed to be done and people they needed to see. During the other trips, and during the dozens of phone calls, they had learned a great deal. One witness told Randle that he couldn't help with the investigation. He admitted that he was at the base at the time, but that he, ''can't talk about it.''

Randle finally asked him, point blank, "Were you on the crash site?"

"I can't talk about it. I was sworn to secrecy."

Later, during another discussion, he confirmed that Mac Brazel had been held in the guest house on the base, that material—the metal—had been taken to Wright Field in Ohio, and that his orders had all been verbal from Blanchard. He wrote no reports but did tell Randle that if reports could be located, the whole story would be learned. Those reports, written by others, covered the entire event at Roswell, and those reports had gone to the Pentagon.

In January, Schmitt and Randle returned to New Mexico. They hoped to find answers to the final questions they had. They planned a few interviews with those they had missed during the other trips.

Schmitt and Randle interviewed Frank Joyce again. This time he was more open, sharing his story completely. Again he said that he had interviewed Brazel during the afternoon of the first day and that Brazel told him the whole story of the discovery. Joyce claims that he told Brazel to call the military out at the base. Wilcox's family said it was the sheriff's idea. It doesn't matter now who suggested it because the call was made.

Joyce didn't have much to do with the story during the next couple of days and then all hell broke loose. As the story developed, Joyce began hiding the press releases and the teletype messages so that he could prove later that it had happened. Whitmore, the majority owner of station KGFL, went to Joyce and told him that the military wanted the press releases back. Joyce said the station's offices had been searched and most of the papers he'd hidden were found and taken.

Again he said that Brazel came to him late one night. Given the situation as Schmitt and Randle had pieced it together, it seemed the visit happened on July 9. Brazel told Joyce the weather balloon story. Joyce said that it wasn't the same thing Brazel had said the first time and

Brazel nodded. Brazel said that it would go hard on him if he didn't tell the new story. But then, as he was leaving, Brazel said, "You know how they talk about little green men. They weren't green."

The first interview the next morning was with Phyllis McGuire and her sister Elizabeth Tulk, the daughters of Sheriff Wilcox. Both remembered the incident and both talked about all the people who came into the sheriff's office because of the phone call out to the base.

Both were teenagers at the time and talked about an apartment near the jail. They remembered the activity and that the military had arrived almost as the sheriff hung up the phone. Both said that Wilcox had been annoyed with the way the military handled it. Wilcox was later told not to talk about it. When he discussed in private with his family, he complained about the military and the secrecy. He regretted not going somewhere else first.

Leaving there, Schmitt and Randle drove to an interview with Juanita Sultemeier. In the late forties she, along with her husband, owned a ranch in the Corona area and both of them knew Mac Brazel. She said that Brazel was a down to earth man who worked long and hard. There was nothing in Brazel's background that would suggest flights of fancy or practical jokes. And, like many of the others who lived there in 1947, she remembered finding weather balloons on occasion. No one ever got them confused with something else. Everyone knew what they were the moment they found them.

In fact, the Sultemeiers found a balloon that carried an offer of a hundred dollar reward. Her husband boxed the thing up and took it into Corona, to the railroad depot, and shipped it out. "But we never got the money," she said.

She mentioned one other thing and that was the group of archaeologists who had stayed near her house a few years after the crash. It was important only because it demonstrated that archaeologists were in the area on occasion. It demonstrated that there was a reason for archaeologists to be in the area.

Finished, Schmitt and Randle drove to Frank Kaufman's. On the phone he had been reluctant to talk but in person he was more than happy to share his information.

Again Kaufman ran through his story. Kaufman had been on the outside for most of it. His friend, a warrant officer named Robert Thomas, had come in on a special flight from Washington, D.C. and seemed to be involved in the retrieval in some fashion. Thomas let Kaufman know a few things. He talked about the debris field and suggested that there was a search in progress for the flight crew. When Thomas talked to Kaufman, they hadn't found the bodies, but they were looking for them.

When asked if he knew anything at all about the recovery of the debris, he said, "I know that one crate was taken to a hangar and left there overnight. There were spotlights on it and it was in the center of the floor with MPs around the walls, guarding it."

He didn't know what was in the crate, only that it had gotten special treatment: lots of guards around it and no one being allowed to approach it.

He also said that he had been sworn to secrecy although he didn't know that much. He said that they were taken into a room in small groups, ten or twelve, and told that they had participated in something that was of national security interest. They were not to talk about it to anyone. They were to forget that it had ever happened.

Randle asked if Kaufman had been made to sign anything.

"No. Just told to forget about it."

He also said that he didn't really know the men in the room with him. He believed the authorities did all that for security reasons. That way Kaufman wouldn't know how many others were involved or who most of them were. He could recognize the other nine or ten but that would be it. And no one was supposed to ask anyone about it. That had been part of their orders.

Kaufman was questioned about that, about Thomas, and about the mood on the base in 1947. He thought that Thomas was dead. He remembered the many rumors in 1947. Everyone had a theory or a belief. There was talk of finding bodies, of finding some of them alive. Lots of rumors. The only thing he was sure about was the crate that had spent most of one night in the hangar with MPs watching it.

The last of the interviews that day was with Robert Shirkey. He had been at the base in 1947 and had watched as some of the wreckage had been taken through the Operations building and out onto the ramp where it was loaded into an aircraft.

According to Shirkey, eight or nine guys carried the material from a truck through the building. The debris was grayish and thin. He remembered one man had a piece of it tucked up under his arm.

Blanchard was there, according to Shirkey, and as Shirkey moved into the doorway to see better, Blanchard stepped back out of the hall to clear a path for the men with the material. Shirkey had to step to the side to see what was going on.

Shirkey didn't get a chance to touch the metal. He only got a chance to see it as it was carried past him. He didn't see much of it.

Of course, like the others, he had heard stories after the event. The one that he remembered was that all the MPs were transferred off the base within a month. "They didn't want them sitting around comparing notes."

The next day Schmitt and Randle drove to Capitan to meet with Bud Payne. In the course of the investigation, they had been told a number of times that they had been to the wrong crash site. Juanita Sultemeier hinted that it was east of the ranch headquarters, though she had never been there herself. Tommy Tyree hinted that Bill Brazel didn't know the actual site, though Bill had found scattered debris and had seen the gouge cut as the thing bounced across the desert.

There were others who knew where the debris field had been found. One of them was Bud Payne, a rancher who had been living in New Mexico for more than seventy years. Bud Payne had been taken to the crash site thirty years earlier. Payne also had been thrown off the Foster ranch by the military about the time the debris had been found.

According to Payne, a cow had gotten loose from the ranch where he worked and he had followed it onto the Foster property. As he was approaching the stray animal, a jeep came roaring over one of the rises, bearing down on him. There were military men in it and they were shouting at him. They escorted him physically from the ranch property.

Payne, using the back roads out of Capitan, headed toward the old Foster ranch (where Mac Brazel had lived in 1947). At first it was blacktop and fairly straight and level, but it quickly changed into gravel, dipping into deep canyons and climbing back out.

Payne took them directly to the crash site. Bill Brazel had taken Schmitt and Randle to the northern end of it and Payne drove to the southern end. In fact, the expedition in September hadn't removed all the flags they had planted. Payne stopped inside those flags, on the same three-quarter mile strip of New Mexico. It was further confirmation of the exact location of the debris field.

Leaving the debris field, Schmitt and Randle drove across New Mexico to the next interview. Jerry Brown was a NASA engineer and had worked at the White Sands Missile Range. He believed there was a possibility that Brazel had found the remains of a V-2 rocket.

During the five hour interview, Brown said there were only two pads for launching the V-2s or the later A-9s.

A-9s were a two-staged rocket with a payload of about 2500 pounds. Brown thought that the men from Roswell might have stumbled onto the wreckage of an A-9. With its upper stage that had wings on it, it could guide in and leave the gouge that Brazel among others reported. Brown didn't think a V-2 would land that way. A V-2 would come straight down, creating a crater and a small debris field, which had not been described by anyone on the crash site.

Brown talked about the evidence that would be left in the crash of a A-9, suggesting that Duraluminum would account for the metal that wouldn't melt under a blowtorch. It was designed to withstand the heat of re-entry. But Duraluminum, while heat resistant and tough, would shatter under repeated blows from a sledgehammer.

Brown tried to explain all the debris found. Some of the wiring in the rocket, if heated in the crash, might end up as small hollow tubes that looked nothing like conventional wiring and that would allow a light pointed at one end to reflect through it, giving the impression of fiber optics.

In fact, Brown was able to explain everything to his own satisfaction except for the foil that unfolded itself and resumed its original shape. He could think of nothing to explain that except that the witnesses had been fooled by something else.

And the bodies? Small bodies that didn't look human.

He speculated about that. Could they had been chimpanzees sent up for experimentation? Possibly, but then why all the secrecy after forty years?

That didn't make sense. If the rocket had crashed on a New Mexico ranch and the occupants had been animals, it might have been embarrassing but it was nothing that would remain a secret for forty years. At some point, someone would have discovered the declassified documents. With all the researchers trying to learn about White Sands and the early years of experimental rocketry, something would have come out.

Unless it was still classified, and there was only one reason for that. The occupants blasted into space had not been animals, but had been humans. Small humans who would fit easily into the craft and whose weight wouldn't be prohibitive.

It was an interesting scenario but one for which there was not a single shred of evidence. Nothing had ever been released to suggest that the men at White Sands had launched a human cargo in 1947. A human cargo that would have been, at the most, two humans and not four.

After discussing the whole range of evidence, from the descriptions of the debris field and the involvement of the men of the 509th Bomb Group, Brown finally said, "If you can show that it wasn't an A-9, then I don't know what it could have been."

What Brown didn't know was that there was only a four day window of opportunity for the A-9 crash. Mac Brazel had told the military he had been on that section of the range four days before he found the debris and nothing had been there then.

Schmitt learned there was only a single attempted V-2 launch that fit into the time frame and it had been July 3. That V-2 never left the pad and was accounted for. That meant that White Sands could be ruled out as a source of the debris. Nothing was launched in the time frame to cover it.

The next day Schmitt and Randle were scheduled to meet with one of the counter-intelligence agents. According to a number of witnesses, the man had been at the debris field on more than one occasion, but he denied it, saying that it had to be someone else. Everyone was mistaken about his presence there.

He invited Schmitt and Randle to visit him at his apartment and met them saying that there wasn't anything he could say about the crash. "I wasn't there."

Schmitt suggested the possibility that the crash had

been a V-2 or an A-9. Schmitt asked if they had ever retrieved anything like that anywhere in New Mexico.

"Never." He said that any rocket going off course would be destroyed by the range officer. They wouldn't have wanted to risk injuries to any civilians on the ground.

Randle asked if he remembered any talk at all about a flying saucer crash but he insisted that nothing at all had happened. The former CIC man hadn't heard any rumors and there had been nothing in the newspaper about a crash. All this, including the story as shown on *Unsolved Mysteries* was "a bunch of garbage."

Schmitt and Randle spent two hours with the man. He told them that any reports he wrote in the normal course of his duties were sent to Washington and not to Eighth Air Force in Fort Worth. He was attached to the 509th but his chain of command was different than theirs.

In fact, he talked about many things willingly. He said that the ranks of the CIC agents were all classified at the time. It didn't look right to have a master sergeant investigating a colonel, so no one on the base, except for a few men cleared to know, had any idea what rank he or any of the others were.

He provided the names of others who might be able to help and he described his normal, unclassified duties at Roswell. But, according to him, the crash and the recovery had never happened. There was no investigation on the Foster ranch, no mystery flights, and no discovery of alien bodies. Nothing.

Randle said that he and Schmitt had, literally, two dozen witnesses to the special flights out of Roswell and the special cleanup operation on the ranch.

"Something must have happened," the CIC man finally conceded, "but I don't know what it was."

As they left, the CIC man asked them, "If you boys found something that affected national security, would you keep it to youselves?"

Schmitt said, "If it affected national security, yes."
The former CIC man grinned and said, "Very good."

There were other interviews that were conducted during that trip, but those witnesses confirmed what they had said on the phone. Jud Roberts, for example, said that he had been turned back by the military cordon. And Art McQuiddy confirmed that someone from the military had come to his office and took all the papers that related to the crash.

But even with that, it had been a productive trip. The whole story was getting out. Now it was just a question of putting the facts together to see what the overall picture looked like.

May, 1990

It had taken months to put the trip together. First was the problem of finding an individual qualified in the use of hypnosis. Neither Schmitt nor Randle wanted just any practitioner. They wanted someone with impeccable credentials so that it couldn't be claimed that the person was unqualified. And they needed someone who was willing to do it in Montana.

Schmitt found a woman who agreed. The trip was scheduled, and then rescheduled at her convenience. Then, three days before they were to arrive in Montana, the woman backed out. She claimed pressure from her peers. They believed that by participating in the regression of Jesse Marcel, Jr., she would be dabbling in the paranormal. Her license or certification or standing in her organization would be jeopardized.

Schmitt, with the help of Brad Radcliffe, located Professor John Watkins in Missoula, Montana. According to Schmitt and Radcliffe, Watkins might be willing to do it. Schmitt suggested that Randle call Watkins. After talking to him for thirty minutes, Watkins agreed, providing that Jesse Marcel would call him. Randle set that up.

With everything in place, Schmitt and Randle left for Montana. When they arrived in Missoula, they met with Watkins. He told them more about his background, including his work on the Hillside Strangler case. If nothing else, Watkins was used to controversy.

Watkins also made it clear that he'd spent years as a psychologist. He worked in VA hospitals, treating soldiers for mental disorders stemming from their combat experiences. He is a psychology professor emeritus at the University of Montana. Watkins is the author of six books, over ninety papers, and more than a hundred articles on various aspects of his research and hypnosis.

From Missoula, they drove to Jesse Marcel's home. While Watkins talked to Jesse Marcel, Schmitt and Randle interviewed his mother. They wanted to learn what her impressions were when Major Marcel brought home some of the material recovered on the crash site.

She said that Jesse Sr. was excited about it. He thought that it was something extraordinary, and, of course, she didn't know what it could be. They had spread it out in the kitchen to examine it. Her descriptions of it matched those given by the others who had handled it.

The afternoon session with Jesse Marcel, Jr. produced the best results. Neither Schmitt nor Randle expected anything spectacular. They hoped to learn, in greater detail, what had happened during the early morning examination of the debris by the Marcel family.

Watkins worked with Marcel for nearly an hour, getting him to relax and finally into a light trance. Watkins had Marcel relive a few childhood memories, moving him from an early part of his life in Houston to Roswell, New Mexico. Slowly, Watkins brought Marcel forward until it was the end of the July 4, 1947 weekend.

Watkins, trying not to lead Marcel, suggested that something important was happening. That his father was there, excited about something. Watkins asked, "What is happening?"

It was now as if Jesse Marcel, Jr. was being shaken

from a sound sleep by his father in 1947. He was slightly confused because his father was standing over him, trying to get him to wake up.

Marcel followed his father outside to help carry in a box filled with debris. Jesse Jr. mentioned that his father had not driven a staff car out to the Brazel ranch, but took their Buick convertible.

Back inside the house, they spread the debris over the kitchen floor, trying to fit the pieces together like a giant jigsaw puzzle, but the damage was too great. Nothing fit together.

Schmitt leaned forward then and quietly asked, "How much of the floor was covered?"

Marcel spoke slowly, quietly, as if examining it before he could answer the question. It filled most of the kitchen floor from the back door to the door that led into the living room. It was spread from the stove on the left, across the floor to the sink and refrigerator.

Marcel described some small, black, plastic-like material that was thicker than lead foil and that was much stronger. He said that it looked like "Bake-lite." He also mentioned the lead foil and the I-beams.

Watkins asked what was happening. Jesse Jr. said that his father was crouched near the back door, trying to fit some of the pieces together, but they wouldn't fit. There was too much of it and the damage had been too great.

While Marcel and his son were trying to put together the debris, Marcel's wife picked up one of the I-beams and said, "There's writing on this."

Jesse Jr., looking at one of the I-beams, noticed writing on it, too. Under hypnosis, he said, "I can't read it." He hesitated and added, "Purple. Strange. Never saw anything like it."

Randle asked him what the writing looked like.

"Different geometric shapes, leaves, circles." Under hypnosis, Marcel drew the symbols as they appeared on the I-beam.

Under questioning, Marcel said that the symbols were

a shiny purple and that they were small, less than a fingernail wide. There were many separate figures.

He also described the beam. He said that it was broken at both ends and that it was made of the same material as the lead foil and that it was cold to the touch. It was thicker and tougher than the lead. He couldn't bend it.

While Marcel was still under hypnosis, Schmitt asked Jesse what his father was saying.

"It's a flying saucer."

"Is he using those words?"

"Yes. I ask him what a flying saucer is. I don't know what a flying saucer is."

"What does he say?"

"It's a ship. He's excited."

Schmitt asked, "Does he say anything about a balloon?"

"No. Only flying saucer."

Marcel then described how he assisted his father putting the debris back in a large cardboard box. They carried it out and put in it the trunk of the Buick.

Schmitt asked, "When is the next time you see him?"

"The next day after work."

"What day?"

"Wednesday. I'm not in school. Don't keep track of the days." (Note: According to the chronology devel-

While under hypnosis, Jesse Marcel, Jr. drew the symbols that were on the one I-beam he examined. Interestingly, these symbols do not resemble those published by others claiming to have knowledge of UFO's.

oped, Marcel was both right and wrong. It wasn't the next day, which would have been a Tuesday, but was the day after, Wednesday.)

Marcel then said that his father didn't say anything about the flying saucer. In fact, Major Marcel cautioned his family about mentioning it at all. Major Marcel told them not to talk about it. To "forget it."

With Jesse Jr. still under hypnosis, Schmitt asked him when the next time his father mentioned the crash was. Jesse Jr. said that he was in high school and that his father still didn't know what it was. Marcel Sr. said that it wasn't a balloon. Wasn't a radar target.

Under more detailed questioning, Marcel remembered a few other details. His father told him that there had been "a lot of debris on the ranch." And that soldiers had been sent out to guard the field.

The problem was that Jesse Jr. was only eleven years old. His father talked to his wife, but Jesse Jr. was more of an observer to those discussions and not a participant. In fact, when Schmitt and Randle tried to learn more about what Marcel said on the day of his return, Jesse Jr. told them that his parents were in the kitchen. He was waiting for his friend to come over.

That was the end of the session. Both Schmitt and Randle agreed it had been valuable. If nothing else, they had learned a few more details and gotten the drawing of the symbols Marcel had seen on the I-beam.

Schmitt conducted the final interview during the Montana trip. He visited with Robert Porter, hoping to learn a few new things about the first flight out of Roswell. According to Porter, the flight was authorized by Major Ralph R. Taylor. The material, the triangle-shaped package, and the three or four shoe boxes, were brought to the aircraft by a staff car. Porter was sure that the material had been stored in Building 1034, which was labeled as an engineering building on the base map.

He couldn't add much more to the story of the mate-

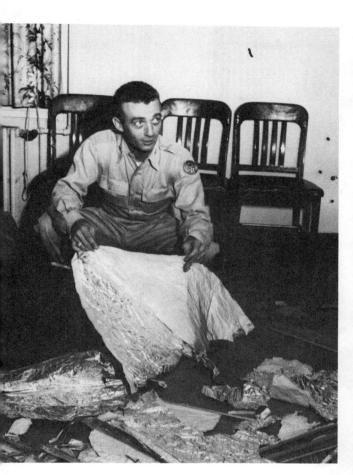

Maj. Jesse A. Marcel with the balloon wreckage in
General Roger Ramey's office.
(Photo courtesy of *Fort Worth Star-Telegram Photograph Collection,*
Special Collections division, University of Texas
at Arlington Libraries)

Maj. Marcel with the remains of the weather balloon in
General Ramey's office. Marcel told friends that the real
wreckage had been removed and the balloon substituted.
(Photo courtesy of *Fort Worth Star-Telegram Photograph Collection*,
Special Collections division, University of Texas
at Arlington Libraries)

General Ramey in his office with the remains of the weather
balloon. There is no doubt that Ramey had the real debris
switched and what was photographed was a Rawin target device.
(Photo courtesy of *Fort Worth Star-Telegram Photograph Collection*,
Special Collections division, University of Texas
at Arlington Libraries)

General Ramey and his chief of staff, Colonel Thomas Dubose,
inspect the remains of a weather balloon.
(Photo courtesy of *Fort Worth Star-Telegram Photograph Collection*
Special Collections division, University of Texas
at Arlington Libraries)

Mac Brazel stored some of the wreckage in a shed before telling military authorities about it. (Photo courtesy of Paul Davids)

One of the few witnesses to see the impact point (second crash site) provided eyewitness testimony about its location and the object seen there. The witness shredded his original drawing. (Drawing courtesy of Don Schmitt)

Marian Strickland (head bowed) said that Mac Brazel sat at her kitchen table to complain about his treatment by the Army in 1947. (Photo courtesy of Juanita Sultemeier)

Lyman Strickland saw Mac Brazel in Roswell in the company of three Army officers. (Photo courtesy of Juanita Sultemeier)

Mac Brazel, closest to the camera.
(Photo courtesy of Juanita Sultemeier)

It was too far to the debris field for Floyd and Loretta Proctor to drive down. (Photo courtesy of Juanita Sultemeier)

Clint Sultemeier listened to Mac Brazel talk about his treatment during the days he was held by the military in Roswell. (Photo courtesy of Juanita Sultemeier)

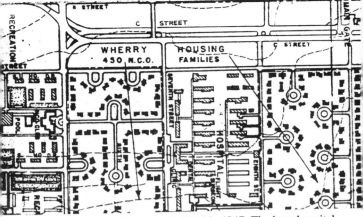

Part of the Roswell Army Air Field in 1947. The base hospital was a group of buildings not far from the front gate. (Map courtesy of Don Schmitt)

The site of the base hospital today. (Photo courtesy of Kevin Randle)

The hangar areas of the Roswell Army Air Field as they appeared in 1947.
(Map courtesy of Don Schmitt)

The section of the runway where bomb pit no. 1 was located. The crate with the bodies was stored there for several hours.
(Map courtesy of Don Schmitt)

Sheriff George A. Wilcox suggested that Mac Brazel call the Army, and then was left out of the investigation. Later, he was sworn to secrecy by the military. (Photo courtesy of Paul Davids)

Don Schmitt listens as one of the witnesses relates her story of the recovery. (Photo courtesy of Paul Davids)

on Schmitt and
evin Randle attempt to
cate other witnesses to
e events at Roswell.
'hoto courtesy of
ul Davids)

yllis McGuire, whose father,
eriff George Wilcox,
id on many occasions
at he wished he had
ver called the Army
th the story. (Photo
urtesy of Paul Davids)

Bud Payne points to the southern end of the debris field. Payne was physically removed by the military in 1947. (Photo courtesy of Paul Davids)

Frank Joyce of radio station KGFL said that Mac Brazel told him two separate stories. Many Joyce's records disappeared as the Army began to destroy the paper trail. (Photo courtesy of Paul Davids)

Juanita Sultemeier told the investigators that archaeologists sometimes stayed overnight at her ranch, not far from the debris field. (Photo courtesy of Paul Davids)

The barren debris field as it appears today. No sign of the wreckage or the military recovery operation remains. (Photo courtesy of Paul Davids)

The airfield at Roswell today. Although it is no longer a military base, military aircraft use the facility.
(Photo courtesy of Kevin Randle)

The main gate of the Roswell Army Air Field as it appears today.
(Photo courtesy of Kevin Randle)

The sign on one of the roads out of Corona attests to the desolate nature of the area. (Photo courtesy of Kevin Randle)

Don Schmitt and Kevin Randle near what was the flightline on the old Roswell Army Air Field.
(Photo courtesy of Kevin Randle)

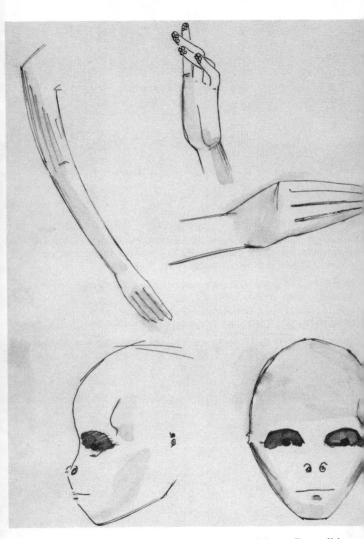

Drawings by Glenn Dennis, formerly a mortician at Roswell in 1947. These illustrations are based on the actual drawings done in Mr. Dennis' presence by the nurse who participated in the preliminary autopsies at Roswell one day later.

rial, but did say his brother, Leonard Porter, who lived south of Brazel, and a friend, Bill Jenkins, had seen Mac in downtown Roswell on July 9. According to Porter, Mac Brazel ignored them, pretending not to see them. According to Jenkins, Brazel was surrounded by military men. That ran the total of people who had seen Brazel with a military escort in Roswell to six.

Schmitt and Randle discussed what they had learned. Everything they had learned. In the months since beginning the investigation, they had realized first that something unusual had happened at Roswell, and then that it had been extraterrestrial in origin. Their attitudes at the beginning of the search, that it couldn't have been the crash of an alien spacecraft, had changed slowly, as all the other explanations vanished under the weight of information.

As they had worked, developing new leads, interviewing more firsthand witnesses, they realized the truth. Too many people had supplied too many pieces of the puzzle. If Major Marcel had been a lone voice, that would have been one thing. But Marcel wasn't alone. Too many others were saying the same things. It boiled down to one fact.

In July, 1947, the United States Army Air Force had participated in the recovery of a craft that defied conventional explanation.

July, 1990

The investigation had progressed well in all aspects. New witnesses had been found, more information had been uncovered, and new details had been given. Schmitt and Randle had followed their own path, searching for their own answers, using the information gained from newspapers, old magazines, and finally the witnesses themselves. Almost every one of them knew of two or three others who had some kind of knowledge about the events of July, 1947.

But in July, 1990, it was time to talk with other investigators. Stanton Friedman, a nuclear physicist who has spent the last two decades lecturing about UFOs, and the last ten years researching the events at Roswell, was one of the first to learn of the crash. It was after a lecture in Minnesota that Vern Maltais came forward to tell him of Barney Barnett. It was Friedman who found Lydia Sleppy, who was the teletype operator in Albuquerque who related the Johnny McBoyle story, and it was Friedman, after a television interview in Louisiana, who learned of Jesse Marcel.

In July, 1990, Schmitt and Randle interviewed Friedman informally. Friedman told them of first hearing the Maltais story after a lecture. Maltais himself related how he almost didn't say a word about it, but decided that someone with an interest in the topic should know.

Alone, the Maltais story was of almost no use. The problem was that Barnett had died in 1969 and couldn't be interviewed for confirmation.

Then, talking to people in California about a UFO case, one of the men told Friedman that he should talk to his mother, Lydia Sleppy. Again, she had an interesting story, but couldn't remember the exact date of the event. She told of having Johnny McBoyle on the phone, telling of a downed saucer, and then him retracting his statements. And again, it was interesting, but there wasn't much of a way to get a handle on it.

But that wasn't the end. Friedman, in Louisiana for a lecture, was doing a television interview. The station manager told Friedman that he knew a ham radio operator, living in Houma, Louisiana, who claimed to be the intelligence officer who had picked up the debris in the late 1940s. Friedman asked for the name, got it, and called Jesse Marcel.

Marcel couldn't remember the date, except that it was in the late 1940s, but he did remember the place, Roswell, New Mexico, and he knew that it was no weather balloon. A search of the newspapers revealed enough additional information to get a handle on it. Once the initial articles, on July 8, 9, and 10, 1947, were found, the time and location had been confirmed. And, some of those articles revealed other names such as Walter Haut, William Blanchard, and Irving Newton.

Friedman alerted a reporter, Steve Tom, who in turn called Len Stringfield. It turned out that Stringfield and Marcel had been on the same Pacific island during the Second World War. They began to talk at length about many things, including the crash near Roswell. Marcel told Stringfield the same things that he'd told Friedman.

Now there was enough information for real research to begin. The names of the units involved were learned. Walter Haut had a yearbook, produced during the summer of 1947, that listed the majority of the people who were at the Roswell Army Air Field during that time. With that, more witnesses were found.

But the initial information was found because Stan Friedman was on the lecture circuit. Friedman listened to those witnesses, filed away the information, holding it until more could be added to it. Had it not been for Friedman finding Marcel and talking to him, no one would have heard of Roswell, New Mexico or the events that took place during the summer of 1947.

March, 1991

As the book went to press, Schmitt and Randle were still in the field following new leads, interviewing new witnesses, and attempting to further verify all the information. They learned, as a result of the UNSOLVED MYSTERIES broadcast, that a man, Gerald F. Anderson, claimed that he had seen the bodies. As a six year old child, he, along with his family, had stumbled upon the crashed saucer on the Plains of San Agustin. According to Anderson, there were four aliens, two obviously dead, one dying, and one that looked in bad shape, but which seemed like it would survive military recovery.

According to Anderson, the archaeologists described earlier appeared a few minutes later coming from an old cliff dwelling area. Later still, one man appeared, coming up over a rise. Anderson believed that this was Barney Barnett. Anderson claimed that the archaeologists saw the object crash and that was why they had come to investigate.

The problem with Anderson's statements, and the belief that Barnett was part of this account, was the discovery of Ruth Barnett's (Barney's wife) diary. Uncovered on September 16, 1990, it eliminated a number of dates for Barnett's involvement. On July 3, he stayed in the office and on July 5, Jerry Anderson's date for the crash, Barnett was in Socorro, New Mexico, working on his new house. Both dates supplied witnesses to his whereabouts.

The diary, and Anderson's involvement, tend to create more questions than they answer. Anderson's story was unconfirmed and some of the details supplied Randle in a February 4, 1990, interview, were contradictory to what he was saying in September, 1990.

Schmitt and Randle also had the opportunity to reinterview Alice Knight, niece of Barney Barnett. Since they were unconvinced that there was a second crash near the Plains of San Agustin, one question that had to be asked was if Knight was sure that Barnett had given that as a location. Knight said that she believed that he had.

Vern Maltais, who heard the story of the crash from Barnett, said that Barney never provided the location. Barnett was the first on the scene. When he found the object, there was no one else there. The archaeologists, four or five, arrived moments later. No one else appeared until the military roared up. All these statements made Schmitt and Randle suspicious of Anderson's report.

Anderson, however, offered some documentation. He

gave Stan Friedman, a diary that supposedly proved his story. Testing of the diary showed that the paper was pre-1947, but the ink was post-1970. In other words, it meant that the diary had been written sometime after 1970.

Still unconvinced about that end of the report, they had one other man to interview. Interviewed earlier, in January, 1990, he was one of the intelligence operatives who had been assigned to the Roswell Army Air Field in 1947. Again, he mentioned that he had been sworn to secrecy, and again, explained that the men had been taken, in small groups, into a room at the Roswell Army Air Field for their debriefing.

But then he revealed, in a roundabout fashion, information he felt safe in discussing. First he said that the news release issued by Walter Haut was damage control. It had been created to end the rumors circulating around Roswell. For a few hours it was exciting, but then the answer was released and interest quickly died.

Second, he sketched in a basic line drawing, the object found at the second site on the Brazel ranch. The disc-shaped object was seemingly squared off at its visible end which might have been a result of the impact. It had a slight dome on top and was tipped up at an angle. Very few were allowed close to the impact he said. Guards were posted and men were organized to clean up the debris but they were kept away from the object.

The interview, like so many other, had been cryptic in nature. The information, however, had been consistent with that provided by others. The only real problem was the discussion of the bodies. He told them flatly that they would never find anyone from the military who would provide first hand testimony about the bodies.

As they left this major witness, both Schmitt and Randle realized that the story was so complex, so involved, with so many witnesses that they could continue to work on it for another ten years and still find new information. The investigation of the crash at Roswell would continue, but the writing of the book had to end. They wanted to get it published in the hope that new sources would be encouraged to come forward. They felt they knew the whole story. It was the fine tuning that would continue.

Explanations

The event at Roswell is not without a series of explanations that suggest the mundane. Within six hours of the announcement that a flying saucer had been captured, the military was telling all who would listen that it was a weather balloon.[1] In the following years there were those who claimed it was a secret government experiment, a V-2 gone off course, or the remains of a Japanese Balloon Bomb. Before moving into the realm of the exotic all mundane answers had to be exhausted. If one of them fit the facts perfectly, then all the other arguments fell by the wayside.

In fact, the skeptics and the non-believers felt that the case was open and shut. On July 9, the day after the *Roswell Daily Record* announced that a flying saucer had been captured, they told the public that "Gen. Ramey Empties Roswell Saucer." According to the skeptics, that article solves the mystery once and for all. There was no crash, just a weather balloon that those with more enthusiasm than sense turned into something spectacular.

On the surface, that paper from July 9, 1947 is a devastating document. Mac Brazel talks about finding the object on June 14, that his wife, a son, and daughter were with him, and that they carried most of it to ranch headquarters. He mentioned that the material was flimsy, that it was basically aluminum foil and balsa, and that he thought nothing of it until he heard about "flying saucers" a couple of weeks later. Then, while in Roswell to sell wool on July 7, 1947, he mentioned to the sheriff, "kind of confidential," that he had found something unusual.[2]

The article describes the material at length, saying that the rubber was smoky gray and that it was scattered over an area about two hundred yards in diameter. There were no words or writing on it although there were some letters on some of the parts. Considerable Scotch tape and some tape with flowers printed upon it had been used in the construction. According to the article, there were no strings or wires but there were some eyelets in the paper to indicate that some sort of attachment may have been used.

The story ends with Brazel saying that he had found weather observation devices on two other occasions but what he found this time did not resemble those. "I am sure what I found was not any weather observation balloon," he said, "but if I find anything else besides a bomb they are going to have a hard time getting me to say anything about it."

For any investigation into the Roswell affair to be valid, it must encompass all the evidence and explain all the facts. The article from July 9 is one area that most of the researchers have ignored.

In an interview conducted by Schmitt, he learned that Brazel had been in the field only four days prior to the discovery of the debris.[3] That meant that there was no wreckage there on June 14, as the article had claimed. Brazel himself told investigators from the Roswell Army Air Field that he knew the material hadn't been there more than four days.

Schmitt also learned from a variety of sources, including Bill Brazel and Jesse Marcel, Jr., that the debris was scattered over an area three-quarters of a mile long and two or three hundred feet wide, and that there was a gouge in the ground about five hundred feet long.[4] Major Marcel, in taped interviews, often said that the debris field was quite large. Others who were also interviewed said the debris was dense.[5] Marcel said that after a full day of collecting debris there was still a great deal of it at the site.

According to Lewis Rickett, they were dispatched the next morning to recover more of it. Bill Brazel said that his father had carted the largest piece from the field to store in a livestock shed. This was certainly more material than would be found in a simple balloon.

Tommy Tyree, who was Mac Brazel's hired hand, but who did not come to work for Brazel until after this event, said that Mac told him he was annoyed by the find. The material spread out over the field formed a barrier that the sheep would not cross. According to Tyree, Brazel had to drive the sheep around the debris field to get them to water. That suggests that whatever had fallen in the field was much larger than any kind of weather balloon.[6]

Descriptions of the material, coming both from Mac Brazel and Jesse Marcel, and from those who saw it later, do not agree with what was printed in the newspaper. Bill Brazel described metal that was so tough that he couldn't cut it. It was lightweight, like balsa, but was much stronger. Bill Brazel also talked about material that sounds suspiciously like fiber optics.

In taped interviews, Major Marcel described metal that was as thin as newsprint but that couldn't be dented. Marcel himself described how they used a sixteen pound sledgehammer without results.

There was lettering on some of the wreckage. Jesse Marcel, Jr. described that as geometric symbols. He drew those he could remember on a pad for Randle. They were embossed on an I-beam and were purplish. The I-beam itself was very strong and slightly flexible.

In a confidential interview, one man who had been on the crash site on the morning of July 8 told Schmitt that the material was not shiny. It did not reflect the sun. Yet the pictures that do exist show the remains of a balloon that is very fragile and very shiny.[7]

But maybe the most devastating testimony comes from Major Marcel. He said, "It was not anything from this Earth. That I'm quite sure of. Because being in intelligence, I was familiar with all materials used in aircraft and in air travel. This was nothing like this. It could not have been."

Other portions of the newspaper story also fall apart. There are six witnesses to Mac Brazel in Roswell on July 9. Floyd Proctor said that Brazel was escorted by several military officers and that he did not acknowledge his friends. Lyman Strickland, who also saw Brazel in Roswell, said that Brazel was in the company of three military officers.[8] Frank Joyce claimed that Brazel visited him at the local radio station and told him a story that was significantly different than the one he had given on July 6. And Paul McEvoy mentioned the military officers who brought Brazel by the offices of the *Roswell Daily Record*. And both Leonard Porter and Bill Jenkins saw Brazel surrounded by military officers.[9] For a story that was unimportant, the Army went out of its way to make sure that the new "facts" were published.

There are other things about the story that are wrong. The newspaper claims that Brazel was not alone at the ranch when he found the object. According to his son, Bill, and according to the neighbors, including the Proctors, there was no one at the ranch house other than Mac Brazel. The family was living in Tularosa, New Mexico in July, 1947.

In a number of interviews, Bill Brazel said that not only was his father alone at the ranch, but when Bill read the story in an Albuquerque newspaper, he decided that someone had to go to the ranch. There was no one around it when he arrived on July 12 or 13.

Inside the story are a few clues about what the Army was trying to accomplish. On July 5, 1947, Sherman Campbell found a strange object on his farm in Circleville, Ohio. Both Campbell and the local sheriff identified it immediately and on July 6, 1947, there were pictures of Jean Campbell holding a kite-like structure printed in papers around the country. The military did not get involved in that report and in fact, the Campbells kept the balloon for years afterward. [10]

According to the *Roswell Daily Record* of July 9, Mac Brazel, accompanied by Marcel and the counter-intelligence agent, took the material to the ranch head-quarters and tried to make a kite out of it but couldn't get the pieces to fit together. In the following days, the type of balloon changed until it was finally identified as a Rawin target device. [11]

That demonstrates that the balloon explanation hadn't fully evolved at the time Brazel gave his story to the *Daily Record*. There is no reason for him, or the military officers, to try to make a kite out of it, unless they were trying to duplicate the explanation from the Circleville find.

The question that no asks about that is why both the farmer and the sheriff in Circleville could identify the balloon but the officers at Roswell were so surprised that they announced they had a flying saucer. It's not only Marcel who was fooled, but also the counter-intelligence agents, Colonel William Blanchard, and his staff. No one at Roswell was able to identify the balloon. It had to be flown to Fort Worth where a rather low ranking officer, Warrant Officer Irving Newton, announced that it was a weather balloon.

In interviews with Bill Brazel, he said that his dad would not have gone into Roswell to sell wool. The ranchers in the area sold the wool to the highest bidder, who then toured ranches shearing the sheep and gather-ing the wool himself. Brazel did not shear sheep and take the wool anywhere.

In studying the July 8 article announcing the discovery of a flying saucer, there are no facts to dispute. A rancher in the Roswell area did find something, he did tell Sheriff George A. Wilcox, who did notify authorities at the Roswell Army Air Field. The material was loaded on a plane and flown to higher headquarters just as the story claims.

With the July 9 article it seemed that nearly everything is in dispute. It appears that the July 9 report is the result of a cover story that had not yet solidified. It is filled with lies that eyewitness testimony has recently revealed. It is obvious that Mac Brazel told the July 9 story under duress while in the company of officers from the 509th Bomb Group, that he lied during the interview and that those officers knew he was lying. It was the beginning of the cover-up that lasted, almost intact, for forty years.

There are those researchers who say that Mac Brazel, with his own words, destroys the theory that he found a flying saucer. They point to the July 9 article which they had not bothered to research any further and then ignore the fact that Bill Brazel stressed his father had taken an oath that he would not reveal the details of the find.[12]

To quote one of the skeptics, ''I'll let Mac Brazel tell the story in his own words.''

''I am sure what I found was not any weather observation balloon,'' Brazel told reporters to end their new article.[13]

And there are those researchers who think Brazel was right about that. It wasn't a weather observation device. But it was something else. John Keel said he believed he had come up with an explanation for Roswell twenty years ago and recently published an article about that. In his attempt to explain Roswell with the mundane he didn't even review the current state of the investigation except to quote from *Majestic*, a work of fiction.

Keel's theory is that Mac Brazel came across a rice paper Japanese Balloon Bomb some two years after the war had ended. He concluded that the object was kept aloft by freakish winds and that government embarrassment about the Japanese project kept the officers of the 509th Bomb Group from revealing the real nature of Brazel's find. Keel suggests that Army Air Force officers at Eighth Air Force headquarters in Fort Worth substituted a weather balloon for the balloon bomb to keep the myth of American invulnerability alive.

To make his theory work, he has to accept the idea that in post-war America, there was a reason to keep this a secret. He quotes from *Japan's World War II Balloon Bomb Attacks on North America* by Robert C. Mikesh, published by the Smithsonian Institution in 1973. It was part of their multi-volume *Annals of Flight* series. In that quote, dated January 4, 1945, it explains how the Office of Censorship asked newspaper editors and radio broadcasters to give no publicity whatsoever to the balloon incidents.

That same publication also points out the reason for the request. The government feared that spies for the Japanese would read the stories and report to their headquarters that the Balloon Bombs were reaching the United States. Documents secured after the war told of Japanese plans to use biological warfare against the United States if the bombing was successful. But the Japanese abandoned the plan when they could confirm no reports of any of their balloons reaching the North American continent. They assumed, falsely, that all the Balloon Bombs had fallen harmlessly into the ocean.

The plan of censorship was abandoned in the summer of the 1945 when six (not four, as Keel writes) picnickers (not campers, as Keel claimed) were killed by a Balloon Bomb in Oregon (not Montana, as Keel suggested). According to the Reverend Archie Mitchell, he was on a picnic with his wife and several children. While he was parking the car his wife and the kids found the balloon in the woods. Tugging on it, they triggered one of the bombs, causing an explosion that killed Elsie Mitchell, Jay Gifford, Eddie Engen, Sherman Shoemaker, Joan Patzke, and Dick Patzke.[15]

These six deaths were the only casualties recorded in the continental United States resulting from enemy action during World War II. In 1949, a Senate committee approved a House bill to pay $20,000 to the families of those killed.

The deaths caused one other action. The War Department began a "whispering campaign" to alert the general public about the dangers from the Balloon Bombs. Programs were presented in schools, in public halls, and through various civilian agencies so that the public would be aware of the danger. They felt that a well planned, well coordinated, low key program could inform the public without letting the Japanese know the balloons were reaching the United States.[16]

And when the war ended, the secrecy was lifted. Grace Maurer of Laurens, Iowa, remembered the balloon bombs. She had written an article for a local newspaper telling of the discovery of a balloon bomb on February 2, 1945. Other balloons fell near Holstein and Pochahontas, Iowa, and Civil Defense Director George Buckwalter carried the debris away.

Those finds are relatively unimportant except that Maurer was visited by the FBI in February, 1945, who asked that she file her story. They explained the situation and Maurer complied, waiting until August 16, 1945, after the end of the war, to publish her article, a full account of the Japanese bombing of Iowa.

Maurer's story wasn't the only one published right after the war. The *Washington Post* on January 16, 1946 carried a report that "Nine Thousand Balloon Bombs were used against the United States." The *New York Times* of February 9, 1946 reported "Raids by Japanese Balloons."

There were also magazine articles about them. The *Engineering Journal* of September, 1945 reported on "Japanese Paper Balloons," and George E. Weider in an unclassified report for the U.S. Army wrote about "Japanese Bombing Balloons" in January, 1946.

These, plus other stories carried in local newspapers, told the public about the Balloon Bombs. The secrecy imposed was only for the time of war and did not extend beyond the signing of the Japanese surrender in 1945. After the war was won, there was no reason for secrecy, no reason to deny that the bombs had been launched and had reached the United States, and more importantly, no evidence that the topic was still classified.

Keel claimed that Mac Brazel found a pile of rice paper in his field, which was in keeping with his Balloon Bomb theory and that "the myth goes marching on." But Keel never bothers with descriptions of the crash site. He dismisses the testimony of more than a half dozen witnesses who said the debris was scattered over a wide area. That was too much debris for one of the Japanese Balloon Bombs, which were about thirty feet in diameter. In fact, in the very beginning of Mikesh's Japanese Balloon Bomb report there is a picture of about a dozen military and government officials inspecting one of the balloons. It did not come apart, it did not scatter debris over a large area, and it is easily identifiable as a balloon.

Marcel said in many recorded interviews that they had tried to burn some of the material found on the ranch but could not. Rice paper would have burned easily. They tried to dent some of the larger pieces with a sixteen pound sledgehammer and could not. Rice paper would have torn and if the material was some of the rubberized stuff used on a few of the balloons, it certainly would have shown the effects of the hammer.

Marcel had no idea what the material was and loaded as much as he could into the back of his Buick. A counter-intelligence agent with him filled the jeep carryall and they drove the wreckage to the Roswell Army Air Field.

Bill Brazel later reported that he had found some additional pieces that the military had failed to pick up. He described a slender strand that he called monofilament fishing line but that sounded suspiciously like fiber optics. He also had a small piece that he tried to whittle with his Buck Knife (which he had used in the past to cut barbed wire) but that would not cut. And finally Brazel described the lead-foil-like material that when wadded into a ball would unfold itself with no sign of a crease.

As mentioned earlier, Pappy Henderson said that he had flown some of the wreckage from Roswell to Wright Field. He described it as something he had never seen before: dull colored metal that was very thin and very lightweight. Certainly not the remains of a paper and rubber balloon launched by the Japanese during the war.

It is interesting that in Keel's list of articles about the Balloon Bombs there is nothing earlier than 1953. In addition to the newspaper and journal articles mentioned earlier (selected only because they pre-dated the July, 1947 find by Brazel), there is a *Reader's Digest* article from August, 1950, and an article by Dr. Lincoln LaPaz from *Collier's* on January 17, 1953. There are also unpublished histories of several military units from 1945, 1946, and 1947 that make reference to the Balloon Bombs.

In 1947, there was no reason for secrecy if what was found was in fact of Japanese manufacture. The story of the Balloon Bombs had already been released. Stories had appeared in major newspapers throughout the country and in many of the smaller, local papers. The Balloon Bombs were no longer a secret.

But even when one Axis Power weapon was proven not to be the culprit, another came along. Ron Schaffner now suggests that it was nothing more extraordinary than the nose cone and parachute from a stray V-2 launched from White Sands. That launch, for security reasons, was classified and when the missile went astray, the military failed to declassify records of it. According to Schaffner, they were protecting their jobs.

Unfortunately Schaffner, along with most of the others with a theory about Roswell, has done no firsthand research. He quickly dismisses as hearsay the reports of the men who were there. He ignores Stringfield, implies that the dead aliens might be the burned results of failed V-2 experiments, and suggests that Marcel might not have been fully aware of all the facts about the find.

Schaffner does make a good case for the reasons the government, the military, or the range officers and scientists at White Sands might have wanted to cover up an errant rocket. If, as he says, there was an ordered suspension of firings, and a rocket was fired in violation of those orders only to fall onto range land in central New Mexico, the men involved would certainly want that information kept secret. Schaffner points out that a V-2 was tested on July 3, 1947, and if there was a mistake by a few of the witnesses about the date, the V-2 might account for the debris found by Mac Brazel on the afternoon of July 3.

Except there is much more to the story. The descriptions of the material recovered, the scene on the crash site, and the crude experiments performed by the Army have all been recounted. When all the facts are brought into play, the area for speculation shrinks to non-existence.

The facts alone, based on the direct testimony of the participants, suggests that Schaffner's theory is incorrect. While it is certainly possible that Marcel, even as the head of the intelligence section of the 509th Bomb Group, might not have known about the experiments with the V-2, he certainly would have been able to identify the components as being of terrestrial manufacture.

And even if Marcel had somehow been fooled, would the other officers of the 509th Bomb Group, including the commander, been unable to identify the foil and capsule as being something made on Earth? The important point is that they don't have to know it came from a V-2, only that it was made of materials like those manufactured elsewhere on the planet.

Marcel said that he had found some metal that was as thin as newsprint but that could not be dented with a sixteen pound sledgehammer. He said that they had tried to burn it, and that they had tried to cut it, and that they had failed. What could a V-2 have contained that had those extraordinary properties?

The second question is whether or not the V-2 would have spread debris over an area that was more than one million square feet in size. Mac Brazel was furious when he saw it because the sheep on the ranch would not cross the field.[17]

There are other hints about the amount of debris. Marcel said that he filled the back of his Buick with it, the counter-intelligence agent filled a jeep carryall, and there was still a great deal of it left.

And finally, there is the credibility of Barney Barnett, among others. If he was the only witness to the bodies, then his story would be suspect. But now there are others who have come forward telling what they had seen. Melvin Brown, a member of Squadron K of the 509th Bomb Group, told his family that he guarded the bodies as they were driven from the crash site to the Roswell Army Air Field.[18] There is testimony from one of the crewmen who flew the bodies from Roswell to Fort Worth.

All this proves that it was not a V-2 that crashed on the ranch managed by Mac Brazel. The descriptions of the material, the size of the debris field, and the testimony of more than two hundred others involved in this show that it was something extraordinary. While it is true that men would try to protect their careers after an errant V-2 crashed, it is not true that the cover-up would extend for over forty years. At some point the men interested in protecting their careers would be transferred or retired and that information would have leaked out. There are no classified records involving a V-2 launch on July 3. In fact, the July 3 launch attempt has been accounted for. The rocket never got off the pad.

These are three of the theories offered to explain Roswell. Others have suggested that it was an experimental aircraft, but there are no records of an experimental crash in the Roswell area in July, 1947.

Marcel said, "This was not from this Earth. That I'm quite sure of."

With that, Marcel dismissed the mundane and left us with only the extraordinary. If he had been the only one with that claim, he might have been ignored. But there are so many others. Too many to be ignored.

Part IV:

The Time Line

July, 1947:
The Sequence of Events

Wednesday, July 2, 1947

9:50 P.M. Mr. and Mrs. Dan Wilmot reported an oval-shaped object, "like two invert saucers faced mouth-to-mouth," moving at a high rate of speed, flew over their house in Roswell, New Mexico. The object was heading to the northwest.

During a thunderstorm in the Corona, New Mexico area, W.W. (Mac) Brazel heard a tremendous thunderclap that sounded like an explosion but that was somehow different than the rest of the thunder. Others in the area reported the same phenomenon.

William Woody reported that he and his father watched a bright meteor, described as white with a red tail streak across the sky, falling to the horizon.

Thursday, July 3, 1947

Because of the rain the night before, Brazel was inspecting the pastures. July and August are the rainy months and Brazel planned to move the livestock onto the fields that had received the rain. During the inspection he discovered a large debris field. Scattered on the slopes and into the sinkholes and depressions was metal, plastic-like beams, pieces of lightweight material, foil, and string. The debris was thick enough that the sheep refused to cross the field and had to be driven around it to water more than a mile away.

Brazel, taking a few scraps of the material, headed to the home of his closest neighbors, Floyd and Loretta Proctor. He showed them "a little sliver" of material that refused to burn and that couldn't be cut. The Proctors suggested that he take it into town to show the sheriff. Loretta Proctor also remembered the rewards being offered for proof of the flying disc's reality and thought that Mac should try to claim the money.

Later that evening, Brazel removed the large circular piece of the debris from the range. According to Bill Brazel, his father either loaded it into the back of his truck or dragged it along behind. He stored it in a livestock shed about three miles north of the crash site.

Saturday, July 5, 1947

Military bases along the west coast had fighters on standby in case the flying discs were seen. A few of the bases in Oregon and Washington had planes equipped with gun cameras on airborne alert.

Sherman Campbell of Circleville, Ohio reported to the sheriff that he thought he had an explanation for some of the flying disc sightings. He'd found a weather balloon on his farm. It was metallic, with a kite-like appendage on it. Under the right conditions, as it drifted on the upper atmosphere winds, it could look like a flying disc. The device was on display at the local newspaper office and then returned to Campbell. Jean (Campbell) Romero, Campbell's daughter, reported that it had been kept in the barn for years afterward.

Sunday, July 6, 1947

Brazel got up early, as was his habit according to Norris Proctor, completed his chores, and then drove into Roswell, about seventy-five miles away. He stopped at the office of Sheriff George A. Wilcox. Contrary to published reports, Wilcox was excited about the find and suggested they call the military.

While they were waiting for the military officers to arrive, Wilcox dispatched two deputies to the ranch. They had only the directions given by Brazel but both men were familiar with the territory and Wilcox thought they'd be able to find the debris field that Brazel described.

Frank Joyce, a reporter and announcer for radio station KGFL, said that he called the sheriff and asked if there was anything interesting happening at the office. According to Joyce, Wilcox told him that there was someone there that he should interview. Joyce talked to Brazel, but said that he didn't pay much attention to what Brazel was saying. He was busy trying to run the station, get the records changed, and listen to the story that Brazel was telling.

Colonel William Blanchard (commander of the 509th Bomb Group), Major Jesse A. Marcel (the air intelligence officer), and a man in civilian clothes (a counter-intelligence agent) responded to the sheriffs' call. According to Phyllis McGuire, daughter of the sheriff, the military arrived almost as soon as the sheriff had hung up the phone. The officers interviewed Brazel, examined some pieces of the material, and then Blanchard ordered Marcel and the CIC man to accompany Brazel to the ranch.

Blanchard, sure that he was in possession of something unusual, alerted the next higher headquarters. According to Blanchard's first wife, Ethyl, he thought that they might have found something that belonged to the Soviets. No one mentioned any type of balloon.

Blanchard, acting on orders from General Clements McMullen, passed to him by Colonel Thomas DuBose, sealed in a bag some of the material Brazel had brought to the sheriff's office. The material was then flown on to the Fort Worth Army Air Field.

After the military officers left along with Brazel, the two deputies returned. They hadn't found the debris field but they did find a burned area in one of the pastures. The sand had been turned to glass and blackened. It looked as if something circular had touched down.

The aircraft from Roswell was met at the Fort Worth Army Air Field by DuBose and Colonel Alan D. Clark. Clark received the plastic bag with the debris and walked to the "command" B-26 to fly it on to Washington, D.C. and General McMullen.

Because it was so far out to the ranch over roads that were less than adequate, Brazel, Marcel, and the CIC agent didn't arrive until after dark. They stayed at the ranch house, ate cold beans and crackers, and waited for daylight. Marcel used a Geiger counter on the large piece of wreckage that Brazel had stored in the cattle shed. He detected no sign of radiation.

Monday, July 7, 1947

Brazel took the two military officers out to the crash site. According to Marcel, the debris field was three-quarters of a mile long and two to three hundred feet wide. There was a gouge starting at the northern end of it that extended for four or five hundred feet toward the other end. Bill Brazel said that it looked as if something had touched down and skipped along. The largest piece of debris was found at the southern edge of the gouge.

Marcel described the debris as being as thin as newsprint but so strong he couldn't bend it. There was foil that when crumbled would unfold itself without a sign of a wrinkle. And there were I-beams that would flex slightly and that had some sort of writing or symbols on them. The descriptions of the debris were confirmed by Bill Brazel, Loretta Proctor, Tommy Tyree, Walt Whitmore, Sr., Jesse Marcel, Jr., Mrs. Viaud Marcel, Robert Shirkey, Robert Smith, O.W. Henderson, and Lewis S. Rickett.

Marcel and the CIC agent walked the perimeter of the field and then ranged out looking for more debris or another crash site but found nothing. Finally, they returned and spent the remainder of the day collecting the debris they could. They loaded the rear of Marcel's '42 Buick and then the jeep carryall driven by the CIC man. About dusk they left the debris field for Roswell.

Lieutenant General Nathan F. Twining, the commander of the Air Materiel Command, the parent organization at Wright Field, Ohio, changed his plans suddenly and flew into the Alamogordo Army Air Field, (later Holloman Air Force Base) New Mexico. Twining was just a short drive from the Roswell Army Air Field.

Tuesday, July 8, 1947

2:00 A.M. Marcel, excited by the find, stopped at his house on the way to the base. He awakened his wife and son to show them the material. They spent an hour examining it, scattered on the kitchen floor. Marcel was not breaking regulations since nothing he brought in had yet been classified. Marcel then collected it all, loaded it into the car, and drove to the base.

* * *

6:00 A.M. Marcel and the CIC agent visited with Blanchard in his quarters, telling him what they've seen. In later years, Marcel would insist that they knew the moment they saw the debris field that the crash was of something that had not been manufactured on Earth.

Blanchard called the Provost Marshal, identified in the 509th Unit History as Major Edwin Easley. Blanchard ordered Easley to post guards on the roads around the crash site, denying access to anyone without official business. He ordered Easley to find Brazel and have him escort the MPs to the crash site.

Blanchard also called Eighth Air Force Headquarters and advised them that Marcel had returned with more of the debris. By this time Blanchard and Marcel knew that it was not a Russian device.

Eighth Air Force Headquarters in Fort Worth relayed Blanchard's message up the chain of command, alerting the Pentagon about the strange material. A special flight from Andrews was arranged for men coming from the Pentagon.

7:30 A.M. The regular morning staff meeting had been moved up. Blanchard discussed what they had found and what they should do about it. Attending that meeting were Marcel, the CIC man, Lewis S. Rickett, Lieutenant Colonel James I. Hopkins, the Operations Officer; Major Patrick Saunders, the Base Adjutant; Major Isidore Brown, the Personnel Officer; and Lieutenant Colonel Ulysses S. Nero; the Supply Officer. There is reason to believe that Lieutenant Colonel Charles W. Horton, Lieutenant Colonel Fernand L. Andry, and Lt. Walter Haut, the PIO, were also in attendance. During the meeting they decided how to handle the retrieval and who would be accomplishing which tasks.

9:00 A.M. The CIC agent and his assistant drew a staff car and drove to the crash site. Following them was another contingent of MPs. They were stopped by the guards that had been posted earlier. When they arrived, they saw that MPs had already been stationed around the debris field to protect it.

Blanchard and members of his staff were on the phones conferring with higher headquarters. Marcel and some of the wreckage were ordered to Fort Worth so that Brigadier General Roger Ramey could inspect it.

11:00 A.M. Walter Haut finished the press release and was preparing to take it into town. The first paragraph, said, ''The many rumors regarding the flying disc became a reality yesterday . . .'' He took it first to one of the radio stations. By noon he had given a copy of the release to both radio stations and to both daily newspapers.

The CIC men at the ranch checked the ground again. The guards were posted around the gouge, around the debris field, and finally on the hills surrounding the area. The CIC men located Mac Brazel and took him back to Roswell.

12:00 P.M. Every point of contact in Roswell reported that they were swamped by calls. Sheriff Wilcox reported calls from Europe and Asia. Art McQuiddy, editor of the *Roswell Morning Dispatch* said that from the moment the press release hit the wire, he was on the phone. Walter Haut said the same thing. The world was trying to learn what happened in Roswell.

The first of the special flights from Washington arrived. On the plane was Warrant Officer Robert Thomas. Thomas and the men were in uniform upon arrival, but quickly changed to civilian clothes. These men would remain at Roswell throughout the retrieval.

* * *

The phones at the base had started to ring. Blanchard, irritated because he couldn't get a phone line, ordered Haut to do something about all the incoming calls. Haut said there was nothing he could do about the incoming calls.

Sheriff Wilcox, wondering what happened out at the crash site, sent two more deputies out. This time they ran into the cordon thrown up by the Army and were turned back. The Army was letting no unauthorized personnel onto the crash site.

Mid-afternoon Brazel was flown back toward the ranch. His was not the first flight back as the 509th tried to find the flight crew of the craft. They were all sure that there had to be one.

The second crash site was located and men on the ground were directed toward it. Brazel, because he knew the land well, was helping to direct them in toward the second site.

Before the Army could arrive, others in the area stumbled onto the second site. Grady L. "Barney" Barnett was surveying the ranches for the suitability of irrigation. According to Vern Maltais, a close friend, Barnett found the remains of the disc. Maltais never asked about the craft because Barnett told him about the occupants: small men, four or five feet tall, thin, with big heads. They were lying outside the craft.

While Barnett was standing there, close enough to touch the bodies, a group of students and archaeologists arrived. They, too, saw the bodies and the strange craft.

The Army arrived at the second crash site and was horrified to find civilians there already. The civilians were rounded up and told that they had stumbled upon something that had national security aspects. They were never to mention what they had seen. The officer in charge told them that the government would be able to find them if they talked. They were escorted off the site as the Army moved in and began to cover the bodies.

Robert Shirkey, standing in the Operations building, watched as MPs began carrying wreckage through to load onto a C-54 of the First Air Transport Unit. To see better, he had to step around Colonel Blanchard.

Pappy Henderson (Captain O.W. Henderson) then took the material to Wright Field in Ohio. He had a chance to see some of the material and described it as something very strange and like nothing he'd ever seen.

2:30 P.M. Blanchard decided that it was time to go on leave. There were too many phone calls into the base asking to speak to him. He, along with a few members of the staff, drove out to the crash site. Those left at the base are told to inform the reporters that the Colonel was now on leave.

3:00 P.M. Marcel who had been told that he was going to Fort Worth with the wreckage, took off for the Fort Worth Army Air Field.

According to Sergeant Robert Porter (one of the flight crew), there were only a few packages loaded onto the plane. One, a triangular package about two feet long, was wrapped in brown paper. The other three were about shoe-box-sized and also wrapped. Porter said that it seemed that there was nothing in them.

Johnny McBoyle, a reporter for radio station KSWS in Roswell, tried to reach the crash site. According to Merle Tucker and Lydia Sleppy, who worked at the parent station in Albuquerque, McBoyle mentioned an object that looked like a crushed dishpan and then told her to hang on. There was an argument with someone close and then McBoyle told her to never mind. He had made a mistake.

Moments later, as she was trying to get something out over the teletype, it began to type out an incoming message from the FBI. She was ordered not to complete the transmission because the item is of national security interest.

Marcel was in Ramey's office with some of the debris. The general wanted to see where it had been found, and Marcel was taken to a map room. Once Ramey was satisfied, they walked back to the office, but the debris was gone. In its place was a weather balloon that had been ripped apart.

Late afternoon Brazel was back in Roswell, having helped find the second crash site. Now the military dropped the ball. No one told him to stay close, so Brazel left. Walt Whitmore found him in Roswell and took him to the radio station, KGFL. Whitmore and another reporter interviewed Brazel using the wire recorder. On it, Brazel told them the whole story. Whitmore then took Brazel to his house to keep him out of the hands of the military.

In Fort Worth, reporter J. Bond Johnson of the *Fort Worth Star-Telegram* was told to drive to the base. His editor said that they had a flying saucer coming in from Roswell and he wanted Johnson out there to cover the story.

Johnson arrived at the Fort Worth air base and was told to head straight up to Ramey's office for the interview. On the floor were the remains of a weather balloon. Part of the rubber in it had burned and Johnson was surprised that Ramey would keep it in his office. Johnson took four pictures of Ramey and the wreckage and then headed back to his office.

* * *

More people arrived at the crash site and they were cleaning it up. Men with wheelbarrows were moving across the field, throwing the debris in. When filled, they took the debris to collection points. The debris was then loaded into covered trucks to be driven into Roswell.

Warrant Officer Irving Newton was ordered from the weather station to Ramey's office. Newton, in front of a small number of reporters and officers of the Eighth Air Force, identified the wreckage on the office floor as a Rawn target balloon. He was photographed and then sent back to his regular duties.

Ramey, with the identity of the wreckage established, announced to the world that the officers at Roswell were fooled by a weather balloon. Ramey also appeared on local radio station WBAP.

Blanchard and members of his staff arrived at the ranch and were taken to the second crash site where the bodies were located. The bodies were loaded into the back of a truck and then covered by a tarp.

In Roswell, the base hospital began to call a local mortuary, asking questions about the preservation of tissue and what specific chemicals would do to the tissue. The mortician, Glenn Dennis, reported he received four or five such phone calls about it and decided there had been a fatal crash at the base.

Lewis S. Rickett said an unscheduled flight from Bolling Field (Washington, D.C.) arrived. He gave the crew a sealed box with wreckage in it.

Melvin E. Brown, a member of Squadron K, 509th Bomb Group, was told to climb into the back of a truck at the second crash site. He was told not to look under the tarp but the moment everyone's back was turned, he did. Under the tarp were the bodies of the alien flight crew. Brown said that they were small, with large heads, and that he thought the skin was yellow or orange.

The bodies arrived at the base and were taken to the hospital for examination. Dr. Jesse Johnson pronounced them dead and did the preliminary work on them.

The mortician, Glenn Dennis, still believing there had been a fatal crash on the base, drove out. The MP on the gate, recognizing him, waved him through and he drove to the hospital. There, he entered and was met by an Army nurse. She told him to get out before he got himself into trouble. Two MPs spotted him and bodily threw him out of the hospital.

A guard at the gate reported that a truck carrying dry ice entered late in the evening. He was surprised by the late hour of the delivery. A check of the local ice house revealed no records available for the 1940s.

The bodies were sealed into a long crate, fifteen feet by three feet by four feet, and the crate was moved to a hangar. It was left there, with spotlights playing on it while MPs stood guard. They never approached it.

Brown was given the task of guarding the outside of the hangar. Brown's commanding officer approached and said, "Come on, Brownie, let's have a look inside." But there was nothing to see then because everything had been packed and crated and was ready for shipment out of there.

Wednesday, July 9, 1947

Morning newspapers were carrying the story that the flying saucer found in Roswell was a weather device. Some quoted Ramey while others quoted sources, including senators, in Washington.

Brazel was still in Roswell, but still in the company of Walt Whitmore, Sr. Whitmore was trying to protect his exclusive interview with Brazel.

Cleanup at the ranch resumed with sun up. The military was trying to get everything picked up before any more civilians stumbled across it.

Robert Smith of the First Air Transport Unit, said that they began loading crates into C-54s about eight o'clock in the morning. The problem wasn't the weight, but the size of the crates. They felt as if they were empty. They loaded three aircraft, all destined to Kirtland and then on to Los Alamos.

According to Roswell Army Air Field head secretary Elizabeth Kyle, the telephones at the base were still tied up by the incoming calls from around the world.

The military found Brazel again and this time took steps to ensure that he didn't get away from them. They interrogated him at the base, asking him the same questions over and over.

More of the wreckage was brought into the base and was now being taken to a different location where it was boxed into crates of various sizes and shapes. The crates were built at Roswell and conformed to the standards used to ship other cargo.

Bud Payne, a rancher in the Corona area, was chasing a stray cow. As he crossed onto the Foster ranch, a jeep carrying soldiers roared over a ridgeline, bearing down on him. He was carried from the Foster ranch.

* * *

Brazel was taken into town, into the offices of the *Roswell Daily Record*. There he gave reporters, including Jason Kellahin and R.A. Adair from Albuquerque, a new story. He told them that he'd found the balloon on June 14 and hadn't taken it into Roswell until three weeks later because he had no phone and no radio and didn't know the world was looking for flying discs. Brazel in that article, however, said that he had found weather balloons on other occasions and what he'd found this time was no weather balloon.

Ramey's weather officer, Newton, claimed that the weather balloon was a special kind and said, "We use them because they go much higher than the eye can see."

Floyd Proctor and Lyman Strickland were in Roswell and saw Mac Brazel. He was being escorted around by three military men. He ignored both Proctor and Strickland, something that he wouldn't normally have done.

Whitmore, at radio station KGFL, got a phone call from Washington telling him not to air the interview with Brazel. According to Jud Roberts, "If we played the interview, we could expect to lose our license the next day."

According to Art McQuiddy, an officer from the base swept through Roswell picking up copies of Haut's press release. Frank Joyce confirmed it, saying that someone had searched the offices of KGFL. The military searched all the radio stations and the newspapers, taking anything that related to the story.

At noon, the crate that had been sitting in the empty hangar guarded by the MPs was moved out to bomb pit number one. According to the men who were there, nothing other than weapons was ever stored in the bomb pit.

* * *

Late in the afternoon, a flight crew at the skeet range was told they had a special flight coming up. The squadron operations officer, Major Edgar Skelley, told the aircraft commander to keep everyone together.

Three C-54s from the First Air Transport Unit took off on short flights to Los Alamos. All three aircraft were loaded with crates holding the wreckage and all the crates were marked with stencils saying, "Top Secret." Armed guards watched the loading of the aircraft. Smith was sure the crates held debris because he was shown a small piece of the foil that could be wadded and then would straighten itself out.

The flight crew pulled from the skeet range was told to quickly preflight their aircraft. Once that was done and they had the engines running, they taxied out to the bomb pit. According to one of the crewmen on that flight, the only places on the base where the bomb pit could be observed were the tower and portions of the flightline.

A sealed, wooden, unmarked crate was brought out and loaded into the bomb bay of B-29 tail number 7301. It was guarded by six MPs, an officer, two NCOs, and three enlisted men, all armed. They never let the crate out of their sight.

At Fort Worth, the aircraft was met by a number of officers, including a mortician. The bombardier recognized the man because he had gone to school with him.

The crate was unloaded and the flight crew was told to head back to Roswell. There was no debriefing given to them at Fort Worth.

According to one of the crewmen, and confirmed by Robert Slusher, Marcel returned with them on that flight. He was in Fort Worth for about twenty-four hours, and that had kept him out of the reporters' line of fire until the cover story could be put into place.

* * *

Frank Joyce reported that officers brought Mac Brazel to radio station KGFL to be interviewed. This time Brazel had a new story, one that was significantly different than the one he'd told on Sunday. Joyce pointed that out and Brazel responded that it would go hard on him if he didn't tell the new story.

By 8:00 P.M., the flight crew was back. Again, they were not debriefed but were told that they had flown the general's furniture to Fort Worth. They were cautioned not to tell anyone what they had done, including their families. The flight had not taken place.

Upon his return, Marcel headed to the CIC office and confronted the officer there. Marcel wanted to see the reports that had been filed in his absence, but the CIC officer refused. Marcel pointed out that he was the senior officer but the CIC agent claimed his orders were from Washington. "Take it up with them."

John Tiffany, Sr., a crew chief assigned to Wright Field, flew on a special mission to the south. They picked up debris that none of them could identify, and a huge, Thermos-like jug. Tiffany told family members about the bodies, his descriptions matching those of the other witnesses.

The *Las Vegas Review Journal* carried a story quoting a UP (United Press) report that said, "Reports of flying saucers whizzing through the sky fell off sharply today as the army and navy began a concentrated campaign to stop the rumors." The story also said that AAF Headquarters in Washington "delivered a blistering rebuke to officers at Roswell." That same article was printed in other newspapers around the country.

Thursday, July 10, 1947

Bill Brazel, reading the morning paper, learned about his father's activities at Roswell. He realized that no one would be at the ranch and made plans to get down there to help.

At both crash sites, the men were working to get everything cleaned up. They wanted no bit of wreckage left and no signs that they were there.

Mac Brazel was being held in the guest house on the base. The officers there were still trying to convince him that he was not to say anything about what he'd seen. They were also trying to keep him out of the way of reporters still searching for a story. He was given a physical by doctors at the base hospital.

There were rumors flying around Roswell about the event. People began to hear that there were bodies and there was even talk that one of them was alive when the military got there. (That has yet to be confirmed.)

Major W.D. Prichard from Alamogordo claimed that there had been a unit from his base in Roswell launching balloons around June 14. That was undoubtedly what Brazel found.

Friday, July 11, 1947

The debriefings of all the participants was underway. According to Frank Kaufman, they were taken into a room in small groups and told that the recovery was a highly classified event. No one was to talk about it to anyone. They were to forget that it ever happened.

Saturday, July 12, 1947

Bill Brazel and his wife, Shirley, arrived at the ranch but there was no one around. Brazel began to work, first surveying the ranch to see what needed to be done. He saw no evidence that the military was still around. The trucks, people, and the cordon were gone.

On this weekend, there were no aircraft with gun cameras searching for flying discs. There were no aircraft on standby waiting for orders to take off. In fact, there were reports that an order went out grounding all aircraft to keep them out of the sky and the search.

Tuesday, July 15, 1947

Bill Brazel reported that his dad returned from Roswell. He would not say much, except that they kept asking him the same questions over and over again, and to say that Bill Brazel was better off not knowing what had happened. Besides, Mac Brazel took an oath that said he would never reveal, in detail, what he had seen. By now most of the world had forgotten that a flying saucer had been reported to have crashed in New Mexico.

Late July, 1947

Mac Brazel visited the Lyman Stricklands and told them what had gone on in Roswell. Marian Strickland said that Mac was upset over being in jail and the shabby way he had been treated by the military. He sat in the kitchen, at the table, drinking coffee as he complained about the military. He would say nothing about what he'd found, other than he'd been sworn to secrecy.

August, 1947

Mac Brazel and ranch hand Tommy Tyree spotted a piece of wreckage floating in the water at the bottom of a sinkhole. Neither man bothered to climb down to retrieve it.

September, 1947

Lewis S. Rickett was assigned to assist Doctor Lincoln LaPaz from the University of New Mexico. LaPaz's three week assignment was to determine, if possible, the speed and trajectory of the craft when it hit. According to Rickett, they discovered a touchdown point five miles from the debris field where the sand was crystallized, apparently from the heat, and they discovered more of the foil-like material. Given all that, LaPaz, not knowing that bodies had been recovered, was convinced that it had been an unoccupied probe from another planet.

September, 1948

Lewis S. Rickett, while in Albuquerque, met with Lincoln LaPaz. According to Rickett, LaPaz told him that he, LaPaz, was still convinced what they had found was an unoccupied probe from another planet. In the year that had passed, LaPaz, in his secret dealings with various government projects, had found nothing to cause him to change his mind.

October, 1948

Lewis S. Rickett met with John Wirth, another CIC man. Rickett asked Wirth about the status of the material recovered at Roswell and was told that they had yet to figure it out. According to Wirth, they hadn't been able to cut it.

Summer, 1949

Bill Brazel, in the two years following the crash, found ''scraps'' of the craft. His dad confirmed it, saying, ''That looks like some of the contraption I found.'' Brazel, in Corona, mentioned that he had found some of the pieces. According to him, the next day Captain Armstrong and three others from the Roswell base arrived and asked for the material. Armstrong reminded Brazel that his dad had cooperated with them. It was Brazel's patriotic duty to give it up. Brazel couldn't think of a good reason to deny it to them and surrendered it.

1961

UPI stringer Jay West reported that he was working in Alamogordo, in the area of the White Sands Proving Ground, when he became friendly with the base public information officer. The PIO had found a file that mentioned the Roswell crash that included a map. The PIO got a topographical map of the crash site. According to West, they made trips out to try to locate the crash. West described the map as showing the debris field and then, two and a half miles to the east, a second crash site.

1978

Pappy Henderson confided in his close friend, John Kromschroeder, that he flew wreckage from a crashed saucer from Roswell, New Mexico to Dayton, Ohio. He showed Kromschroeder a fragment of the debris and told his friend that he'd seen the bodies.

Jesse Marcel was located by researcher Stan Friedman. Marcel told Friedman that he was sure that the debris was nothing from Earth. Later, Marcel granted interviews to various news organizations, but those reports did not gain wide dissemination.

May, 1979

Bob Pratt interviewed Jesse Marcel and published an article in which Marcel "admitted that he was the intelligence officer who had recovered the parts of a flying saucer."

1980

In Search Of aired a program about UFO cover-ups and interviewed Marcel. In the course of that interview, Marcel again said that whatever was found, he was sure that it was nothing from Earth.

January, 1980

Len Stringfield published the second of his status reports on crash retrievals. Included in it was a report from Major Jesse A. Marcel, telling of his experiences on the debris field in July, 1947.

September, 1980

Charles Berlitz and William L. Moore publish *The Roswell Incident,* the first attempt at a comprehensive analysis of the event at Roswell. In the course of the research, Moore and Stanton Friedman located more than sixty witnesses who had some knowledge of the event.

1982

After reading a story about the events at Roswell in a tabloid newspaper, Pappy Henderson told his wife about his role. He told her that everything in the story was true, which surprised him. He hadn't expected them to get the facts right, and that included the descriptions of the bodies.

October, 1988

Jim Parker reported that his son had seen a strange pickup truck on the ranch. Parker chased it down and discovered two men sitting in a U.S. Air Force pick up with a camper on the back. There were maps of the local area in it. He described the men as in their late twenties or early thirties and thought they were both low ranking. They claimed they were surveying the area to put in a

radar site to monitor low flying aircraft, but then asked
if Parker knew about the Roswell crash, mentioning that
the crash site was somewhere close. Parker had never
heard of it and didn't know what they were talking about.
The men left the ranch then. No one from the Air Force
had asked permission to enter the ranch from the ranch
owners, and no one had checked with the Bureau of Land
Management about the availability of property in the
area.

September, 1989

The CUFOS scientific expedition to the Roswell crash
site was made. This was only the preliminary investigation that discovered nothing new. Weeks after they were
gone, the ranch foreman reported that someone had been
out there driving all over the site where the expedition
had been searching.

June, 1991

Avon Books released a detailed account of the Roswell
crash with the supporting testimony of more than two
hundred witnesses.

1991: Conclusions

If the crash and retrieval of a UFO in New Mexico in 1947 actually happened, shouldn't there be other reliable reports from other reliable sources since then? The answer is yes, if the statement is true. There should be many good, reliable reports from solid citizens, from men and women whose credentials are impeccable. Men and women who have nothing to gain by claiming they saw a flying saucer. And some of those sightings should have been made by highly respected sources.

General Michael Rexrold said that he viewed Chester Lytle as one of the great, unsung heroes of this country. Lytle was a key player in the Manhattan Project and developed the radio commands that detonated the first atomic bomb dropped on Japan.

In the years that followed, Lytle served in government, designing and engineering communication systems for the old Atomic Energy Commission. The military called on him many times for secret projects at different bases across the country.

Lytle is, therefore, one of those impeccable sources. Lytle said that while he was on assignment at Wright-Patterson Air Force Base in the late 1950s, the base suddenly went on alert. Lytle and a number of officers were escorted to a special radio room in the operations building. Inside, while the military personnel worked, Lytle watched an intercept by jet fighters, on a small television monitor.

According to Lytle, one of the jet interceptors was equipped with a television camera in the gun camera position. He was transmitting the intercept to the operations radio room. In the clear daylight, Lytle watched a smooth, metallic disc play cat and mouse with the lead fighter. For a moment, Lytle thought he had to be watching some kind of science fiction movie, but there was no doubt that the intercept was real. Everyone around him acted as if the event was routine. Then, suddenly, the UFO disappeared, leaving the interceptors far behind it.

Afterward, Lytle was told by the base commander that this type of activity was a regular event, not only at Wright-Patterson, but at other Air Force bases as well. In fact, over the years, Lytle had heard numerous, similar accounts from both military officers and governmental officials.

Today, Lytle, who is the president of a telecommunications company, is adamant about what he knows to be the truth. What he witnessed defied all conventional explanation. He faces the same problem that researchers face—lack of physical evidence. While it is true that all efforts by civilian researchers have yielded no tangible proof, it is also true that Roswell demonstrates that the "nuts and bolts" evidence does exist. For the first time the "smoking gun" has been found. It has been documented.

With the Roswell case, the enigma of UFOs is no longer spurious or abstruse. Answers, though known only by a select few, are still being withheld. However, we can now, in total confidence and conviction, direct the public to the undeniable source of the proof: proof which would enable us to finally lift the veil of secrecy that surrounds Roswell. Put aside all political agenda, all preconceived opinions, all bias, and consider the following.

• If the debris originated from a top secret test, why was there no recovery or search operation under way until Brazel reported the debris to Sheriff Wilcox four days after the find? Aerial search over open range and high desert would have taken a few hours to locate any downed object. This has been confirmed by retired military officers, who were involved in actual search and rescue missions in New Mexico. We have flown a private plane over the crash area. Given that the debris field was three-quarters of a mile long, a search and recovery team would have located it easily long before Brazel did.

• Weather balloons had fallen onto Brazel's ranch on a number of occasions, and he turned them in for the rewards offered. This time, however, he was angry because of the amount of debris. His sheep would not cross the pasture because of the material. It is interesting to note that weather balloons are still dropping on the ranch. The current owners store them in an old silo. One large balloon, about twenty feet in diameter, took one man two minutes to retrieve.

• After examining samples of the material, why did Brazel's neighbors encourage him to report the crash as physical evidence of a flying disc and not for the five dollar balloon reward?

• How did highly trained and experienced military officers, the elite in their fields, mistake a conventional weather instrument for an object they all, without exception, concluded to be an actual flying disc? Those who believe that it was a special radar reflecting balloon have said that the men, Blanchard, Marcel, and the CIC man, were not familiar with the specialized equipment. Marcel, who, had a radar interpretation officer assigned to his office, was himself trained in radar operations. He would have been able to recognize the balloon, even if the others were fooled.

• What type of balloon could scatter debris over an area three-quarters of a mile long and could make a 150-yard gouge in the tough New Mexican soil?

• What type of balloon would fill a the trunk of Marcel's car, a jeep carryall box, and then require fifty to sixty troops two days to complete the cleanup?

• Why did the military check the site for possible radiation if the downed object was nothing more than a common weather balloon?

• On the morning of July 8, Brazel was picked up at his ranch house by CIC agents and taken back to Roswell. Why was Brazel flown over the ranch on that afternoon? And why were there at least three other flights over the area? Aerial reconnaissance? Aerial photography? What else were they searching for? A CIC officer from Washington, D.C., named Thomas, told Frank Kaufman at the Roswell base that same afternoon, "We don't know if there are bodies, but we're looking for them."

• After his flight over the ranch, why was Brazel held in detention at the base for another seven to eight days? According to Brazel, he was not allowed to place any outside calls, not even to his wife. He was also given a physical examination. His family and neighbors remember that he later complained how he had been asked the same questions over and over, and that he described the experience by saying he "was in jail."

• Why the need for extreme security measures at the crash site of a downed meteorological instrument? There were measures such as: armed guards surrounding the inner gouge area, another cordon around the perimeter, riflemen posted on the surrounding hills, and MPs stationed on the outlying roads.

• Why was Bud Payne, a hired hand at one of the neighboring ranches, bodily removed from the Brazel ranch during the military occupation of the site? As Payne was attempting to round up a stray cow, a military jeep roared up to him and an MP physically forced him off the ranch.

• Why were there eight (possibly nine) confirmed flights to transport the remains of a balloon? Most of the wreckage was flown out under high security. Rather extreme treatment even within the confines of the top security base in the world at the time.

• If the object was nothing more than a weather balloon, or even a Rawin target device, why would Colonel Blanchard drive out to the recovery site? As the commanding officer of the 509th Bomb Group, the only atomic bomb group in the world in 1947, Blanchard would have had better things to do with his time.

• Why were the farmer, Sherman Campbell, and the local sheriff in Circleville, Ohio able to identify the Rawin target device that crashed there while the officers and sheriff in Roswell were not?

• Why did a special photo team from Washington, D.C. arrive in New Mexico to photograph the site and record the subsequent events? Against standard operating procedure, the Third Photo Lab at the Roswell base was never called in to photograph the crash site or the material.

• If the recovery was of nothing more unusual than a weather balloon, why did the military, on July 9, tour the various news media in Roswell retrieving copies of Walter Haut's press release? If there was nothing to the story, why did the military search radio station KGFL, taking everything that related to the crash, including the documents that Frank Joyce tried to hide?

• There was definitely talk at the base during the recovery concerning bodies involved in the crash. Rumors circulated through the town of Roswell about one of the aliens being alive. One day after the first press release, the Army and Navy, as reported by the Associated Press, moved to ''Shut down the rumors.''

• Secrecy oaths would not have been required for the recovery of a weather balloon, or any other conventional device, unless it was a highly classified subject. Why were the men involved taken into a conference room in groups of ten to twelve and verbally sworn to protect the truth concerning what actually happened? Others at Roswell and Fort Worth were ordered not to discuss it, or ever bring it up again.

• In 1947, there were only two rocket launch sites in New Mexico. Both were at the White Sands Proving Grounds, where they averaged two launches per month. On July 3, 1947, an attempted V-2 test at White Sands failed when the rocket exploded on its pad.

• Ed Reese, in charge of the now declassified Project Blue Book files at the National Archives, told us that he, too, was surprised that Roswell is not included in the Blue Book system with all other explained reports.

• Neighbors of Mac Brazel, including Loretta Proctor and her son, Norris, reported that Mac Brazel returned from his detention driving a new pickup truck. According to Norris Proctor, Brazel, who had been dirt poor, suddenly had the money to buy a new house in Tularosa and a meat locker in Las Cruces.

• The daughter of Melvin Brown reported that her father, who had seen the bodies the day they were discovered along with the MPs at the crash site, was paid off. She said that a special trust account was established in Roswell for the guards.

• There are two, possibly three sites involved with the crash at Roswell. First is the debris field. Two and a half miles to the southeast where the remains of the craft and the bodies were located is the second. A few miles to the northwest is the original touchdown point that was first seen by Chaves County deputies and then by Lewis S. Rickett and Dr. Lincoln LaPaz.

• Pieces of small wreckage Bill Brazel Jr. had managed to collect were confiscated by the military in 1949. Why was the military still monitoring the situation two years later? Hadn't everything been explained?

• If the Roswell device was nothing more than a weather balloon, why bring in Dr. Lincoln LaPaz, a noted expert in the discovery and recovery of meteorites? LaPaz had worked on dozens of classified government projects including the ultra-classified Manhattan Project. If it was nothing more unusual that a balloon, the government wouldn't have wasted his time.

• A rather strange situation exists concerning the Roswell base pathologist, Jesse B. Johnson, Jr., M.D. Dr. Johnson died in 1987, but his last listing in the *ABMS Compendium of Certified Medical Specialists* raises major questions. Dr. Johnson completed his internship in 1946, but there is no listing for 1947 when he was stationed at Roswell. Military service is otherwise noted, but not for Dr. Johnson. In 1948, he's listed as a staff pathologist at the University of Texas Medical Branch in Galveston. From 1949 until going into private practice, he allegedly practiced radiology at numerous hospitals across the country. Yet, when we made inquiries, none of the hospitals had any record of him. Dr. Johnson did not have a driver's license registered in any state. The Texas Motor Vehicle Administration Office informed us that this was possible only through government exemption, or if he didn't drive. Even his wife remains unaware of any government affiliation after his military service.

• We submitted the names and documented serial numbers of over two dozen military personnel stationed at Roswell in July, 1947 to both the Defense Department and the Veteran's Administration for further confirmation of military service. The list included Charles E. Hanshaw, James W. Hundley, William J. Cardell, Lee J. Mulliner, Melvin E. Brown, Ernest O. Powell, Clyde M. Robertson, Cecil T. Yoakum, Harold T. Hastings, Edward M. Sager, and Donald E. Carroll. Why does neither the Defense Department nor the Veteran's Administration have records of any of these men when we can document that each served at the Roswell Army Air Field?

• Why are the key military witnesses telling us that they are still sworn to secrecy? Others will not even talk to former 509th Bomb Group members concerning any recollections about Roswell.

• If there was nothing to the Roswell case other than a misidentification of a weather balloon, why have witnesses, on their deathbeds, denied that? Melvin E. Brown spent the last four days of his life telling his family that it wasn't a weather balloon. Why was the dying archaeologist in Florida telling the nurses she had seen the bodies and then warning them about the government?

• The unusual qualities of the material described to date by fourteen known eyewitnesses are consistent in every detail. In appearance, tensile strength, apparent weightlessness, memory characteristics, uninterpretable symbology, and plastic-like, metal-like composition, its physical makeup would be difficult to duplicate even by today's standards.

• Each description of the bodies from the witnesses from Roswell is consistent. Interestingly, they do not entirely resemble what has been commonly described by witnesses in the other reported humanoid cases, as well as the alleged abduction stories. This tends to rule out contamination from these sources.

Public apathy often causes an inconsistent approach to important issues. Certainly, an event such as Roswell would have profound ramifications on our way of viewing the universe and humanity's place in it. It is because of this potential impact on our lives that it deserves to be discussed openly and honestly.

It is time that government officials acknowledge their responsibility for their actions—and their failure. No one can question the rational motivation and benign intent behind withholding, at first, the truth. Until the true nature of the Roswell wreckage was identified, it was the duty of government officials and military officers to safeguard national security through whatever means they believed prudent, including absolute secrecy and denial of the facts. But they have failed. Absolute secrecy has not been maintained, and the complete truth must be told. No longer should half-truths, rumors, and innuendo take center stage in the public forum. The whole story must be revealed.

The facts have been presented for your consideration. Our investigation led us to a conclusion we would present in any court of law, or, if possible, before Congress. We are confident that you, too, will demand a complete account. With sufficient public support, this can indeed happen.

The Roswell case rests on a wealth of evidence which we have attempted to present in a scientific and objective manner. We welcome any conventional explanation for these events that disproves, with solid evidence, what we have outlined.

However, until such proof is forthcoming, we will continue to present the facts as we have seen them. We will continue to believe that Roswell respresents the recovery of an alien spacecraft by the United States government. For when all possible explanations have been ruled out, whatever remains, however impossible, must be the truth.

Or, as UFO skeptic, Dr. Jerry Brown of NASA told us when asked if the Roswell debris could have been caused by a flying saucer, "If you can rule out an A-9 rocket with a crew, gentlemen, I don't know what else it could have been."

Postscript:
The Unholy Thirteen

The interviews with Brigadier General Arthur Exon revealed surprising as well as corroborative information. First was his confirmation, from Wright Field, of the Roswell event and the things we had learned during our investigation. He confirmed the two separate sites, the debris field, and the main crash where the bodies were found. He confirmed that material, contrary to what General Ramey said, had gone to Wright Field, and he confirmed that the bodies also arrived there. Coupled with all the other information, it only strengthens the case.

But the most surprising revelation was the acknowledgement of an official group that controlled access to the wreckage, bodies, and information about the crash. He referred to them as the unholy thirteen, only because he didn't know the actual name of the group. (And, after studying what he said, it seems that the name, Majestic Twelve, does not fit. Majestic Twelve, or MJ-12, was allegedly the group created to study the Roswell material, according to a briefing document released in the late 1980s. There is no evidence that the document is authentic.)

According to Exon, once the nature of the crash at Roswell was understood, the information would have been passed up the chain of command. Ramey probably called the Army Chief of Staff, Dwight Eisenhower.

The General identified others on the committee, men

who held high positions in the government. Carl Spaatz, the head of the Army Air Force in July, 1947, who became the first Chief of Staff of the Air Force in September, 1947, was mentioned as a committee member.

Exon named several others, including James Forrestal in his role as Secretary of War (later Defense), Stuart Symington, at that time the Under Secretary of War for Air, and President Truman. Given the nature of the crash and the preliminary conclusions being drawn, the president had to be included.

Additional names were not supplied for the remaining members, but he knew which offices were represented. These included the head of the CIA in the fall of 1947, Admiral Roscoe Hillenkoetter. Exon said there were representatives of the military intelligence community. Nathan F. Twining, as the head of the Air Materiel Command, would be another obvious choice.

There are other men who may have had a major role. Brigadier General Roger Ramey eventually left the Eighth Air Force, moving to Washington and duties in the Pentagon. In 1952, Major General Roger Ramey, Deputy Chief (of Staff) for Operations, was involved in UFO research. Ramey's inclusion would have been natural. He was involved almost from the beginning, had managed to bury the story with the balloon explanation, and the bodies did transit Fort Worth Army Air Field.

Major General John Samford, the Chief of Air Intelligence, might not have been an original member of the team, but by 1952 may have held one of the second echelon seats.

Exon's information only provided a few names: Spaatz, Symington, Truman, and Hillenkoetter. But he also said Ramey would have contacted the Army Chief of Staff, Eisenhower, upon learning of the Roswell recovery.

Exon said, ''I just know there was a top intelligence echelon represented and the President's office was represented and the Secretary of Defense's office was represented and these people stayed on it in key positions even though they might have moved out.''

One thing that Exon made clear was that no elected officials, outside the President, were ever included as a member of the top echelon. Elected officials were excluded from knowing anything about it.

Confirmation of that comes partially from Barry Goldwater. His attempts to learn more about it were turned back by Air Force Chief of Staff General Curtis LeMay. Goldwater, who was a United States senator and reserve major general, didn't have the clout, or the security clearances to get in to learn more about it.

In 1955, Exon moved to the Pentagon as a full colonel. While there, he ran into the controlling committee again. They were still in operation and still concerned with UFOs.

And when he moved on to Wright-Patterson as the base commander in 1964, UFOs were still of major interest. He said that he would receive a call from Washington, D.C. ''A team of uniformed officers would arrive on a commercial flight. We would ready a T-39, and occasionally a Convair 240.'' Eight to fifteen men would make up the team and they'd be gone for three days to a week. ''We were never informed about any reports. They all went to Washington.''

It was Exon's belief that the committee was created because of the Roswell crash. They not only controlled all access to Roswell but all highly classified UFO reports. Exon thought that the head of Blue Book would have been aware of the second, more highly classified study. He assumed that Blue Book was a part of it, an office that had a more public relations aspect than that of a real investigative arm. The real investigations were controlled from Washington, and not Wright-Patterson, where Blue Book was headquartered.

This major relevation totally contradicts the government public position on UFOs. Exon's startling testimony confirms what many researchers have always believed; that Blue Book was only a front for the actual investigation and that a special committee was designed to study the UFO crash at Roswell.

Exon's brush with the controlling committee—he didn't know the name or the code word—was limited. But it was the first outside confirmation of such a committee that had been found. It provided revelations we intend to pursue, information that with help we will develop into the next phase of UFO research: The Government's "Secret UFO Investigation."

As we go to press, we are still learning more about the event at Roswell and this special committee. Once the door of secrecy is cracked, there may be others who can provide new information that will make the Roswell case absolutely conclusive. For this to happen we need your help. Anyone who has additional information should write or call the J. Allen Hynek Center for UFO Studies, 2457 West Peterson Avenue, Chicago, Illinois 60659. Confidentiality will be respected but this has remained a secret too long. The truth must be learned.

Part V:

The Appendices

Appendix A:
Project Blue Book

For twenty-two years the United States Air Force actively and publicly investigated unidentified flying objects, spending millions of dollars and thousands of man-hours studying some of the most puzzling sightings ever reported. They recovered a wide variety of physical evidence, collected films and photos, and heard thousands of eyewitness statements. Sighting reports came from everyone including military personnel, scientists, police officers, and average citizens.

After a series of UFO reports in 1964 and 1965, the Air Force, feeling the sting of public pressure, commissioned a civilian study at the University of Colorado headed by astrophysicist Dr. Edward U. Condon. When the scientists working on the Condon Committee claimed they could find no evidence proving UFOs real or hostile, they recommended the Air Force close Project Blue Book. On December 17, 1969, the anniversary of the first powered flight at Kitty Hawk, and the anniversary of the formation of the Air Force as a separate service in 1947, the Pentagon officially announced the termination of Project Blue Book.

It seemed, based on the investigations of the Air Force and the Condon Committee, that the UFO phenomenon was nothing more than misidentifications by the ill-informed and the ravings of those who craved public attention. UFOs were no more real than the Easter Bunny and the Tooth Fairy.

But the real story of Project Blue Book isn't quite that cut and dried. From the very beginning, there have been researchers who suggested that a release of all the information in Project Blue Book would answer all the questions about the UFO phenomenon. Or they suggested that Project Blue Book was nothing more than a cover for the real investigation. The really good reports, the really hot ones, went somewhere else.

Project Blue Book was an outgrowth of Project Sign, the official study of the flying discs first sighted in the summer of 1947. Records show an unnamed intelligence study was made before the beginning of Sign, but the conclusions of that study are absent from the official files.[1]

Several months after Kenneth Arnold reported the nine silver objects over Mount Rainier, Washington, on June 24, 1947, Lieutenant General Nathan F. Twining forwarded a report (stamped SECRET) through channels that claimed the flying discs were "something real and not visionary or fictitious."[2] Twining urged the creation of a project to study the phenomenon, suggested a code name, and an overall security classification. The recommendation was accepted and Project Sign was born.[3]

Sign's files, however, begin before the project was even created. The first sighting recorded was early June, 1947. Several cases without specific dates were listed, including sightings from Hamburg, New York; Seattle, Washington; and Rehoboth Beach, Delaware. All these cases are missing from the Blue Book files and only the notations that they were once there remain. The Arnold sighting is the tenth logged into Project Sign.[4]

According to the Sign files, the flying saucers did not fade away by the end of the summer of 1947 as many expected. Sightings continued through the summer of 1947 and into 1948. During those months, an object would be found near Roswell, New Mexico and newspapers all over the country would pick up the story. Project Sign files would contain no mention of the report.[5]

It was also in those first few months that an Air Force

pilot would be killed chasing a UFO. Captain Thomas Mantell, flying an F-51, chased a large, glowing object over Godman Army Air Field, Kentucky. Mantell, according to official records, flew too high without oxygen equipment, blacked out, and was killed when his plane came apart in an uncontrolled power dive.[6]

By the summer of 1948, dozens of puzzling reports had been made to the Air Technical Intelligence Center (ATIC) in Dayton, Ohio, but it wasn't until a DC-3 was buzzed that ATIC decided to make an estimate of the situation. Officers at ATIC, assembling the best data they had, wrote a report concluding that UFOs were real and interplanetary and shipped it up to General Hoyt S. Vandenberg. According to Captain Ed Ruppelt, former head of Project Blue Book, Vandenberg said that the conclusions were not warranted by the evidence presented and rejected the report. It was declassified and destroyed.[7]

Others, including a colonel who was a lieutenant in 1948, claimed that Vandenberg required the mention of all physical evidence including the Roswell case removed from the study, and then rejected the report. No one felt the urge to rewrite it when all their best evidence had been removed on the orders of the Commanding General.[8]

By the end of 1948, the UFO phenomenon was losing ground. Officers at Sign claimed to have studied 122 sightings and had identified all but 7. Believing that the UFO phenomenon was about to disappear, project officers recommended that Sign by continued at a lower classification level and at a lower priority. In 1949, Project Sign was downgraded and the name changed to Grudge.[9]

With the new name came a new attitude. All reports were now evaluated on the premise that they were simply misidentifications of natural phenomena. If a report claimed that the UFO acted as if it might be a specific natural phenomenon, it became that phenomenon. Many of the reports coming into ATIC were not investigated because they could be explained without an investigation.

This lack of concern worked well through 1950 and into 1951. There were only a few reports of UFOs and they were rarely reported in the newspapers. The major exception to this was a series of articles written by Major Donald E. Keyhoe, a retired Marine who had accompanied Lindbergh on some of his cross country flights. Those articles became the basis of a book, *Flying Saucers Are Real*, which caused a minor stir.

Interest was also generated by the book written by Frank Scully. *Behind the Flying Saucers* was the story of the recovery of a crashed flying saucer with its dead flight crew. It became a minor bestseller and Scully hit the lecture circuit. Not long after, *True* ran an expose trashing Scully's book, claiming it was a hoax from the very beginning. Scully, according to the *True* story, had been duped by a couple of con men. There was no crash and no little bodies hidden anywhere.

The story of the crash and the bodies would continue to pop up in various forms for years. Each time it did, serious researchers attacked, dismantling the claim and then dismissing it. There could be no such thing as crashed flying saucers.

About that same time, early 1951, a general in the Pentagon asked what "was happening with the flying saucers." The answer he received didn't please him. He ordered the project re-evaluated and re-organized. Project Grudge became Project Blue Book and a new study began.[10] The new project was to be another serious attempt at research, but sightings were not being reported. In 1950 and 1951 combined, there were only 379 cases reported. All but 49 were explained.

In 1952 the situation changed. By the end of the year, there would be another 1500 reports in the files and 303 of them would be unexplained. That might not have been significant, if the sightings had been filed away without the public knowledge. However, at the end of July, formations of UFOs were buzzing Washington, D.C. and the military seemed powerless to stop them.

It was twenty minutes after midnight on July 19, 1952 when eight objects appeared on the radar screens at Washington's National Airport. Airline crews also reported seeing lights. A supervisor in the airport control room thought the radar might be malfunctioning, but technicians could find nothing wrong. As the radar operators watched, the UFOs poked along at just over 100 miles an hour and then accelerated to 7000 miles an hour. Before the night was over, radar technicians at Bolling AFB, Andrews AFB, and several other airports and bases sighted the objects both visually and on radar.

A week later, the saucers were back, but this time a procedure had been established. One of the civilian radar operators, following instructions from his superiors, called for military help. The reporters, who had arrived to watch the intercepts, were removed at the insistence of the Pentagon. "They'll be using classified orders," said a spokesman. "Newsmen are to be barred."[11]

All through the night, sightings were made and intercepts attempted. Fighter pilots reported both visual sightings and that their on-board radar locked onto the targets but they were unable to catch the UFOs. As the sun came up, the saucers vanished and the interceptors returned to base, but the mystery remained.

In the days that followed, the press pushed the Air Force for an answer. At a hastily called press conference, Air Force officials suggested some of the sightings might have been the result of temperature inversions. A heavy inversion layer had been over Washington at the time. But both radar operators and fighter pilots didn't believe they could have spent the night chasing something they knew was a natural phenomenon.[12] The sightings were listed in the Blue Book files as "unidentified."

Press and public interest increased. Newspapers bannered the Washington National sightings with headlines claiming "Saucers Swarm Over Capital."[13] During August the sightings throughout the country continued, as they did in September. By the end of 1952, the Air Force added over 300 new, unidentified cases to the Project Blue Book files—a situation the Air Force could not tolerate.

Their solution was the creation of the Robertson Panel. A CIA sponsored investigation, it would look at the best of the Blue Book cases presented by the project officers. The panel would evaluate the Mantell incident of January, 1948, a 1950 movie taken over Great Falls, Montana by Nick Mariana, the 1952 Tremonton, Utah movie, and the multiple witness, radar confirmed sightings over Washington. [14]

Since the CIA salted the panel with scientists who were friendly to their point of view, the discussions were fairly easy to direct. Dr. J. Allen Hynek, the Air Force consultant in astronomy, attended the conference, but was not allowed to participate. [15] He could only watch as the CIA scientists ridiculed the cases and then offered explanations that seemed to almost fit the facts. In three days the Robertson Panel did what the Air Force had been unable to do in five years. They explained the whole UFO phenomenon.

But the panel also made several recommendations. One of these was the establishment of a training program that would help the general public identify many of the objects reported as flying saucers. In the final report, the panel said, ''The Panel's concept of a broad education program integrating efforts of all concerned agencies was that it should have two major aims: training and 'debunking.' ''[16]

They explained the debunking by saying, ''The 'debunking' aim would result in reduction in public interest in 'flying saucers' which today evokes a strong psychological reaction. This education could be accomplished by mass media such as television, motion pictures, and popular articles. Basis of such education would be actual case histories which had been puzzling at first but later explained. As in the case of conjuring tricks, there is much less stimulation if the 'secret' is known. Such a program should tend to reduce the current gullibility of the public and consequently their susceptibility to clever hostile propaganda. The Panel noted that the general absence of Russian propaganda based on a subject with so many obvious possibilities for exploitation might indicate a possible Russian policy."[17]

In very simple terms, the Panel suggested that UFOs were not real and they wanted the Air Force to debunk them. It marked a definite shift of emphasis that can be seen in the Blue Book files. The Panel was followed with Air Force Regulation (AFR) 200-2 and Joint Army, Navy and Air Force Publication (JANAP) 146, that made it a crime to release information about unidentified sightings.

Prior to the Robertson Panel, Air Force officers had tried to make Project Blue Book a serious study. Afterwards, it became little more than a public relations gimmick with almost no manpower or responsibility. UFO sightings were to be identified in the mundane. Suddenly, Kenneth Arnold saw a mirage. Thomas Mantell chased a balloon and the Montana movie showed jet fighters. All these cases were explained by the "improved methods of scientific research now employed by Blue Book officers."[18] These new methods also demonstrated how all sightings were to be explained without regard to the facts.

In fact, looking at the history of the project only as it appears in the Blue Book files suggests the investigations weren't as thorough as they could have been and that there was a calculated effort to explain all the sightings. An understanding of the way the military mind works suggests that nothing more nefarious was going on than a high ranking officer impressing his opinion on those who serve under him. The general doesn't believe and therefore it is a good idea for no one else to believe.

With that kind of logic, and with no physical evidence that would prove, beyond a doubt, that UFOs were extraterrestrial, this attitude could be understandable. The point is, Blue Book was a project hampered by those who had already reached conclusions. The search was not for information but for proof that there was nothing to UFOs.

However, in all the discussion about early cases and explanations, no one mentioned Roswell. It had faded into oblivion and the powers directing UFO research from the Pentagon and CIA headquarters were happy to leave it right there.

It can be shown the good civilian sightings never went to Project Blue Book. The strangest of the military sightings never went to Blue Book. Dr. Hynek was quoted many times as saying that the really good cases were directed somewhere other than Blue Book.[19]

It is fairly obvious that Blue Book was designed so that another, more highly classified project could be hidden. In other words, Blue Book was a cover for the real UFO investigation. The missing cases, the poorly handled investigations, and the out-and-out lies issued by the Air Force show that. In 1957, during the wave of sightings that began with the Levelland reports, Assistant Air Force Secretary Richard Horner said, ''The Air Force is not hiding UFO information. And I do not have to qualify that in any way.''[20]

He made that statement knowing full well that there had been at least two separate studies that concluded UFOs were extraterrestrial in origin. It makes no difference that both reports were later rejected. It is only important to remember that the reports had been made and that Horner had said that didn't exist.

After 1953, Project Blue Book became an agency for debunking UFO sightings. Its purpose was not to investigate UFO sightings but to explain them. It was a policy that was seldom questioned and it allowed Blue Book to continue its distortion of the facts.

It makes no sense, however, until the Roswell sighting is plugged into the equation. Then, suddenly, it's all very clear. If Roswell was a crash of a flying saucer, then the policy is understandable. The Air Force and the government didn't have to investigate. They already had the answers. Physical evidence had dropped into their hands, by accident. It was better to keep the public out of it. Tell them anything but the truth.

Appendix B:
The UFO Crashes

There are those who say that they don't believe UFOs are extraterrestrial spacecraft because there have been no crashes. No matter how good their technology, no matter how far advanced they are, there is always the possibility of mechanical failure or pilot error according to those skeptics. Without the story of a crash, the skeptics just will not accept the idea of space flight.

As the investigation began, Schmitt and Randle learned that there had been reports of UFO crashes almost from the moment that newspapers began reporting the phenomenon. In fact, the Roswell story pushed the report of a crash near Bozeman, Montana off the front pages. Although there is no evidence that Bozeman was a real crash, there is unquestionable evidence that something happened at Roswell.

And, if it happened once, within two weeks of the Kenneth Arnold sighting, why not several times? The following list contains information about the best known or the best documented of the UFO crashes. Information on the hoaxes has been included because they have been reported in several magazine articles and in several books. Where there is a conclusion about the authenticity of the information, it has been included. Where the authenticity is still open to debate, the case has been labeled that way.

July 2, 1947: Roswell, New Mexico

The best documented and best researched of the UFO crash stories. There is every indication that this is the proof positive that UFO researchers have wanted for years and the study of this case explains the trend in the field since 1947. There is no longer any doubt that this marked the first recovery of a craft built on another planet.

March 25, 1948: Aztec, New Mexico—Hoax

Frank Scully, in his book, *Behind the Flying Saucers*, reported a flying saucer crash near Aztec, New Mexico. His sources, Silas Newton and Leo GeBauer, reported that government radar had tracked the object as it flew over New Mexico. Apparently there was something wrong because it fell out of the sky, hitting the ground. Because it had been tracked on three radars, it wasn't hard for the military to locate the crash site. Using that information, they triangulated and headed out into the desert.

Scientists, police officers, and soldiers surrounded the craft, watching it. It was described as disc-shaped, about a hundred feet in diameter, and had portholes. After two days, the scientists and the military approached. Looking through a broken porthole, they spotted sixteen bodies inside. Probing through the porthole with a stick, they hit something that opened a hatch, allowing the scientists to enter.

The bodies were removed and laid on the ground. According to one of the scientists, Doctor Gee (Leo GeBauer), all the beings were small, 38 to 42 inches tall, but unlike the bodies recovered near Roswell, these were perfectly formed humans.

The military removed the craft and the bodies, taking them away for study. Doctor Gee said that at one time he had been in charge of 1700 scientists working on the project.[1]

But that crash disappeared into oblivion. Unlike Roswell there were no firsthand witnesses to be interviewed. There were no newspaper reports about the crash, and there was no military activity at Aztec. No firsthand witnesses have come forward and there were no newspaper articles from the newspapers. The owner of the land where the craft supposedly crashed refuses to talk about anything except to say it never happened. He just wants to be left alone.[2]

The only conclusion possible is that this case, like the two related to it from Paradise Valley, Arizona, and near Phoenix, Arizona, is a hoax. No evidence to support any of those reports has ever surfaced, and it is now believed by some that the information was filtered through government sources to discredit leaks about Roswell.

December 1950: Del Rio, Texas

The second legitimate crash seems to be the one claimed near Del Rio, Texas. Like Roswell, there are firsthand witnesses to this report. One researcher has identified more than two dozen military men, including Colonel Robert Willingham, who were involved in the retrieval.[3]

In 1977 Willingham went on the record describing his handling of the wreckage. In a signed affidavit, he stated:

"Down in Dyess Air Force Base in Texas, we were testing what turned out to be the F-94. They reported on the scope that they had an unidentified flying object flying at a high speed going to intercept our course. It came visible to us and we watched it and we wanted to take off after it. Headquarters wouldn't let us go after it and it played around a little bit. We got to watching how it made 90 degree turns at this high speed and everything. We knew it wasn't a missile of any type. So then, we confirmed it with the radar control station on the DEW

Line (NORAD) and they kept following it and they claimed that it crashed somewhere off between Texas and the Mexican border. We got a light aircraft, me and my co-pilot, and we went down to the site. We landed out in the pasture right across from where it hit. We got over there. They told us to leave and everything else and then the armed guards came out and they started to form a line around the area. So, on the way back, I saw a little piece of metal so I picked it up and brought it back with me. There were two sand mounds that came down and it looked to me like this thing crashed right in between them. But it went into the ground, according to the way people were acting around it. So we never did actually get up to the site to see what had crashed. But you could see for, oh I'd say, three to five hundred yards where it had went across the sand. It looked to me, I guess from the metal that we found, chunks of metal, that it either had a little explosion or it began to disintegrate. Something caused this metal to come apart.''

After leaving the crash site, Willingham and his co-pilot examined the metal.

''It looked like it was something that was made because it was honeycombed. You know how you would make a metal that would cool faster. In a way it looked like a magnesium steel but it had a lot of carbon in it. I tried to heat it with a cutting torch. It just wouldn't melt. A cutting torch burns at anywhere from 3200 to 3800 degrees Fahrenheit and it would make the metal hot but it wouldn't even start to make the metal yield.''

Willingham took the metal to a Marine Corps metallurgy lab in Hagerstown, Maryland, for analysis. Several days later he was told the man he had contacted at the lab never worked there and no one else at the lab knew anything about the piece of metal. Willingham was ordered never to discuss it and signed an oath of secrecy.

Warren Smith also knew of a firsthand witness to the information. A man Smith worked with was receiving letters from his wife at a dude ranch in Texas. She wrote that they had seen a fiery crash and that the cowboys were going to ride out to see if it had been an airplane. They returned with a story of a flying saucer and the dead pilot.[4]

According to sources, there was a fight over the jurisdiction since the craft had crashed in Mexico, but apparently the Americans won. The craft and the occupant were removed to a base in Texas.[5]

Although not as well documented as the Roswell case, there is good reason to believe that something extraordinary happened there.

September 12, 1952: Spitsbergen Island—Possible Hoax

According to press reports, Norwegian soldiers had found a disc-shaped object crashed in the snowy wastes of Spitsbergen Island. Project Blue Book files show that on September 12, 1952, the Air Force received word that the crash story was a hoax.[6] John Keel, a well known UFO writer, confirmed, to his satisfaction in 1967, that it was a hoax.[7]

The original story, according to both the Air Force and Keel, which appeared in a West German magazine, was that the craft contained Russian writing, log books in Russian, and that it could fly 20,000 kilometers without refueling.

There were other reports about Spitsbergen but they bore no resemblance to the case as the Air Force had related it. The September 5, 1955 issue of the *Stuttgarter Tageblatt* told of a badly damaged disc being found in 1952 and that U.S. and British experts were brought in to study it.

Then, in 1955, in a story datelined Oslo, Norway, they told of a board of inquiry of the Norwegian General Staff that was preparing for the publication of a report on the examination of the remains of a UFO that had crashed on Spitsbergen. Colonel Gernod Darnbyl, who headed the investigation, reported that the Spitsbergen disc was not built by any country on Earth. "The materials used in the construction are completely unknown to all experts who participated in the investigation."

The findings of the board were not going to be published until "some sensational facts have been discussed with US and British officials."[8]

Darnbyl also claimed that the disc had been falsely identified as Soviet by someone at the Pentagon in Washington. That means the story in the Blue Book files about the crash being a hoax could be wrong. And it could also mean that John Keel made a mistake when he did his research in 1967. Like so many cases in the field, this one must be reviewed.

May 21, 1953: Kingman, Arizona

The Kingman crash falls into that category of not having a lot of documentation or firsthand witnesses, though this is slowly changing. In the last few months another firsthand witness has appeared. There are no supporting documents like those available about Roswell, but unlike Aztec, there are people who claim to have participated in the recovery. Because of that, the case must be examined.

According to a firsthand witness, he was working on another government project in Nevada when he and 15 or 20 others were driven to an Air Force base, put on a plane and flown to Arizona.

On arrival, they were escorted to a field 20 miles northwest of Kingman where they saw a disc-shaped object that had crashed with some force into the desert. It was about 30 feet in diameter, and was stuck in the sand without any apparent structural damage.

Nearby was a tent where the single occupant of the craft lay. According to the source, he was about four feet tall, had two eyes, two ears, and a round mouth.

Once everyone had finished his task, all of them were

put on the plane and flown back to their original duties, with instructions to forget everything that had just happened and to forget everything they had seen.[9]

Again, if this was a single source case, it would almost demand to be labeled a hoax, but with Roswell suggesting that UFOs do crash and pending additional witnesses to this activity, this case must remain open.

September 15, 1957: Ubatuba, Brazil

It was early in September, 1957, when a Rio de Janeiro columnist received a strange letter from several men who claimed they had been fishing when they spotted a flying disc. It was approaching at high speed, dived at them, made a tight turn, and then began a rapid climb. Moments later it exploded, showering the beach and the ocean near Ubatuba with thousands of fragments. The men picked up dozens of them, enclosed a couple of the smallest pieces in the letter, and mailed it to the reporter.

The columnist wrote his story and Doctor Olavo Fontes, the Aerial Phenomena Research Organization's (APRO) Brazilian representative, saw it. He believed the story to be a hoax, but decided he should check it. If true, there was the possibility he could actually touch something manufactured on another planet. He contacted the columnist and asked to see the metal.[10]

Working with the columnist, Fontes had a portion of the metal examined by a local chemist. The preliminary study showed that it wasn't from a meteorite because it was too light. It was obviously metal and it had been burned. It was not aluminum so they made several additional tests.

Spectroscopic analysis revealed that the sample was magnesium of a purity believed to be unobtainable at the time. That, along with the evidence that the columnist had not invented the story to fill space, suggested that the report was true. Fontes sent a complete report, along with a detailed analysis, to APRO Headquarters in Tucson, Arizona.

APRO tried to interest the Air Force in a joint analysis of the sample. A small piece was sent to an Air Force laboratory, but the spectrograph operator destroyed the sample without getting an exposed plate. The Air Force requested another sample, but APRO declined.

Next, APRO tried the Atomic Energy Commission. A density test was made and the Ubatuba metal was found to be slightly more dense than would be expected of normal samples. This was an interesting result that could be accounted for by oxide on the magnesium.[11]

While the sample was at the AEC labs, another spectroscopic analysis was run. The presence of minute quantities of several trace elements were found, but the technician said that they could have been the result of comtamination on the electrodes and not impurities in the sample. Another test wasted.[12]

Lab analysis showed that the metal came from an object that had broken up rapidly. There was no evidence of melting, so it was believed that an explosion had torn apart a larger object. They didn't say it was a UFO because the sample did not show it to be a spacecraft. They just said that whatever it was, it had blown up.

While this was going on, Fontes was trying to track down the witnesses to the explosion. There were questions that he wanted to ask them, but they had disappeared. Fontes suspected that Brazilian intelligence officials had ordered them to forget about the sighting.[13]

Later, during the University of Colorado UFO (Condon Committee) study, samples were loaned to them for further analysis. The report released at the termination of the project did not agree with all APRO's findings. According to them, magnesium of equal purity was available in small, laboratory amounts in 1957. Doctor R.S. Busk of the Condon Committee also reported there was a high content of strontium in the sample. Strontium was not an expected impurity found in magnesium made under normal methods. The report also said that they didn't believe the metal came from a larger object.[14] In other words, it was not part of an exploding UFO.

Because of the negative results, APRO decided to have the metal subjected to non-destructive analysis. The new results showed that the fragments were directionally solidified castings. That was something that was not being studied in 1957. Doctor Walter W. Walker wrote, "This might be interpreted as meaning that the samples are from a more advanced culture."[15] He wasn't saying that the object and the samples came from another planet, but he was leaving that impression.

The other negative results from the Colorado study were also refuted by APRO. They were surprised by the statement from the Colorado scientists that the Ubatuba metal did not come from a fabricated metal object. Walker said that apparently the Colorado scientists did not accept castings as a method of fabrication.

Researchers, studying the Ubatuba case, say that it is not the proof positive that they have been looking for. The chain of evidence, from the exploding disc to the columnist, can't be established. There is the possibility of a hoax. Given the qualities of the sample, a hoax is unlikely.

April 18, 1962: Las Vegas, Nevada

On April 18, 1962, an object was reported to have exploded over the deserts of Nevada. The roar was heard for miles and the flash of light was so bright that it lit the streets of Reno like the noonday sun.

The story actually began near Oneida, New York. A spokesman for the North American Air Defense Command in Colorado Springs, Colorado, Lieutenant Colonel Herbert Rolph, told reporters that the first observers had seen a glowing red object, heading to the west, over the Oneida area.[16] It was at great altitude.

Radar picked up the object. Operators watched as it streaked above the midwest, and the Air Defense Command alerted a number of Air Force bases, including Nellis in Las Vegas. Interceptors were scrambled from Phoenix.

In Nephi, Utah, witnesses reported the glowing red object flew overhead. When it was gone, there was a rumbling like that from jet engines. That might have been the interceptors as they chased the UFO.

The UFO landed near Eureka, Utah and interrupted the electrical service from a power plant close to the landing site. The craft took off a few minutes later, continuing on toward the west. [17]

The object suddenly disappeared from the radar screens seventy miles northwest of Las Vegas. That coincided with reports of a brilliant explosion. [18]

The original report came from Frank Edwards. So many of Frank Edwards' stories were impossible to check. Edwards wrote from memory and sometimes his memory let him down. And the Las Vegas crash presented problems because most of the major UFO researchers knew nothing about the case. That ended, however, when a man who was in Eureka, Utah the night the object landed was interviewed.

According to the source, he was traveling south when he saw the object coming down. It wasn't just a bright light, but an oval-shaped, orange object that was making a quiet whirring sound. The ground around it was lighted as if the sun was coming up. The man said that the UFO came from the east, landed, then took off and continued on to the west, disappearing in the distance. [19]

Edwards claimed that others heard a roar that he attributed to fighters in the air giving chase. The source didn't hear the jets, and didn't see them.

He continued on to his destination, stopping in the larger cities, buying newspapers and searching for stories of the saucer sighting. He found nothing, though he continued to look. Only Frank Edwards mentioned the case.

Reports of the story were missing from most newspapers, just as the source said. Only the *Las Vegas Sun* reported it. In that report, two individuals who had seen the object were named. Both men were living in Las Vegas. One confirmed his description of an orange craft.[20] The other talked about the search he led to look for wreckage. Nothing was found.

One man, who refused to be identified, claimed that he had been stationed at Nellis Air Force Base at the time of the crash. He had been awakened, and along with thirty other officers, was driven into the desert. The men were used to clean a field filled with debris. They used flashlights as they crawled from one end to the other.

As the sun came up, the men were loaded on a bus. The windows had been covered with dark paper. The source said that he could see through a place where the paper didn't quite cover the whole window. Through that, he could see a smashed, disc-shaped craft.[21]

At the base, the men were all debriefed. They were warned about telling anyone about anything they had seen. According to the officer in charge, the men had recovered wreckage from a secret craft that crashed. Anything said about it could help the Soviets determined the direction of research.

The whole story was pieced together from various sources and seems to be just one more example of how fast the public relations machinery can be put into motion to suppress the data. With the exception of the story in the *Sun*, the majority of the country heard nothing about it.

December 9, 1965:
Kecksburg, Pennsylvania

About dusk a brilliant fireball flashed across the sky. It was described by the witnesses as orange, leaving a smoky trail behind it. The object headed south over Michigan, crossed into Ohio and then apparently turned, striking the ground southeast of Pittsburgh. Some kind of metal strips fell to the ground near Lapeer, Michigan, setting a number of small fires.[22]

At 4:47 P.M. a woman living near Kecksburg, Pennsylvania, saw something slam into the woods near her home. From her porch she could see a column of blue smoke and her children wanted to go down to see what it was. She let them and then decided there might be something dangerous down there and ran after them. As she caught them she saw something like a five-pointed star over the trees.[23]

By 7:00 P.M., the Pennsylvania State Police were trying to find the crash site. There were stories that the military would be arriving soon but the State Police were now telling reporters that a thorough search of the woods had failed to find anything. There was talk that the military was coming in to search the woods themselves.

Upon arriving, the military took over the Kecksburg Volunteer Fire Department. Witnesses saw a great deal of equipment brought in, including radio gear. Others reported both Air Force and Army personnel and equipment. Later that night jets arrived carrying NASA people.[24]

There were witnesses, firsthand witnesses, who saw something lying in a stream bed, hidden in the woods. It was described as acorn shaped, golden in color, with a band of writing around it.[25]

The military and the police kept people from getting in close to it. Witnesses reported that the military later took something out on a flatbed truck. They had gotten into the area, secured it, retrieved whatever fell, and were gone by four in the morning.

Stan Gordon of the Pennsylvania Association for the Study of the Unexplained spent twenty years studying the case. Gordon believes that what came down near Kecksburg might have been a nuclear powered satellite launched by either the United States or the Soviet Union.

Kecksburg is important for one reason. It showed that

the military could get to a crash site quickly, seal it off, and retrieve whatever came down. Newspapers around the country, including the *Boston Record American* carried headlines that said, "Army, Police Seal Off Woods in UFO Probe."

Again, here is a case where something unexpected happened and the military and the government explained it as a meteor, one that turned a corner and crashed into the woods. The Pennsylvania State Police and the military responded to the crash. A full recovery operation was undertaken. It's a case that must remain open until more facts are presented.

February 12, 1968: Orocué, Colombia

Residents reported hearing three loud explosions in the area where a metallic-looking, disc-shaped object had been only moments before. They began to search the area where they saw debris falling and recovered a large piece of metal. It was lightweight and very hard. Attempts to cut it failed, so it was transported intact to Bogotá. The American Air Attache there claimed that the metal was from a spacecraft of some kind. The metal was smooth, except for tiny grooves that might have been the result of the explosion. It had green and orange hues and when struck with a hammer, it seemed to magnify the sound. Official statements released later claimed the metal to have come from a disintegrating American satellite.[26]

July 15, 1974: Spain

There are reports from Spain that military experts and scientists have recovered the wreckage of a disc-shaped craft. It was moved to a military base for study. Currently no further information is available.

August 8, 1976: Presidente Prudente, São Paulo, Brazil

Witnesses reported that a flying object exploded over the town. It was claimed that the explosion was quite spectacular but there are no other details. There was a suggestion that it might have been a Soviet or an American satellite.[27]

May 6, 1978: Bolivia

Hundreds of people saw a strange, elongated object fly over them. Moments later it crashed into the jungle. Besides the natives in the area, three engineers from a mining company and personnel from Bolivian customs saw the object fall. When the government officials arrived, they sealed off the area, keeping newsmen and tourists away. There is some speculation that the object might have been a satellite, but there are also reports of disc-shaped UFOs in the area.[28]

August 22, 1981: Argentina

Several witnesses claimed they saw a stricken, disc-shaped object as it plunged to Earth. It halted the descent, but then exploded, the debris raining down. Military jets were seen in the area shortly after the explosion. A search of the area revealed metal fragments and several large pieces of equipment that weren't identifiable. Military authorities moved in quickly, surrounding the area and barring the curious. There were reports that two badly burned bodies were also recovered.[29]

Appendix C:
The Press Accounts

There are those who say they don't believe in UFOs and the stories of the crashes because there was nothing about the crashes in the newspapers. In an era with more leaks in security than plumbing in a hundred-year-old building, they expect that something should have leaked.

They are, of course, correct. The answer to that problem is threefold. One is to say that the subject is a self-keeping secret. That is, those who do talk out of turn are ignored because the subject is so fantastic. A witness to the retrieval of a crashed disc or the recovery of the bodies won't mention it because he or she knows that no one will believe the story. Such things just do not happen.

Normally, the military, or the agency controlling the retrieval also swear the participants to secrecy. That has been demonstrated over and over. Men at Roswell told us that they can't talk about it because they are sworn to secrecy. Mac Brazel refused to tell his son because he took an oath. And Mary Ann Gardner said that her patient, even on her deathbed, was frightened of the government learning that she had mentioned the crash.

The final point, that there is never anything in the papers or in magazines, is untrue. Several times over the last forty years, the stories of crash retrievals have appeared in the national press, and each time the stories have dried up quickly with no one remembering that they had been published.

The first published report of a flying saucer crash came

on July 7, 1947. In an AP story out of Bozeman, Montana, there was a report that a pilot of a civilian P-38 had been paced by a formation of "clam-shaped" objects. One of the objects flew too close to his propwash and had been destroyed. The wreckage spiraled into the Tobacco Root Mountains near Bozeman. Searchers failed to locate the wreckage.[1]

The Bozeman report disappeared when Walter Haut issued his press release on July 8. That story was published in newspapers around the country. Again, an answer was offered quickly, but the point is, there were newspaper accounts of a flying saucer crash.

But even ignoring the Roswell stories, there were other early reports in the newspapers. As early as 1949, Frank Scully, writing in *Variety,* mentioned a crashed saucer and the recovered bodies of the dead crew. He went into little detail about it and wrote part of the story tongue in cheek.

There was apparently enough interest in the story that Scully followed up on it, writing a book, *Behind the Flying Saucers.* In it, he detailed three crashes in the United States, either in New Mexico or Arizona. There are just enough similarities between what Scully wrote and what happened at Roswell to indicate that someone might have accidentally leaked some of the Roswell information.

After the publication of Scully's book, there were dozens of reviews and newspaper articles examining the premise. Most "serious" journalists had decided that such things do not happen and therefore Scully's book must be a hoax. Few of them bothered to check any of the facts. It could not have happened and therefore did not happen.

On January 6, 1950, the *Wyandotte Echo* in Kansas City, Kansas published an article that mentioned Scully's crashed saucers and the dead pilots of them. An engineer by the name of Coulter (Koehler?) claimed to have seen two saucers and the bodies. One of the ships had been badly damaged in the crash and the bodies were so badly charred that little could be learned from them.

In March, 1950, Silas Newton, one of Scully's original sources, talked, informally, with the students of the University of Denver, in Denver, Colorado. That led to a series of articles in the *Denver Post* about the ''secret'' lecture, who Newton was, and a discussion of the reports of crashed saucers and the bodies from them.

A month later, *Newsweek* reported the story of a crashed saucer and the recovery of a 23-inch-tall occupant. Although shorter than those normally reported by Scully, this time they mentioned the head being larger than normal.

It is obvious that by 1950, there were many stories circulating that the U.S. government, and most probably the Air Force, had recovered one, possibly more, downed saucers. And there were stories circulating about the dead flight crews from those saucers.

That, however, was a story that the government couldn't afford to have leaked. If ''serious'' researchers believed in crashed saucers, it wouldn't be long before reporters would be on the trail, too. The problem was that the trail could lead right back to Wright-Patterson Air Force Base. The debunking went into high gear.

A number of high ranking officers, in offical statements, said that there was no truth to the rumors that the government had captured a flying saucer or recovered the bodies. There were no hidden bases, no secret rooms, and no special studies. All the stories were the work of the over-active imaginations of men who would be better off writing science fiction.

But still the rumors persisted, and after the massive sightings of July, 1952, more people than ever were convinced that something was being hidden.

In September, 1952, *True* magazine commissioned J.P. Cahn of the *San Francisco Chronicle* to look into Scully's story of downed discs and dead aliens. Cahn followed the trail of Newton and the mysterious Dr. Gee, tracking them down and interviewing them. The proof that Newton claimed he had turned out to be poorly focused photographs and poor-grade aluminum that melted at 600 degrees. No one accepted Newton's proof.

That article, and Cahn, proved to many that there had been no flying saucer crashes. There were no hidden government labs and no research studies on the material recovered. When both Newton and Dr. Gee, identified as Leo GeBauer, were tried on fraud in a Colorado court, the stories end.[2]

It also soured legitimate researchers on the possibility that there was something to the crash retrieval stories. Any mention of flying saucers and little bodies was met with scorn. Even those in the UFO field willing to admit to landings, occupant reports, and, later, abduction accounts, refused to listen when someone talked about the bodies at Wright-Patterson Air Force Base.

But the stories persisted. In 1954, there were a number of accounts that then President Eisenhower traveled secretly to Edwards Air Force Base. According to the stories, Eisenhower was taken there to look at the remains of a downed disc and the crew from it.[3] Again it was a story that got some play in the press, but always with the tongue in cheek. The serious researcher never considered it to be true.

Dorothy Kilgallen reported in her column that she had heard the strangest tale in 1954. According to her, a British subject of "cabinet rank" had told her the story of a crashed saucer and the recovery of the dead pilots. She never identified her source, which made the story suspect. Interestingly, Kilgallen, who had a national audience, never caused a stir with the report.[4]

In October, 1974, Robert Carr made national headlines when he reported that the stories of alien bodies at Wright-Patterson were true. According to Carr, he had found five firsthand witnesses who had either been part of the recovery effort in Aztec, New Mexico or who had seen the corpses at Wright-Patterson.[5]

But Carr cut his own throat. He refused to reveal a single source, and on a story like that, sources are needed. He could have had a hundred sources but without a name to verify or a way to check the facts, his release was no more impressive than that made by Frank Scully nearly twenty-five years earlier.

In fact, when the Carr story surfaced, almost everyone assumed that it was the Scully reports updated for an audience that had seen Americans on the moon and who had seen pictures transmitted from Mars.

The APRO Bulletin, the official publication of the Aerial Phenomena Research Organization, in the January-February 1975 issue, attacked Carr's statements. According to sources interviewed by Coral Lorenzen, APRO's Director, Carr had been telling the same stories for years.

In the October, 1975 issue of *Official UFO,* a magazine devoted to UFO reports, Mike McClellan researched the Aztec story and could find nothing to suggest that it had ever taken place. Carr, in response, said that he had never been sure of the location of the crash and that Aztec might not have been right. Other researchers ignored it because Carr gave them nothing that could be verified.

The following April, in what they labeled an exclusive, *Official UFO* printed an article about the recovery of a crashed saucer and a body near Kingman, Arizona. To the UFO community the words were the same but the song had changed. There were not many who would believe that one, especially when the author, Ray Fowler, refused to identify his source. An unidentified source is, once again, no source at all.

There were many such stories circulating. A half dozen or more witnesses or researchers that claimed the government had captured a saucer or two saucers and they had found bodies in them. Even the *Book of Scientific Knowledge* from Grolier's carried a brief account of a crash and the retrieval of the dead. A great deal had been published but there still were no witnesses who would let their names be used.

In 1979, the *Denver Post* published a story about the search of the body of a spaceman killed when his ship exploded near Aurora, Texas. Unlike those stories reported by Scully and Carr, this was not derivative of the Aztec case. This dealt with the Great Airship of 1897. Researchers had long ago dismissed the idea that the Great Airship of 1897 was any kind of space vehicle, but that didn't stop modern investigators from making a grandstand play to exhume the body and capture a few headlines. And, it was another newspaper account of a spaceship crash.

In 1980, Ronald Story published the *Encyclopedia of UFOs*. In it was a brief mention of the stories of crashed saucers and the hidden bodies. Kevin Randle, writing the entry, related all the stories to the Scully book of 1950. Quoting Hector Quintanilla, a former chief of Project Bluebook, "We don't have any little bodies in our cellar." Randle concluded that if no one would come forward to be quoted about a retrieval, if there was no way to verify any of the facts, then there probably was nothing to the stories.

Also in 1980, Charles Berlitz and William Moore published *The Roswell Incident* about a flying saucer crash. Those in the "know" rejected the book as one more Scully update. The difference this time was that a few names were named. Even so, the book disappeared quickly.

There were more stories and talk about crashed saucers in the later 1970s and the 1980s. Len Stringfield started the trend, writing about the rumors and the stories in a series of papers and status reports. Stringfield, in a few cases, named the names of those making the reports.

With that, the floodgates were opened. There were press accounts of UFO crashes, most of them centering on the Roswell area. But where there had been almost no information in the past, now there was a wealth of it. Witnesses were being identified, and when those witnesses were interviewed, they claimed to have firsthand knowledge of the event.

Those who claimed that nothing had appeared in the newspaper, the news magazines, or on television, are wrong. Reports about the bodies and the crashes have been printed and have been aired. The skeptics may not have read or seen them, but they were there. The fact the skeptics didn't see them is now irrelevant.

Appendix D:
The Reluctant Witnesses

Not everyone contacted during the search for information was willing to help. A few of them, remembering the oaths they had taken forty years earlier, refused to talk. Others remembered the threats that had been made and were still frightened by them. And the rest felt it was their duty not to talk, saying that they had been sworn to secrecy and they were going to maintain that silence even in the face of proof they had to know something about the case.

Edgar Skelley was an operations officer at Roswell in 1947. Witnesses have reported that he instructed a flight crew to stay on the base because there might be an emergency flight. One of the crew members later reported that a single crate was loaded into the bomb bay and it's possible the crate contained the bodies. Skelley briefed them before the pre-flight.

When Schmitt contacted Skelly's wife and mentioned the 509th Bomb Group, she kept asking, "Are you sure you're not with the Air Force?" When Schmitt spoke to Skelley directly, he denied any such flight took place and denied that any such incident happened in Roswell. Skelley insisted that a man named MacPherson might be able to answer the questions. MacPherson was not at Roswell in July, 1947.

Concerning that same flight, Felix Martucci had said nothing to anyone about his role in July, 1947. He knew that something extraordinary had happened and commented about it to his fellow crewmen. Martucci, when first contacted, had an answering machine and a friendly voice. He admitted that he had been a member of the 509th Bomb Group during the summer of 1947 but when given the names of the crew he normally flew with, he claimed to remember none of them. "It was a long time ago, after all."

The feeling was that Martucci might be reluctant to talk to strangers on the phone, but might respond to a fellow crew member, the man who had identified him in the first place. But Martucci didn't have an answering machine anymore and didn't answer his phone.

It took several weeks but the man finally got an answer. It was a young woman who wanted to know what the caller wanted. When he mentioned the 509th Bomb Group, she screamed, "No, no," into the phone and hung up.

Subsequent attempts to contact Martucci have failed. Any mention of Roswell or the 509th Bomb Group caused him to hang up without another word. It seemed that Martucci, now that he had been inadvertently warned, no longer wanted phone calls from his old buddies.

But Martucci isn't the only one. One man who was identified as being on the crash site denied, at first, he had even been in Roswell in July, 1947. According to him, nothing extraordinary happened in Roswell, there was no talk of alien spacecraft, and nothing published in either of the Roswell daily newspapers. He finally admitted that he had been there, but insisted he knew nothing of the crash and hadn't heard about it until UFO researchers began to call him.

Wives and relatives aren't immune either. Thaddeus Love flew with the bodies from Roswell to Fort Worth. Those on the aircraft remembered him, and the only name that Martucci could recall, when he still talked, was Love's. Thaddeus Love died in May, 1989, but his wife hadn't moved so the phone number was still good.

Like the others, Mrs. Love knew that her husband had

been a member of the 509th in July, 1947. She was willing to talk about it, right up to the first mention of the special flight. Then she said, "You'll have to talk to someone else. One of the officers."

She was told that others had been contacted and they had talked, but again she said that there was nothing she could say. She became frightened and agitated. She didn't want to talk, insisting that she didn't know anything. "Talk to officers."

It was obvious that Thaddeus Love had told her something and it was equally obvious that he'd told her never to mention it. Thinking that she might respond to another member of her husband's flight crew, that was tried. Her answer was to shout, "No, no, no. Leave me alone."

It could be argued that there was another reason for the agitation shown by each of these people. It could be a coincidence that the mere mention of the 509th and the events of July, 1947, caused a reluctance to talk. The 509th was, at that time, the only atomic bomb group in the world. The men assigned to it all had top secret atomic clearances. They lived with secrets and atomic weapons and security. They knew that the slightest mention of an atomic secret could result in court martial. And their wives were aware of the regulations, too.

But the atomic secrets and the normal security that surrounded the 509th had evaporated over the years. Secrets that had to maintained in 1947 had fallen to improvements to the weapons through the years and the formation of other atomic squadrons. Almost everything that had been classified at Roswell in 1947 had been declassified. Even the unit history that had once been secret was available to anyone who wanted to see it.

There seemed to be only a single secret left from those days, and it revolved around what had happened in July, 1947. When questioned specifically about the crash, more than one man said that he couldn't talk about it. They had been sworn to secrecy.

Sheridan Cavitt, for example, said that he remembered

nothing about it. As far as he knew, it had never happened. There was no talk of flying saucers or crashes near the Roswell base.

The Provost Marshal, who had been identified as being on the debris field by two witnesses, didn't deny it. Instead he said that he had been sworn to secrecy and that he couldn't talk about it. That was all he would say. Even when asked directly about being on the crash site, he said that he couldn't talk about it. He couldn't talk about it forty-three years after the event.

Frank Kaufman confirmed the secrecy, explaining that the men had been taken in small groups into a room for their debriefings. When that was finished, they were warned that everything they had seen or heard was classified. They were not to mention anything about it, ever.

And that secrecy extended beyond the military men and their wives and family. The archaeologists who stumbled onto the second crash site were sworn to secrecy and none of them broke that. They were frightened by the military.

Mary Ann Gardner, the nurse from the cancer ward, said that the dying archaeologist who told of seeing the bodies said the same thing over and over. "Don't tell anyone that I said anything." Even as she lay dying, she was reluctant to talk. She was afraid the government would still be able to do something to her.

The only other archaeologist to talk refuses to let his name be used because he is afraid for his government grants and the reactions of his colleagues. For forty years he kept quiet and then, after a great deal of thought, made a single phone call to tell his story. He stressed that he was afraid of what would happen to his reputation if he was identified.

Melvin Brown's wife and oldest daughter still refuse to talk about what he told them on his deathbed. They think the government can still do something to him or his records. And they remember Brown's statements after saying that he'd seen the bodies. "Don't tell anyone or you'll get daddy in trouble."

And that's the interesting thing about the Roswell crash. Witnesses who are obviously lying maintain those lies in the face of evidence. Men say they weren't in Roswell in July, 1947, when the records clearly prove they were there. Others admit to being in Roswell but remember nothing about the events. "It was too long ago," they claim.

But even those who deny knowledge help advance the case. Remember Circleville, Ohio. The farmer found a balloon, the sheriff confirmed it, and the newspaper printed pictures of it. Those people are willing to talk and the military made no attempt to classify the find or collect the evidence.

At Roswell, they moved in and swore everyone to secrecy even though the balloon supposedly found in Roswell was similar to the one found in Ohio. In one case, the witnesses were sworn to secrecy and in the other they were not.

When considering the Roswell case, one question must be addressed. If nothing extraordinary happened at Roswell, why the extraordinary efforts to keep it secret? Why are the people afraid to talk forty-three years later?

Appendix E:
The Interviews

In the course of completing this work, more than two hundred people were contacted and interviewed. Some of them feared ridicule, some of them wanted to tell their stories and not be deluged with inquiries about the subject, and others feared losing military and government pensions. Some witnesses, fearing, with some justification, this kind of harassment, asked that their names be withheld. Reluctantly, we agreed.

It must be stressed that every bit of information from those anonymous sources has been confirmed through discussions with others.

The following is a list containing the names and the number of interviews conducted with those who granted permission to use their names. Remember, this is not the entire list.

ANDERSON, Gerald: conducted by phone, Feb 1990

ARGENBRIGHT, E.J.: conducted by phone, Aug 1990, Dec 1990

ARNER, Harold: conducted by phone, Sep 1990

BEAN, Beverly: conducted in person, Mar 1990, Jan 1991

BEBRICH, Carl: conducted by phone, Aug 1989, Sep 1989

BENNETT, Charles: conducted by phone, Dec 1990

BERLINER, Don: conducted in person, July 1990, Sep 1990

BIESIOT, A.C.:   conducted in person, Jan 1990

BLAKE, Harry: conducted in person, Aug 1989, Sep 1989

BLANCHARD, Anne: conducted by phone in Aug 1989

BOGEL, Bill: conducted by phone, Feb 1989; in person, Sep 1989

BOGEL, Don: conducted by phone, Feb 1989, Oct 1989

BRAZEL, Shirley: conducted in person, Feb 1989, Sep 1990; by phone, March 1989, Aug 1989, Jan 1990

BRAZEL, William: conducted by phone, 1988, conducted in person, Feb 1989, March 1989, Sep 1990; on phone, March, 1989, April 1989, May 1989, June 1989, Oct 1989

BRILEY, Joe: conducted by phone, Oct 1989, Apr 1990, Dec 1990

BROWN, Jerry: conducted in person, Jan 1990

BROWN, Ada: conducted in person, Jan 1991

BURTON, Wayne: conducted by phone, Feb 1990

BUTT, Walter: conducted in person, 1988

CARLTON, Paul: conducted in June 1991

CAVITT, Mary: conducted by phone, Aug 1989, in person, Jan 1990

CAVITT, Joe: conducted by phone, Dec 1989

CAVITT, Sheridan: conducted by phone, Aug 1989; in person, Jan 1990

CASHON, Charles A.: conducted by phone, Jan 1990, Dec 1990

CRUIKSHANK, Arthur W.: conducted by phone, Jul 1990

DALEY, William: in person Nov 1990

DANLEY, J. F. (Fleck):   conducted by phone, Oct 1990

DENNIS, Glenn: conducted in person, Nov 1990, Mar 1991

DENNIS, Robert: conducted by phone, Sept 1990

DE VAUGHN, Bill: conducted in person, Jan 1990, Jul 1990, Feb 1991

DICK, Herbert: conducted by phone, July 1989

DOBSON, S. M. "Sav":   conducted in person, Sept 1990

DOUD, Donald: conducted by phone, Dec 1989

DUBOSE, Thomas: conducted in person, Aug 1990, by phone Feb 1991

DUGGER, Barbara: conducted in person, Mar 1991

DUTTON, Bertha: conducted by phone, Feb 1990

EASLEY, Edwin: conducted by phone, Oct 1989, Feb 1990, May 1990

ECCLESTON, Charles: conducted by phone, Aug 1989

ELLIS, Eddie: conducted by phone, Oct 1990

EXON, Arthur: conducted by phone, Jul 1989, May 1990; conducted in person, Jun 1990, July 1990

FOSTER, Iris: conducted by phone Feb 1990

FRIEDMAN, Stanton: conducted in person, Aug 1989, Jul 1990, Sep 1990

FRIEND, Robert: conducted by phone, Aug 1990

FUMIHIKO, Fujiki: conducted in person, July 1989

GARCIA, David: conducted in person, Dec 1989

GARDNER, Mary Ann: conducted by phone, Feb 1989, April 1990

GATES, Robert: conducted by phone, Aug 1989, Sep 1989

GLOVER, Don: conducted in person July 1989

GOOD, Timothy: conducted in person, July 1989

GREENEN, James S.: conducted in person, Oct 1989

GROODE, Mary Katherine: conducted by phone, May 1990

HAMILTON, Colin: conducted by phone, Sep 1990

HARTINGER, Robert: conducted by phone, Feb 1990, March 1990

HAUT, Walter: conducted by phone, Dec 1988; in person, April 1989, Aug 1989, Jan 1990, Jul 1990

HEICK, Ralph: conducted in person, Feb 1989, Aug 1989; by phone, March 1990

HENDERSON, Anna: conducted by phone, Sep 1990

HENDERSON, Bill: conducted by phone, Aug 1990

HENDERSON, Ned: conducted by phone, May 1990

HENDERSON, Sappho: conducted in person, Aug 1989, by phone, Dec 1989, Jan 1990, April 1990, Jul 1990, Feb 1991

HILLMAN, Imholtz: conducted by phone, Sep 1990

HOBBS, Alma: conducted in person, Sep 1990

HODAM, John: conducted by phone, Aug 1990

HOPPER, Jeff: conducted by phone, Nov 1990

HUDON, Betsy: conducted by phone, Feb 1989, June 1989, Feb 1990

JEFFERY, Arthur: conducted by phone, Feb 1991

JEFFREYS, Kenneth: conducted by phone Oct 1989

JOHNSON, J. Bond: conducted by phone, Feb 1989, May 1989, Dec 1989, May 1990, Aug 1990

JOHNSON, Mrs Jesse B., Jr.: conducted by phone, April 1989

JONES, Bessie: conducted by phone, Dec 1989

JONES, Loretta: conducted in person, Jul 1990

JONES, Milton: conducted by phone, Aug 1989

JOSEPH, Paul: conducted in person Feb, 1991

JOYCE, Frank: conducted by phone, Jan 1990

KAUFMAN, Frank: conducted by phone, Jan 1990; in person, Jan 1990

KEEL, John: conducted by phone, Nov 1989

KELLY, J.H.: conducted by phone, Dec 1989

KEYHOE, Donald E.: conducted by phone, 1976

KIRKPATRICK, Sheila: conducted by phone, Dec 1989

KNIGHT, Alice: conducted by phone, Aug 1990, Sep 1990; in person, Sep 1990, Oct 1990

KROMSCHROEDER, John: conducted by phone, Jan 1990, in person, Jul 1990

KYLE, Elizabeth: conducted by phone, Aug 1989

LINDE, Shirley: conducted by phone, Jan 1991

LINDER, David: conducted in person, Dec 1989; by phone, Feb 1990, March 1990

LITTELL, Max: conducted by phone, Aug 1990

LORENZEN, Coral: conducted at APRO Headquarters, 1972, 1983.

LOUNSBURY, W.E.: conducted in person, Jul 1990

LOVE, Thaddeus: conducted by phone, May 1989

LYTLE, Chester: conducted by phone, Jan 1989, Aug 1990; in person, Feb 1989, April 1989, Jan 1990

LYTLE, Steve: conducted by phone, Feb 1990

MACK, John: conducted in person, Nov 1990, by phone Feb 1991

MACPHERSON, Clarence M.: conducted by phone, July 1989

MANN, Allene: conducted in person, Nov 1990

MANN, Johnny: conducted by phone, Oct 1989, Dec 1989

MARCEL, Viaud: conducted in person, May 1990

MARCEL, Jesse, Jr.: conducted in person, Aug 1989, May 1990, Jul 1990; by phone, Nov 1989, Jan 1990, April 1990

MARTIN, Francis: conducted by phone, April 1989

MAGGIO, Frank: conducted in person, Nov 1988

MALTAIS, L. W.: conducted in person, Aug 1989, Jul 1990

MARTUCCI, Felix: conducted by phone, Dec 1989

MCBOYLE, Johnny: conducted by phone May, 1990, Dec 1990

MCEVOY, Paul: conducted by phone, April 1989

MCGUIRE, Phyllis: conducted by phone, Aug 1989; in person, Jan 1990, Jul 1990

MCQUIDDY, Art: conducted by phone, Jan 1990; in person, Jan 1990

MILLEN, Ernest: conducted by phone, Dec 1989

MITCHELL, Don: conducted in person, Feb 1989, April 1989

MITCHELL, Richard: conducted by phone, Sep 1989, Oct 1989, Nov 1989, Dec 1989, Jan 1990, Feb 1990, Mar 1990; in person, Jul 1990

MUNDE, Ruben: conducted in person, Nov 1990, by phone Dec 1990, Feb 1991

NEAL, David: conducted by phone, Dec 1990

NEWTON, Irving: conducted by phone, Mar 1990

ORR, David: conducted by phone, Dec 1990

PARKER, Jim: conducted by phone, Sep 1989; in person, Sep 1989

PAYNE, Bud: conducted by phone, Dec 1989; in person, Jan 1990

PERKINS, Archie: conducted by phone, Oct 1989

PLATT, Curtiss: conducted in person, Jul 1989

PORTER, Leonard: conducted in May, 1990

PORTER, Robert: conducted by phone, Jan 1990, in person, April 1990, Jul 1990

PROCTOR, Loretta: conducted by phone, April, 1989, Jan 1990; in person, Jul 1990

PROCTOR, Norris: conducted by phone, Jan 1990

RAGSDALE, Betty: conducted by phone, Aug 1990

RAYNES, Jock: conducted by phone Nov 1990

REESE, Ed: conducted by phone, Jan 1990, Feb 1990, Jul 1990

REXROLD, Mike: conducted by phone, Nov 1989, Jan 1990

RICHARDS, Myra: conducted by phone, Jan 1990

RICKETT, Lewis: conducted by phone, May 1989, Nov 1989, Dec 1989, Jan 1990, Feb 1990, March 1990; in person, Nov 1989, Jan 1990

RICKETT, Lewis, Mrs.:   conducted in person, Oct 1989, Jan 1990

ROBERTS, Jud: conducted by phone, Jan 1990; in person, Jan 1990

RODDEN, Jack: conducted by phone, Aug 1989; in person, Sep 1989

ROMERO, Jean: conducted by phone, Mar 1990

ROWE, Frankie: conducted in person Nov 1990

RUNYARD, Gerald: conducted by phone Nov 1989

SAGER, Edward M.:   conducted by phone, Aug 1990

SAUNDERS, Patrick: conducted by phone, June 1989, Dec 1990

SCHREIBER, Bessie: conducted by phone, Mar 1989, July 1989

SCHERRER: conducted in person Nov 1990

SEIFRIED, Richard D.:   conducted by phone, Dec 1989, Jan 1990

SHIRKEY, Robert: conducted in person, Jan 1990; by phone, Sep 1989, Dec 1989; in person, Jul 1990

SHORTRIDGE, Lacey: conducted by phone, Oct 1989

SKELLEY, Edgar: conducted by phone, Nov 1989

SLUSHER, Robert: conducted by phone, Oct 1990

SMITH, David: conducted by phone, Jul 1990

SMITH, Laurence: conducted by phone, Nov 1989

SMITH, Louise: conducted by phone, June 1990

SMITH, Robert E.: conducted by phone, Dec 1989, Jan 1990, in person, Mar 1991

SMITH, Warren: conducted in person, Oct 1988; by phone, Dec 1989

SNYDER, Gene: conducted by phone, May 1989, Sep 1989

SPARKS, Elaine: conducted by phone, Dec 1989

SPURLIN, F.L.: conducted by phone, Feb 1990

STONE, Clifford: conducted in person, Feb 1989; by phone, Aug 1990

STRICKLAND, Marian: conducted by phone, Jan 1990

STRINGFIELD, Leonard: conducted by phone, Feb 1989, March 1989, May 1989, Aug 1989, Sep 1989, Oct 1989, Nov 1989, Dec 1989, Jan 1990, April 1990; in person, June 1989, Feb 1990

STUBBS, Al: conducted by phone, Jan 1989

SWEDMARK, Jean A.: conducted by phone, April 1989

SWORE, Robert, Mrs.: conducted by phone, Feb 1991

SULTEMEIER, Daniel: conducted by phone, Aug 1990

SULTEMEIER, Frank: conducted by phone, July 1989

SULTEMEIER, Juanita: conducted in person, Jan 1990

TAYLOR, William: conducted by phone, Apr 1990

THOMPSON, Tommy: conducted by phone, Jan 1990

TIFFANY, John G.: conducted in person, Sep 1990

TILLEY, John: conducted by phone, Aug 1989

TOOMAN, Bill: conducted by phone, Aug 1989

TORRES, Robert: conducted by phone, Dec 1990

TOULESE, Carmy: conducted by phone, Oct 1989

TUCKER, Merle: conducted in person, Aug 1989; by phone, April 1989, Dec 1989

TULK, Christine: conducted in person, Jul 1990

TULK, Jay: conducted in person, Jan 1990

TULK, Elizabeth: conducted in person, Jan 1990, Jul 1990

TYREE, June: conducted in person, Aug 1989

TYREE, Tommy: conducted in person, Aug 1989; by phone, Sep 1989, Dec 1989

VEGH, Elaine: conducted by phone, Feb 1990, Mar 1990

WACHTER, Helen: conducted by phone, Mar 1990

WADE, Cory: conducted in person, Nov 1990

WALKER, Jim: conducted by phone Nov 1990

WALSH, George: conducted by phone, May 1990

WATKINS, John: conducted in person, May 1990

WELLS, Jeff: conducted in person, Feb 1989, Sep 1990; by phone, Aug 1989, Sep 1989, Dec 1989, Feb 1990

WEST, Jay: conducted in person, Nov 1989

WILLIAMS, Lyle: conducted by phone Nov 1989

WILMOT, Terry: conducted by phone, Aug 1989

WILSON, Wallace: conducted by phone, Aug 1989

WOODY, William: conducted in person, Nov 1990

ZORN, Vernon D.:   conducted in person, April 1990, by phone, Oct 1989

In addition, the following individuals were contacted in an attempt to learn more about the events of July, 1947.

William Adams
James M. Anderson
Harold W. Arner
Cory Beck
Pat Beckett
Joe Bergoich
W. Bischoff
Dale Bocock
Chester Bohart
Donald Carroll
Bill Cassidy
Dick Chapman
Albert Clayton
Robert T. Dardan
George Davis
Lyman Deford
Jesse M. Delozier
Harold Denning
Nancy Dumas
Ed Dunn
E. R. Eggert
Florence Ellis
Orville Gardner
Robert Gilman
Stan Gordon
Hoyt S. Griffith
Bruce Groesbeck
Elizabeth Hackworth
Colin C. Hamilton
Charles E. Hanshaw
Elizabeth Hart
Harold T. Hastings
Robert Hastings

Emil Haury
James Hendley
Dick Henry
Ray Howard
Anthony Ivens
Bruce Johnson
Henry Jones
Ralph Jordon
Mrs. Arnold Kalp
Edwin R. Kellogg
James Kolb
Milton Knight
Tom Kurns
James Lamb
Elmer L. Landry
Paul Martin
Vere McCarty
Sean McLaughlin
David Miles
Robert Murray
John Nalda
Arnold Pfeiffer
Mrs. Archie Perkins
Fred Plog
Timothy D. Proctor
Tim Rasmussen
Royal Reese
James E. Rogers
Justin Rose
John Rudowski
Joe C. Shackelford
John Simonson
John Skinner

William Sonntag
Avritz Sparks
Florian J. Spiczka
Milton Sprouse
Mary Strode
Peter Sturrock
Russell Snyder
Rosemary Talley
James Taylor
William Taylor
Robert Terrell
Fred Van Devender

Gene Wagner
Arthur T. Walters
Charles J. Warth
Kay Whitman
Walt Whitmore, Jr.
John Wilson
Joseph Wirth
Fred Windorf
Steven Wright
Robert Wyatt
John Wyth
Donald B. Yeager

Appendix F: The Intelligence Function in July, 1947

509th Bomb Group

MAJ Jesse A. Marcel - OIC

CPT James R. Breece
1LT Charles V. Swanson
1LT Floyd D. Powell
1LT Victor G. Thiel

COUNTER-
INTELLIGENCE:
CPT Sheridan Cavitt
MSG Lewis S. Rickett
SGT Jack Williams

SQUADRON
INTELLIGENCE:
Emory R. Wells

In from Washington DC:
WO Robert Thomas

Eighth Air Force

COL Alfred F. Kalberer - OIC

MAJ Edwin M. Kirton
MAJ George W. Kinney
1LT Robert B. Wilson
MSG George R. Bremer, Jr.
MSG Herbert M. Harwood, Jr.

COUNTER-
INTELLIGENCE:
MAJ Milton R. Knight
MAJ John C. Campbell
CPT Louis J. Schiavo
MSG Robert A. Marco
MSG Milo D. Hodges
TSG Wilbur R. Stephens
TSG William H. Valentine
SSG Roderick B. Pierce
SSG John J. Guilfoyle

Appendix G:
Relevant Persons

ARMSTRONG, Captain—Collected pieces of the crash from the Brazels' two years after the crash.

BARNETT, Grady L. "Barney"—Claimed to have found wreckage and bodies on the Plains of San Agustin, about 120 miles from where Mac Brazel found wreckage.

BARROWCLOUGH, Lt. Colonel Robert—Executive Officer of Roswell Army Air Field, Roswell, New Mexico. He flew on the first B-29 flight from Roswell to Fort Worth Army Air Field.

BLANCHARD, Colonel William—Commander, 509th Bomb Group, Roswell Army Air Field. Upon seeing the material collected at the site by Major Jesse A. Marcel, he ordered the roads leading to the crash site blocked. He later made a special trip to the site.

BRAZEL, W.W. "Mac"—Foreman at the Foster ranch in Lincoln County, near Corona, New Mexico. He found the crash site on the ranch.

BRAZEL, Bill—Son of Mac Brazel and a major witness.

BRILEY, Lt. Colonel Joe—In mid-July, 1947, he became Operations Officer at Roswell Army Air Field.

BROWN, Dr. Jerry—NASA engineer who had worked at White Sands Missile Range. He has speculated that the metal found was Duraluminum alloy or a V-2 rocket.

BROWN, Sergeant Melvin E.—Was at the second site, guarding the truck containing alien bodies. He also guarded the hanger at Roswell Army Air Field while crates from the site were held there.

CHAVEZ, Senator Dennis—U.S. Senator from New Mexico. He supposedly called Walter Whitmore, Sr. and suggested he not air the recorded interview with Mac Brazel.

CLARK, Deputy, B.A.—Took the initial report from Mac Brazel at the Chaves County sheriff's office.

DUBOSE, Colonel Thomas J.—Chief of Staff to Brigadier General Roger Ramey. He was photographed in Ramey's office with the "debris."

EASLEY, Major Edwin D.—Provost Marshal in charge of the troops clearing the crash site.

FOSTER, Iris—Owned a cafe in Taos, New Mexico. She often heard a man named "Cactus Jack," an amateur archaeologist, talk about seeing a downed alien ship.

GARDNER, Mary Ann—Nurse at St. Petersburg Hospital, Florida. She heard an archaeologist on her deathbed tell about discovering an alien ship and bodies.

GARDNER, Norma—Typist with a top security clearance at Wright-Patterson Air Force Base. She typed autopsy reports on alien beings and saw two bodies.

HAUT, 1st Lieutenant Walter—Public Information Officer at Roswell Army Air Field. He was ordered by Colonel Blanchard to issue a press release stating that a flying disc had been recovered.

HENDERSON, Captain Oliver W. "Pappy"—Member, First Air Transport Unit, Roswell Army Air Field, and co-pilot of the first B-29 flight from Roswell to Fort Worth. He also was the pilot of a C-54 flight carrying wreckage from Roswell to Wright Field, Dayton, Ohio.

HENDERSON, Sappho—Wife of Pappy Henderson. She was told by her husband that he had flown the C-54 to Wright Field.

JENNINGS, Colonel Payne—Deputy base and group commander at Roswell Army Air Field. He was the pilot of the first B-29 flight from Roswell to Fort Worth.

JOHNSON, J. Bond—Staff reporter for the *Fort Worth Star Telegram*. He took four photographs of the "wreckage" in General Ramey's office.

JOHNSON, Dr. Jesse B.—Base pathologist at Roswell Army Air Field. He performed the preliminary studies on the bodies.

JOYCE, Frank—Reporter and announcer for Roswell radio station KGFL. He interviewed Mac Brazel on the telephone before the military arrived and was later told a different story.

KAUFMAN, Frank—Friend of Warrant Officer Robert Thomas. He said that the bodies were sealed in a wooden crate while still at the hospital.

LAPAZ, Dr. Lincoln—Expert in meteoritics; degrees in mathematics and astronomy. He was called in to investigate the crash site.

MALTAIS, L.W. "Vern"—Said Barney Barnett had told him he had seen bodies in one-piece gray suits, after which archaeologists and the military arrived.

MARCEL, Major Jesse A.—Intelligence Officer at Roswell Army Air Field, 509th Bomb Group Intelligence Office. He picked up material at the ranch and later flew it to Forth Worth Army Air Field.

MARCEL, Jesse, Jr.—Son of Jesse A. Marcel. He saw debris samples his father brought home and, under hypnosis, was able to recall the designs marking the I-beam.

MCBOYLE, Johnny—Station manager of radio station KSWS, Roswell, New Mexico. He attempted to put the Roswell story out over the wire.

MCGUIRE, Phyllis—Daughter of Sheriff George A. Wilcox. She saw the military arrive very soon after her father called them.

MCQUIDDY, Art—Editor, *Roswell Morning Dispatch*. Walter Haut delivered a press release to him, which other military personnel later tried to retrieve.

NEWTON, Warrant Officer Irving—Weather officer at Fort Worth Army Air Field. He was ordered to General Ramey's office to identify the "wreckage," a Rawin target balloon.

PARKER, Jim—Ranch hand of Mac Brazel's. His son came home from school one day in 1988 reporting an Air Force truck in the area.

PAYNE, Bud—Neighbor of Mac Brazel. He had gotten thrown off the Foster ranch by the military while chasing a stray cow. He knew exactly where the crash site was.

PORTER, Sergeant Robert—Crewman on the B-29 that flew packages from Roswell Army Air field to Fort Worth Army Air Field. He claims Jesse Marcel was on the flight.

PROCTOR, Floyd—Mac Brazel's nearest neighbor and husband of Loretta Proctor. Brazel came to their house to show them a piece of metal.

PROCTOR, Loretta—Mac Brazel's nearest neighbor and wife of Floyd Proctor. She said she remembers her husband trying to whittle on the metal but failing to make a mark.

PROCTOR, Timothy D.—Son of Floyd and Loretta. He found the crash site with Mac Brazel.

RAMEY, Brigadier General Roger—Commander, Eighth Air Force, of which the 509th Bomb Group was a part.

RICKETT, Lewis S.—Army counter-intelligence (CIC) agent, who assisted in the retrieval of debris from the crash site.

ROBERTS, Jud—Minority owner of radio station KGFL, Roswell, New Mexico. He said the military picked up copies of Haut's press release from the media there.

SHIRKEY, Robert—Saw wreckage taken by eight or nine men through the Operations Building at Roswell Army Air Field.

SLEPPY, Lydia—Secretary to Merle Tucker in Albuquerque, New Mexico. She was ordered over the teletype to stop transmitting the crash story.

SMITH, Sergeant Robert E.—Member of the First Air Transport Unit at Roswell Army Air Field. He spent an entire day loading three aircraft with the material from the crash site.

STRICKLAND, Lyman—Neighbor of Mac Brazel. He saw Brazel in Roswell being escorted out of the newspaper offices by three military officers.

STRICKLAND, Marian—Neighbor of Mac Brazel, wife of Lyman Strickland. An upset Brazel visited them after his release from custody at Roswell Army Air Field.

STRINGFIELD, Len—Researcher and writer in the UFO field. He interviewed Major Jesse Marcel in 1978.

THOMAS, Robert—Warrant Officer who came in on a special flight to assist in recovery of the debris.

TUCKER, Merle—Owner of several New Mexico radio stations. He arrived back from out of town to find that his Roswell station manager had tried to put the crash story out over the wire.

TYREE, Tommy—Hand for Mac Brazel. He began work about one month after the crash and remembers that Brazel was irritated because the sheep would not cross the debris field and had to be driven the long way around to water.

WHITMORE, Walter, Sr.—Majority owner of radio station KGFL in Roswell, New Mexico. He hid Mac Brazel from the military.

WILCOX, Sheriff George A.—Sheriff of Chaves County, in which Roswell is located. Mac Brazel showed him a piece of the debris and he suggested Brazel contact the military.

WILMOT, Dan—Resident of Roswell, N.M. He and his wife saw an oval-shaped object fly over their house on July 2, 1947, the probable date of the crash.

ZORN, Vernon D.—Non-commissioned officer in charge of the Third Photo Unit at Roswell Army Air Field. He said no photos of the crash site were taken by his men.

Notes

Part I: A Historical Perspective

CHAPTER ONE—THE SUMMER: 1947

1. Ted Bloecher, *Report on the UFO Wave of 1947* (Washington, D.C., Author, 1967)
2. "Mystery Objects Seen In Fast Flight," *Cedar Rapids Gazette,* 26 June 1947
3. Bloecher, 1967
4. *Cedar Rapids Gazette,* 9 July 1947
5. "Army Planes Comb Skies for Flying Discs," *Des Moines Register, The,* 7 July 1947
6. *Clinton Herald,* 6 July 1947
7. "Flying Discs Still Puzzling U.S. Residents," *Circleville Herald,* 7 July 1947
8. "Flying Saucer Hoax Is Told," *Des Moines Register, The,* 8 July 1947
9. Bloecher, 1967
10. Ruppelt, Edward J., *The Report on Unidentified Flying Objects* (New York: Ace Books, 1956)
11. *Las Vegas Review-Journal,* 9 July 1947

CHAPTER TWO—ROSWELL REVISITED

1. "RAAF Captures Flying Saucer," *Roswell Daily Record,* 8 July 1947

2. " 'Disk-overy' Near Roswell Identified As Weather Balloon by FWAAF Officer,'' *Fort Worth Star-Telegram,* 9 July 1947

3. Frank Edwards, "Lecture on UFOs," Convention, Indianapolis, Indiana, 27 Oct 1955

4. Len Stringfield, personal interview, 9 Feb 1990

5. Charles Berlitz and William Moore, *The Roswell Incident* (New York: Berkley Books, 1988)

6. Lewis S. Rickett, personal interview, Nov 1989

Part II: Roswell, the Real Story

CHAPTER THREE—JULY 3–14, 1947: MAC BRAZEL

1. "Weather Briefs," *Roswell Daily Record,* 1–30 July 1947

2. Loretta Proctor, personal interview, 20 April 1989

3. Bill Brazel, personal interview, 31 March 1989

4. Tommy Tyree, personal interview, 12 Aug 1989

5. Norris Proctor, personal interview, 12 Aug 1989

6. Phyllis McGuire, personal interview, 27 Jan 1990

7. Lewis S. Rickett, personal interview, Nov 1989

8. Phyllis McGuire, personal interview, 27 Jan 1990

9. Lewis S. Rickett, personal inteview, Nov 1989

10. "Send First Roswell Wire Photos from Record Office," *Roswell Daily Record,* 9 July 1947

11. "Harassed Rancher who Located 'Saucer' Sorry He Told About It," *Roswell Daily Record,* 9 July 1947

12. Frank Joyce, personal interview, 26 Jan 1947

13. Bill Brazel, personal interview, 19 Feb 1989

14. Tommy Tyree, personal interview, 12 Aug 1989

CHAPTER FOUR—JULY 6–10, 1947:
  CHAVES COUNTY SHERIFF

1. Phyllis McGuire, personal interview, 27 Jan 1990

2. Juanita Sultemeier, personal interview, 27 Jan 1990

3. Phyllis McGuire, personal interview, 27 Jan 1990
4. Elizabeth Tulk, letter to authors, 28 Jan 1990

CHAPTER FIVE—JULY 7, 1947: THE DEBRIS FIELD

1. Personal observation, 31 March 1989
2. Bill Brazel, personal interview, 19 Feb 1989
3. Leonard H. Stringfield, *UFO Crash/Retrieval Syndrome* (Seguin Tex: MUFON, 1980)
4. Bill Brazel, personal interview, 31 March 1989
5. Stringfield, *Syndrome*
6. Bill Brazel, personal interview, 19 Feb 1989
7. Lewis S. Rickett, personal interview, Nov 1989
8. Jesse Marcel, Jr., personal interview, 3 Aug 1989
9. Bill Brazel, personal interview, 31 March 1989
10. Bill Brazel, personal interview, 19 Feb 1989
11. Lewis S. Rickett, personal interview, Nov 1989

CHAPTER SIX—JULY 8, 1947: THE MORNING BRIEFING

1. Patrick Saunders, personal interview, 20 June 1989
2. Roswell Army Air Field Phone Book, Aug 1947
3. Lewis S. Rickett, personal interview, Nov 1989
4. George "Jud" Roberts, personal interview, 31 Jan 1990
5. Sheridan S. Cavitt, personal interview, 29 Jan 1990

CHAPTER SEVEN—JULY 8, 1947: THE DEBRIS FIELD

1. Lewis S. Rickett, personal interview, Jan 1990
2. George "Jud" Roberts, personal interview, 31 Jan 1990
3. Lewis S. Rickett, personal interview, Jan 1990
4. Lewis S. Rickett, personal interview, Nov 1989
5. Vernon D. Zorn, personal interview, Feb 1990
6. Robert E. Smith, personal interview, 19 Jan 1990
7. Robert E. Smith, personal interview, 19 Jan 1990
8. Lewis S. Rickett, personal interview, Jan 1990

9. Loretta Proctor, personal interview, 20 April 1989
10. Jerry Brown, personal interview, 28 Jan 1990
11. Lewis S. Rickett, personal interview, Jan 1990
12. Robert E. Smith, personal interview, 19 Jan 1990
13. Patrick Saunders, personal interview, 20 June 1990
14. Joe Briley, personal interview, 20 Oct 1989
15. Edwin D. Easley, personal interview, 4 Feb 1990

CHAPTER EIGHT—JULY 8-10, 1947: THE PRESS BRIEFINGS

1. Walter G. Haut, personal interview, 1 April 1989
2. "Roswell Statement," *San Francisco Chronicle*, 9 July 1947
3. Joe Briley, personal interview, 20 Oct 1989
4. George "Jud" Roberts, personal interview, 31 Jan 1990
5. J. Bond Johnson, personal interview, 27 Feb 1989
6. Irving Newton, personal interview, 25 March 1990
7. Thomas DuBose, personal interview, 31 March 1990
8. Copy, FBI Teletype Message, 7 July 1947
9. Walter G. Haut, personal interview, 1 April 1989
10. "Flying Discs Still Puzzling U.S. Residents," *Circleville Herald*, 7 July 1947
11. Walter G. Haut, personal interview, 20 April 1989
12. "Local Weatherman Believes Disks to Be Bureau Devices," *Roswell Daily Record*, 9 July 1947
13. "Disk-overy' Near Roswell Identified As Weather Balloon by FWAAF Officer," *Fort Worth Star-Telegram*, 9 July 1947
14. Frank Joyce, personal interview, 31 March 1989
15. George "Jud" Roberts, personal interview, 31 Jan 1990

CHAPTER NINE—JULY 8-10, 1947: THE FLIGHTS OUT

1. Thomas DuBose, personal interview, 16 Aug 1990
2. Jesse Marcel, Jr., personal interview, 2 Aug 1989
3. Robert Porter, personal interview, 8 April 1990

4. Sappho Henderson, personal interview, 3 Aug 1989
5. Vere McCarty, letter, 12 July 1989
6. Lewis S. Rickett, personal interview, Nov 1989

CHAPTER TEN—JULY 8, 1947: THE BODIES

1. Berlitz and Moore, 1988
2. Lewis S. Rickett, personal interview, Jan 1990
3. Beverly Bean, personal interview, March 1990
4. John Kromschroeder, personal interview, 29 Jan 1990
5. Beverly Bean, personal interview, Jan 1990

CHAPTER ELEVEN—JULY, 1947–PRESENT: THE BODIES

1. Len Stringfield, personal interview, 8 June 1989
2. Stringfield, *Syndrome*
3. John Timmerman, personal interview, 4 Feb 1990
4. Helen Wachter, personal interview, 4 April 1990
5. Bill de Vaughn, personal interview, 3 Feb 1990

CHAPTER TWELVE—JULY, 1947:
THE WRIGHT FIELD CONNECTION

1. Official Air Force biography of Arthur Exon
2. Letter from Twining to BG George Schulgen, 23 Sep 1947
3. Arthur Exon, personal interview, 19 July 1990

CHAPTER THIRTEEN—JULY, 1947: THE ARCHAEOLOGISTS

1. Lewis S. Rickett, personal interview, Jan 1990
2. Dick Chapman, personal interview, 19 May 1989
3. J.H. Kelly, personal interview, 12 Dec 1989
4. Fred Windorf, personal interview, 19 Oct 1989
5. Mary Ann Gardner, personal interview, 10 Feb 1990
6. Iris Foster, personal interview, 12 Feb 1990

CHAPTER FOURTEEN—SEPTEMBER, 1947:
  RICKETT AND LAPAZ

1. 509th Unit History, July and Aug, 1947.
2. Lincoln LaPaz with Albert Rosenfeld, "Japan's Balloon Invasion of America," *Collier's,* 17 Jan 1953
3. Bill Cassidy, personal interview, 19 Nov 1989
4. Ruppelt, 72–73
5. Lewis S. Rickett, personal interview, Jan 1990
6. Lewis S. Rickett, personal interview, Nov 1989
7. Lewis S. Rickett, personal interview, Jan 1990
8. Correspondence from personal files of Alexander D. Mebone 15 Jan 1954

Part III: The J. Allen Hyneck Center for UFO Studies Investigation

CHAPTER SIXTEEN—EXPLANATIONS

1. "General Ramey Empties Roswell Saucer," *Roswell Daily Record,* 9 July 1947
2. "Harassed Rancher who Located 'Saucer' Sorry He Told About It," *Roswell Daily Record,* 9 July 1947
3. Lewis S. Rickett, personal interview, Nov 1989
4. Bill Brazel, personal interview, 31 March 1989
5. Tommy Tyree, personal interview, 12 Aug 1989
6. Tommy Tyree, personal interview, 12 Aug 1989
7. Lewis S. Rickett, personal interview, Nov 1989
8. Mrs. Lyman Strickland, personal interview, 4 Jan 1990
9. Paul McEvoy, personal interview, Apr 1989
10. "Flying Discs Still Puzzling U.S. Residents," *Circleville Herald,* 7 July 1947
11. Irving Newton, personal interview, 21 Mar 1989
12. Bill Brazel, personal interview, 19 Feb 1989
13. "Harassed Rancher who Located 'Saucer' Sorry He Told About It," *Roswell Daily Record,* 9 July 1947
14. John Keel, personal interview, 19 Nov 1989

15. Robert C. Mikesh, *Japan's World War II Balloon Bomb Attacks On North America,* Vol. 9 (Washington D.C.: Smithsonian Institution, 1973)
16. Mikesh, 1973
17. Tommy Tyree, personal interview, 12 Aug 1989
18. Beverly Bean, personal interview, March 1990

Part V: The Appendices

APPENDIX A: PROJECT BLUE BOOK

1. "Project Blue Book" (microfilm). National Archives, Washington, D.C.
2. Nathan F. Twining, letter to BG George Schulgen, 23 Sep 1947
3. Ruppelt, 26.
4. "Project Blue Book" (microfilm). National Archives, Washington, D.C.
5. "Project Blue Book Master Index," (microfilm). National Archives, Washington, D.C.
6. Kevin Randle, *The UFO Casebook,* (New York: Warner Books, 1989), 19–27
7. Ruppelt, 64
8. Randle, *Casebook,* 28–31
9. Ruppelt, 81–85
10. Ruppelt, 113–130
11. Randle, *Casebook,* 64–71
12. Randle, *Casebook,* 64–71
13. "Saucers Swarm Over Capital, *Cedar Rapids Gazette,* 29 Jul 1947
14. Randle, *Casebook,* 74–77
15. J. Allen Hynek, personal interview, Dec 1982
16. Daniel S. Gillmor, ed., *Scientific Study of Unidentified Flying Objects* (New York: Bantam Books, 1969), 525
17. Gillmor, 525
18. Kevin D. Randle and Robert Charles Cornett, "The

Project Blue Book Cover-up: Pentagon Suppressed UFO Data," *UFO Report,* Fall 1975, 27
19. J. Allen Hynek, personal interview, Jan 1983
20. Randle and Cornett, *UFO Report,* 28

APPENDIX B: THE UFO CRASHES

1. J.P. Cahn, "The Flying Saucers and the Mysterious Little Men," *True,* Sep 1952, 4
2. Harold Dunning, personal interview, Aug 1985
3. Robert Hastings, personal interview, 28 Jan 1990
4. Warren Smith, personal interview, 27 Oct 1988
5. Randle, *Casebook,* 54–56
6. "Project Blue Book" (microfilm) National Archives
7. John Keel, personal interview, Nov 1989
8. Frank Edwards, *Flying Saucers—Serious Business* (New York: Bantam Books, 1966), 45
9. Raymond Fowler, "What About Crashed UFOs?" *Official UFO,* April 1976, 24–25
10. Coral Lorenzen, *Flying Saucers: The Startling Evidence of the Invasion from Outer Space* (New York: Signet, 1966), 104–105
11. Lorenzen, *Evidence,* 143
12. Lorenzen, *Evidence,* 142
13. Lorenzen, *Evidence,* 130–142
14. Gillmor, 94–96
15. Randle, *Casebook*, 97
16. "Brilliant Red Explosion Flares in Las Vegas Sky," *Las Vegas Sun,* 19 April 1962
17. Randle, *Casebook*
18. "Project Blue Book" (microfilm) National Archives
19. Ralph Jordan, personal interview, 12 Feb 1989
20. Walter Butt, personal interview, 9 Nov 1988
21. Letter to author, 12 May 1989
22. "Widespread Sightings of 'Fireballs' Reported," *Denver Post,* 10 Dec 1965
23. Mrs. Arnold Kalp, interview, 10 Dec 1965
24. Stan Gordon, personal interview, 12 Oct 1989

25. Stan Gordon, personal interview, 12 Oct 1989
26. "Remains Of Crashed UFO In Columbia," *A.P.R.O. Bulletin,* March–April 1968
27. "The UFO Crashes," privately published, 1989
28. "Object Falls in Bolivia," *A.P.R.O. Bulletin,* May 1978
29. "The UFO Crashes," privately published, 1989

APPENDIX C: THE PRESS ACCOUNTS

1. "Flying Saucer Hoax Is Told," *Des Moines Register,* 8 July 1947
2. J.P. Cahn, "The Flying Saucers and the Mysterious Little Men," *True,* Sep 1952, 4
3. Berlitz and Moore, 129
4. Column by Dorothy Kilgallen, *Fort Worth Star-Telegram,* 24 May 1954
5. "What On Earth?" *Clearwater Sun,* 27 Oct 1974

Glossary

APRO—Aerial Phenomena Research Organization. The first of the civilian groups devoted to the study of UFOs and founded by Jim and Coral Lorenzen.

ATIC—Air Technical Intelligence Center at Wright-Patterson Air Force Base in Dayton, Ohio. At one time it was the controlling agency of Project Blue Book.

Atomic Blast—The base newspaper of the 509th Bomb Group in Roswell in 1947.

Avionics—A contraction of Aviation Electronics. It refers to the radios and the electronic equipment in an aircraft.

B-25—A twin engine Army Air Force bomber used widely during the Second World War.

B-29—A four engine bomber used by the Army Air Force at the end of the Second World War. A B-29 Superfortress dropped the atomic bombs on Japan.

C-54—A four engine cargo plane used by the Army Air Force in 1947.

CIC—Army's Counterintelligence Corps.

Condon Committee—An Air-Force-sponsored scientific study of UFOs made by the University of Colorado. The results of the study were released in 1969.

Duraluminum—A strong, hard, lightweight alloy of aluminum that is used in aircraft construction.

Eighth Air Force—Parent unit to the 509th Bomb Group. It was located at the Fort Worth Army Air Field.

Extraterrestrial—Anything or anyone that comes from anywhere but the Earth. Meteors and comets have extraterrestrial origins.

First Air Transport Unit—located at the Roswell Army Air Field in July, 1947. First Air Transport aircraft flew much of the wreckage out of Roswell.

509th Bomb Group—In July, 1947, it was the only atomic bomb group in the world. The 509th was responsible for dropping the bombs on Hiroshima and Nagaski.

flying disc—one of the first names applied to UFOs.

flying saucers—one of the first names applied to UFOs. In time, it became a derogatory term.

IUR—International UFO Reporter. The official publication of the Center for UFO Studies.

Majestic Twelve, or MJ-12—The alleged committee organized by President Truman to investigate the craft discovered at Roswell. In the last few months the authenticity of the MJ-12 has been seriously questioned.

Project Blue Book—The Air Force's study of UFOs. It was officially terminated in December, 1969.

RAAF—Roswell Army Air Field.

Rawin Target Device—The weather balloon that skeptics claim was recovered at Roswell.

SETI—Search for Extraterrestrial Intelligence. The scientific search for life elsewhere in the universe.

UFO—Unidentified Flying Object. Official term used by the Air Force.

Bibliography

ABNEY, David L. "Expert Testimony and Eyewitness Identification," *Case and Comment* (March–April 1986)

BARKER, Gray. "America's Captured Flying Saucers—The Cover-up of the Century," *UFO Report* (May 1977)

BARNETT, Ruth. Personal Diary, 1947

BERLITZ, Charles and MOORE, William L. *The Roswell Incident*. New York: Berkley Books, 1988

BINDER, Otto. *What We Really Know about Flying Saucers*. Greenwich, Conn.: Fawcett Gold Medal Books, 1967

BLOECHER, Ted. *Report on the UFO Wave of 1947*. Washington D.C.: Author, 1967.

BLUM, Ralph, with BLUM, Judy. *Beyond Earth: Man's Contact with UFOs*. New York: Bantam Books, 1974

BROWN, Fred R. *National Security Management*. Washington D.C.: Industrial College of the Armed Forces, 1972

BRUNVAND, Jan Harold. *The Choking Doberman and Other "New" Urban Legends*. New York: W.W. Norton & Co., 1984

CAHN, J.P. "The Flying Saucers and the Mysterious Little Men," *True* (September 1952)

DIXON, Robert T. *Dynamic Astronomy*. Englewood Cliffs, New Jersey: Prentice-Hall, Inc., 1971

EDWARDS, Frank. *Flying Saucers—Here and Now!* New York: Bantam Books, 1968

——. *Flying Saucers—Serious Business.* New York: Bantam Books, 1966

——. *Strange World.* New York: Bantam Books, 1969

Eighth Air Force Staff Directory, Texas: June 1947

FALK, Stanley L. and BAUER, Theodore W. *The National Security Structure.* Washington D.C.: Industrial College of the Armed Forces, 1972

FAWCETT, Lawrence and GREENWOOD, Barry J. *Clear Intent: The Government Cover-up of the UFO Experience.* New Jersey: Prentice-Hall, 1984

FORD, Brian. *German Secret Weapons: Blueprint for Mars.* New York: Ballantine Books, 1969

FOWLER, Raymond E. *Casebook of a UFO Investigator.* Englewood Cliffs, New Jersey: Prentice-Hall, 1981

——. "What about Crashed UFOs" *Official UFO* (April 1976)

GILLMOR, Daniel S., ed. *Scientific Study of Unidentified Flying Objects.* New York: Bantam Books, 1969

GOLDSMITH, Donald. *Nemesis.* New York: Berkley Books, 1985

GOOD, Timothy. *Above Top Secret.* New York: Morrow, 1988

HALL, Richard. *Uninvited Guests.* Santa Fe, New Mexico: Aurora Press, 1988

——. "Crashed Discs—Maybe," *International UFO Reporter,* Vol. 10, No. 4, July–August, 1985.

"History of the Eighth Air Force, Fort Worth, Texas," (Microfilm) Air Force Archives, Maxwell Air Force Base, AL

"History of the 509th Bomb Group, Roswell, New Mexico," (Microfilm). Air Force Archives, Maxwell Air Force Base, AL

HOGG, Ivan U. and KING, J.B. *German and Allied Secret Weapons of World War II.* London: Chartwell Books, 1974

HYNEK, J. Allen. *The UFO Experience: A Scientific Inquiry.* Chicago: Henry Regnery, 1972

JACOBS, David M. *The UFO Controversy in America.* New York: Signet, 1975

KEYHOE, Donald E. *Aliens From Space.* New York: Signet, 1974

KLASS, Philip J. *UFOs Explained.* New York: Random House, 1974

——. "Crash of the Crashed Saucer Claim," *The Skeptical Enquirer,* Vol 10, 1986.

LANG, Daniel. *The Man in the Thick Lead Suit.* New York: Oxford University Press, 1954

LORENZEN, Coral and Jim. *Abducted!* New York: Berkley Medallion Books, 1977

——. *Encounters with UFO Occupants.* New York: Berkley Medallion Books, 1976

——. *Flying Saucer Occupants.* New York: Signet, 1967

——. *Flying Saucers: The Startling Evidence of the Invasion from Outer Space.* New York: Signet, 1966

MCCLELLAN, Mike. "The Flying Saucer Crash of 1948 is a Hoax," *Official UFO* (October 1975)

MCDONOUGH, Thomas R. *The Search for Extraterrestrial Intelligence.* New York: John Wiley & Sons, 1987

MENZEL, Donald H. and TAVES, Ernest H. *The UFO Enigma.* Garden City, New York: Doubleday and Co., 1977

MICHEL, Aimé. *The Truth about Flying Saucers.* New York: Pyramid Books, 1967

National Security Agency. Presidential Documents. Washington D.C.: Executive Order 12356 1982

PRICE, Alfred. *Luftwaffe.* New York: Ballantine Books, 1969

"PROJECT BLUE BOOK" (microfilm). National Archives, Washington, D.C.

RAAF Base Phone Book, New Mexico: Aug 1947

RAAF Yearbook, Roswell, New Mexico: 1947

RANDLE, Kevin D. "The Flight of the Great Airship,"

True's Flying Saucers and UFOs Quarterly (Spring 1977)

——. "Mysterious Clues Left Behind by UFOs," Saga's *UFO Annual* (Summer 1972)

——. *The October Scenario.* Iowa City, Iowa: Middle Coast Publishing, 1988

——. "The Pentagon's Secret Air War Against UFOs," *Saga* (March 1976)

RANDLE, Kevin D. and CORNETT, Robert Charles. "Project Blue Book Cover-up: Pentagon Suppressed UFO Data," UFO Report Vol. 2 No. 5 (Fall 1975)

——. *The UFO Casebook.* New York: Warner Books, 1989

RANDLES, Jenny. *The UFO Conspiracy.* New York: Javelin Books, 1987

RUPPELT, Edward J. *The Report on Unidentified Flying Objects.* New York: Ace Books, 1956

——. "Rocket and Missile Firings," White Sands Proving Grounds, Jan 30-Jul 1947, Listing

SAGAN, Carl and PAGE, Thornton, eds. *UFO's: Scientific Debate.* New York: W.W. Norton & Co. 1974

SCULLY, Frank. *Behind The Flying Saucers.* New York: Henry Holt, 1950

SNIDER, L. Britt. "What Are We Doing About Espionage?" *Defense* (November 1985)

SPENCER, John and EVANS, Hilary. *Phenomenon.* New York: Avon Books: 1988

STEIGER, Brad. *Project Blue Book.* New York: Ballantine Books, 1976

——. *Strangers From The Skies.* New York: Award Books, 1966

STORY, Ronald D. *The Encyclopedia of UFOs.* Garden City, New York: Doubleday and Co., 1980

STRINGFIELD, Leonard H. *Situation Red: The UFO Siege!* Garden City, New York: Doubleday, 1977

——. *UFO Crash/Retrieval Syndrome: Status Report II.* Seguin, Tex.: Mutual UFO Network, 1980

——. *UFO Crash/Retrievals: Amassing the Evidence: Status Report III*. Cincinnati, Ohio: The Author, 1982

SUTHERLY, CURT. "Inside Story of the New Hampshire UFO Crash," *UFO Report*, July 1977

U.S. Congress House Committee on Science and Astronautics. *Symposium on Unidentified Flying Objects*. July 29, 1968, Hearings, Washington, D.C.: U.S. Government Printing Office, 1968

VALLEE, Jacques. *Anatomy of a Phenomenon*. New York: Ace Books, 1966

WILCOX, Inez, personal writings 1947–1952

WILKINS, Harold T. *Flying Saucers on the Attack*. New York: Citadel Press, 1954

WILSON, Colin. *Mysteries*. New York: Perigee Books, 1978

Other Periodicals and Research Sources:

A.P.R.O. Bulletin March–April 1968, July–August 1970, May 1978

Atomic Blast, RAAF Base Newspaper, July–August 1947

International UFO Reporter, 1987–1989

Alamogordo News, July 1947

Albuquerque Journal, July 1947

Boston Advertiser, Dec 1965

Bozeman Daily Chronicle, July 1947

Cedar Rapids Gazette, March–April 1897, June 24, 1947–July 30, 1947

Chicago Daily News, July 1947

Chicago Sun, July 1947

Chicago Daily Times, July 1947

Circleville Herald, July 1947

Clinton Herald, July 1947

Dalhart Texan, July 1947

Dallas Morning News, July 1947

Dallas Times Herald, July 1947

Dallas Morning News, July 1947

Dayton Daily News, July 1947

Denver Post, July 1947, March 1950, June 1979
Des Moines Register, June 24, 1947–July 20, 1947
Detroit Free Press, July 1947, Dec 1965
Flint Journal, Dec 1965
Fort Worth Star-Telegram, March–April 1897, July 1947
Houston Chronicle, July 1947
Las Vegas Review-Journal, July 1947
Las Vegas Sun, April 19, 1962–April 20, 1962
London Times, July 1947
Los Angeles Herald Express July 7, 1947–July 10, 1947
Los Angeles Times, July 1947, Dec 1965
Louisville Courier-Journal, July 1947
Rocky Mountain News, July 1947
Roswell Daily Record, July 1947
Roswell Morning Dispatch, July 1947
New York Herald Tribune, July 1947, Dec 1965
New York Times, July 1, 1947–July 15, 1947
San Francisco Chronicle, July 1947
Seattle Daily Times, July 1947
St. Paul Pioneer Press, July 1944
Syracuse Herald-American, July 1947
Syracuse Herald-Journal, July 1947
Toronto Daily Star, Dec 1965
Washington Post, July 1947

Acknowledgments

A work of this nature cannot be completed without the assistance of dozens of others. A few of those people supplied information that was invaluable.

CARL BEBRICH—Scientific consultant.

BILL AND DON BOGEL—For allowing us to get started.

BILL BRAZEL—Without whose help the investigation would have stalled before it got started.

RICHARD BUDEMAN—Associate.

J. ALLEN HYNEK CENTER FOR UFO STUDIES—2457 West Peterson Ave, Chicago, Illinois 60659. A special thanks to Mark Rodeghier, the scientific director, George Eberhart, and John Timmerman. The Center is also the repository for copies of all tapes, notes and interviews relating to the Roswell investigation.

JAMES CLEARY, M.D.—Associate.

SUE ANN CURTIS—Scientific consultant.

PAUL DAVIDS—For his appreciation of the Roswell event and his invaluable help in completing this work.

GEORGE M. EBERHART—Creating the Index for this book.

R.T. EIERMANN—Editorial assistance.

STANTON FRIEDMAN—Nuclear physicist and UFO researcher, who first learned of the events at Roswell and through persistence was able to find the key witnesses that broke the story wide open.

306

STAN GORDON—Pennsylvania Association for the Study of the Unexplained, 6 Oak Hill Avenue, Greensburg, Pennsylvania 15601.

BARRY GREENWOOD—For his valuable assistance.

ROBERT HASTINGS—Has spoken at over 300 colleges and universities nationwide. His lecture program, "UFOs: The Hidden History," is based on previously classified CIA, Air Force, and FBI documents about UFOs that have now been released through the Freedom of Information Act. He has asked that anyone having information regarding these cases to contact him at 40 Evergreen Circle, Caropines, Myrtle Beach, South Carolina 29575.

WALTER HAUT—The PIO at the RAAF during July, 1947. His assistance in tracking down witnesses, and his advice has been invaluable.

RICHARD HEIDEN—Research assistant.

RALPH HEICK—Who provided numerous leads and assistance in tracking down first-hand witnesses. His knowledge of the 509th Bomb Group and the operations at the Roswell Army Air Field were invaluable.

CHESTER LYTLE—Who has become a trusted ally and major supporter.

DON MITCHELL—Who assisted in the investigations and who provided the use of his oil-eating crew-cab pick-up truck. His knowledge of New Mexico made it easier to reach the witnesses.

JEFF PERONTO—Associate

BRAD RADCLIFFE—Assistant to Don Schmitt; for his tremendous efforts throughout the entire project.

BILL RAMSEYER—Associate.

SUSAN ROCKHILL—Editorial assistant.

ROUNDTOWN UFO SOCIETY—PO Box 52, Circleville, Ohio 43113. Pete Hartinger, Director; Delbert Anderson, Chief Investigator; Jon Fry, Chief Researcher. They provided valuable information about the Sherman Campbell discovery in July, 1947.

CLIFFORD STONE—For his valuable support and assistance.

LEONARD STRINGFIELD—4412 Grove Avenue, Cincinnati, Ohio 45227. His CRASH/RETRIEVAL Status Reports provided a valuable source of information. Copies of the reports, as well as other UFO-related material is available for a fee from Stringfield.

DR. MICHAEL SWORDS—For all his great advice and his encouragement.

JERRY VERMEULEN, M.D.—Even if he didn't bring the anti-venom to the crash site.

JEFF WELLS—Who helped with the leads and whose support is truly appreciated.

STEVE ZALEWSKI—For his valuable assistance

Several universities and institutions provided research assistance for us. Although none of them subscribed to the theory of extraterrestrial intervention at Roswell, all were willing to provide what assistance they could.

Air Force Archives, Maxwell Air Force Base, Alabama
Albuquerque City Library, Albuquerque, New Mexico
Arizona State Museum, Tempe, Arizona
Bettmann Photo Archives, New York
Carswell Air Force Base, Fort Worth, Texas
Cedar Rapids Public Library, Cedar Rapids, Iowa
Chaves County Historical Society, Roswell, New Mexico
Clark County Public Library, Las Vegas, Nevada
Communications Diversified, Inc., Albuquerque, New Mexico
Dayton and Montgomery County Library, Dayton, Ohio
Fate Magazine, Chicago, Illinois
FOIA Officers, U.S. Army, Navy and Air Force, Washington, D.C.
Paul Harvey News, Chicago, Illinois
Holloman Air Force Base, Alamogordo, New Mexico

Institute of Meteoritics, Alberquerque, New Mexico
Kirtland Air Force Base, Albuquerque, New Mexico
Museum of New Mexico, Santa Fe, New Mexico
National Aeronautics and Space Administration
National Archives, Washington, D.C.
NBC Television, including the staff and crew of *Unsolved Mysteries*
New Mexico Military Institute, Roswell, New Mexico
Offutt Air Force Base, Omaha, Nebraska
OMNI Magazine, New York, New York
Pease Air Force Base, New Hampshire
Pentagon, Dep't of Army Intelligence, Washington, D.C.
Roswell Chamber of Commerce, Roswell, New Mexico
Roswell Public Library, Roswell, New Mexico
Smithsonian Institution, Washington, D.C.
Southern Methodist University, Dallas, Texas
University of Arizona, Tucson, Arizona
University of Iowa, Iowa City, Iowa
University of New Mexico, Albuquerque, New Mexico
University of Texas—Arlington, Arlington, Texas
University of Wisconsin, Madison, Wisconsin
Wall Street Journal, New York, New York
White Sands Proving Grounds, New Mexico
Wright-Patterson Air Force Base, Dayton, Ohio

Index

Astonishing UFO Reports
from Avon Books

COMMUNION: A TRUE STORY
  by Whitley Strieber   70388-2/$4.95 US/$5.95 Can

TRANSFORMATION: THE BREAKTHROUGH
  by Whitley Strieber   70535-4/$4.95 US/$5.95 Can

THE GULF BREEZE SIGHTINGS: THE MOST
ASTOUNDING MULTIPLE UFO SIGHTINGS
IN U.S. HISTORY
  by Ed Walters and Frances Walters
                          70870-1/$5.95 US/$6.95 Can

PHENOMENON: FORTY YEARS
OF FLYING SAUCERS
  edited by John Spencer and Hilary Evans
                          70654-7/$4.95 US/$5.95 Can

REPORT ON COMMUNION
  by Ed Conroy   70811-6/$4.95 US/$5.95 Can